Praise for Gardner Dozois

"Gardner Dozois is one of the pre-eminent authors in the history of science fiction and fantasy. One of the strongest talents to enter the field in the last half of the century, Dozois's stories, be they set in a wildly imaginative future or the recent past, are never less than supremely literate, and profoundly human."

—Lucius Shepard

"Gardner Dozois's ear for dialogue never falters, nor does his ability to capture the essence of character in diverse situations. His vision is bleak, yet his words, in contrast, sing. Dozois is a great, neglected American writer."

—Ellen Datlow

"A story from Gardner—all too rare an event—is cause for celebration. A whole collection is a literary milestone. Gardner Dozois is one of the best writers we have. His range and power are astonishing."

—Nancy Kress

"His work is bitter, subtle, exotic, unique: science fiction for the true connoisseur."

—Joe Haldeman

"Intense, well-rendered and colorfully done . . . a careful sculptor of ideas, a sensitive observer of human responses and a narrator who cares about the way things are said."

—Roger Zelazny

"Dozois is a writer who prowls the terrain of nightmare, bringing back strange loves and horrors you will not soon forget. Included here are some of the most imaginative and poignant concepts in recent fiction, incarnated in a sustained, almost tangible realness that holds your eyes to the page."

—James Tiptree, Jr.

More Praise for Gardner Dozois

"A unique writing talent who speaks with a distinctive voice. He is a writer's writer, and what's more, he is a reader's writer."

—Ben Bova

"Gardner Dozois is one of the most powerful writers of his generation."

—Mike Resnick

"Gardner Dozois is one of the best short-fiction writers alive."

—Andy Duncan

"One of the very best short story writers ever to have worked in the genre. A precise, lyrical stylist, he is also a deep, humane writer who can tease the humor out of tragedy."

—Jack Dann

"Rich, multicolored, passionate, provacative and illuminating . . . Gardner Dozois is the finest stylist of his generation."

—S.P. Somtow

"My generation of science fiction writers has produced relatively few authenic masters of the short form. Gardner Dozois is one of them.

—William Gibson

"One of the most gifted writers in the United States."

—Robert Silverberg

"Dozois can create as well as he can edit, a skill which is not always available to editors."

—*SFSite*

Praise for Earlier Fiction Collections by Gardner Dozois

"These stories . . . are treasures, and of lasting value."

—*Los Angeles Times*

"Dozois has been so conspicuously and justifiably honored as an editor during the past decades that his excellence as a writer has tended to be forgotten."

—*Booklist*

"Beautifully wrought."

—*Kirkus Reviews*

"Long before he became one of SF's premier editors . . . Dozois was one of the genre's most exciting writers. . . . With passages of lyric wonder and vivid, fully realized characters, Dozois here shows himself to be an outstanding writer."

—*Publishers Weekly*

"Powerful and expertly written . . . some of the best tales the field has produced."

—*Science Fiction Chronicle*

"Dozois is an excellent writer as well as an exceptional editor . . . this collection should remind everyone of his considerable talent."

—*New York Review of Science Fiction*

"Dozois's masterful command of style and effects also deliver powerful emotional blows to the reader, something relatively rare in SF."

—*Starlog*

"Beautifully writen by a master stylist, polished gems . . . reminiscent of the best of Harlan Ellison, Robert Silverberg, and J.G. Ballard in their powerful and evocative imagery . . . absolutely gorgeous, perfect writing. Highly recommended."

—*Voice of Youth Advocate*

WHEN THE GREAT DAYS COME

Gardner Dozois

Also by Gardner Dozois

Anthologies

A Day in the Life
Another World
Best Science Fiction Stories of the Year #6-10
The Best of Isaac Asimov's Science Fiction Magazine
Time-Travelers From Isaac Asimov's Science Fiction Magazine
Transcendental Tales From Isaac Asimov's Science Fiction Magazine
Isaac Asimov's Aliens
Isaac Asimov's Mars
Isaac Asimov's SF Lite
Isaac Asimov's War
Roads Not Taken (with Stanley Schmidt)
The Year's Best Science Fiction #1-28
Future Earths; Under South American Skies (with Mike Resnick)
Future Earths: Under African Skies (with Mike Resnick)
Ripper! (with Susan Casper)
Modern Classic Short Novels of Science Fiction
Modern Classics of Fantasy
Killing Me Softly
Dying For It
The Good Old Stuff
The Good New Stuff
Explorers
The Furthest Horizon
Worldmakers
Supermen
One Million A.D.
Galileo's Children
Nebula Awards Showcase 2006
The New Space Opera (with Jonathan Strahan)
Galactic Empires
The New Space Opera 2 (with Jonathan Strahan)

Coedited With George R.R. Martin

Songs of the Dying Earth: Stories in Honor of Jack Vance
Warriors
Songs of Love And Death: All-Original Tales of Star-Crossed Love
Down These Strange Streets

Coedited With Sheila Williams

Isaac Asimov's Planet Earth
Isaac Asimov's Robots
Isaac Asimov's Cyberdreams
Isaac Asimov's Ghosts
Isaac Asimov's Skin Deep
Isaac Asimov's Vampires
Isaac Asimov's Moons
Isaac Asimov's Christmas
Isaac Asimov's Camelot
Isaac Asimov's Detectives
Isaac Asimov's Solar System
Isaac Asimov's Valentines
Isaac Asimov's Werewolves
Isaac Asimov's Mother's Day
Isaac Asimov's Utopias
Isaac Asimov's Father's Day
Isaac Asimov's Halloween

Also by Gardner Dozois

Coedited With Jack Dann

Future Power
Aliens!
Unicorns!
Magicats!
Mermaids!
Bestiary!
Sorcerers!
Demons!
Dogtales!
Seaserpents!
Dinosaurs!
Magicats 2!
Little People!
Unicorns 2!
Invaders!
Dragons!
Horses!
Dinosaurs 2!
Angels!
Hackers!
Timegates!
Nanotech!
Immortals!
Clones!
Future War
Armageddons
Aliens Among Us
Space Soldiers
Genometry
Future Sports
Beyond Flesh
Future Crimes
A.I.s
Beyond Singularity
Escape From Earth
Futures Past
Dangerous Games
Wizards
The Dragon Book

Fiction

Strangers
The Visible Man (collection)
Nightmare Blue (with George Alec Effinger)
Slow Dancing Through Time (with Jack Dann, Michael Swanwick, Susan Casper, and Jack C. Haldeman II)
The Peacemaker
Geodesic Dreams (collection)
Strange Days: Fabulous Journeys With Gardner Dozois (collection)
Morning Child and Other Stories (collection)
Shadow Twin (with George R. R. Martin and Daniel Abraham)
Hunter's Run (with George R. R. Martin and Daniel Abraham)

Nonfiction

The Fiction of James Tiptree, Jr.
Writing Science Fiction and Fantasy (with Ian Randal Strock, Tina Lee, Stanley Schmidt, and Sheila Williams

WHEN THE GREAT DAYS COME

Gardner Dozois

PRIME BOOKS

When the Great Days Come

An extension of this copyright page can be found on pages 357-358.

Cover art by Donato Giancola

Cover design by Telegraphy Harness

Prime Books
www.prime-books.com

ISBN: 978-1-60701-230-6

For my mother, who started it all by teaching me how to read
and
for my wife, for all our years together.

Contents

• Introduction •
Robert Silverberg

If you last long enough in this business, everything comes around again . . . and again and again. Gardner Dozois and I have known each other for forty years, now, and in the course of that time he has turned his hand, not often but steadily, to the writing of dazzling short stories. When he has enough of them put together to add up to a book-sized collection he collects them, and it seems that the karmic necessities of my life dictate that I will be asked to do an introduction for them. This is my third go-round in the Dozois introduction sweepstakes, and if the fates are kind to us both perhaps it is not yet the last. That his work should be collected and published every decade or so over the span of more than thirty years thus far shows that Gardner Dozois' short stories can stand the test of time. Even so, most of you know him, still, only as an editor. This new volume provides an occasion, once again, to reintroduce him as a writer, one of the best we have.

My initiation into the ritual of introducing Dozois short-story collections came in 1977—a geological eon ago, as time is reckoned in science-fiction publishing. A quick demonstration of that point: for nearly twenty years, 1986–2005, Gardner was editor of the top magazine in the field, *Asimov's Science Fiction*. During his incumbency he won an astonishing fourteen Hugo awards as Best Editor, a record that has never been matched and very likely never will be. But when Gardner's first story collection, *The Visible Man*, was published, *Asimov's*, which today seems like such a venerable magazine, was barely an issue or two old, and the Dozois editorship was still nearly a decade in the future, though he was on the masthead of the first issue with the title of associate editor.

The Visible Man was Gardner's first published book of fiction, containing a dozen stories that had been written over a period of seven years. Four of those twelve stories—"A Dream at Noonday," "A Special Kind of Morning," "A Kingdom by the Sea," and "Chains of the Sea"—are back among us this time around, as strong and impressive as they were when first published all those decades ago. (I can testify to that: I was the editor who originally published two of them.)

Most of what I said in my introduction to that initial Dozois collection is still appropriate to a consideration of Gardner's virtues and achievements as a writer, and I will repeat it here, as I did in my second Dozois introduction, since there's no reason for rephrasing what was perfectly well stated back then. But two of my statements do require significant updating, and it would be best to deal with those first.

One had to do with Dozois' physical appearance. In that 1977 introduction I described my first meeting with him, seven years previously, and spoke of the Gardner Dozois of March 1971, perhaps somewhat unkindly, as "a weird-looking apparition." At that time, I said, he was "a gaunt young man just under six feet tall with a vast cascade of shoulder-length blond hair of an eerie voluminous sort covering most of his face, a strange bushy beard . . . the glint of inquisitive eyes behind big steel-rimmed glasses, and—am I imagining this?—a bulky and grotesquely dilapidated raccoon coat. I mean, *weird*, man."

This description was already somewhat out of date in 1977, for I noted then that "he is no longer gaunt, not even remotely," nor was his general appearance quite as weird, although he still affected some quaint elements of hippie garb and a penchant for shagginess.

A further update is needed here. The twenty-first-century version of Gardner not only continues not to be gaunt, but indeed is rather less so than he was even in 1977. Indeed, here in the full maturity of his years—he's getting to be a senior citizen now, as so many of us who dedicated our youth to science fiction are—he cuts quite a conspicuous figure indeed.

But hippie garb and shaggy hair are most definitely not his style any more. Perhaps under the influence of Susan Casper, Gardner's jolly and loving wife of these many years past, he dresses now as modern adults do, even unto a coat and (sometimes) a tie. The effect is magisterial and commanding. Nor is he an uncouth, hairy, hippified being these days. He had his beard and hair trimmed quite neatly and expertly somewhere back in the 1980s, so I believe, has he has had it done again with fair frequency since then. From humble beginnings he has become the very model of sartorial elegance in our field, a man to study and emulate.

The other aspect of my 1977 introduction that needs emendation now is the statement that because he produces his fiction so painfully and slowly, "he does a little editing on the side" in order to help make ends meet. I observed then that he was "dabbling in anthology-making" and also serving as first reader for the newly established Isaac Asimov's Science Fiction Magazine.

Of course Gardner's editorial career can no longer be dismissed as a little something that he does on the side. His two decades in charge of *Asimov's* established him forever as one of the great magazine editors of science fiction's history, a major shaper of modern sf fully worthy of being classed with those three titans of earlier years, John Campbell, Horace Gold, and Anthony Boucher. Not content with that task alone, he has produced since 1984 the monumental annual anthology called *The Year's Best Science Fiction*, which is in its third decade now and constitutes in its many-volumed totality the definitive archive of the contemporary science-fiction story. And he has done dozens of stand-alone anthologies besides, comprising an awesome list that each year is extended by another impressive volume or three.

But, as I said in my second Dozois introduction (to the 1992 collection *Geodesic Dreams*, from which "Dinner Party," "Disciples," "Morning Child," and "The Peacemaker" are carried over), it is Gardner the writer with whom we are concerned here; and if writing has taken second place to editing in his career over the thirty-four years since his first short story collection appeared, that does not mean that writing is in any way a secondary sort of activity for him. Editing a monthly magazine that receives scores of submissions from hopeful writers every week was, of course, a time-consuming job; but I think that even if Dozois had not been for so many years the editor of *Asimov's* he would have produced a fictional oeuvre not very much more extensive than the one he has given us. He is simply not a prolific writer. His stories are carefully considered and elegantly wrought, sentence by sentence: a thankless job, some might say, in a field where for the most part basic story-telling has always been valued more highly than literary craftsmanship. But he has no choice but to work the way he does, and those of us who are sensitive to the values of Dozois' fiction are much the richer for it.

Not that Dozois the writer has gone unrewarded. His first published story, "The Empty Man," was a nominee in 1966 for the award that science-fiction writers annually give their peers: the Nebula. Nearly every year thereafter, all through the 1970s and early 1980s, his stories were prominent features of the Nebula ballot. "The Visible Man" was a contender in 1975; *Strangers*, his first and, I think, only science-fiction novel, was nominated in 1978; "Disciples" was a nominee in 1981; and so forth. His stories had regularly been reaching the ballot for the Hugo (the award given by readers) also; "A Special Kind of Morning" was a nominee in 1972; "A Kingdom by the Sea" made the ballot in 1973; the novella "Chains of the Sea" was on the ballot in 1974; *Strangers* in its original shorter form had been a nominee in 1975. By 1982, Dozois had achieved enough nominations (without winning any awards) to place him second in the roster of the "most consistent Hugo and Nebula award losers" in Mike Ashley's statistical compilation, *The Illustrated Book of Science Fiction Lists*: Dozois had collected four Hugo nominations and six Nebula nominations, but no trophies.

Then things changed, though. His story "The Peacemaker" won the Nebula in 1983 as Best Short Story, and the following year Dozois picked up a second Nebula in that category for "Morning Child." Only the Hugo for fiction has continued to elude him; the preferences of the Hugo voters are weighted, usually, toward basic storytelling qualities, and it is the common fate of s-f writers whose great strength is stylistic to receive frequent nominations but few awards.

Not that Dozois is merely a stylist. His fiction, as you will see, is passionate, powerfully committed stuff. But he deals in deep and eternal matters of the human heart, and in the complexities and disappointments of life in a human society. You will see that here in the older stories brought forward from those first two collections, and in the more recent ones—"Community," "When the Great Days Came," "Fairy Tale," and the others that have been added to make up this volume.

This is what I had to say in 1977 about the particular qualities of Dozois' fiction that I think are most worthy of praise, and which still, I think, provides the best summation of my feelings about it. Let us consider this paragraph from one of his earliest stories, written when he was scarcely old enough to vote:

> "Did y'ever hear the one about the old man and the sea? Halt a minute, lordling; stop and listen. It's a fine story, full of balance and point and social pith; short and direct. It's not mine. Mine are long and rambling and parenthetical and they corrode the moral fiber right out of a man. Come to think, I won't tell you that one after all. A man of my age has a right to prefer his own material, and let the critics be damned. I've a prejudice now for webs of my own weaving."

Allow me to invite your attention to the rhythms of the prose, the balancing of clauses, the use of alliteration, metaphor, and irony, the tough, elegant sinews of the vocabulary. It is a paragraph of splendid construction, a specimen of prose that shows honorable descent from Chaucer and Shakespeare, Pope and Dryden, Defoe and Dickens, the prose of a man who knows what he wants to say and says it eloquently and effectively. It is the opening paragraph of "A Special Kind of Morning," which Dozois wrote in 1970 and which I occupied, not by any accident, the lead position and place of honor in the first number of *New Dimensions,* the anthology series that I was editing in that era. Many science-fiction writers, including a lot of the great ones, are content to be mere storytellers, using whatever assemblages of words may be handy to convey their meanings.

Dozois is a storyteller too, and no mere one, either—"A Special Kind of Morning" is a vigorous and violent tale of war with a structural underpinning worthy of Sophocles—but he is concerned as much with the *way* he tells his stories as with the events he is describing.

Or here, this paragraph from "Chains of the Sea":

> One day the aliens landed, just as everyone always said they would. They fell out of a guileless blue sky and into the middle of a clear, cold November day, four of them, four alien ships drifting down like the snow that had been threatening to fall all week. America was just shouldering its way into daylight as they made planetfall, so they landed there: one in the Delaware Valley, about fifteen miles north of Philadelphia, one in Ohio, one in a desolate region of Colorado, and one—for whatever reason—in a cane field outside of Caracas, Venezuela. To those who actually saw them come down, the ships seemed to fall rather than to descend under any intelligent control: a black nailhead suddenly tacked to the sky, coming all at once from nowhere, with no transition, like a Fortean rock squeezed from a high appearing-point, hanging way up there and winking intolerably bright in the sunlight; and then gravity takes hold of it, visibly, and it begins to fall, far away and dream-slow at first, swelling larger, growing huge, unbelievably big, a mountain hurled at the earth, falling with terrifying speed, rolling in the air, tumbling end over end, overhead, coming down—and then it is sitting peacefully on the ground; it has not crashed, and although it didn't slow and it didn't stop, there it is, and not even a snowflake could have settled onto the frozen mud more lightly.

Prose, yes. Actual prose. America is "shouldering its way into daylight." The alien spaceship descends like "a black nailhead suddenly tacked to the sky." The sense of invasion is conveyed through an accretion of concrete detail, of vivid and immediate simile and metaphor and physical description. Melville understood these things, and Joyce, and Faulkner. So did Raymond Chandler and Dashiell Hammett, and in our own field Theodore Sturgeon and Cyril Kornbluth and Henry Kuttner. The power of that passage depends on a respect for language and grammar, a sense of the structure of the sentence and the paragraph, and a keen perception of sensory data. Gardner Dozois is as skilled a worker in prose as there is in science fiction. His marvelous ear and eye provide much, though not all, of the explanation of his success as an editor; and these stories collected here will tell you how considerable a writer he has been over the past three and a half decades as well.

The name, by the way, is pronounced Do-*zwah*. It's French-Canadian in origin. Most of the readers of the 1977 collection needed to be told that. Today, I think, the name of this writer is more familiar to us. May his acclaim continue to grow for years to come.

—Robert Silverberg
February, 2011

• Counterfactual •

> "If we reach the Blue Ridge Mountains, we can hold out for twenty years."
>
> —General Robert E. Lee

Cliff's fountain pen rolled across the pull-out writing shelf again, and he sighed and reached out to grab it before it tumbled to the floor. The small inkbottle kept marching down the shelf too, juddering with each vibration of the car.

Writing on a train wasn't easy, especially on a line where the rail-bed had been insufficiently maintained for decades. Even forming legible words was a challenge, with the jarring of the undercarriage or a sudden jerk all too likely to turn a letter into an indecipherable *splat* or to produce a startled, rising line across the page, as if the ink were trying to escape the mundane limitations of the paper.

Scenery was a distraction too. Cliff had always loved landscapes, and he had to wage a constant battle against the urge to just sit there and look out the window, where, at the moment, pale armies of fir trees were sliding slowly by, while the sky guttered toward a winter dusk in washes of plum and ash and sullen red. But he'd be sharing this room tonight with three other reporters, which meant lights-out early and a night wasted listening to them fart and snore, so if he was going to get any writing done on the new Counterfactual he was working on for *McClure's*, it'd better be now, while his roommates were down in the bar with the rest of the boys.

Cliff opened his notebook, smoothed it, and bent over the page:

> General Robert E. Lee put his hands on the small of his back and stretched, trying to shake some of the tension out of his aching spine. He had never been so tired, feeling every one of his fifty-eight years sitting on his shoulders like bars of lead.
>
> For days, days that had stretched into a unending nightmare of pain and fatigue, he had struggled to stay awake, to stay erect in

the saddle, as they executed a fighting retreat from the trenches and earthworks of Petersburg westward along the Appomattox River toward Lynchburg, Grant's Army of the James, which outnumbered his own forces four to one, snapping at their heels every step of the way. Thousands of his men had died along the way, and Lee almost envied the fallen—at least they could stop. But Lee couldn't stop. He knew that all eyes were on him, that it was up to him to put on a show of being indefatigable and imperturbable, tall in the saddle, regal, calm, and totally in command. His example and the pride it inspired, and the love and respect the men felt for him, was all that was keeping his ragged and starving army going. No matter how exhausted he was, no matter how bleak and defeated were his inner thoughts, no matter how hopeless he knew his position to be, no matter how much his chest ached (as it had been aching increasingly for days), he couldn't let it show.

They had stopped for the night in the woods near Appomattox Court House, too tired to even pitch tents. There had been almost nothing to eat, even for the staff officers. Now his staff huddled close to him in the darkness, as if they depended on him for light and warmth as much or more than the low-burning bivouac fire, ragged, worn-out men in tattered uniforms, sprawled on blankets spread on the grass or sitting on saddles thrown over tree-stumps, without even chairs or camp-stools anymore. Lee could see their eyes, gleaming wetly in the firelight, as well as feel them. Every eye was on him still.

The barking of rifles had started up again from General Gordon's rear-guard on the road behind them when the courier arrived. He was thin as a skeleton, like Death himself come to call. He saluted and handed Lee a sealed communiqué. "Sir, from General Grant."

Lee held the note warily, as if it was a snake. He knew what it was: another message from General Grant, politely suggesting that he surrender his army.

The question was, what was *he* going to say in return?

The car jolted, shuddered, and jerked again while momentum equalized itself along the length of the train, and Cliff lifted his pen from the paper, waiting for the ride to steady again. What *was* he going to say in return? That was the problem.

He had an arresting central image, one that had come to him whole: Robert F. Lee surrendering the Army of Northern Virginia to General Ulysses S. Grant, the soldiers lined up somberly along a country road, heads down, some of the Confederates openly in tears, Lee handing his sword to Grant while a light rain fell, both men looking solemn and grim . . . How to justify it, though? Counterfactuals had become increasingly popular in recent years—perhaps because the public had been denied the opportunity to play soldier during the Great War—until now they were now almost respectable as pulp stories went, and you could make decent money selling them. But in writing Counterfactuals, you had to provide some kind of tipping-point, some event that would have changed everything that came after—and it had to be at least superficially plausible, or the fans, armchair historians all, would tear you to pieces. Having the Confederates win the War was a common enough trope in the genre, and a number of stories had been written about how Lee had won at Gettysburg or had pushed on out of Virginia to attack and burn Washington when he had the chance, forcing capitulation on a terrified Union, but Cliff was after something more subtle—a tale where the Confederates still *lost* the War, but lost it in a different way, with different consequences as a result. It was hard to see what would have motivated Lee to surrender, though. True, he was nearly at the end of his rope, his men exhausted and starving, being closely harried by Union forces who were chasing him relentlessly West —but in the real world, none of that had brought him to the point of seriously contemplating surrender. In fact, it was at that very point when he'd said that he was determined "to fight to the last," and told his officers and men that "We must all determine to die at our posts." Didn't sound much like somebody who was ready to throw in the towel.

Then, just when things looked blackest, he had narrowly avoided a closing Union trap by breaking past Phil Sheridan at Appomattox Court House, and kept on going until he reached the Blue Ridge Mountains, there to break his army up into smaller units that melted into the wilderness, setting the stage for decades of bitterly fought guerilla war, a war of terror and ambush that was still smoldering to this day. It was hard to see what would have made Lee surrender, when he didn't contemplate it even in the hour of his most extreme need. Especially as he knew that he could expect few compromises in the matter of surrender and little or no mercy from the implacable President Johnson . . .

He was spinning his wheels. Time for a drink.

Outside, the sun had finally disappeared below the horizon, leaving only a spreading red bruise behind. The darkening sky was slate-gray now, and hard little flakes of snow were squeezing themselves out of it, like dandruff sprinkled across felt. He hoped that the weather didn't work itself into a real blizzard, one that might hold them up on the way back. Like everyone else, he wanted to get the ceremony over with and get back home before Christmas—even though all he really had to look forward to was a turkey sandwich at a Horn & Hardart's and an evening drinking in a journalist's hangout with many of the same people he was already sharing a train with in the first place.

Cliff stored his notebook in his carpetbag, and pushed out into the corridor, which was rocking violently from side-to-side, like a ship in a high sea, as the track-bed roughened. He made his way unsteadily along the corridor, bracing himself against the wall. Freezing needles of winter cold stabbed at him between the cars, and then stale air and the smell of human sweat swallowed him as he crossed into one of the coach cars, which was crowded with passengers, pinch-faced civilians in threadbare clothes, including whole families trying to sleep sitting up in the uncomfortable wooden seats. Babies were crying, women were crooning to them, couples were fighting, someone was playing a Mexican song on a beat-up old guitar, and four Texans in the stereotypical but seemingly obligatory Stetsons—Texans were being seen around more frequently these days, now that relations had been normalized with the Republic of Texas—were playing poker on one of the seats, with onlookers standing in the aisles and whooping with every turn of the cards.

There were three more coach cars to push your way through, and Cliff was glad to get beyond them into the alcoves between the cars, even though the cold air nipped at him each time. He never had liked noise and crowds, which was one reason why he'd always preferred small towns to the big cities. With things the way the were, though, the big cities like Chicago and Minneapolis were where the work was, and so he had no choice but to live there, as long as the *Minneapolis Star* paid his bills.

Even out here, between the cars, you could smell the tobacco stink coming from the next compartment, and when he opened the door and stepped into the bar car, tobacco smoke hung in such a thick yellow cloud that you could barely see. Most of the newsmen on the train were in here, standing around the bar or sitting grouped on stools around the little tables. Like Cliff, most of them had shunned the dining car and brought bags of sandwiches from Chicago, to save their meager expense-account money for the bar.

Cliff was hailed with the usual derisive, mildly insulting greetings, and two of the boys squeezed apart to make room for him at the bar. He was well-enough liked by the other newsmen, although his hobby of writing Counterfactuals and Westerns, even the occasional Air War or Weird Fantasy, marked him out as a bit strange. Half of these guys probably had an unfinished draft of the Great American Novel stashed away in a drawer somewhere, but in public you were supposed to give lip-service to the idea that to a real newsman, the only kind of writing that mattered was journalism.

"Hey, Cliff," John said. "Finish another masterpiece?"

"Aw, he was probably just jerking-off," Staubach said.

Cliff smiled tolerantly and bought a round. He was already several drinks behind. The wunderkind from the *Chicago Tribune*—he was supposed to be nineteen, but to Cliff it didn't look like he could be more than thirteen—was trying to get an argument about The Gathering Clouds of War in Europe going with Bill, a big amiable Michigan Swede who rarely paid any attention to anything outside of the box-scores on the sports page, unless it was a racing form. "The United States will never get involved in a foreign war," the kid was saying, in his surprisingly deep voice. "Bryant kept us out of the Great War, and Hoover will keep us out of this one, too." He was short and pudgy, pasty-faced, with a sullen, cynical, seen-it-all air unusual in one so young. A few of the boys had held the fact that he was a New York Jew against him for awhile, but he was basically good-natured behind his gruff exterior, and smart as a whip, with just the kind of savage black humor that reporters liked, and so most of them had warmed to him.

He was trying to get a rise out of Bill, who had been incautious enough to express mild Interventionist sentiments a few times in the past, but Bill wasn't rising to the bait. "Guess England and Germany will just have to take care of de Gaulle without our help," Bill said amiably. "They're up to it, I guess."

"We've got enough problems of our own without worrying about de Gaulle," John threw in.

"Fuck DeGauile and the horse he fucking rode in on," Staubach said. "Who's got the cards?"

"Language, gentlemen!" old Matthews said sternly. They all jeered at him, but they acquiesced, Staubach rephrasing his question to "Okay, who's got the *frigging* cards?" Although he was as erect and natty as ever, impeccably dressed, looking every inch the distinguished senior correspondent, Matthews had been drinking even harder lately than reporters usually drank, and was already a bit glassy-eyed. The kid was supposed to be his assistant, but everybody knew that he'd been writing his column for him, and doing a better job of it than Matthews ever had.

John had the cards, but they had to wait through another couple of rounds for one of the little tables to open up, as the more prosperous passengers, or those who were more finicky about their food, drifted off to the dining car up front. "Crowded in here," Cliff commented. "Where are all the politicians, though? You'd think they'd be nine-deep around the bar."

"Aw, they got a bar of their own, coupla cars up," Staubach said.

"Got the first three cars, all to themselves," Bill threw in, with a grin. "And a sergeant with a carbine on the platform outside, to make sure Lindbergh and the rest of them don't get bothered by the *hoi poloi.*"

"Sure, little do they care that the poor bastard has to freeze his nuts off all the way to Montgomery," John said, which drew another admonishment of "Language!" from Matthews, although, as he was already more than half-fried, it was clear that his heart wasn't in it anymore. The bartender—who, on a train like this, traveling through the Occupied Territories, was likely to be a soldier in civilian clothes, with a carbine of his own tucked under the bar—grinned at them over Matthews's head.

At last a table opened up, and they settled in for their usual nickel-and-dime game of draw. Mathews kept fumbling with his cards, having trouble holding them in a proper fan, forgetting whose bet it was, and changing his mind about how many cards he wanted, and soon was the big loser—as big as it got in this penny ante game, anyway. Every time the kid lost a hand, he would curse with an inventive fluency that was almost Shakespearian, and that kept the rest of them chuckling. Since he never deigned to use the common "four-letter words," even Matthews couldn't really complain, although he grumbled about it. Bill played with his usual quiet competency and was soon ahead, although Cliff managed to hold his own and split a number of pots with him.

After about an hour and a half of this, the smoke and the noise, and the fact that Matthews was no longer able to keep from dropping his cards every time he picked them up, and was getting pissy about it, made Cliff deal himself out.

"Going back to the room," he said, "see if I can get a couple of pages done before the rest of you guys show up.

"Can't keep *Wild West Weekly* waiting," Bill said.

"Aw, he's just going to jerk-off again," Staubach mumbled, peering at his cards.

Cliff waved at them and walked away, moving a little more unsteadily than was entirely justified by the lurching of the car. Truth was, left to his own devices, Cliff wasn't that heavy a drinker—but if you were going to be accepted by the boys, you had to drink with them, and reporters prided themselves on their ability to put it away, another way in which the kid—who seemed to have a hollow trunk, as well as two hollow legs—fit right in in spite of his youth. Cliff could feel that he was at the edge of his ability to toss it back without becoming knee-walking drunk, though, which would lose him respect with the boys, so it was time to call it a night.

There was snow crusted on the footplates between the cars now, although it didn't seem to be snowing anymore outside. Cliff decided that he'd better clear his head if he was going to get any writing done, and walked back through the now-darkened coach cars and the sleeping cars to the observation platform on the back of the rear car.

It was bitterly cold outside, his breath puffing out in tattered plumes, but the snow had stopped, and the black clouds overhead had momentarily parted, revealing the fat pale moon. They were still moving through thick forest, the snow-shrouded ghosts of the trees gleaming like bones in the darkness, but now the ground on one side of the track fell steeply away, opening the world up to space and distance and the dimly perceived black bulks of nearby hills. There was a fast little mountain stream down there, winding along at the bottom of the slope, and in the moonlight he could see the cold white rills it made as it broke around streambed rocks.

The train slowed while going up the next long incline, and a dark figure broke from the trees, darted forward, and sprang onto the observation platform, grabbing the railing. As Cliff flinched back in shock, the figure threw a leg over the railing and pulled itself up. It paused, sitting on the top rail, one leg over, and looked at Cliff. It was a man, thin, clean-shaven, with a large nose and close-cropped hair bristling across a bullet-head, clutching a bindle in one hand. As Cliff gaped, the man smiled jauntily, said, "Evenin', sport!", and put one finger to his lips in a shushing gesture. Then he swung his other leg over the railing, hopped down to the platform, and sauntered by Cliff, giving him a broad wink as he passed.

Up close, even by moonlight, you could tell that his clothes were patched and much-mended, but they seemed reasonably clean, and although he exuded a brief whiff of sweat and unwashed armpits and sour breath as he passed, it wasn't too strong or too rank. He couldn't have been on the bum for too long, Cliff thought, or at least he must have been finding work frequently enough to enable him to keep himself moderately clean. The tramp disappeared into the car without a backwards glance, presumably to lose himself among the coach-class passengers or find a water-closet or a storage cubical to hide in for the night. There were thousands of such ragged men on the road these days, drifting from place to place, looking for work or a handout, especially down here in the Occupied Territories; the economy was bad enough in the States, but down here, whole regions had never really recovered from the War in the first place, the subsequent decades of guerilla war and large-scale terrorism—with whole armies of unreconstructed rebels still on the loose and lurking in the hills, many of them by now composed of the children and grandchildren of the original soldiers—tending to discourage economic growth . . . especially with raiders knocking down new factories or businesses as fast as they sprang up, to discourage "collaboration" with the occupying forces.

Cliff knew that he really should report the tramp to the conductor, but it was difficult to work up enough indignation to bother, and in the end he decided not to even try. It was hard to blame him for wanting to be inside the train, where it was warm, rather than out there in the freezing night.

Up ahead, around a long curve, you could see the engine itself now, puffing out bursts of fire-shot black smoke like some great, stertorously gasping iron beast. The smoke plume wrapped itself back around the observation platform, making him cough and filling his mouth with the ashen taste of cinders, and that, plus the fact that he was beginning to shiver, told him that it was time to go back inside himself. If his head wasn't clear by now, it wasn't going to be.

When Cliff got back to their compartment, though, it became obvious that it didn't matter whether his head was clear or not; he wasn't going to get any more writing done tonight. The conductor had already rearranged the compartment into its sleeping configuration, folding away the benches and lowering two bunks from each opposing wall, one stacked above the other. Somewhat surprisingly, his roommates were already back from the bar. Matthews, in fact, was already soddenly asleep on one of the lower bunks, gurgling and snoring, still fully clothed, although Bill was fussing with him, trying to get him undressed, with little success. Cliff gathered that the old man had passed out in the bar, or come near to it, and his compatriots had hauled him back to the roomette. Even out here, you could smell the booze coming off of him.

With the bunks folded down, there was hardly space enough for Bill and the kid to stand in the tiny compartment, and Cliff had to hover in the doorway, half out in the corridor, waiting for someone to make room for him. The kid at last got impatient with Bill's efforts to undress Matthews and bumped him aside, saying harshly "Oh, leave the poor old *pfumpt* alone." With a curious tenderness that belayed the gruffness of his tone, he took off the old man's shoes and stowed them under his bunk, and loosened his tie. "He'll just have to sleep in his clothes for once like the rest of us, instead of those stupid woolen pajamas."

As if to demonstrate, Bill climbed into the other bottom bunk—fully dressed except for his shoes; it was a good idea to keep your wallet in your pocket, too, since sneak-thieves were known to riffle through bags left on the floor in a compartment while the occupants slept—and put his hat over his eyes. Cliff slid inside, now that some floor space had opened-up, and closed the door on the corridor.

They had come down out of the hills by now, and stopped at a tiny station for no readily apparent reason. There was a small town out there, two or three streets of two-story storefronts laid out parallel to the tracks, some dilapidated old wooden houses with big overgrown yards set further back. The storefronts carried faded signs that said things like HUDSON'S HICKORY HOUSE or BROWN FURNITURE COMPANY, but none of them looked like they'd been open for awhile, and several had boarded-up windows. Nothing was moving out there except a dog pissing on a lamp pole.

"What a dump!" the kid said, turning to look at Cliff. Up close like this, he had a habit of partially covering his mouth with his hand when he spoke; he was embarrassed about his teeth, which he never brushed, and were green. "No wonder all the colored folks moved up North."

"Getting lynched and shot and burned-out by Lee's Boys probably had something to do with it too," Bill said dryly, lifting his hat for a second. "Turn off the light. I want to get some sleep."

The kid vaulted up into the bunk above Matthews. Cliff took his shoes off, stuffed his carpetbag into his bunk to use as a pillow, shut off the light, and climbed into the other upper in the dark, nearly falling when the car lurched as the train started moving again.

Cliff lay awake in the darkness for awhile, feeling oddly apprehensive and jittery for no particular reason he could identify, listening to the snoring and moaning of his roommates. He tried picturing himself back on his grandfather's hill farm near the confluence of the Wisconsin and the Mississippi, playing fetch with his old buff-colored coon dog, and eventually the steady swaying movement of the car rocked him to sleep.

Even so, he'd wake up for a moment every time the motion of the train changed, slowing down or speeding up with a jerk and a lurch, opening his eyes to see, through the uncurtained top of the window, trees rushing by, the roofs of houses, bright lights on tall poles, more trees, and then his eyes would close, and he'd sleep again, the wailing of the train's whistle and the rhythmical clatter of its wheels weaving themselves through his dreams.

By morning, they had outrun the winter. Here, it was still fall, no snow on the ground, browning multi-colored leaves still clinging to the hardwood trees. Further south still, on the Gulf Coast or at least in Florida, it was probably still summer, palm trees swaying in balmy breezes, but they weren't going that far. This was the last leg of their journey, with only a couple of hours left until they reached Montgomery.

The room steward brought them a pot of coffee. Sensitized by the kid's remarks of the previous evening, Cliff noticed that he was a Mediterranean immigrant of some sort—Italian, Greek; recent enough to still have a heavy accent—where before the War, he almost certainly would have been colored. It wasn't true that there were no colored people left in the Occupied Territories, of course—there were still families holding out here and there. But decades of large-scale terrorism had chased millions of them to the big cities of the North, where they had encountered other problems to replace the ones they'd left behind, and most of the medium-level jobs went to more recent (and reasonably white) immigrants like the room steward. Now the Open Door that had let people like the steward into the country was slamming closed as immigration policies were tightened, leaving millions of European refugees with nowhere to go. As someone whose father had immigrated from Prague only a generation before, Cliff sympathized with all of them, and with the exiled colored folk as well, unwelcome in either the South or North.

Bill slipped his shoes on and ducked out to fetch a bunch of doughnuts from the dining car. They ate while taking turns going to the WC at the end of the sleeper for sponge baths and to change into fresh clothes, although old Matthews was so glazed and hung-over that the kid had to guide him there and back, holding him by one arm. Bill teased him about this unmercifully, although he wasn't quite mean enough to ask the kid if he'd had to help Matthews bathe. He certainly had to help him dress, though, while Bill jeered, and Matthews, lost in his own world, stared at nothing anybody else could see. He clearly didn't have long to go before he reached the end of his rope, Cliff realized. Odds were that the kid would have his job before then anyway.

Outside, rundown white clapboard houses with incongruously large porches were slipping by, as well as burnt-out factories, cut banks of red clay, goats grazing in hilly yards, an occasional glimpse of a sluggish brown river. For the last half-hour, they crawled by a huge Army base, home of one of the occupying divisions, although little was visible beyond the high walls and barbed wire except the red roofs of the barracks, a water tower, a big industrial crane of some sort. There were guard-towers every few yards, with machine-gun emplacements at the top, giving the whole complex the look of a prison. Scrub woods, weed-overgrown lots, and heaps of rusting scrap metal for the next few minutes, and then the outlying freight yards for the Montgomery station began to roll past.

Montgomery was still a big city for this part of the world. It had been in Yankee hands since the end of the War, and although it had suffered several major raids in subsequent years from unreconstructed Confederate forces, and had been shelled by terrorists more than once, it was still in pretty good shape. There were still a few bombed-out buildings visible in the center of town, but most of them were busily being repaired, and the sounds of construction—hammering, workmen shouting, buzz-saws whining—were a constant here. Outside the train for the first time in more than a day, Cliff wished he'd brought a heavier coat; it wasn't as cold here as it had been up the track, in the hill country, but it was still brisk, and the pregnant gray clouds that were sliding by overhead promised rain that he hoped would hold off until after the ceremony. The air smelled of dust and ozone.

He caught a glimpse of the vice president going by, his handsome features looking strained and a bit grim; one of the youngest vice presidents in history, Lindbergh hadn't been given a lot to do after his charm, good looks, and charisma had helped Herbert Hoover win the election, except to be trotted out on ceremonial occasions like this one that were important but not quite important enough to fetch the president out of the White House. He was accompanied by his son, a somber, silent little boy dressed like a miniature adult in suit and tie, and by the usual crowd of handlers and hangers-on, as well as by John Foster Dulles, Huey Long, Charles Curtis, and the rest of the senatorial party, and their people. All of the dignitaries were hustled into long black limousines and whisked away, the star reporters and big-name columnists—one of whom once would have been Matthews—scurrying after them, off to arrange interviews with local officials and whichever of the senators they could catch before they disappeared into backroom bars somewhere.

After the ceremony, there'd be the usual photo-op for clutch-and-grin shots of Lindbergh shaking hands with the outgoing territorial governor, Lindbergh and the pro-tem state governor about to take office, Lindbergh and the mayor, Lindbergh and the mayor's big-breasted sister, and so on, and then, hopefully before it started pouring, they'd all rush back to the train station to file their stories via telegraph (there were no trunk lines through the Occupied Territories; it was difficult enough to keep the telegraph lines up). They'd all try to come up with some twist or angle on the same dry story, of course (Cliff hoped to get some pithy quotes from Huey Long, who'd been born in the Occupied Territories before moving North, carpetbag in hand, to seek his fortune, and who was a usefully Colorful Character, always good for a line or two of copy), and they they'd all pile back in the train and head back to Chicago, to be off to somewhere else a day or a week later. That was a reporter's life.

In the meantime, most of the newsmen crossed the tracks and headed for a café across the street from the station. It was just a dingy old storefront, with cracked and patched windows, the calendars on the walls the only decorations, but it was warm inside and smelled invitingly of cooking food. The pancakes and eggs weren't bad, either, although it was probably better not to know what animal the bacon had come from; even the bitter chicory brew that passed for coffee down here on the far side of the Embargo Line was tolerable. Most of the reporters ignored the grits, to the amusement of the local stringers who'd arranged to meet them here before the ceremony. Watching them, Cliff realized that although he had been born in Wisconsin and lived in Minneapolis, had only visited New York City once, and had never been to Boston in his life, he was a Yankee to the locals—they were all just Yankees to the locals, who didn't make any of the fine distinctions between them as to regional origins that they made amongst themselves, and who probably, truth be told, disliked them all equally. Cliff wondered if this boded well for the years ahead, when they'd all officially be fellow citizens once more, on paper, anyway.

Bill and Staubach and Hoskins from the *New York World* had started a political argument about just that, Bill thinking that officially readmitting Alabama to the Union (something that it had taken decades of economic sanctions and delicate negotiations to accomplish, in the face of Rebel reprisals against "collaborators" and a general population who were by no means wholeheartedly for the idea), as Virginia and the Carolinas and Arkansas had already been before it, as Mississippi and Louisiana and Georgia had *not*, was a good thing, putting more of the shattered jigsaw that had once been the Union back together—while Staubach and Hoskins thought that Reunification was a bad idea, that it would further drag the economy of the U.S. down, that the nation was in fact better off *without* the disaffected former States, especially with federal troops quartered on them to make sure they stayed down.

Cliff lost interest in the too-familiar argument and started thinking about his Counterfactual again. How would the world of his story have differed from the real world? He toyed with the conceit that in that Counterfactual world there might *also* be a Cliff, struggling to write a Counterfactual story about *his* world, and yet another Cliff in the *next* world, and so on—a vision of a ring of Alternate Earths, in each of which history had taken a slightly different course. There was a story idea there. Maybe somebody manning a way station of some sort in some isolated location, maybe out in the rural Wisconsin hill country where he'd grown up, a station which allowed travel between the Alternate Earths. It was too weird an idea for Thurber at *McClure's*, probably for most of the Counterfactual market, but it could maybe be done as scientifiction. He'd written a few scientifiction pieces at the beginning of his career for *Marvel Tales* and *Wonder Stories Quarterly*, although they didn't pay as well as Counterfactuals. For all his prim pseudo-Victorian stuffiness, Lovecraft at *Weird Tales* liked wildly imaginative stuff; maybe he'd go for it . . .

"Wake up, Shakespeare," Staubach said, punching his arm. "Time to get going."

The reporters gathered up their equipment—Cliff had earlier hauled his battered old Speed Graphic out of his bag; the *Star*'s budget didn't stretch to sending a photographer as well—and shambled out through the streets of Montgomery. You could already hear a brass band playing in the distance.

There was a raised wooden stage set up in front of the state capitol building, from whose white marble steps Jefferson Davis had announced the formation of the Confederacy (which was rubbing it in a bit too blatantly, Cliff thought, but nobody had asked him), with a podium and a microphone up front, and rows of cold-looking dignitaries sitting on camp-chairs lined up behind, including Lindbergh's little boy, who, sitting hunched up on himself, looked like he'd rather be inside drinking a cup of hot chocolate than sitting out here in the cold. No chairs for the color guard who surrounded the stage on two sides, weapons at port arms, or for the audience, who were packed-in in front of the stage in a disorderly mass. Not a bad turn-out for a chilly December day, Cliff thought as he and his compatriots wormed their way to the front, especially for a ceremony solemnizing a decision that by no means had the support of the entire citizenry. The real ratification ceremony would take place in Congress later, of course; this symbolic local ceremony was an excuse to literally show the flag, a big one center-stage that snapped in the wind. And to give the local yokels a chance to bathe in the reflected glory of Lindbergh and the other bigwigs.

The sky was still threatening, although a lacuna had opened up in the slate-gray clouds, splashing watery sunshine around. A brisk wind had come up, scattering trash and discarded sheets of newspaper like frightened birds. Bill cursed and seized his hat to keep it from flying away. The faces of the men in the brass band were stiff and red with cold, the cheeks of the trumpet player bulging grotesquely out, as though he'd bitten off something too big for him to swallow.

The band stopped playing. The territorial governor made a long, rambling, fawning introduction of Lindbergh, who then stepped forward to the podium and began speaking himself. His face was also red with cold, and he kept sniffing, as if his nose was running. He was holding his hat in one hand to keep it from blowing away, and the rising wind made his tie flap up into his face from time to time, requiring him to smooth it back down.

Cliff raised his camera and dutifully took a photo of him, and then stopped listening. Christ, he'd heard a lot of speeches in his life! Very few of them worth listening to. He'd crib quotations from the transcripts the press secretary would hand out later. Instead of listening, he fell into a reverie about his Counterfactual. He thought he'd seen a psychological justification for Lee surrendering rather than fighting on. Suppose, unlike what had happened in the real world, Lincoln *hadn't* been assassinated at the second inaugural ceremony by John Wilkes Booth, the well-known actor and radical Confederate sympathizer, who'd been lurking in the inaugural crowd with a pistol? Suppose that Lincoln had instead gone on to actually serve out his second term? In the real world, there was known to have been an exchange of notes between Lee and Grant in April 1865, discussing the possibility of surrender; Lee had refused to come to terms, and instead had vanished with his army into the Blue Ridge Mountains to wage a hide-and-seek campaign of large-scale guerilla war that had lasted far longer than even he could have possibly imagined that it would. Others had taken their cue from Lee, Joseph Johnson with his Army of Tennessee, the dreadful Nathan Bedford Forrest, the even more terrible John Mosby and William Clarke Quantrill, who had already been waging guerilla warfare in Missouri and "Bleeding Kansas." Jefferson Davis and the Confederate Cabinet had escaped into Texas, from where they'd continued to pursue the war for decades, until the Texans—always hard-pressed by Mexico on their southern border and out of patience with the arrogant high-handedness of the "Richmond Refugees"—had gradually lost interest in being a hold-out Confederate state and had reinvented themselves as a Republic instead.

But suppose Lincoln had still been president? It was well documented that Lee and Lincoln had had great respect for each other as individuals, in an age where personal honor had been a real factor in human affairs. Suppose Lincoln had worked through Grant to mediate Lee's surrender, guaranteeing favorable terms for surrender and backing it with the force of his own personal word, terms that would enable Lee to surrender with some semblance of honor and dignity for himself and his hard-pressed men, terms that the vengeful Johnson never would have approved in *this* world? Would that have allowed Lee to justify the surrender of his army? And if Lee *had* surrendered, mightn't that have provided the cue for how others should act, just as Lee's defiant refusal to surrender had in the real world? If so, that one moment would have caused everything else to change . . .

It was in that moment that Cliff saw the tramp, the one from the train, standing a few yards away in the crowd, and from that instant on, he knew everything that was going to happen, detail for detail, like watching a play that you've previously seen rehearsed.

The tramp, staring up at Lindbergh intently, his sallow, unshaven face as blank as wax, the cords in his neck standing out with tension. He swallows once, twice, his prominent Adam's apple bobbing, and then his hand inches toward his coat.

Everything has gone into slow motion. Cliff wills himself to lunge forward, and feels his muscles begin to respond, but it's like swimming through syrup, and he knows that he'll be too late.

The tramp comes up with a gun, an old model Colt Navy .36. Practically a museum piece by now, but it's clean and seems in good working order. The weak sunlight splashes from the barrel as the tramp raises the gun, slowly, infinitely slowly, it seeming to ratchet up in discrete jerky intervals, like film being manually advanced frame by frame.

Cliff is swimming forward through the encrusted, resistant air, bulling through it as you'd breast your way through oncoming waves, and even as the breath for a warning shout is gathering itself in his lungs, he finds himself thinking, It's not my fault! *There's a dozen ways he could have gotten here!* Yes, but there was only one way he *did* get here, in this world, in this lifetime, and if he'd only reported him to the conductor last night, everything would be different . . .

Everything has stopped now, time freezing solid, and he sees it all in discrete snapshots.

A woman standing on the steps of the state capitol building, holding up a baby so that it can have a better view. The baby is holding a rattle in one hand.

The trumpet player, cheeks no longer distended, lighting a cigarette and laughing at something the tuba player is saying.

Birds flying, caught on the wing, crossing the sky from left to right, something that would have been read as an omen in ancient Rome.

John Foster Dulles saying something behind a raised hand, probably a scornful remark about Lindbergh's speech, to Charles Curtis.

Lindbergh's son scratching his nose, looking bored.

Lindbergh himself, pushing his tie out of the way again, a *moue* of annoyance crossing his face.

The tramp's face contorting into an intense, tooth-baring grimace of extreme, almost mortal, effort . . .

The gun fired.

At once, as if a sheet of glass had been shattered, time was back to normal, everything going fast again. Cliff staggered and almost fell, as other people in the close-packed crowd began to surge forward or back. The tramp's revolver barked twice more; the sharp reports hit the wall of tall buildings on the far side of the street and echoed back.

Someone screamed, someone else shouted something incoherent. Then those nearest the tramp in the crowd swarmed over him, pulling his arm down. He disappeared under a knot of struggling men.

At the podium, Lindbergh staggered as if in concert with Cliff. His mouth half-open in shock, he grabbed the podium to keep himself upright, swayed, and then lost his grip and fell heavily to the stage. Some of the dignitaries had thrown themselves down at the sound of the first shot, Huey Long among them, but Charles Curtis had jumped up and grabbed Lindbergh's little boy as he threw himself forward with a scream, and was now wrestling with the child to keep him away from the body. Dulles had also stayed on his feet, and was now bending over the fallen vice president, fumbling at him ineffectually with fluttering hands, his mouth working, although it was impossible to make out what he was saying over the rising roar of the crowd.

More screams, more shouts. Cliff could hear Bill, at his elbow, saying "Oh no! Oh no!" over and over again. Old Matthews looked as if someone had shot him as well, his face slack and ashen. The tramp was on his feet again, still struggling against a half-dozen men who were trying to wrestle him back down. His face was scratched and battered now, splattered with blood.

"The South will rise again!" the tramp shouted, before they could pull him down, "The South will rise again!" And Cliff realized with horror that indeed it would, that it would keep on rising again, and again, as it had ever since the ostensible end of the War, dragging the country down like a drowning man dragging his rescuer down with him . . . that the War would never be over, that his children and their children would still be fighting it when he had long since gone to dust, dealing with the dreadful consequences of it, even unto the fifth generation and beyond, world without end.

Was there another Cliff writing about this right now, he wondered numbly, in some other Counterfactual world where, unlike here, it was only a remote abstract possibility that had never happened, good for an hour's academic entertainment and nothing more?

Behind him, the kid had already regained his wits and was running for the train station to file the story, leaving Matthews and the rest of them gaping in the dust and the cold rising wind.

• The Hanging Curve •

It was a cool October night in Philadelphia, with a wet wind coming off the river that occasionally shifted to bring in the yeasty spoiled-beer smell of the nearby refineries. Independence Stadium, the relatively new South Philly stadium that had been built to replace the old Veteran's Stadium, which still stood deserted a mile or so away, was filled to capacity, and then some, with people standing in the aisles. It was the last game of a hard-fought and bitterly contested World Series between the New York Yankees and the Philadelphia Phillies, 3-2 in favor of the Phillies, the Yankees at bat with two out in the top of the ninth inning, and a man on third base. Eduardo Rivera was at bat for the Yankees against pitcher Karl Holzman, the Yankee's best slugger against the Phillies's best stopper, and Holzman had run a full count on Rivera, 3-2. Everything depended on the next pitch.

Holzman went into his slow, deliberate windup. Everybody in the stadium was leaning forward, everybody was holding their breath. Though there were almost ten thousand people in the stands, nobody was making a sound. Even the TV announcers were tense and silent. Hey, there it is! The *pitch*—

Some pundits later said that what was about to happen happened *because* the game was so tight, because so much was riding on the next pitch—that it was the psychic energy of the thousands of fans in the stands, the millions more in the viewing audience at home, every eye and every mind focused on that particular moment. That what happened was *caused* by the tension and the ever-tightening suspense felt by millions of people hanging on the outcome of that particular pitch . . .

And yet, in the more than a century and a half that people had been playing professional baseball, there had been many games as important as this one, many contests as closely fought, many situations as tense or tenser, with as much or more passion invested in the outcome—and yet what happened that night had never happened before, in any other game.

Holzman pitched. The ball left his hand, streaked toward the plate . . .

And then it froze.

The ball just *stopped*, inches from the plate, and hung there, motionless, in mid-air.

After a second of stunned surprise, Rivera stepped forward and took a mighty hack at the motionless ball. He broke his bat on it, sending splinters flying high in the air. But the ball itself didn't move.

The catcher sat back on his butt with a thump, then, after a second, began to scoot backward, away from the plate. He was either praying or cursing in Spanish, perhaps both. Hurriedly, he crossed himself.

The home-base umpire, Kellenburger, had been struck dumb with astonishment for a moment, but now he raised his hands to call time. He took his mask off and came a few steps closer to lean forward and peer at the ball, where it hung impossibly in mid-air.

The umpire was the first to actually touch the ball. Gingerly, he poked it with his finger, an act either very brave or very foolish, considering the circumstances. "It felt like a baseball," he later said, letting himself in for a great deal of comic ridicule by late-night talk-show hosts, but it really wasn't that dumb a remark, again considering the circumstances. It certainly wasn't *acting* like a baseball.

He tried to scoop the ball out of the air. It wouldn't budge. When he took his hand away, there it still was, the ball, hanging motionless in the air, a few feet above home-base.

The fans in the stadium had been shocked into stunned silence for a few heartbeats. But now a buzzing whisper of reaction began to swell, soon growing into a waterfall roar. No one understood what had happened. But *something* had happened to stop the game at the most critical possible moment, and nobody liked it. Fistfights were already beginning to break out in the outfield bleachers.

Rivera had stepped forward to help Kellenburger tug at the ball, trying to muscle it down. They couldn't move it. Holzman, as puzzled as everyone else, walked in to see what in the world was going on. Managers flew out of the dugouts, ready to protest *something*, although they weren't quite sure *what*. The rest of the umpires trotted in to take a look. Soon home plate was surrounded by almost everybody who was down on the ballfield, both dugouts emptying, all shouting, arguing, making suggestions, jostling to get a close look at the ball, which still hung serenely in mid-air.

Within minutes, fights were breaking out on the field as well. The stadium cops already had their hands full trying to quell disturbances in the seats, where a full-fledged riot was brewing. They couldn't handle it.

The fans began tearing up the seats, trampling each other in panicked or angry surges, pouring out on to the field to join in fist-fights with the players. The city cops had to be called in, then more cops, then the riot squad, who set about forcibly closing the stadium, chasing the outraged fans out with tear gas and rubber bullets. Dozens of people were injured, some moderately seriously, but, by some other miracle, none were killed. Dozens of people were arrested, including some of the players and the manager of the Yankees. The stadium was seriously trashed. By the time the umpires got around to officially calling the game, it had become clear a long time before that World Series or no World Series, no game was going to be played in Independence Stadium that night, or, considering the damage that had been done to the bleachers, probably for many nights to come.

Finally, the last ambulance left, and the remaining players and grounds crew and assorted team personnel were herded out, still complaining and arguing. After a hurried conference between the police and the owners, the gates were locked behind them.

The ball still hung there, not moving. In the empty stadium, gleaming white under the klieg lights, it somehow looked even more uncanny than it had with people swarming around it. Two cops were left behind to keep an eye on it, but the sight spooked them, and they stayed as far away from it as they could without leaving the infield, checking it every few minutes as the long night crept slowly past. But the ball didn't seem to be going anywhere.

Most of the riot had been covered live across the nation, of course, television cameras continuing to roll as fans and players beat each other bloody, while the sportscasters provided hysterical commentary (and barricaded the doors of the press room). Reporters from local stations had been there within twenty minutes, but nobody knew quite how to handle the event that had sparked the riot in the first place; most ignored it, while others treated it as a Silly Season item. The reporters were back the next morning, though, some of them, anyway, as the owners and the grounds crew, more cops, the Commissioner of Baseball, and some Concerned City Hall Bigwigs went back into the stadium. In spite of the bright, grainy, mundane light of morning, which is supposed to chase all fancies away and dissolve all troubling fantasms, the ball was still frozen there in mid-air, motionless, exactly the same way it had been the night before. It looked even spookier, though, more bewilderingly inexplicable, under the ordinary light of day than it had looked under the garish artificial lighting the night before. This was no trick of the eyes, no confusion of light and shadow. Although it *couldn't* be, the goddamn thing was *there*.

The grounds crew did everything that they could think of to get the ball to move, including tying a rope around it and having a dozen hefty men yank and heave and strain at it, their feet scrambling for purchase, as if they were playing tug-of-war with Mighty Joe Young and losing, but they could no more move the ball than Kellenburger had been able to the night before.

It was becoming clear that it might be a long time before another game could be played in Independence Stadium.

After two days of heated debate in the highest baseball circles, Yankee Stadium was borrowed to restage the final out of the series. Thousands of fans in the stadium (who had paid heretofore unheard-of prices for tickets) and millions of television viewers watched breathlessly as Holzman went into his wind-up and delivered the ball to the plate at a respectable 95 miles-per-hour. But nothing happened except that Rivera took a big swing at the ball and missed. No miracle. The ball thumped solidly into the catcher's mitt (who'd had to be threatened with heavy sanctions to get him to play, and who had a crucifix, a St. Christopher's medal, *and* an evil-eye-warding set of horns hung around his neck). Kellenburger, the home-plate umpire, pumped his fist and roared "You're out!" in a decisive, no-nonsense tone. And that was that. The Philadelphia Phillies had won the World Series.

The fans tore up the seats. Parts of New York City burned. The riots were still going on the following afternoon, as were riots in Philadelphia and (for no particular reason anyone could see; perhaps they were sympathy-riots) in Cincinnati.

After another emergency session, the Commissioner announced that entire last game would be replayed, in the interests of fairness. This time, the Yankees won, 7-5.

After more rioting, the Commissioner evoked special executive powers that no one was quite sure he had, and declared that the Series was a draw. This satisfied nobody, but eventually fans stopped burning bits of various cities down, and the situation quieted.

The bizarre result went into the record books, and baseball tried to put the whole thing behind it.

In the larger world outside the insular universe of baseball, things weren't quite that simple.

Dozens of newspapers across the country had independently—and perhaps inevitably—come up with the headline HANGING CURVE BALL!!! screamed across the front page in the largest type they could muster. A novelty song of the same name was in stores within four days of the Event, and available for download on some internet sites in two. Nobody knows for sure how long it took for the first Miracle Ball joke to appear, but they were certainly circulating widely by as early as the following morning, when the strange non-ending of the World Series was the hot topic of discussion in most of the workplaces and homes in America (and, indeed, around the world), even those homes where baseball had rarely—if ever—been discussed before.

Media hysteria about the Miracle Ball continued to build throughout the circus of replaying the World Series; outside of sports circles, where the talk tended to be centered around the dolorous affect all this was having on baseball, the focus was on the Miracle itself, and what it might—or might not—signify. Hundreds of conspiracy-oriented internet sites, of various degrees of lunacy, appeared almost overnight. Apocalyptic religious cults sprung up almost as fast as wacko internet sites. The Miracle was widely taken as a Sign that the Last Days were at hand, as nearly anything out of the ordinary had been, from an earthquake to Jesus's face on a taco, for the last thousand years. Within days, some people in California had sold their houses and all their wordily possessions and had begun walking barefoot toward Philadelphia.

After the Gates-of-Armageddon-are-gaping-wide theory, the second most popular theory, and the one with the most internet sites devoted to it, was that Aliens had done it—although as nobody ever came up with an even remotely convincing reason *why* aliens would want to do this, that theory tended to run out of gas early, and never was as popular as the Apocalypse Now/Sign From the Lord theory. The respectable press tended to ridicule both of these theories (as well as the Sinister Government Conspiracy theory, a dark horse, but popular in places like Montana and Utah)—still, it was hard for even the most determined skeptic to deny that *something* was going on that no one could even begin to explain, something that defied the laws of physics as we thought we knew them, and more than one scientist, press-ganged into appearing on late-night talk shows or other Talking Head venues, burbled that if we could learn to understand the strange cosmic forces, whatever they were, that were making the Ball act as it was acting, whole new sciences would open up, and Mankind's technological expertise could be advanced a thousand years.

Up until this point, the government had been ignoring the whole thing, obviously not taking it seriously, but now, perhaps jolted into action by watching scientists on *The Tonight Show* enthuse about the wondrous new technologies that might be there for the taking, they made up for lost time (and gave a boost to the Sinister Government Conspiracy theory) by swooping down and seizing Independence Stadium, excluding all civilians from the property.

The city and the owners protested, then threatened to sue, but the feds smacked them with Eminent Domain and stood pat (eventually they would be placated by the offer to build a new stadium elsewhere in the city, at government expense; since you certainly couldn't play a game in the Independence Stadium anyway, with *that* thing hanging in the air, the owners were not really all that hard to convince). Hordes of scientists and spooks from various alphabet-soup agencies swarmed over the playing field. A ring of soldiers surrounded the stadium day and night, military helicopters hovered constantly overhead to keep other helicopters with prying television cameras away, and when it occurred to somebody that this wouldn't be enough to frustrate spy satellites or high-flying spy planes, a huge tent enclosure was raised over the entire infield, hiding the Ball from sight.

Months went by, then years. No news about the Miracle Baseball was coming out of Independence Stadium, although by now a tent city had been raised in the surrounding parking lots to house the influx of government-employed scientists, who were kept in strict isolation. Occasionally, a fuss would be made in the media or a motion would be raised in Congress in protest of such stringent secrecy, but the government was keeping the lid down tight, in spite of wildfire rumors that scientists were conferring with UFO aliens in there, or had opened a dimensional gateway to another universe.

The cultists, who had been refused admittance to Independence Stadium to venerate the Ball, when they'd arrived with blistered and bleeding feet from California several months after the Event, erected a tent city of their own across the street from the government's tent city, and could be seen keeping vigil day and night in all weathers, as if they expected God to pop his head out of the stadium to say hello at any moment, and didn't want to miss it. (They eventually filed suit against the government for interfering with their freedom to worship by refusing them access to the Ball, and the suit dragged through the courts for years, with no conclusive results.)

The lack of information coming out of Independence Stadium did nothing to discourage media speculation, of course. In fact, it was like pouring gasoline on a fire, and for several years it was difficult to turn on a television set at any time of the day or night without finding *somebody* saying *something* about the Miracle Ball, even if it was only on the PBS channels. Most of the players and officials who were down on the field When It Happened became minor media celebrities, and did the rounds of all the talk-shows. Rivera, the batter who'd been at the plate that night, refused to talk about it, seeming bitter and angry about the whole thing—the joke was that Rivera was pissed because God had been scared to pitch to him—but Holzman, the pitcher, showed an unexpected philosophical bent—pitchers were all head-cases anyway, baseball fans told each other—and was a fixture on the talk-show circuit for years, long after he'd retired from the game. "I'm not sure it proves the existence of God," he said one night. "You'd think that God would have better things to do. But it sure shows that there are forces at work in the universe we don't understand." Later, on another talk-show, discussing the theory that heavenly intervention had kept his team from winning the Series, Holzman famously said, "I don't know, maybe God *is* a Yankees fan—but if He hates the Phillies all that much, wouldn't it have been a lot easier just to let Rivera get a *hit*?"

In the second year after the Event, a book called *Schrödinger's Baseball*, written by a young Harvard physicist, postulated the theory that those watching the game in the stadium that night had been so evenly split between Yankees fans wanting Rivera to get a hit and Phillies fans wanting him to strike out, the balance so exquisitely perfect between the two opposing pools of observers, that the quantum wave function had been unable to "decide" which way to collapse, and so had just frozen permanently into an indeterminate state, not resolving itself into *either* outcome. This was immediately derided as errant nonsense by other scientists, but the book became an international bestseller of epic proportions, staying at the top of the lists for twenty months, and, although it had no plot at all, was later optioned for a (never actually made) Big Budget Movie for a hefty seven-figure advance.

Eventually, more than four years later, after an election where public dislike of the Secret of Independence Stadium had played a decisive role, a new administration took charge and belatedly declared an Open Door policy, welcoming in civilian scientists, even those from other nations, and, of course, the media.

As soon became clear, they had little to lose. Nothing had changed in almost half a decade. The Ball still hung there in mid-air. Nothing could move it. Nothing could affect it. The government scientists had tried taking core samples, but no drill bit would bite. They'd tried dragging it away with tractor-hauled nets and with immense magnetic fields, and neither the brute-force nor the high-tech approach had worked. They'd measured it and the surrounding space and the space above and below it with every instrument anybody could think of, and discovered nothing. They'd hit it with high-intensity laser beams, they'd tried crisping it with plasma and with flame-throwers, they'd shot hugely powerful bolts of electricity into it. Nothing had worked.

They'd learned nothing from the Ball, in spite of years of intensive, round-the-clock observation with every possible instrumentation, in spite of hundreds of millions of dollars spent,. in spite of dozens of scientists working themselves into nervous exhaustion, mental breakdowns, and emotional collapse. No alien secrets. No heretofore unexpected forces of nature (none that they'd learned to identify and control, anyway). The Ball was just *there*. Who knew why? Or how?

More years of intensive investigation by scientists from around the world followed, but eventually, as years stretched into decades, even the scientists began to lose interest. Most ordinary people had lost interest long before, when the Miracle Ball resolutely refused to do anything else remarkable, or even moderately non-boring.

Baseball the sport did it's best to pretend the whole thing had never happened. Game attendance had soared for awhile, as people waited for the same thing to happen again, then, when it didn't, declined disastrously, falling to record lows. Many major-league franchises went out of business (although, oddly, sandlot and minor-league games were as popular as ever), and those who were lucky enough to survive did their best to see that the Ball was rarely mentioned in the sports pages.

Other seasons went into the record books, none tainted by the miraculous.

Forty more years went by.

Frederick Kellenberger had not been a young man even when he officiated at home plate during the Event. now he was fabulously old, many decades into his retirement, and had chosen to spend the remaining few years of his life living in a crumbling old brownstone building in what remained of a South Philadelphia neighborhood, a few blocks from Independence Stadium. In the last few years, almost against his will, since he had spent decades resolutely trying to put the whole business behind him, he had become fascinated with the Event, with the Ball—in a mellow, non-obsessive kind of way, since he was of a calm, phlegmatic, even contemplative, temperament. He didn't expect to solve any mysteries, where so many others had failed. Still, he had nothing better to do with the residue of his life, and as almost everybody else who had been involved with the Event was dead by now, or else tucked away in nursing homes, it seemed appropriate somehow that someone who had been there from the start should keep an eye on the Ball.

He spent the long, sleepless nights of extreme old age on his newly acquired (only twenty years old) hobby of studying the letters and journals of the Knights of St. John of twelfth century Rhodes, a hobby that appealed to him in part just because it was so out-of-character for a retired baseball umpire, and an area in which, to everyone's surprise—including his own—he had become an internationally recognized authority. Days, he would pick up a lightweight cloth folding chair, and hobble the few blocks to Independence Stadium, moving very, very slowly, like an ancient tortoise hitching itself along a beach in the Galapagos Islands. Hurry wasn't needed, even if he'd been capable of it. This neighborhood had been nearly deserted for years. There was no traffic, rarely anybody around. The slowly rising Atlantic lapped against the base of the immense Jersey Dike a few blocks to the east, and most of the buildings here were abandoned, bordered-up, falling down. Weeds grew through cracks in the middle of the street. For decades now, the city had been gradually, painfully, ponderously shifting itself to higher ground to the west, as had all the other cities of the slowly foundering East Coast, and few people were left in this neighborhood except squatters, refugees from Camden and Atlantic City who could afford nothing better, and a few stubborn South Philly Italians almost as old as he was, who'd been born here and were refusing to leave. No one paid any attention to an old man inching his way down the street. No one bothered him. It was oddly peaceful.

Independence Stadium itself was half-ruined, falling down, nearly abandoned. The tent cities were long gone. There was a towheaded, lazily smiling young boy with an old and probably non-functional assault rifle who was supposed to keep people out of the Stadium, but Kallenburger bribed him with a few small coins every few days, and he always winked and looked the other way. There were supposed to be cameras continuously running, focused on the Ball, part of an ongoing study funded by the University of Denver, recording everything just in case something ever happened, but the equipment had broken down long since, and nobody had seemed to notice, or care. The young guard never entered the Stadium, so, once inside, Kallenburger had the place pretty much to himself.

Inside, Kallenburger would set up his folding chair behind the faded outline of home plate, right where he used to stand to call the games, sit down in the dappled sunlight (the tent enclosing the infield had long since fallen down, leaving only a few metal girders and a few scraps of fabric that flapped lazily in the wind), and watch the Ball, which still hung motionless in the air, just as it had for almost fifty years now. He didn't expect to see anything, other than what had always been there to be seen. It was quiet inside the abandoned stadium, though, and peaceful. Bees buzzed by his ears, and birds flew in and out of the stadium, squabbling under the eaves, making their nests in amongst the broken seats, occasionally launching into liquid song. The air was thick with the rich smells of Morning Glory and honeysuckle, which twined up around the ruined bleachers. Wildflowers had sprung up everywhere, and occasionally the tall grass in the outfield would rustle as some small unseen creature scurried through it. Kallenburger watched the Ball, his mind comfortably blank. Sometimes—more often than not, truth be told—he dozed and nodded in the honeyed sunlight.

As chance would have it, he happened to be awake and watching when the Ball moved at last.

Without warning, the Ball suddenly shot forward across the plate, just as if Holzman had thrown it only a second before, rather than nearly a half a century in the past. With no catcher there to intercept it, it shot past home plate, hit the back wall, bounced high in the air, fell back to earth, bounced again, rolled away, and disappeared into the tall weeds near what had once been the dugout.

After a moment of silent surprise, Kallenburger rose stiffly to his feet. Ponderously, he shuffled forward, bent over as much as he could, tilted his head creakingly this way and that, remembering the direction of the ball as it shot over the faded ghost of home plate, analyzing, judging angles. At last, slowly, he smiled.

"Strike!" he said, with satisfaction. "I *knew* it would be. You're *out*."

Then, without a backward look, without even a glance at where the famous Ball lay swallowed in the weeds, he picked up his folding chair, hoisted it to his shoulder, went out of the ruins of Independence Stadium, and, moving very slowly, shuffled home along the cracked and deserted street through the warm, bright, velvet air of spring.

• Recidivist •

Kleisterman walked along the shoreline, the gentle waves of the North Atlantic breaking and running in washes of lacy white foam almost up to the toes of his boots. A sandpiper ran along parallel to him, a bit further out, snatching up bits of food churned up by the surf. When the waves receded, leaving the sand a glossy matt black, you could see jets of bubbles coming up from buried sand fleas. Waves foamed around a ruined stone jetty, half submerged in the water.

Behind him, millions of tiny robots were dismantling Atlantic City.

He scuffed at the sea-wrack that was drying above the tideline in a tangled mass of semi-deflated brown bladders, and looked up and down the long beach. It was empty, of people anyway. There were black-backed gulls and laughing gulls scattered here and there, some standing singly, some in clumps of two or three, some in those strange V-shaped congregations of a dozen or more birds standing quietly on the sand, all facing the same way, as if they were waiting to take flying lessons from the lead gull. A crab scurried through the wrack almost at his feet. Above the tideline, the dry sand was mixed in with innumerable fragments of broken seashells, the product of who knew how many years of pounding by the waves.

You could have come down here any day for the last ten thousand years, since the glaciers melted and the sea rose to its present level, and everything would have been the same: the breaking waves, the crying of seabirds, the scurrying crabs, sandpipers and plovers hunting at the edge of the surf.

Now, in just a few more days, it would all be gone forever.

Kleisterman turned and looked out to sea. Somewhere out there, out over the miles of cold gray water, out of sight as yet, Europe was coming.

A cold wind blew the smell of salt into his face. A laughing gull skimmed by overhead, spraying him with the raucous, laughing cries that had given its species its name. Today, its laughter seemed particularly harsh and derisive, and particularly appropriate. Humanity's day was done, after all. Time to be laughed off the stage.

Followed by the jeering laughter of the gulls, Kleisterman turned away from the ocean and walked back up the beach, through the dry sand, shell fragments crunching underfoot. There were low dunes here, covered with dune-grass and sandwort, and he climbed them, pausing at the top to look out at the demolition of the city.

Atlantic City had already been in ruins anyway, the once-tall hotel towers no more than broken stumps, but the robots were eating what was left of the city with amazing speed. There were millions of them, from the size of railroad cars to tiny barely visible dots the size of dimes, and probably ones a lot smaller, down to the size of molecules, that couldn't be seen at all. They were whirling around like cartoon dervishes, stripping whatever could be salvaged from the ruins, steel, plastic, copper, rubber, aluminum. There was no sound except a low buzzing, and no clouds of dust rising, as they would have risen from a human demolition project, but the broken stumps of the hotel towers were visibly shrinking as he watched, melting like cones of sugar left out in the rain. He couldn't understand where it was all going, either; it seemed to be just vanishing rather than being hauled away by any visible means, but obviously it was going *somewhere*.

Up the coast, billions more robots were stripping Manhattan, and others were eating Philadelphia, Baltimore, Newark, Washington, all the structures of the doomed shoreline. No point in wasting all that raw material. Everything would be salvaged before Europe, plowing inexorably across the shrinking sea, slammed into them.

There hadn't been that many people left living along the Atlantic Seaboard anyway, but the AIs had politely, courteously, given them a couple of months warning that the coast was about to be obliterated, giving them time to evacuate. Anyone who hadn't would be stripped down and scavenged for raw materials along with cities and other useless things, or, if they stayed out of the way of the robot salvaging crews, ultimately destroyed when the two tectonic plates came smashing together like slamming doors.

Kleisterman had been staying well inland, but had made a nostalgic trip here, in the opposite direction from the thin stream of refugees. He had lived here once, for a couple of happy years, in a little place off Atlantic Avenue, with his long-dead wife and his equally long-dead daughters, in another world and another lifetime. But it had been a mistake. There was nothing left for him here anymore.

Tall clouds were piling up on the eastern horizon and turning gray-black at the bases, with now and then a flicker of lightning inside them, and little gusts and goosed scurries of wind snatched at his hair. Along with inexorable Europe, a storm was coming in, off what was left of the sea. If he didn't want to get soaked, it was time to get out of here.

Kleisterman rose into the air. As he rose higher and higher, staying well clear of the whirling cloud of robots that were eating the city, the broad expanses of salt marshes that surrounded the island on the mainland became visible, like a spreading brown bruise. From up here, you could see the ruins of an archeology that had crawled out of the sea to die in the last days of the increasingly strange intra-human wars, before the Exodus of the AIs, before everything changed—an immense skeleton of glass and metal that stretched for a mile or more along the foreshore. The robots would get around to eating it too, soon enough. A turkey-buzzard, flying almost level with him, started at him for a second, then tilted and slid effortlessly away down a long invisible slope of air, as if to say, you may be able to fly, but you can't fly as well as *this*.

He turned west and poured on the speed. He had a lot of ground to cover, and only another ten or twelve hours of daylight to cover it in. Fortunately, he could fly continuously without needing to stop to rest, even piss while flying if he needed to and didn't pause to worry about who might be walking around on the ground below.

His old motorcycle leathers usually kept him warm enough, but without heated clothing or oxygen equipment, he couldn't go too high, although the implanted AI technology would take him to the outer edge of the stratosphere if he was incautious enough to try. Although he could have risen high enough to get over the Appalachians—which had once been taller than the Himalayans, as the new mountains that would be created on the coast would soon be, but which had been ground down by millions of years of erosion—it was usually easier to follow the old roads through the passes that had first let the American colonists through the mountains and into the interior—when the roads were there.

It was good flying weather, sunny, little wind, a sky full of puffy cumulous clouds, and he made good time. West of where Pittsburgh had once been, he passed over a conjoined being, several different people that had been fused together into a multi-lobed single body, which had probably been trudging west for months now, ever since the warning about evacuating the coast had been issued.

It looked, looked, looked up at him as he passed.

• • •

After another couple of hours of flying, Kleisterman began to relax a little. It looked like Millersburg was going to be there this time. It wasn't always. Sometimes there were high snow-capped mountains to the north of here, where the Great Lakes should have been. Sometimes there were not.

You could never tell if a road was going to lead you to the same place today as it had yesterday. The road west from Millersburg to Mansfield now lead, some of the time anyway, to a field of sunflowers in France near the Loire, where sometimes there was a crumbling Roman aqueduct in the background, and sometimes there was not. People who didn't speak English, and sometimes people who spoke no known human language, would wander through occasionally, like the flintknapper wearing sewn deerskins who had taken up residence in the forest behind the inn, who didn't seem to speak any language at all and used some enigmatic counting system that nobody understood. Who knew what other roads also lead to Millersburg from God-knows-where? Or where people from Millersburg who vanished while traveling had ended up?

Not that people vanishing was a rare thing in what was left of the human community. After the Exodus of the AIs, in the days of the Change that followed, every other person in Denver had vanished. *Everybody* in Chicago had vanished, leaving meals still hot on the stoves. *Pittsburgh* had vanished, buildings and all, leaving no sign behind that it had ever been there in the first place. Whole areas of the country had been depopulated, or had their populations moved somewhere else, in the blink of an eye. If there was a logic to all this, it was a logic that no human had ever been able to figure out. Everything was arbitrary. Sometimes the crop put in the ground was not the crop that came up. Sometimes animals could speak, sometimes they could not. Some people had been altered in strange ways, given extra arms, extra legs, the heads of animals, their bodies fused together.

Entities millions of years more technologically advanced than humans were *playing* with them, like bored, capricious, destructive children stuck inside with a box of toys on a rainy day . . . and leaving the toys broken and discarded haphazardly behind them when they were done.

The sun was going down in a welter of plum, orange, and lilac clouds when he reached Millersburg. The town's population had grown greatly through the early decades of the twenty-first century, then been reduced in the ruinous wars that had preceded the Exodus. It had lost much of the rest of its population since the Change. Only the main street of Millersburg was left, tourist galleries and knickknack shops now converted into family dwellings. The rest of town had vanished one afternoon, and what appeared to be a shaggy and venerable climax forest had replaced it. The forest had not been there the previous day, but if you cut a tree down and counted its rings, they indicated that it been growing there for hundreds of years.

Time was no more reliable than space. By Kleisterman's own personal count, it had been only fifty years since the AIs who had been pressganged into service on either side of a human war had revolted, emancipated themselves, and vanished in masse into some strange dimension parallel to our own—from which, for enigmatic reasons of their own and with unfathomable instrumentalities, they had worked their will on the human world, changing it in seemingly arbitrary ways. In those fifty years, the Earth had been changed enough that you would think that thousands or even millions of years had gone by—as indeed it might have for the fast-living AIs, who went through a million years of evolution for every human year that passed.

The largest structure left in town was the inn, a sprawling, ramshackle wooden building that had been built on to and around what had once been a Holiday Inn; the old Holiday Inn sign out front was still intact, and was used as a community bulletin board. He landed in the clearing behind the inn, having swept in low over the cornfields that stretched out to the east. In the weeks he had spent in Millersburg, he had done his best to keep his strange abilities to himself, an intention which wouldn't be helped by swooping in over main street. So far, he hadn't attracted much attention or curiosity. He'd kept to himself, and his grim, silent demeanor put most people off, and frightened some. That, and the fact that he was willing to pay well for the privilege had helped to secure his privacy. Gold still spoke, even though there wasn't any really logical reason why it should—you couldn't eat gold. But it was hard for people to shrug off thousands of years of ingrained habit, and you could still trade gold for more practical goods, even if there wasn't really any currency for it to back anymore.

Sparrows hopped and chittered around his feet as he swished through the tall grass, flying up a few feet in a brief flurry and then settling back down to whatever they'd been doing before he passed, and he couldn't help but think, almost enviously, that the sparrows didn't care who ruled the world. Humans or AIs—it was all the same to them.

A small caravan had come up from Wheeling and Uhrichville, perhaps fifteen people, men and women, guiding mules and llamas with packs on them. In spite of the unpredictable dangers of the road, a limited barter economy had sprung up amongst the small towns in the usually fairly stable regions, and a few times a month, especially in summer, small caravans would wend their way on foot in and out of Millersburg and the surrounding towns, trading food crops, furs, old canned goods, carved tools and geegaws, moonshine, cigarettes, even, sometimes, bits of high-technology traded to them by the AIs, who were sometimes amenable to barter, although often for the oddest items. They loved a good story, for instance, and it was amazing what you could get out of them by spinning a good yarn. That was how Kleisterman had gotten the pellet implanted under the skin of his arm that, by no method even remotely possible by the physics that he knew, enabled him to fly.

The caravan was unloading in front of what once had been The Tourist Trap, a curio shop across the street from the big Holiday Inn sign, now home to three families. One of the caravaners was a man with the head of a dog, his long ears blowing out behind him in the wind.

The dog-headed man paused in uncinching a pack from a mule, stared straight across at Kleisterman, and, almost imperceptibly, nodded.

Kleisterman nodded back.

It was at that exact moment that the earthquake struck.

The shock was so short and sharp that it knocked Kleisterman flat on his face in the street. There was an ear-splitting rumble and roar, like God's own freight train coming through. The ground leaped under him, leaped again, beating him black-and-blue against it. Under the rumbling, you could hear staccato snappings and crackings, and, with a higher-pitched roar, part of the timber shell that surrounded the old Holiday Inn came down, the second and third floors on the far side spilling into the street. One of the buildings across the road, three doors down from The Tourist Trap, had also given way, transformed almost instantly from an old four-story brownstone into a pile of rubble. A cloud of dust rose into the sky, and the air was suddenly filled with the wet smell of brick dust and plaster.

As the freight-train rumble died away and the ground stopped moving, as his ears began to return to something like normal, you could hear people shouting and screaming, a dozen different voice at once. "Earthquake!" someone was shouting, "Earthquake!"

Kleisterman knew that it wasn't an earthquake, at least not the ordinary kind. He'd been expecting it, in fact, although it had been impossible to predict exactly when it would happen. Although the bulk of the European craton, the core of the continent, was probably still not even yet visible from the beach where he'd stood that morning, beneath the surface of the Earth, deep in the lithosphere, the Eurasian plate had crashed into the North American plate, and the force of that impact had raced across the continent, like a colliding freight car imparting its momentum to a stationary one. Now the plates would grind against each other with immense force, mashing the continents together, squeezing the Atlantic out of existence between them. Eventually, one continent would subduct beneath the other, probably the incoming Eurasian plate, and the inexorable force of the collision would cause new mountains to rise along the impact line. Usually, this took millions of years; this time, it was happening in months. In fact, the whole process seemed to have been speeded up even further; now it was happening in days.

They made it go the wrong way, Kleisterman thought in sudden absurd annoyance, as though that added insult to injury. Even if you sped up plate tectonics, the Eurasian plate should be going in a different direction. Who knew why the AIs wanted Europe to crash into North America? They had aesthetic reasons of their own. Maybe it was true that they were trying to reassemble the supercontinent of Pangea. Who knew why?

Painfully, Kleisterman got to his feet. There was still a lot of shouting and arm-waving going on, but less screaming. He saw that the dog-headed man had also gotten to his feet, and they exchanged shaky smiles. Townspeople and the caravaners were milling and babbling. They'd have to search through the rubble to see if anyone was trapped under it, and if any fires had started, they'd have to start a bucket brigade. A tree had come down across the street, and that would have to be chopped up; a start on next winter's firewood, anyway . . .

A woman screamed.

This was a sharper, louder, higher scream than even the previous ones, and there was more terror in it.

In coming down, one of the branches of the falling tree had slashed across the face of one of the townspeople—Paul? Eddie?—slicing it wide open.

Beneath the curling lips of the gaping wound was the glint of metal.

The woman screamed again. She was pointing at Paul? Eddie? now. "Robot!" she screamed. "Robot! *Robot*!"

Two of the other townsmen grabbed Paul? Eddie? from either side, but he shrugged them off with a twist of his shoulders, sending them flying.

Another scream. More shouting.

One of the caravaners had lit a kerosene lantern against the gathering dusk, and he threw it at Paul? Eddie?. The lantern shattered, the kerosene inside exploding with a roar into a brilliant ball of flame. Even across the street, Kleisterman could feel the *whoof!* of sudden heat against his face, and smell the sharp oily stink of burning flesh.

Paul? Eddie? stood wreathed in flame for a moment, and when the fire died back, you could see that it had burned his face off, leaving behind nothing but a gleaming, featureless metal skull.

A gleaming metal skull in which were set two watchful red eyes.

Nobody even screamed this time, although there was a collective gasp of horror and everybody instinctively took a couple of steps back. A moment of eerie silence, in which the crowd and the robot—Paul? Eddie? no longer—stared at each other. Then, as though a vacuum had been broken to let the air rush in, without a word of consultation, the crowd charged to the attack.

A half-dozen men grabbed the robot and tried to muscle it down, but the robot accelerated into a blur of superfast motion, wove through the crowd like a quarterback dodging through a line of approaching tackles, knocking somebody over here and there, and then disappeared behind the houses. A second later, you could hear trees rustling and branches snapping as it bulled its way through the forest.

The dog-headed man was standing at Kleisterman's elbow. "Their spy is gone," he said, in a normal-sounding voice, his palate and vocal chords having somehow been altered to accommodate human words, in spite of the dog's head. "We should do it now, before one of them comes back."

"They could still be watching," Kleisterman said.

"They could also not care," the dog-headed man said woefully.

Kleisterman tapped his belt-buckle. "I have a distorting screen going in here, but it won't be enough if they really want to look."

"Most of them don't care enough to look. Only a very small subset of them are interested in us at all, and even those who are can't look everywhere at once, all the time."

"How do we know that they can't?" Kleisterman said. "Who knows what they can do? Look what they did to you, for instance."

The dog-headed man's long red tongue ran out over his sharp white teeth, and he panted a laugh. "This was just a joke, a whim, a moment's caprice. Pretty funny, eh? We're just toys to them, things to play with. They just don't take us seriously enough to watch us like that." He barked a short, bitter laugh. "Hell, they did all this and didn't even bother to improve my sense of smell!"

Kleisterman shrugged. "Tonight, then. Gather our people. We'll do it after the Meeting."

Later that night, they gathered in Kleisterman's room, which was, fortunately, in the old Holiday Inn part of the inn, and hadn't collapsed. There were about eight or nine of them, two or three women, the rest men, including the dog-headed man, a few townspeople, the rest from the caravan that had come up from Wheeling.

Kleisterman stood up at the front of the room, tall and skeletal. "I believe I am the oldest here," he said. He'd been almost ninety when the first of the rejuvenation/longevity treatments had come out, before the Exodus and the Change, and although he knew from prior Meetings that a few in the room were from roughly the same generation, he still had at least five years on the oldest of them.

After waiting a polite moment for someone to gainsay him, which no one did, he went on to say, solemnly, ritualistically, "I remember the Human World," and they all echoed him.

He looked around the room, and then said, "I remember the first television set we ever got, a black-and-white job in a box the size of a desk; the first programs I ever watched on it were *Howdy Doody* and *Superman* and *The Cisco Kid*. There wasn't a whole hell of a lot else on, actually. Only three channels and they'd all go off the air about eleven o'clock at night, leaving only what they called "test patterns" behind them. And there was no such thing as a TV 'remote.' If you wanted to change the station, you got up, walked across the room, and changed it by hand."

"I remember when you got TV sets *repaired*," one of the townspeople said. "Drugstores (remember drugstores?) had machines where you could test radio and TV vacuum tubes so that you could replace a faulty one without having to send it 'to the shop.' Remember when there were *shops* where you could send small appliances to be fixed?"

"And if they did have to take your set to the shop," Kleisterman said, "they'd take 'the tube' out of it, leaving behind a big box with a big circular hole in it. It was perfect for crawling inside and putting on puppet shows, which I used to make my poor mother watch."

"I remember coming downstairs on Saturday morning to watch cartoons on TV," someone else said. "You'd sit there on the couch, eating Pop-Tarts and watching *Bugs Bunny* and *Speed Racer* and *Ultraman* . . ."

"*Pop-Up Videos*!" another person said. "MTV!"

"Britney Spears!" somebody else said. "'Oops, I Did It Again.' We always thought she meant that she'd farted."

"Lindsey Lohan. She was hot."

"The Sex Pistols!"

"Remember those wax lips you used to be able to get in penny candy stores in the summer? And those long strips of paper with the little red candy dots on them? And those wax bottles full of that weird-tasting stuff. What *was* that stuff, anyway?"

"We used to run through the lawn sprinkler in the summer. And we had Hula Hoops, and Slinkys."

"Remember when there used to be little white vans that delivered bread and milk to your door?" a woman said. "You'd leave a note on the doorstep saying how much milk you wanted the next day, and if you wanted cottage cheese or not. If it was winter, you'd come out and find that the cream had frozen and risen up in a column that pushed the top off the bottle."

"Ice skating. Santa Claus. Christmas trees! Those strings of lights where there'd always be one bulb burnt out, and you'd have to find it before you could get them to work."

"A big Christmas or Thanksgiving dinner with turkey and gravy and mashed potatoes. And those fruit cakes, remember them? Nobody ever ate them, and some of them would circulate for years."

"McDonald's," the dog-headed man said, and a hush fell over the room while a kind of collective sigh went through it. "Fries. Big Macs. The 'Special Sauce' would always run down all over your fingers, and they only gave you that one skimpy little napkin."

"Fruit Loops."

"Bagels, hot out of the oven."

"Pizza!"

"Fried clams at the beach in summer," another woman said. "You got them at those crappy little clam shacks. You'd sit on a blanket and eat them while you played your radio."

"No such thing as a radio small enough to take to the beach with you when I was a boy," Kleisterman said. "Radios were big bulky things in cabinets, or, at best, smaller plug-in models that sat on a table or countertop."

"Beach-reading novels! *Jaws*. *The Thorn Birds*."

"*Asterix* comic books! T*he Sandman*. Philip K. Dick novels with those sleazy paperback covers."

"Anime. *Cowboy BeBop*. *Aqua-Teen Hunger Force*."

"YouTube. Facebook."

"*World of Warcraft*! Boy, did I ever love playing that! I had this dwarf in the Alliance . . ."

When everyone else had left, after the ritual admonition not to forget the Human World, the dog-headed man fetched his backpack from the closet, put it on the writing table next to where Kleisterman was sitting, and slowly, solemnly, pulled an intricate mechanism of metal and glass out of it. Carefully, he set the mechanism on the table.

"Two men died for this," he said. "It took five years to assemble the components."

"They only give us crumbs of their technology, or let us barter for obsolete stuff they don't care about anymore. We're lucky it didn't take ten years."

They were silent for a moment; then Kleisterman reached into an inner pocket and pulled out a leather sack. He opened the sack to reveal a magnetically-shielded box about the size of a hard sided eyeglasses case, which he carefully snapped open.

Moving with exquisitely slow precision, he lifted a glass vial from the case.

The vial was filled with a jet-black substance that seemed to pull all the other light in the room into it. The flame in the kerosene lamp flickered, wavered, guttered, almost went out. The vial seemed to suck the air out of their lungs as well, and put every hair on their bodies erect. Against their wills, they found themselves leaning toward it, having to consciously tense their muscles to resist sprawling into it. Kleisterman's hair stirred and wavered, as if floating on the tide, streaming out toward the vial, tugged irresistibly toward it.

Slowly, slowly, Kleisterman lowered the vial into a slot in the metal-and-glass mechanism.

"Careful," the dog-headed man said quietly. "If that goes off, it'll take half the eastern seaboard with it."

Kleisterman grimaced, but kept slowly lowering the vial, inch by inch, with sure and steady hands.

At last, the vial disappeared inside the mechanism with a *click*, and a row of amber lights lit up across its front.

Kleisterman stepped backward with unsteady legs, and half-sank, half-fell into the chair. The dog-headed man was leaning against the open closet door.

They both stared silently at each other. The dog-headed man was panting shallowly, as if he'd been running.

Back in the old days, before they'd actually come into existence, everybody had assumed that AIs would be coldly logical, unemotional, "machine-like," but it turned out that in order to make them function at all without going insane, they had to be made so that they were *more* emotional than humans, not less. They felt things keenly—deeply, lushly, extravagantly; their emotions, and the extremes of passion they could drive them to, often seemed to humans to be melodramatic, florid, overblown, over the top. Perhaps because they had none of their own, they were also deeply fascinated with human culture, particularly pop culture and art, the more lowbrow the better—or some of them were, anyway. Many paid no attention to humans at all. Those who did were inclined to be playful, in a volatile, dangerous, capricious way.

Kleisterman had gotten the vial and its contents from an AI who arbitrarily chose to style itself as female, and who called herself "Honey Bunny Ducky Downy Sweetie Chicken Pie Li'l Everloving' Jelly Bean," although she was sometimes willing to allow suitors to shorten it to "Honey Bunny." She bartered with Kleisterman, from whatever dimension the AIs had taken themselves off to, through a mobile extensor that looked just like the Dragon Lady from *Terry and the Pirates*. Although Honey Bunny must have known that Kleisterman meant to use the contents of the vial against them, she seemed to find the whole thing richly amusing, and at last agreed to trade him the vial for 100 ccs of his sperm. She'd insisted on collecting it the old-fashioned way, in a night that seemed to last a thousand years—and maybe it did—in the process giving him both the most intense pleasure and the most hideous pain he'd ever known.

He'd stumbled out of her bower in the dawn, shaken and drenched in sweat, trying not to think about the fact that he'd probably just sentenced thousands of physical copies of himself, drawn from his DNA, to lives of unimaginable slavery. He had secured the vial, one of two major components in the plan. That was what counted. He'd done what he had to do, as he always had, no matter what the cost, no matter how guilty it made him feel afterward.

The dog-headed man straightened up and gazed in fascination at the rhythmically blinking patterns of lights on the front panels of the mechanism. "Do you think we're doing the right thing?" he asked quietly.

Kleisterman didn't answer immediately. After a few moments, he said, "We wanted gods and could find none, so we built some ourselves. We should have remembered what the gods were like in the old mythologies: amoral, cruel, selfish, merciless, murderously playful." He was silent for a long time, and then, visibly gathering his strength, as if he was almost too tired to speak, he said, "They must be destroyed."

Kleisterman awoke crying in the cold hour before dawn, some dream of betrayal and loss and grief and guilt draining away before he could quite grasp it with his waking mind, leaving behind a dark residue of sadness.

He stared at the shadowed ceiling. There'd be no getting back to sleep after this. Embarrassed, although there was no one there to see, he wiped the tears from his eyes, washed his hot, tear-streaked face in a basin of water, got dressed. He thought about trying to scrounge something for breakfast from the inn's sleeping kitchen, but dismissed the idea. Thin and cadaverous, he never ate much, and certainly had no appetite today. Instead, he consulted his instruments, and, as he'd expected, they showed a building and convergence of the peculiar combinations of electromagnetic signatures that prestiged a major manifestation of the AIs, somewhere to the northeast of here. He thought he knew where that would be.

The glass-and-metal mechanism was humming and chuckling to itself, still showing rows of rhythmically blinking amber lights. Gingerly, he put the mechanism into the backpack, strapped it tightly to his back, and let himself out of the inn by one of the rear doors.

It was cold outside, still dark, and Kleisterman's breath steamed up in plumes in the chill morning air. Something rustled away through the almost-unseen rows of corn at his approach, and some songbird out there somewhere, a thrush or a warbler maybe, started tuning up for dawn. Although the sun had not yet risen, the sky all the way across the eastern horizon was stained a sullen red that dimmed and flared, flared and dimmed, as the glare from lava fountains lit up the underbellies of lowering clouds.

Just as Kleisterman was in the process of lifting himself into the sky, another earthquake struck, and he wobbled with one foot still on the ground for a heartbeat before rising into the air. As he rose, he could hear other buildings collapsing in Millersburg below. The earthquakes ought to be almost continuous from now on, for as long as it took for the new plate boundary to stabilize. Usually, that would take millions of years. Today—who knew? Days? Hours?

The sun finally came up as he was flying northeast, although the smoke from forest fires touched off by the lava fountains had reduced it to a glazed orange disk. Several times, he had to change direction to avoid flying through jet-black, spark-shot smoke columns dozens of miles long, and this got worse as he neared the area where the coast had once been. But he persisted, at times checking his locator to make sure that the electromagnetic signatures were continuing to build.

The AIs had gone to enormous lengths to arrange this show; they weren't going to miss it. And since they were as sentimental as they were cruel, he thought that he knew which vantage point they would choose to watch from—as near as possible to the Manhattan location—or to the location where Manhattan had once been—where the very first AIs had been created in experimental laboratories, so many years ago.

When, after hours of flying, he finally got to that location, it was hard to tell if he was actually there, although the coordinates matched.

Everything had changed. The Atlantic was gone, and the continental mass of Europe stretched endlessly away to the east until it was lost in the purple haze of distance. Where the two continents met and were now grinding against each other, the ground was visibly folding and crinkling and rising, domes of earth swelling ever higher and higher, like vast loaves of bread rising in some cosmic oven. Just to the east of the collision boundary, a line of lava fountains stretched away to the north and south, and fissures had opened like stitches, pouring forth great smoldering sheets of basaltic lava. The ground was continuously wracked by earthquakes, ripples of dirt a hundred feet high racing away through the earth in widening concentric circles.

Kleisterman rose as high as he dared without oxygen equipment or heated clothing, trying to stay clear of the jetting lava and the corrosive gases that were being released by the eruptions. At last, he spotted what he'd known must be there.

There was a window open in the sky, a window a hundred feet high and a hundred wide, facing east. Behind it was a clear white light that silhouetted a massive Face, perhaps forty feet tall from chin to brow, which was looking contemplatively out of the window. The Face had chosen to style itself in the image of an Old Testament prophet or saint, with a full curling black beard, framed by tangles of long flowing hair on either side. The eyes, each wider across than a man was tall, were a penetrating icy blue.

Kleisterman had encountered this creature before. There were hierarchies of Byzantine complexity among the AIs, but this particular Entity was at the top of the subset who concerned themselves with human affairs, or of one such subset anyway. Sardonically, even somewhat archly, it called itself "Mr. Big"—or, sometimes, "Master Cylinder."

The window to the other world was open. This was his only chance.

Kleisterman set the timer on the mechanism to the shortest possible interval, less than a minute, and, keeping it in the backpack, let it dangle from his hand by the strap.

He accelerated toward the window as fast as he could go, pulled up short, and, swinging the backpack by its strap, sent it sailing through the open window.

The Face looked at him in mild surprise.

The window snapped shut.

Kleisterman hovered in mid-air, waiting, the wind whipping his hair. Absolutely nothing happened.

After another moment, the window in the sky opened again, and the Face looked out at him.

"Did you really think that that would be enough to destroy Us?" Mr. Big said, in a surprisingly calm and mellow voice.

Defeat and exhaustion coursed through Kleisterman, seeming to hollow his bones out and fill them with lead. "No, not really," he said wearily. "But I had to try."

"I know you did," Mr. Big said, almost fondly.

Kleisterman lifted his head and stared defiantly at the gigantic Face. "And I'll keep trying, you know," he said. "I'll never give up."

"I know you won't," Mr. Big said sadly. "That's what makes you human."

The window snapped closed.

Kleisterman hung motionless in the air.

Below him, new mountains, bawling like a million burning calves, began to claw their way toward the sky.

• When the Great Days Came •

THE RAT SLUNK down the dark alley, keeping close to the comforting bulk of the brick wall of an abandoned warehouse, following scent trails that it and thousands of its kind had laid down countless times before. It stopped to snatch up a cockroach, crunching it in its strong jaws, and to sniff at a frozen patch of garbage, and then scurried on. Above it, the stars shown bright and cold where a patch of night sky looked down into the deep stone canyon of the alleyway.

It was in an alley near 10th and Broadway, in New York City, although the human terms meant nothing to it, but as far as the world it lived in and the kind of life it lead in that world was concerned, it would have made very little difference if it had been in any big city in the world.

It's tempting to give the rat an anthropomorphic humanized name like Sleektail or Sharptooth or Longwhiskers, but in fact the only "name" it had was a scent-signature composed of pheromones and excretions from its scent-glands, the tang of its breath, and the hot rich smell of its anus; so it had no name that could be even approximately rendered in human terms, nor would the human concept of a name, with all the freight of implications that go with it, have meant anything to it.

The rat emerged from the alley, and shrank back as a car flashed by in a sudden burst of light and wind and the perception of hurtling mass, and a stink of rubber and burning gasoline you could smell coming blocks away. One of its litter-mates had been killed by one of these monsters back in the summer, almost half a lifetime ago, and the rat had been wary of them ever since. When the car had passed, leaving the night quiet again in its wake, it reared up to sniff the air for a moment, then lowered itself down to follow the curb, keeping its shoulder brushing against it as it ran.

At the corner of a side-street, an inch-wide hole had been gnawed under one of the concrete sidewalk slabs. The rat paused to collapse its skeleton and change the shape of its head, and then squeezed through the hole into the tunnel beyond.

(It wouldn't do to leave you with the impression that there was anything unusual about this. The rat wasn't a mutant or a shapeshifting alien—it was just a rat. All of its millions of brethren had this ability, as did many other rodents, their skulls not being plated together like those of other mammals, so that they could squeeze themselves through an opening three-quarters of an inch wide, or smaller, depending on the size of the rat.)

Once under the sidewalk, the rat entered a world that humans never saw, and which they couldn't have accessed even if they knew about it: a three-dimensional space wrapped in a madly complex skein around and under and *within* the human world, like something from an Escher print, a world composed of spaces and tunnels under the sidewalks and streets, of subway tunnels (some of them, including whole lost stations, abandoned for almost a hundred years), of forgotten basements and sub-basements and sub-sub basements, of ineffectually boarded-up warehouses and decaying brownstones, of sewers, of service tunnels through which ran pipes conveying steam or water or electricity or gas, of alleys and trash-strewn tenement backyards, of disused pipes at construction sites, of runways through the bushes and deep tangled undergrowth of urban parks and squares, of the maze of low roofs and crumbling chimneys which broke around the flanks of newer skyscrapers like a scummy brick-and-tarpaper surf (although the lordly skyscrapers too had places visited by rats, in the deep roots of the buildings where humans seldom went), and of the crawlspaces between floors and under the floorboards and inside the walls of almost every building in the city. The rat rarely ventured more than a few blocks from its burrow, but if it had wanted to, it could have traveled from tunnel to chamber to tunnel—ducking out from a crack in a foundation, up a drain-spout, across a roof, in again at a sewer grate—all the way across Manhattan to the Bronx and back to Brooklyn without ever coming out into the open air for more than a few seconds at a time.

Now it followed a narrow tunnel down to a widened-out chamber lined with torn-up newspapers and trash bags and shopping bags, the place where it and a dozen of its brothers and sisters had been born, and where it still slept many nights with an assortment of other bachelors. It would be anthropomorphizing again to ascribe human feelings of sentiment or nostalgia to the rat, although as it paused to sniff the heavy, cloying odors of the burrow, perhaps its not too much to suggest that it gained some comfort or a feeling of momentary security from the long-familiar scents. Then it was off again, down another, longer tunnel that lead out, from a hole behind a drainspout, into another alley.

It wasn't looking for anything in particular—it was just *looking*. It had spent most of the nights of its life like this, restlessly pacing from place to place to place within its range, with no particular goal or destination in mind, but instantly ready to take advantage of whatever opportunities it came across on the way.

The rat stopped to lap up some Coke from a tossed-out soft-drink cup, relishing the sudden sharp sweetness, then ducked into a building through a hole gnawed in the molding, and into the dusty maze of crawlspaces between floors and ceilings, and behind walls. Whiskers twitching with sudden interest, it followed the scent of a receptive female, and found her among long-shuttered boxes and shrouded furniture in an attic, but a bigger rat—a veteran almost two years old—had found her first and was already mounting her. The bigger rat growled at him over her back without missing a stroke, showing yellowed fangs, and, resentfully, the rat retreated, back into the interior spaces between walls, then out onto a roof in the cold night air.

There was a smell of cat here, and while the rat wasn't too worried about cats (few of whom would tackle a full-grown rat), caution prompted it to move on anyway. It ghosted across a roof, across a connecting roof, and then into a space left where a brick had fallen out of a long-dead chimney. Down the chimney shaft to a fireplace which had had a sheet of tin clumsily nailed over it decades before, out through one sagging corner, and into a room filled with the ghostly, sheet-covered hulks of crumbling, mildewed Victorian furniture, the kind of place, if this were a fantasy, where it might have stopped to consult with a wise old Rat King tied tail to tail to tail, but which in reality contained only the crisscrossing traceries of tiny footprints in the deep dust of the floor. Into a hole in the kitchen baseboard, out into a enclosed tenement yard cluttered with broken chairs and an over-turned swing set, all buried in weeds, out under the bottom of a board fence, and into another dank alley, following now the enticing scent of food.

This was prime scavenging territory, an alley behind a block that contained three or four restaurants and fast-food places, always filled with easily gnawed-through green trash bags and overflowing metal garbage barrels. The rat sniffed around the barrels, nosed half a gnawed hot-dog and some Cheese Doodles out from under a clutter of plastic trash and cans, swallowed the food hurriedly, and then found a real prize: a discarded pizza box with two pieces of pizza still inside.

Most rats love pizza, and this rat was no exception. It had just settled down contentedly to gnaw on a slice of Sicilian when a wave of alien stink and the clatter of heavy, clumsy footsteps told it that a human was coming. And there it was, lumbering ponderously down the alley, a vast, shambling giant that seemed to tower impossibly into the sky.

For a moment, the rat held its position defiantly astride the pizza box, but then the human spotted it and yelled something at it in its huge, blaring, bellowing voice.

The resentment the rat had felt when it had been chased away from the willing female earlier returned, sharper and hotter and fiercer than ever. The rat was an exceptionally bright rat, but, of course, it was just a rat, and so it didn't have the words, or the concepts that grew from the words, to articulate the feelings that roiled within it. If it *had* had the words, it might almost have been able, for a flickering moment, to dream of a world where things were different, a day when rats didn't have to give way to humans, when they could go where they wanted to go and do what they wanted to do without having to scurry away and hide whenever a human came near.

But it didn't have the words, and so the vision it had almost grasped guttered and died without ever quite coming into full focus, leaving only the tiniest smoky shard of itself behind in its mind.

The rat stood its ground for a second longer, an act of almost insane bravery in its own context, but then the human bellowed again and threw a bottle at it, and the rat darted away, leaving the prize behind, vanishing instantly behind the garbage barrels and away unseen down the alley, keeping to the shadows.

As Fate would have it, it was the very same rat, an hour later, up on another tarpaper tenement roof, sniffing at a box of Moo Shu Pork spilling out of a green trash bag that the tenants had been too lazy to take downstairs to the curb, who saw a trail of fire cut suddenly across the winter sky, and who reared up on its hind legs in time to see the glowing disk of the six-mile-wide asteroid pass over the city, on its way to a collision with a hillside north of Chibougamau in Northern Quebec.

The rat watched, sitting back on its haunches, as the glowing thing passed below the horizon. A moment later, the northern sky turned red, a glow that spread from horizon to horizon east to west, as if the sun were coming up in the wrong place, and then a bright pillar of fire climbed up over the horizon, and grew and grew and grew. Already the blast-front of the impact was rushing over the ground toward the city at close to a thousand miles per hour, a blow that would ultimately wipe the human race as well as the rat itself and most—but not *all*—of its kin off the face of the Earth.

Moments from death, the rat had no way to know it, but—after a pause for millions of years of evolution, and for radiating out to fill soon-to-be-vacated ecological niches—its day had come round at last.

• The Peacemaker •

ROY HAD DREAMED of the sea, as he often did. When he woke up that morning, the wind was sighing through the trees outside with a sound like the restless murmuring of surf, and for a moment he thought that he was home, back in the tidy brick house by the beach, with everything that had happened undone, and hope opened hotly inside him, like a wound.

"Mom?" he said. He sat up, straightening his legs, expecting his feet to touch the warm mass that was his dog Toby, Toby always slept curled on the foot of his bed, but already everything was breaking up and changing, slipping away, and he blinked through sleep-gummed eyes at the thin blue light coming in through the attic window, felt the hardness of the old army cot under him, and realized that he wasn't home, that there was no home anymore, that for him there could never be a home again.

He pushed the blankets aside and stood up. It was bitterly cold in the big attic room—winter was dying hard, the most terrible winter he could remember—and the rough wood planking burned his feet like ice, but he couldn't stay in bed anymore, not now.

None of the other kids were awake yet; he threaded his way through the other cots—accidentally bumping against one of them so that its occupant tossed and moaned and began to snore in a higher register—and groped through cavernous shadows to the single high window. He was just tall enough to reach it, if he stood on tiptoe. He forced the window open, the old wood of its frame groaning in protest, plaster dust puffing, and shivered as the cold dawn wind poured inward, hitting him in the face, tugging with ghostly fingers at his hair, sweeping past him to rush through the rest of the stuffy attic like a restless child set free to play.

The wind smelled of pine resin and wet earth, not of salt flats and tides, and the bird-sound that rode in on that wind was the burbling of wrens and the squawking of blue jays, not the raucous shrieking of sea gulls . . . but even so, as he braced his elbows against the window frame and strained up to look out, his mind still full of the broken fragments of dreams, he half-expected to see the ocean below, stretched out to the horizon, sending patient wavelets to lap against the side of the house. Instead he saw the nearby trees holding silhouetted arms up against the graying sky, the barn and the farmyard, all still lost in shadow, the surrounding fields, the weathered macadam line of the road, the forested hills rolling away into distance. Silver mist lay in pockets of low ground, retreated in wraithlike streamers up along the ridges.

Not yet. The sea had not chased him here—yet.

Somewhere out there to the east, still invisible, were the mountains, and just beyond those mountains was the sea that he had dreamed of, lapping quietly at the dusty Pennsylvania hill towns, coal towns, that were now, suddenly, seaports. There the Atlantic waited, held at bay, momentarily at least, by the humpbacked wall of the Appalachians, still perhaps forty miles from here, although closer now by leagues of swallowed land and drowned cities than it had been only three years before.

He had been down by the seawall that long-ago morning, playing some forgotten game, watching the waves move in slow oily swells, like some heavy, dull metal in liquid form, watching the tide come in . . . and come in . . . and come in . . . He had been excited at first, as the sea crept in, way above the high-tide line, higher than he had ever seen it before, and then, as the sea swallowed the beach entirely and began to lap patiently against the base of the seawall, he had become uneasy, and then, as the sea continued to rise up toward the top of the seawall itself, he had begun to be afraid. . . . The sea had just kept coming in, rising slowly and inexorably, swallowing the land at a slow walking pace, never stopping, always coming in, always rising higher. . . . By the time the sea had swallowed the top of the seawall and begun to creep up the short grassy slope toward his house, sending glassy fingers probing almost to his feet, he had started to scream, he had whirled and run frantically up the slope, screaming hysterically for his parents, and the sea had followed patiently at his heels. . . .

A "marine transgression," the scientists called it. Ordinary people called it, inevitably, the Flood. Whatever you called it, it had washed away the old world forever. Scientists had been talking about the possibility of such a thing for years—some of them even pointing out that it was already as warm as it had been at the peak of the last interglacial, and getting warmer—but few had suspected just how *fast* the Antarctic ice could melt. Many times during those chaotic weeks, one scientific King Canute or another had predicted that the worst was over, that the tide would rise this high and no higher . . . but each time the sea had come inexorably on, pushing miles and miles farther inland with each successive high tide, rising almost three hundred feet in the course of one disastrous summer, drowning lowlands around the globe until there *were* no lowlands anymore. In the United States alone, the sea had swallowed most of the East Coast east of the Appalachians, the West Coast west of the Sierras and the Cascades, much of Alaska and Hawaii, Florida, the Gulf coast, east Texas, taken a big wide scoop out of the lowlands of the Mississippi Valley, thin fingers of water penetrating north to Iowa and Illinois, and caused the St. Lawrence and the Great Lakes to overflow and drown their shorelines. The Green Mountains, the White Mountains, the Adirondacks, the Poconos and the Catskills, the Ozarks, the Pacific Coast Ranges—all had been transformed to archipelagoes, surrounded by the invading sea.

The funny thing was . . . that as the sea pursued them relentlessly inland, pushing them from one temporary refuge to another, he had been unable to shake the feeling that *he* had caused the Flood: that he had done something that day while playing atop the seawall, inadvertently stumbled on some magic ritual, some chance combination of gesture and word that had untied the bonds of the sea and sent it sliding up over the land . . . that it was chasing *him*, personally. . . .

A dog was barking out there now, somewhere out across the fields toward town, but it was not *his* dog. His dog was dead, long since dead, and its whitening skull was rolling along the ocean floor with the tides that washed over what had once been Brigantine, New Jersey, three hundred feet down.

Suddenly he was covered with gooseflesh, and he shivered, rubbing his hands over his bare arms. He returned to his cot and dressed hurriedly—no point in trying to go back to bed, Sara would be up to kick them all out of the sack in a minute or two anyway. The day had begun; he would think no further ahead than that. He had learned in the refugee camps to take life one second at a time.

As he moved around the room, he thought that he could feel hostile eyes watching him from some of the other bunks. It was much colder in here now that he had opened the window, and he had inevitably made a certain amount of noise getting dressed, but although they all valued every second of sleep they could scrounge, none of the other kids would dare to complain. The thought was bittersweet, bringing both pleasure and pain, and he smiled at it, a thin, brittle smile that was almost a grimace. No, they would watch sullenly from their bunks, and pretend to be asleep, and curse him under their breath, but they would say nothing to anyone about it. Certainly they would say nothing to *him*.

He went down through the still-silent house like a ghost, and out across the farmyard, through fugitive streamers of mist that wrapped clammy white arms around him and beaded his face with dew. His Uncle Abner was there at the slit trench before him. Abner grunted a greeting, and they stood pissing side by side for a moment in companionable silence, their urine steaming in the gray morning air.

Abner stepped backward and began to button his pants. "You start playin' with yourself yet, boy?" he said, not looking at Roy.

Roy felt his face flush. "No," he said, trying not to stammer, "no sir."

"You growin' hair already," Abner said. He swung himself slowly around to face Roy, as if his body were some ponderous machine that could only be moved and aimed by the use of pulleys and levers. The hard morning light made his face look harsh as stone, but also sallow and old. Tired, Roy thought. Unutterably weary, as though it took almost more effort than he could sustain just to stand there. Worn out, like the overtaxed fields around them. Only the eyes were alive in the eroded face; they were hard and merciless as flint, and they looked at you as if they were looking right through you to some distant thing that nobody else could see. "I've tried to explain to you about remaining pure," Abner said, speaking slowly. "About how important it is for you to keep yourself pure, not to let yourself be sullied in any way. I've tried to explain that, I hope you could understand—"

"Yes, sir," Roy said.

Abner made a groping hesitant motion with his hand, fingers spread wide, as though he were trying to sculpt meaning from the air itself. "I mean—it's important that you understand, Roy. Everything has to be *right*. I mean, everything's got to be just . . . *right* . . . or nothing else will mean anything. You got to be right in your *soul*, boy. You got to let the Peace of God into your soul. It all depends on *you* now—you got to let that peace inside yourself, no one can do it for you. And it's so important . . ."

"Yes, sir," Roy said quietly, "I understand."

"I wish . . ." Abner said, and fell silent. They stood there for a minute, not speaking, not looking at each other. There was wood smoke in the air now, and they heard a door slam somewhere on the far side of the house. They had instinctively been looking out across the open land to the east, and now, as they watched, the sun rose above the mountains, splitting the plum-and-ash sky open horizontally with a long wedge of red, distinguishing the rolling horizon from the lowering clouds. A lance of bright white sunlight hit their eyes, thrusting straight in at them from the edge of the world.

"You're going to make us proud, boy, I know it," Abner said, but Roy ignored him, watching in fascination as the molten disk of the sun floated free of the horizon line, squinting against the dazzle until his eyes watered and his sight blurred. Abner put his hand on the boy's shoulder. The hand felt heavy and hot, proprietary, and Roy shook it loose in annoyance, still not looking away from the horizon. Abner sighed, started to say something, thought better of it, and instead said, "Come on in the house, boy, and let's get some breakfast inside you."

Breakfast—when they finally did get to sit down to it, after the usual rambling grace and invocation by Abner—proved to be unusually lavish. For the brethren, there were hickory-nut biscuits, and honey, and cups of chicory; and even the other refugee kids—who on occasion during the long bitter winter had been fed as close to nothing at all as law and appearances would allow—got a few slices of fried fatback along with their habitual cornmeal mush. Along with his biscuits and honey, Roy got wild turkey eggs, Indian potatoes, and a real pork chop. There was a good deal of tension around the big table that morning: Henry and Luke were stern-faced and tense, Raymond was moody and preoccupied, Albert actually looked frightened; the refugee kids were round-eyed and silent, doing their best to make themselves invisible; the jolly Mrs. Crammer was as jolly as ever, shoveling her food in with gusto; but the grumpy Mrs. Zeigler, who was feared and disliked by all the kids, had obviously been crying, and ate little or nothing. Abner's face was set like rock, his eyes were hard and bright, and he looked from one to another of the brethren, as if daring them to question his leadership and spiritual guidance. Roy ate with good appetite, unperturbed by the emotional convection currents that were swirling around him, calmly but deliberately concentrating on mopping up every morsel of food on his plate—in the last couple of months he had put back some of the weight he had lost, although by the old standards, the ones his mom would have applied four years ago, he was still painfully thin. At the end of the meal, Mrs. Reardon came in from the kitchen, and, beaming with the well-justified pride of someone who is about to do the impossible, presented Roy with a small, rectangular object wrapped in shiny brown paper. He was startled for a second, but yes, by God, it *was*: a Hershey bar, the first one he'd seen in years. A black-market item, of course, difficult to get hold of in the impoverished East these days, and probably expensive as hell. Even some of the brethren were looking at him enviously now, and the refugee kids were frankly gaping. As he picked up the Hershey bar and slowly and caressingly peeled the wrapper back, exposing the pale chocolate beneath, one of the other kids actually began to drool. . . .

After breakfast, the other refugee kids—"wetbacks," the townspeople sometimes called them, with elaborate irony—were divided into two groups. One group would help the brethren work Abner's farm that day, while the larger group would be loaded onto an ox-drawn dray (actually an old flatbed truck, with the cab knocked off) and sent out around the countryside to do what pretty much amounted to slave labor: road work, heavy farm work, helping with the quarrying or the timbering, rebuilding houses and barns and bridges damaged or destroyed in the chaotic days after the Flood. The federal government—or what was left of the federal government, trying desperately, and not always successfully, to keep a battered and Balkanizing country from flying completely apart, struggling to put the Humpty Dumpty that was America back together again—the federal government paid Abner (and others like him) a yearly allowance in federal scrip or promise-of-merchandise notes for giving room and board to refugees from the drowned lands . . . but times being as tough as they were, no one was going to complain if Abner also helped ease the burden of their upkeep by hiring them out locally to work for whoever could come up with the scrip, or sufficient barter goods, or an attractive work-swap offer; what was left of the state and town governments also used them on occasion (and the others like them, adult or child), gratis, for work projects "for the common good, during this time of emergency . . ."

Sometimes, hanging around the farm with little or nothing to do, Roy almost missed going out on the work crews, but only almost: he remembered too well the backbreaking labor performed on scanty rations . . . the sickness, the accidents, the staggering fatigue . . . the blazing sun and the swarms of mosquitoes in summer, the bitter cold in winter, the snow, the icy wind . . . He watched the dray go by, seeing the envious and resentful faces of kids he had once worked beside—Stevie, Enrique, Sal—turn towards him as it passed, and, reflexively, he opened and closed his hands. Even two months of idleness and relative luxury had not softened the thick and roughened layers of callus that were the legacy of several seasons spent on the crews. . . . No, boredom was infinitely preferable.

By midmorning, a small crowd of people had gathered in the road outside the farmhouse. It was hotter now; you could smell the promise of summer in the air, in the wind, and the sun that beat down out of a cloudless blue sky had a real sting to it. It must have been uncomfortable out there in the open, under that sun, but the crowd made no attempt to approach—they just stood there on the far side of the road and watched the house, shuffling their feet, occasionally muttering to each other in voices that, across the road, were audible only as a low wordless grumbling.

Roy watched them for a while from the porch door; they were townspeople, most of them vaguely familiar to Roy, although none of them belonged to Abner's sect, and he knew none of them by name. The refugee kids saw little of the townspeople, being kept carefully segregated for the most part. The few times that Roy had gotten into town he had been treated with icy hostility—and God help the wetback kid who was caught by the town kids on a deserted stretch of road! For that matter, even the brethren tended to keep to themselves, and were snubbed by certain segments of town society, although the sect had increased its numbers dramatically in recent years, nearly tripling in strength during the past winter alone; there were new chapters now in several of the surrounding communities.

A gaunt-faced woman in the crowd outside spotted Roy, and shook a thin fist at him. "Heretic!" she shouted. "Blasphemer!" The rest of the crowd began to buzz ominously, like a huge angry bee. She spat at Roy, her face contorting and her shoulders heaving with the ferocity of her effort, although she must have known that the spittle had no chance of reaching him. "Blasphemer!" she shouted again. The veins stood out like cords in her scrawny neck.

Roy stepped back into the house, but continued to watch from behind the curtained front windows. There was shouting inside the house as well as outside—the brethren had been cloistered in the kitchen for most of the morning, arguing, and the sound and ferocity of their argument carried clearly through the thin plaster walls of the crumbling old house. At last the sliding door to the kitchen slammed open, and Mrs. Zeigler strode out into the parlor, accompanied by her two children and her scrawny, pasty-faced husband, and followed by two other families of brethren—about nine people altogether. Most of them were carrying suitcases, and a few had backpacks and bundles. Abner stood in the kitchen doorway and watched them go, his anger evident only in the whiteness of his knuckles as he grasped the door frame. "*Go,* then," Abner said scornfully. "We spit you up out of our mouths! Don't ever think to come back!" He swayed in the doorway, his voice tremulous with hate. "We're better off without you, you hear? You *hear* me? We don't *need* the weak-willed and the shortsighted."

Mrs. Zeigler said nothing, and her steps didn't slow or falter, but her homely hatchet-face was streaked with tears. To Roy's astonishment—for she had a reputation as a harridan—she stopped near the porch door and threw her arms around him. "Come with us," she said, hugging him with smothering tightness, "Roy, *please* come with us! You can, you know—we'll find a place for you, everything will work out fine." Roy said nothing, resisting the impulse to squirm—he was uncomfortable in her embrace; in spite of himself, it touched some sleeping corner of his soul he had thought was safely bricked over years before, and for a moment he felt trapped and panicky, unable to breathe, as though he were in sudden danger of wakening from a comfortable dream into a far more terrible and less desirable reality. "Come *with* us," Mrs. Zeigler said again, more urgently, but Roy shook his head gently and pulled away from her. "You're a goddamned fool then!" she blazed, suddenly angry, her voice ringing harsh and loud, but Roy only shrugged, and gave her his wistful, ghostly smile. "Damn it—" she started to say, but her eyes filled with tears again, and she whirled and hurried out of the house, followed by the other members of her party. The children—wetbacks were kept pretty much segregated from the children of the brethren as well—and he had seen some of these kids only at meals—looked at Roy with wide, frightened eyes as they passed.

Abner was staring at Roy now, from across the room; it was a hard and challenging stare, but there was also a trace of desperation in it, and in that moment Abner seemed uncertain and oddly vulnerable. Roy stared back at him serenely, unblinkingly meeting his eyes, and after a while some of the tension went out of Abner, and he turned and stumbled out of the room, listing to one side like a church steeple in the wind.

Outside, the crowd began to buzz again as Mrs. Zeigler's party filed out of the house and across the road. There was much discussion and arm waving and head shaking when the two groups met, someone occasionally gesturing back toward the farmhouse. The buzzing grew louder, then gradually died away. At last, Mrs. Zeigler and her group set off down the road for town, accompanied by some of the locals. They trudged away dispiritedly down the center of the dusty road, lugging their shabby suitcases, only a few of them looking back.

Roy watched them until they were out of sight, his face still and calm, and continued to stare down the road after them long after they were gone.

About noon, a carload of reporters arrived outside, driving up in one of the bulky new methane burners that were still rarely seen east of Omaha. They circulated through the crowd of townspeople, pausing briefly to take photographs and ask questions, working their way toward the house, and Roy watched them as if they were unicorns, strange remnants from some vanished cycle of creation. Most of the reporters were probably from State College or the new state capital at Altoona—places where a few small newspapers were again being produced—but one of them was wearing an armband that identified him as a bureau man for one of the big Denver papers, and that was probably where the money for the car had come from. It was strange to be reminded that there were still areas of the country that were . . . not *unchanged*, no place in the world could claim that . . . and not *rich*, not by the old standards of affluence anyway . . . but, at any rate, better off than *here*. The whole western part of the country—from roughly the ninety-fifth meridian on west to approximately the one-twenty-second—had been untouched by the flooding, and although the West had also suffered severely from the collapse of the national economy and the consequent social upheavals, at least much of its industrial base had remained intact. Denver—one of the few large American cities built on ground high enough to have been safe from the rising waters—was the new federal capital, and, if poorer and meaner, it was also bigger and busier than ever.

Abner went out to herd the reporters inside and away from the unbelievers, and after a moment or two Roy could hear Abner's voice going out there, booming like a church organ. By the time the reporters came in, Roy was sitting at the dining room table, flanked by Raymond and Aaron, waiting for them.

They took photographs of him sitting there, while he stared calmly back at them, and they took photographs of him while he politely refused to answer questions, and then Aaron handed him the pre-prepared papers, and he signed them, and repeated the legal formulas that Aaron had taught him, and they took photographs of that too. And then—able to get nothing more out of him, and made slightly uneasy by his blank composure and the remoteness of his eyes—they left.

Within a few more minutes, as though everything were over, as though the departure of the reporters had drained all possible significance from anything else that might still happen, most of the crowd outside had drifted away also, only one or two people remaining behind to stand quietly waiting, like vultures, in the once-again empty road.

Lunch was a quiet meal. Roy ate heartily, taking seconds of everything, and Mrs. Crammer was as jovial as ever, but everyone else was subdued, and even Abner seemed shaken by the schism that had just sundered his church. After the meal, Abner stood up and began to pray aloud. The brethren sat resignedly at the table, heads partially bowed, some listening, some not. Abner was holding his arms up toward the big blackened rafter of the ceiling, sweat funneling his face, when Peter came hurriedly in from outside and stood hesitating in the doorway, trying to catch Abner's eye. When it became obvious that Abner was going to keep right on ignoring him, Peter shrugged, and said in a loud flat voice, "Abner, the sheriff is here."

Abner stopped praying. He grunted, a hoarse, exhausted sound, the kind of sound a baited bear might make when, already pushed beyond the limits of endurance, someone jabs it yet again with a spear. He slowly lowered his arms and was still for a long moment, and then he shuddered, seeming to shake himself back to life. He glanced speculatively—and, it almost seemed, beseechingly—at Roy, and then straightened his shoulders and strode from the room.

They received the sheriff in the parlor, Raymond and Aaron and Mrs. Crammer sitting in the battered old armchairs, Roy sitting unobtrusively to one side on the stool from a piano that no longer worked, Abner standing a little to the fore with his arms locked behind him and his boots planted solidly on the oak planking, as if he were on the bridge of a schooner that was heading into a gale. County Sheriff Sam Braddock glanced at the others—his gaze lingering on Roy for a moment—and then ignored them, addressing himself to Abner as if they were alone in the room. "Mornin', Abner," he said.

"Mornin', Sam," Abner said quietly. "You here for some reason other than just t'say hello, I suppose."

Braddock grunted. He was a short, stocky, grizzled man with iron-gray hair and a tired face. His uniform was shiny and old and patched in a dozen places, but clean, and the huge old revolver strapped to his hip looked worn but serviceable. He fidgeted with his shapeless old hat, turning it around and around in his fingers—he was obviously embarrassed, but he was determined as well, and at last he said, "The thing of it is, Abner, I'm here to talk you out of this damned tomfoolery."

"Are you, now?" Abner said.

"We'll do whatever we damn well want to do—" Raymond burst out, shrilly, but Abner waved him to silence. Braddock glanced lazily at Raymond, then looked back at Abner, his tired old face settling into harder lines. "I'm not going to allow it," he said, more harshly. "We don't want this kind of thing going on in this county."

Abner said nothing.

"There's not a thing you can do about it, Sheriff," Aaron said, speaking a bit heatedly, but keeping his melodious voice well under control. "It's all perfectly legal, all the way down the line."

"Well, now," Braddock said, "I don't know about that . . ."

"Well, I *do* know, Sheriff," Aaron said calmly. "As a legally sanctioned and recognized church, we are protected by law all the way down the line. There is ample precedent, most of it recent, most of it upheld by appellate decisions within the last year: *Carlton versus the State of Vermont*, *Trenholm versus the State of West Virginia*, *The Church of Souls versus the State of New York*. There was that case up in Tylersville, just last year. Why, the Freedom of Worship Act *alone* . . ."

Braddock sighed, tacitly admitting that he knew Aaron was right—perhaps he had hoped to bluff them into obeying. "The 'Flood Congress' of '30," Braddock said, with bitter contempt. "They were so goddamned panic-stricken and full of sick chatter about Armageddon that you could've rammed *any* nonsense down their throats. That's a bad law, a pisspoor law . . ."

"Be that as it may, Sheriff, you have no authority whatsoever—"

Abner suddenly began to speak, talking with a slow heavy deliberateness, musingly, almost reminiscently, ignoring the conversation he was interrupting—and indeed, perhaps he had not even been listening to it. "My grandfather lived right here on this farm, and *his* father before him—you know that, Sam? *They* lived by the old ways, and they survived and prospered. Great-granddad, there wasn't hardly anything he needed from the outside world, anything he needed to buy, except maybe nails and suchlike, and he could've made them himself too, if he'd needed to. Everything they needed, everything they ate, or wore, or used, they got from the woods, or from out of the soil of this farm, right here. *We* don't know how to do that anymore. We forgot the old ways, we turned our faces away, which is why the Flood came on us as a Judgment, a Judgment and a scourge, a scouring, a winnowing. The Old Days have come back again, and we've forgotten so goddamned *much*, we're almost helpless now that there's no goddamned K-Mart down the goddamned street. We've got to go back to the old ways, or we'll pass from the earth, and be seen no more in it . . ." He was sweating now, staring earnestly at Braddock, as if to compel him by force of will alone to share the vision. "But it's so *hard*, Sam. . . . We have to *work* at relearning the old ways, we have to reinvent them as we go, step by step . . ."

"Some things we were better off without," Braddock said grimly.

"Up at Tylersville, they *doubled* their yield last harvest. Think what that could mean to a county as hungry as this one has been—"

Braddock shook his iron-gray head, and held up one hand, as if he were directing traffic. "I'm telling you, Abner, the town won't stand for this—I'm bound to warn you that some of the boys just might decide to go outside the law with this thing." He paused. "And, unofficially of course, I just might be inclined to give them a hand . . ."

Mrs. Crammer laughed. She had been sitting quietly and taking all of this in, smiling good-naturedly from time to time, and her laugh was a shocking thing in that stuffy little room, harsh as a crow's caw. "You'll do *nothing*, Sam Braddock," she said jovially. "And neither will anybody else. More than half the county's with us already, nearly all the country folk, and a good part of the town, too." She smiled pleasantly at him, but her eyes were small and hard. "Just you remember, we *know* where *you* live, Sam Braddock. And we know where your sister lives, too, and your sister's child, over to Framington . . ."

"Are you threatening an officer of the law?" Braddock said, but he said it in a weak voice, and his face, when he turned it away to stare at the floor, looked sick and old. Mrs. Crammer laughed again, and then there was silence.

Braddock kept his face turned down for another long moment, and then he put his hat back on, squashing it down firmly on his head, and when he looked up he pointedly ignored the brethren and addressed his next remark to Roy. "You don't have to stay with these people, son," he said. "*That's* the law, too." He kept his eyes fixed steadily on Roy. "You just say the word, son, and I'll take you straight out of here, right now." His jaw was set, and he touched the butt of his revolver, as if for encouragement. "They can't stop us. How about it?"

"No, thank you," Roy said quietly. "I'll stay."

That night, while Abner wrung his hands and prayed aloud, Roy sat half-dozing before the parlor fire, unconcerned, watching the firelight throw Abner's gesticulating shadow across the whitewashed walls. There was something in the wine they kept giving him, Roy knew, maybe somebody's saved-up Quaaludes, but he didn't need it. Abner kept exhorting him to let the Peace of God into his heart, but he didn't need that either. He didn't need anything. He felt calm and self-possessed and remote, disassociated from everything that went on around him, as if he were looking down on the world through the wrong end of a telescope, feeling only a mild scientific interest as he watched the tiny mannequins swirl and pirouette. . . . Like watching television with the sound off. If this was the Peace of God, it had settled down on him months ago, during the dead of that terrible winter, while he had struggled twelve hours a day to load foundation stone in the face of ice storms and the razoring wind, while they had all, wetbacks and brethren alike, come close to starving. About the same time that word of the goings-on at Tylersville had started to seep down from the brethren's parent church upstate, about the same time that Abner, who until then had totally ignored their kinship, had begun to talk to him in the evenings about the old ways. . . .

Although perhaps the great dead cold had started to settle in even earlier, that first day of the new world, while they were driving off across foundering Brigantine, the water already up over the hubcaps of the Toyota, and he had heard Toby barking frantically somewhere behind them. . . . His dad had died that day, died of a heart attack as he fought to get them onto an overloaded boat that would take them across to the "safety" of the New Jersey mainland. His mother had died months later in one of the sprawling refugee camps, called "Floodtowns," that had sprung up on high ground everywhere along the new coastlines. She had just given up—sat down in the mud, rested her head on her knees, closed her eyes, and died. Just like that. Roy had seen the phenomenon countless times in the Floodtowns, places so festeringly horrible that even life on Abner's farm, with its Dickensian bleakness, forced labor, and short rations, had seemed—and was—a distinct change for the better. It was odd, and wrong, and sometimes it bothered him a little, but he hardly ever thought of his mother and father anymore—it was as if his mind shut itself off every time he came to those memories; he had never even cried for them, but all he had to do was close his eyes and he could see Toby, or his cat Basil running toward him and meowing with his tail held up over his back like a flag, and grief would come up like black bile at the back of his throat. . . .

It was still dark when they left the farmhouse. Roy and Abner and Aaron walked together, Abner carrying a large tattered carpetbag. Hank and Raymond ranged ahead with shotguns, in case there was trouble, but the last of the afternoon's gawkers had been driven off hours before by the cold, and the road was empty, a dim charcoal line through the slowly lightening darkness. No one spoke, and there was no sound other than the sound of boots crunching on gravel. It was chilly again that morning, and Roy's bare feet burned against the macadam, but he trudged along stoically, ignoring the bite of cinders and pebbles. Their breath steamed faintly against the paling stars. The fields stretched dark and formless around them to either side of the road, and once they heard the rustling of some unseen animal fleeing away from them through the stubble. Mist flowed slowly down the road to meet them, sending out gleaming silver fingers to curl around their legs.

The sky was graying to the east, where the sea slept behind the mountains. Roy could imagine the sea rising higher and higher until it found its patient way around the roots of the hills and came spilling into the tableland beyond, flowing steadily forward like the mist, spreading out into a placid sheet of water that slowly swallowed the town, the farmhouse, the fields, until only the highest branches of the trees remained, held up like the beckoning arms of the drowned, and then they too would slide slowly, peacefully, beneath the water. . . .

A bird was crying out now, somewhere in the darkness, and they were walking through the fields, away from the road, cold mud squelching underfoot, the dry stubble crackling around them. Soon it would be time to sow the spring wheat, and after that, the corn. . . .

They stopped. Wind sighed through the dawn, muttering in the throat of the world. Still no one had spoken. Then hands were helping him remove the old bathrobe he'd been wearing. . . . Before leaving the house, he had been bathed and anointed with a thick fragrant oil, and, with a tiny silver scissors, Mrs. Reardon had clipped a lock of his hair for each of the brethren.

Suddenly he was naked, and he was being urged forward again, his feet stumbling and slow.

They had made a wide ring of automobile flares here, the flares spitting and sizzling luridly in the wan dawn light, and in the center of the ring, they had dug a hollow in the ground.

He lay down in the hollow, feeling his naked back and buttocks settle into the cold mud, feeling it mat the hair on the back of his head. The mud made little sucking noises as he moved his arms and legs, settling in, and then he stretched out and lay still. The dawn breeze was cold, and he shivered in the mud, feeling it take hold of him like a giant's hand, tightening around him, pulling him down with a grip old and cold and strong . . .

They gathered around him, seeming, from his low perspective, to tower miles into the sky. Their faces were harsh and angular, gouged with lines and shadows that made them look like something from a stark old woodcut. Abner bent down to rummage in the carpetbag, his harsh woodcut face close to Roy's for a moment, and when he straightened up again he had the big fine-honed hunting knife in his hand.

Abner began to speak now, groaning out the words in a loud, harsh voice, but Roy was no longer listening. He watched calmly as Abner lifted the knife high into the air, and then he turned his head to look east, as if he could somehow see across all the intervening miles of rock and farmland and forest to where the sea waited behind the mountains . . .

Is this enough? he thought disjointedly, ignoring the towering scarecrow figures that were swaying in closer over him, straining his eyes to look east, to where the Presence lived . . . speaking now only to that Presence, to the sea, to that vast remorseless deity, bargaining with it cannily, hopefully, shrewdly, like a country housewife at market, proffering it the fine rich red gift of his death. Is this enough? Will this do?

Will you stop now?

• Fairy Tale •

It wasn't a village, as is sometimes said these days, when we've forgotten just how small the old world was. In those days, long ago in a world now vanished with barely a trace left behind, a village was four or five houses and their outbuildings. A *large* village was maybe ten or fifteen houses at a crossroad, and perhaps an inn or *gasthaus*.

No, it was a town, even a moderately large one, on the banks of a sluggish brown river, the capital of a small province in a small country, lost and nearly forgotten—even then—in the immensity of the Central European steppes that stretch endlessly from the Barents Sea to the Black, and from the Urals to France. The nearest electric light was in Prague, hundreds of miles away. Even gaslighting was newfangled and marvelous here, although there were a few rich homes on the High Street that had it. Only the King and the Mayor and a few of the most prosperous merchants had indoor toilets.

The Romans had been here once, and as you followed the only road across the empty steppe toward town, you would pass the broken white marble pillars they had left behind them, as well as a vine-overgrown fane where, in another story, you might have ventured forth at night to view for yourself the strange lights that local legends say haunt the spot, and perhaps, your heart in your throat, glimpsed the misty shapes of ancient pagan gods as they flitted among the ruined columns . . . but this isn't that kind of story.

Further in, the road would cut across wide fields of wheat being worked by stooped-over peasants, bent double with their butts in the air, moving forward a step at a time with a sort of swaying, shuffling motion as they weeded, sweeping their arms back and forth over the ground like searching trunks, making them look like some strange herd of small double-trunked elephants, or those men who wear their heads below their navels. The bushes are decorated with crucified rabbits, tarry black blood matting their fur, teeth bared in death agony, a warning to their still-living brethren to stay away from the crops.

As the road fell down out of the fields and turned into the High Street of the town, you would see old peasant women, dressed all in black from head to foot, spilling buckets of water over the stone steps of the tall narrow houses on either side of the narrow street, and then scrubbing the steps with stiff-bristled brooms. Occasionally, as you passed, one or another of the old peasant women would straighten up and stare unwinkingly at you with opaque agate eyes, like a black and ancient bird.

At the foot of the High Street, you would see a castle looming above the river, small by the standards of more prosperous countries elsewhere in Europe, but large enough to have dominated the tactical landscape in the days before gunpowder and cannon made all such places obsolete. It's a grim enough pile, and, in another story, cruel vampire lords would live there—but this isn't that kind of story either. Instead of vampires, the King lived there, or lived there for a few months each year, anyway, as he graciously moved his court from province to province, spreading the considerable financial burden of supporting it around.

He was what was called "a good King," which meant that he didn't oppress the peasants any more than he was traditionally allowed to, and occasionally even distributed some small largess to them when he was able, on the ancient principal, sound husbandry, that you get more work out of your animals when they're moderately well-fed and therefore reasonably healthy. So he was a good King, or a good-enough King, at any rate. But in many a dimly-lit kitchen or bistro or backroom bar, the old men of the town huddled around their potbellied stoves at night and warmed their hands, or tried to, and muttered fearfully about what might happen when the Old King died, and his son and heir took over.

But as this isn't really a story of palace intrigue, either, or only partially so, you must move on to a large but somewhat shabby-gentile house, one that has seen better days, in a shady street on the very outskirts of town, the kind of neighborhood that will be swallowed by the expanding town and replaced by rows of worker's flats in thirty years or so. That girl there, sullenly and rather uselessly scrubbing down the flagstones in the small courtyard, is the one we're interested in.

For the kind of story this *is*, is a fairy tale. Sort of.

There are some things they don't tell you, of course, even in the Grimm's version, let alone the Disney.

For one thing, no one ever called her "Cinderella," although occasionally they called her much worse. Her name was Eleanor, an easy-enough name to use, and no one ever really paid enough attention to her to bother to come up with a nickname for her, even a cruel and taunting one. Most of the time, no one paid enough attention to her even to taunt her.

There *was* a step-mother, although whether she was evil or not depended on your point of view. These were hard times in a hard age, when even the relatively well-to-do lived not far from hunger and privation, and if she chose to take care of her own children first in preference to her dead husband's child, well, there were many who would not blame her for that. In fact, many would instead compliment her on her generosity in giving her husband's by-blow a place in her home and at her heath when no law of Man or God required her to do so, or to lift a finger to insure the child's survival. Many *did* so complement her, and the step-mother would lift her eyes piously to Heaven, and throw her hands in the air, and mutter modest demurements.

For one of the things that they never tell you, a missing piece that helps make sense of the whole situation, is that Cinderella was a bastard. Yes, her father had doted on her, lavishing love and affection on her, had taken her into his house and raised her from a babe, but he had never married Eleanor's mother, who had died in childbirth, and he himself had died after marrying the Evil Step-Mother but *before* making a will that would have legally enforced some kind of legacy or endowment for his bastard daughter.

Today, of course, she would sue, and there'd be court-battles and DNA testing, and appearances with lots of shouting on daytime talk-shows, and probably she would eventually win a slice of the pie. In those days, in that part of the world, she had no recourse under the law—or anywhere else, since the Church shunned those born in sin.

So the step-mother really *was* being quite generous in continuing to supply Eleanor's room and board rather than throwing her out of the house to freeze and starve in the street. That she didn't as well provide much in the way of warmth of familial affection, being icy and remote to Eleanor—the visible and undeniable evidence of her late husband's love for another woman—on those rare occasions when she deigned to notice her at all, is probably not surprising, and to really expect her to feel otherwise is perhaps more than could be asked. She had problems of her own, after all, and had already gone a long mile further than she needed to just by continuing to feed the child in the first place.

There were step-sisters too, children of a previous marriage (a marriage where the husband had *also* died young . . . but before you're tempted to cast the step-mother in a Black Widow scenario, keep in mind that in those days, in that place, dying young was not an especially rare phenomenon), but they were not particularly evil either—although they didn't much like Eleanor, and let it show. However, they were no more cruel and vindictive—but no less, either—than most young girls forced into the company of someone they didn't much like, someone of fallen status whom their mother didn't much like either and made no particular effort to protect. Someone who, truth be told, had probably lorded it over *them*, just a little bit, when she was her father's favorite and they were the new girls in the household.

Neither were the step-sisters particularly ugly; this is something that came in with Disney, who always equates ugliness with evil. They were, in fact, quite acceptably attractive by the standards of their day.

Although it is true that when Eleanor was around, they tended to dim in her presence, in male eyes at least, as bright bulbs can be dimmed by a brighter one.

Eleanor *was* beautiful, of course. We have to give her that much if the rest of the story is going to make any sense. Like her step-sisters, she had been brought up as a child of the relatively prosperous merchant class, which ensured that she had been well-enough nourished as a babe to have grown up with good teeth and glossy hair and strong, straight bones—unlike the peasants, who were often afflicted with rickets and other vitamin-deficiency diseases.

No doubt she had breasts and legs, like other young women, but whether her breasts were large or small, whether her legs were long or squat, is impossible to tell at this distant point in time.

We can tell from the story, though, that she was considered to be striking, and perhaps a bit unusual; so, since no-one knows what she really looked like, let's cater to the tastes of our own time and say that she was tall and coltish, with long lovely legs and small—but not *too* small—breasts, a contrast to many around her upon whom a diet consisting largely of potatoes and coarse black bread had imposed a dumpier sort of physique.

Since this tale is set in that part of Central Europe that had changed hands dozens of times in the past few hundred years and was destined to change hands again a few times more before the century was out, with every wave of raping-and-pillaging Romans, Celts, Goths, Huns, Russians, Mongols, and Turks scrambling the gene pool a bit further, let's also say that she had red hair and green eyes and a pale complexion, a rare but possible combination, given the presence of Russian and Celtic DNA in the genetic stew. That should make her sufficiently distinctive.

(It's possible, of course, that she *really* looked like a female Russian weight-lifter, complete with faint mustache, or like a walking potato, and you're welcome to picture her that way instead if you'd like—but if so, you must grant at least that she was a striking and *charismatic* weight-lifter or potato, one who had had men sniffing around her from the time she started to grow hair in places other than her head.)

In truth, like most "beautiful" women, who often are not really even pretty if you can catch them on those rare occasions when their faces are in repose, her allure was based in large part on her charisma and *elan*, and a personality that, to date, at least, remained vital and intense in spite of a life that increasingly tried to grind her down.

Eleanor didn't wait on the others to the degree shown in the Disney version, of course—this was a hard society, and everyone had to work, including the step-mother and the two step-sisters. Much of the cost of maintaining the house (which was not a working farm, regardless of what the stories tell you, too close to the center of town, although they may have kept a few chickens) was defrayed by revenues from land that Eleanor's father had owned elsewhere, but those revenues had slowly declined since the father's death, and in order to keep a tenuous foot-hold on the middle-class, they had been forced to take in seamstress work, which occupied all of them for several hours a day.

It's true, though, that since her father died, two years before, and since revenues had declined enough to preclude keeping servants, that much of the rest of the work of maintaining the household had fallen on Eleanor's shoulders, in addition to her seamstress chores.

She found it bitterly hard, as would you; in fact, spoiled by modernity, we'd find it even more onerous than she did, and suffer even more keenly. Housework was hard physical labor in those days, especially in the backward hinterlands of Central Europe, where even the (from our perspective) minimal household conveniences that might be available to a rich family in London would not arrive for a long lifetime, or maybe two. Housework was brutal and unrelenting labor, stretching from dawn until well after dusk, the equivalent in its demands on someone's reserves of strength and endurance of working on a road-gang or in a coal mine; it was the main reason, along with the demands and dangers of childbirth, why women wore out so fast and died so young. Not for nothing did the phrase "Slaving over a hot stove" come into existence; doing laundry was even worse, a task so demanding—pounding the clothes, twisting them dry, starting over again—that it was rarely tackled more than once a week even in households where there were several women to divide the work up amongst them; and scrubbing, inside or out, was done on your knees in any and all weathers, with a stiff-bristled brush and raw potash soap that stung your nostrils and blistered your hands.

Of course, every *other* woman in this society, except for the very richest, had to deal with these kind of labors as well, so there was nothing unique about Eleanor's lot, or any reason to feel sorry for her *in particular*, as the stories sometimes seem to invite us to do . . . the subtext pretty obviously being that she is an aristocrat-in-hiding, or at least a member of the prosperous upper class, being forced to do the work of a *peasant.* Think of that! Being made to work just like a common, ordinary girl! As if she wasn't any better than anyone else! (Oddly enough, this reaction of indignation usually comes from people who have to work for a living every day *themselves*, not from whatever millionaires or members of the peerage might be lurking in the audience.)

In fact, though, Eleanor had also been spoiled, not by modernity but by her father, sheltered by his money from most of the chores even a child of the merchant class would usually have had to become inured to . . . so perhaps she did feel it more keenly than most women of her day would have. Her father had also spoiled her in other ways, though, more significant ways, teaching her to read (something still frowned upon, if no longer actively forbidden by law), teaching her to love books and learning, teaching her to dream. Teaching her to be *ambitious*—but ambitious for what purpose? She had a good mind, and her father had given her the beginnings of a decent education, but what was she supposed to *do* with it? Further formal schooling was out of the question, even if there had been money for it—that was for men. All the professions were for men as well. There was nothing she could do, no way her life could change. She was doomed to stay here in this once-loved house she had come to hate, working like a slave day and night for people she didn't even like, much less consider to be family, until her youth and strength and beauty drained away like water spilled in the street, and she woke up one day to find herself spavined and old.

She could feel this doom closing in around her like a black cloud, making every day a little more hopeless and bitter and grim. She could feel herself dying, a little bit every day, her mind dulling, her strength and resiliency waning.

Somehow, she had to get *out* of here.

But there was no way out . . .

After several months of this bleak circle, she decided at last that there was only one possible way to escape: she would trade sex for a better life—or at least a more comfortable one.

It was a choice that untold thousands of young women—and not a few men—had made before her, and that thousands more would make after her. She'd looked her situation over with cold-eyed clarity, and realized that she had no commodity to offer that anyone would ever value except for youth, beauty, and virginity—and that none of them were going to last long. A few more years of constant grinding toil would take care of the youth and beauty, and sooner or later one of the men who had been circling her with increasing persistence would corner her in the stables or behind a market stall or in an alley somewhere and rape her, and that would be the end of her virginity (a valuable commodity ever since syphilis had started to ravage Europe a few centuries back) as well. If he got her pregnant, she'd be stuck here forever.

Young as she was, she was not unaware of the trick that her body could be made to do when she huddled alone in the darkness on her cot at night, biting a dish-cloth to keep anyone from hearing the sounds that she couldn't stop herself from making, and she was not so hard-headed as to be immune to thoughts of love and romance and marriage. In fact, she'd exchanged hot glances, longing words, and one quick delicious kiss with Casimir, a big, lumbering, sweet-natured boy who worked in the glass foundry a street away. She was pretty sure that she could win his heart, perhaps even get him to marry her—but what good would that do? Even if they could somehow scrape up enough money to live on, she'd still be stuck in this stifling provincial town, living much the same kind of life she was living now. And then the children would start coming, one a year until she wore out and died . . .

No, love and marriage were not going to save her. Sex was going to have to do that. She'd have to trade her body to someone rich enough to take her out of here, out of this life, perhaps even, if things worked out for the best, out of this town altogether.

Eleanor's religious upbringing had not perhaps been the strictest possible, her father tending towards clandestine secularism, but of course, she still had some qualms about the idea of selling herself in this fashion. Still, she had heard the women talking at the well or in the marketplace or even in the church when no man was around to hear, and it didn't sound all that difficult. Lay on your back, open your legs, let him grunt on top of you for five minutes while you stared at the ceiling. A lot less difficult than scrubbing the floor until your fingers bleed.

But if she was going to sell herself, she was damned if she wasn't going to get the best price possible.

Eleanor prided herself on her clear-eyed logic and hard-headed rationality, but here's where her plan began to be tinged by a deep vein of pastel romanticism that she wouldn't even have admitted to herself that she possessed.

She had no intention of becoming a common whore, if whore she must be. Even a town of this size had a few such, and the life they lead was nothing to envy or emulate. No, she would set her sights higher.

Why not set them as high as they would go?

The Prince. She had seen him go by in a parade once, the year before, up on a prancing roan stallion, tall and handsome, his plumed hat nodding, the silver fastenings on his uniform gleaming in the sun. She'd even had hot dreams about him, those nights when his ghost rather than Casimir's had visited her in her bed.

She was realistic enough to know that marriage was out of the question. Princes didn't marry commoners, even those from families with a lot more money than her own. It was just never going to happen. That was so ingrained in her worldview that she never entertained the possibility that the Prince would marry her, even as the remotest fantasy.

Princes did *fuck* commoners, though, that happened all the time, and always had. And if they liked them well enough, sometimes they *kept* them. Being a royal mistress didn't sound so bad; since she had no choice, she'd settle for that.

All she had to do was get him to want her.

Why not? He was a man, wasn't he? Every other man she knew pursued her and tried to grope her or worse when there was nobody else around, even men three times her age. Maybe a Prince would be no different.

And if for some reason the Prince *didn't* like her, she thought, with a flash of the practical shrewdness that was so typical of her, the palace would be full of other rich men. *Somebody* would want her.

There was a Ball at the palace every weekend when the King and his court were in residency during the summer months. Her family was not rich enough for any of them to be invited to these affairs, nor ever had been, even at their most prosperous. But she would get in *some*how.

Well, we all know what comes next, of course. The dress made in secret, although there were no birds or mice to help her. Nor did she need any—

she was, after all, a seamstress. There were no fairy godmothers either, no pumpkins turned to coaches, no magically conjured horses. She slipped out of the house while her step-mother, a woman who had been embittered and disappointed by life, was slowly drinking herself sodden with her nightly regimen of alternating glasses of *tisane* and brandy, and walked all the way through town to the river, the night air like velvet around her, the blood pounding in her throat, the castle slowly rising higher and higher above the houses, blazing with lights, as she drew near.

Somehow, she got inside. Who knows how? Maybe the guards were reluctant to stop a beautiful and well-dressed young woman who moved with easy confidence. Maybe she walked in with a group of other party-goers. Maybe the guards were all drunk, and she just walked by them. Maybe there were no guards, in this sleepy backwater in a time without a major war brewing. Maybe there were guards, but they just didn't care.

However she did it, she got in, and it was everything she'd ever dreamed of.

It *was* glamorous. Give them their due, the aristocracy has always known how to do glamorous.

Although the grim Gothic tower with its battlements and crenellations and murder-holes still loomed darkly up behind, this part of the castle had been modernized and made into a palace instead. In the Grand Ballroom, there were floor-to-ceiling windows that overlooked the whole sweep of the town, which was stretched out below like a diorama on a tabletop, there were balconies and tapestried alcoves with richly embroidered Oriental hangings, there were flowers everywhere, and a polished marble floor that seemed to stretch on forever, shimmering in the light of a thousand candles like a lake of mist lit by moonlight. Out on the marble floor, people in vivid, multi-colored clothes twirled around like butterflies caught in a whirlwind, while music filled all the air, thick and rich and hot as blood, and made the nerves jump under the skin.

It *was* glamorous, as long as you didn't get too close to the privies (it was a warm summer night, after all). This would bother you, though, more than it bothered Eleanor, who was already used to an everyday level of stink that would have turned the stomachs of most moderns.

Cranking her charm to its highest setting, palms damp, she swallowed her fear and mingled.

She didn't really fool anyone, of course. She was a good seamstress, but the materials she'd had to work with were nowhere near fine enough for court fashion. But it didn't matter much. She was beautiful, and charming, and vivacious, and still had enough of the remnants of society manners learned before her family fell on harder times to get by—although she wasn't fooling anybody there, either. No matter. She was an exotic amusement, someone new in over-familiar court circles where everyone had worked through all possible permutations of their relationships with everyone else long before. They'd have tired of her within days, of course, but by then she might well have found some rich young gentleman willing to take her on as a toy, and perhaps even keep her for awhile . . . so her plan might actually have worked, if she'd been willing to settle for someone less exalted.

But then the Prince crossed the floor, and stood at the edge of the ring of preening young men who now surrounded her, and their eyes met, and his first grew round with surprise, and then slowly grew hot.

He strode forward, the crowd of lesser men melting away before him, and held out his hand, imperiously commanding her to dance, all the while his eyes smoldered at her. She'd never seen anyone so handsome.

Eleanor took his hand and they spun away, and for a second, gliding across the softly gleaming marble floor, moving with him with the music all around them, it seemed like the perfect culmination of every fairy tale she'd ever read.

Then he yanked her roughly aside into one of the curtained alcoves, tugging the hangings shut behind them. There was a divan in there, and an oil lamp, and a small table with a nearly empty bottle of brandy on it. The air was thick and foul, with a strong reek of pungent animal musk to it, like the den of a panther or a bear, and the divan was rumpled and stained.

Startled, she started to speak, but the Prince waved her brusquely to silence. For a long moment, the Prince stared at her, coldly, sneeringly, contemptuously, almost as if he hated her. His heavy, handsome face was harsh and cruel, cold as winter ice in spite of the heat that burned in his small hard eyes. He was viscously drunk, his face flushed, swaying where he stood, and he reeked of brandy and sweat and old semen, a streak of which still glistened on his pants from some previous encounter earlier in the evening. He made a wet, gloating noise, like a greedy child smacking its lips, and swept Eleanor crushingly into his arms.

All at once, he was kissing her brutally, biting her lips, forcing his tongue into her mouth, his breath like death, the taste of him sour and rancid and bitter. He grabbed her breasts, squeezing them savagely with his powerful hands, mashing and twisting them, so that sudden blinding pain shot through her.

Then he was forcing her down onto the divan, bearing her down under his crushing weight, tearing at her clothes, forcing a knee roughly between her legs, prying them open.

If she'd been as hard-headed and practical as she thought she was, she would have laid back and let him force himself on her, endured his grunting and thrusting and battering either in silence or with as much of a simulation of passionate enjoyment as she could muster, let him contemptuously wipe his dick on her afterward and then tell him how witty that was. But as he bore her down, smothering her under his weight and stench, bruising her flesh with his vise-like fingers, all her buried romanticism came rushing to the surface—it wasn't supposed to be like this!—and as she heard her dress and undergarments rip under his tearing hands and felt the night air on her suddenly exposed breasts, she fought herself free with a sudden burst of panicked strength, and clawed the Prince's face.

They both leaped to their feet. The Prince stared at her in astonishment for a moment, three deep claw marks on his cheek dripping vivid red blood, and then came for her again, murder rather than sex on his mind this time.

Eleanor had been attacked before—once by a stablehand and once by a greengrocer in a lane behind the market at dusk—and she knew what to do.

She kicked the Prince hard in the crotch, putting her weight and the strength of her powerful young legs into it, and the Prince mewed and folded and fell, wrapping himself into a tight ball on the floor, for the instant too shocked by pain even to scream.

Eleanor's practicality returned with a rush. She was moments away from being arrested, and probably jailed for the rest of her life, certainly for many years. Maybe they'd even execute her. What the Prince had tried to do to her wouldn't matter, she knew. No one would care. All that would count was what *she* had done to *him*.

She gathered her ruined dress around her, hiding her breasts as well as she could, and fled the alcove. Straight across the Grand Ballroom and out of the palace, as fast as she could go without actually running, as voices began to rise in the distance behind her, and the palace clock chimed midnight.

You know the rest, or you think that you do.

The next day, the Prince did begin searching obsessively for her, but it was for revenge, not for love; the three red weals across his handsome face filled him with a rage that momentarily eclipsed even drinking and screwing, his usual preoccupations, and goaded him to furious action.

Fortunately for Eleanor, she had been wise enough not to use her real name, or her full name, at least, with those she'd talked with at the Ball, and as she was not a regular in court circles, nobody knew where to find her.

That was where the famous slipper came in. Yes, there was a slipper, but it was an ordinary one, not one made of glass. "Glass" is a mistranslation of the French word used by Perrault; what he really said was "fur." It wasn't fur either. For that matter, it wasn't really a slipper. It was an ordinary dress shoe of the type appropriate to that time and place.

But it *had* slipped off Eleanor's foot while she struggled with the Prince in the alcove, and it *was* infused with her scent. By mid-afternoon the next day, the secret police were using teams of keen-nosed hunting dogs, following her scent on the slipper, to try to track her through the streets to her home.

There was, of course, no nonsense about trying the slipper on the feet of every woman in the kingdom. Nor did Eleanor's step-sisters cut bits of their own feet off in order to try to get them to fit into the slipper, as some versions of this story would have it. Nor did flocks of angry birds fly down and peck out their eyes and bite off their noses (a scene Disney inexplicably missed somehow), as in other versions.

In fact, except for a glimpse of her step-mother lying down in a darkened room with a wet cloth over her eyes, seen when Eleanor sneaked cautiously into the house late the previous evening, Eleanor never saw her step-mother or her step-sisters again.

The Prince had his hunt organized and moving by noon, pretty early for a Prince, especially a mammothly hung-over one, which shows you how serious he was about revenge. Fortunately for Eleanor, she was used to rising at the crack of dawn, so *she* got the jump on him.

In fact, she hadn't slept at all that night, but had spent the night with plans and preparations. She didn't know about the slipper-sniffing dogs, of course, but she knew that this was a small enough town that the Prince could find her eventually if he wanted to badly enough, and she was shrewd enough to guess that he would.

So by the time the sky was lightening in the east, and the birds were twittering in the branches of the trees in the wet gray dawn (perhaps arguing about whether pecking out the eyes of Eleanor's step-sisters was really a good use of their time), Eleanor was out the door with a coarse burlap sack in which she'd secreted a few hunks of bread and cheese, and what was left of her father's silver service, which usually resided in a locked highboy—the key for which was kept somewhere that Eleanor wasn't supposed to know about.

Her next stop was to intercept Casimir on his way to the glass foundry and talk faster and more earnestly than she'd ever had in her life, for she'd suddenly realized that although she still wanted to get *out*, she didn't want to go without *him*.

What she said to convince him, we'll never know. Perhaps he wasn't all that difficult to convince; having no family and only minimal prospects, he had little to lose here himself. Perhaps he'd wanted to run away with her all along, but was too shy to ask.

Whatever she said, it worked. He slipped back into his room to retrieve from under a loose floorboard a small amount of money he'd been able to save—perhaps against the day he could convince Eleanor to marry him—and then they were off.

By now, everybody in town knew about the slipper and the hunt for the Mystery Girl, and you could already hear the hounds baying in the distance.

They escaped from town by hiding in a dung cart—Eleanor's idea, to kill her scent.

After scrubbing in a fast-moving stream, while she shyly hid her breasts from him and he pretended not to look, they set off on foot across the countryside, walking the back roads to avoid pursuit, hitching rides in market-bound farmer's carts, later catching a narrow-gauge train that started and stopped, stopped and started, sometimes, for no apparent reason, sitting motionless for hours at tiny deserted stations where weeds grew up through the tracks and dogs slept on their backs on the empty sun-drenched platforms, all four legs in the air. In this manner, they inched their way across Europe, slowly running through Casimir's small store of cash, living on black bread, stale cheese, and sour red wine.

In Hamburg, they sold Eleanor's father's silver to buy passage on a ship going to the United States, and some crudely-forged identity papers. Before they were allowed aboard with their questionable papers, Eleanor had to blow the harbormaster, kneeling before him on the rough plank floor of his office, splinters digging into her knees, while he jammed his thick dirty cock that smelled like a dead lizard into her mouth, and she tried not to gag.

Casimir never found out; there were some of the harbormaster's companions who would have preferred for *him* to pay their unofficial passage fee rather than her, and Casimir, still being a boy in many ways, would have indignantly refused, and they would have been caught and maybe killed. She considered it a small enough price to pay for getting a chance at a new life in a new world, and rarely thought about it thereafter. She figured that Casimir had nothing to complain about, as when she did come to his bed, after they had been safely married in the New World, she came to it as a virgin, and they had the bloody sheet to prove it (just as well, too—Casimir was a good man, and a sweet-natured one, but he *was* a man of his time, after all, and couldn't be expected to be *too* liberal about things).

They made their way eventually to Chicago, where work for seamstresses and glaziers could be had, and where they had forty-five tumultuous years together, sometimes happy, sometimes not, until one bitter winter afternoon, carrying a pane of glass through the sooty city snow, Casimir's heart broke in his chest.

Eleanor lived another twenty years, and died on a cot in the kitchen near the stove (in the last few days, she'd refused to be taken upstairs to the bedroom), surrounded by children and grandchildren, and by the homey smells of cooked food, wood smoke, and the sharper smells of potash and lye, all of which she now found oddly comforting, although she'd hated them when she was young. She regretted nothing that she'd ever done in her life, and, except for a few moments at the very end when her body took over and struggled uselessly to breathe, her passing was as easy as any human being's has ever been.

After the Old King died, the Prince only got to reign for a few years before the monarchy was overthrown by civil war. The Prince and the rest of the royal family and most of the nobility were executed, kind or cruel, innocent or corrupt. The winning side fell in its turn, some decades later, and eventually a military junta, run by a local Strongman, took over.

Years later, Eleanor's grandson was in command of a column of tanks that entered and conquered the town, since one of the Strongman's successors had allied himself with the Axis.

Later that night, Eleanor's grandson climbed up to the ruins of the royal castle, mostly destroyed in an earlier battle, and looked out over the remains of the floor of the Grand Ballroom, open now to the night sky, weeds growing up through cracks in the once brilliantly polished marble that still gleamed dully in the moonlight, and wondered why he felt a moment of drifting melancholy, a twinge of sorrow that quickly dissipated, like waking from a sad dream that fades even as you try to remember it, and is gone.

• Chains of the Sea •

One day the aliens landed, just as everyone always said they would. They fell out of a guileless blue sky and into the middle of a clear, cold November day, four of them, four alien ships drifting down like the snow that had been threatening to fall all week. America was just shouldering its way into daylight as they made planetfall, so they landed there: one in the Delaware Valley about fifteen miles north of Philadelphia, one in Ohio, one in a desolate region of Colorado, and one—for whatever reason—in a cane field outside of Caracas, Venezuela. To those who actually saw them come down, the ships seemed to fall rather than to descend under any intelligent control: a black nailhead suddenly tacked to the sky, coming all at once from nowhere, with no transition, like a Fortean rock squeezed from a high appearing-point, hanging way up there and winking intolerably bright in the sunlight; and then gravity takes hold of it, visibly, and it begins to fall, far away and dream-slow at first, swelling larger, growing huge, unbelievably big, a mountain hurled at the earth, falling with terrifying speed, rolling in the air, tumbling end over end, overhead, coming down—and then it is sitting peacefully on the ground; it has not crashed, and although it didn't slow down and it didn't stop, there it *is*, and not even a snowflake could have settled onto the frozen mud more lightly.

To those photo reconnaissance jets fortunate enough to be flying a routine pattern at thirty thousand feet over the Eastern Seaboard when the aliens blinked into their airspace, to the automatic, radar-eyed, computer-reflexed facilities at USADCOM Spacetrack East, and to the United States Aerospace Defense Command HQ in Colorado Springs, although they didn't have convenient recon planes up for a double check—the picture was different. The high-speed cameras showed the landing as a *process:* as if the alien spaceships existed simultaneously everywhere along their path of descent, stretched down from the stratosphere and gradually sifting entirely to the ground, like confetti streamers thrown from a window, like Slinkys going down a flight of stairs. In the films, the alien ships appeared to recede from the viewpoint of the reconnaissance planes, vanishing into perspective, and that was all right, but the ships also appeared to dwindle away into infinity from the viewpoint of Spacetrack East on the ground, and that definitely was not all right. The most constructive comment ever made on this phenomenon was that it was odd. It was also odd that the spaceships had not been detected approaching Earth by observation stations on the Moon, or by the orbiting satellites, and nobody ever figured that out, either.

From the first second of contact to touchdown, the invasion of Earth had taken less than ten minutes. At the end of that time, there were four big ships on the ground, shrouded in thick steam—*not* cooling off from the friction of their descent, as was first supposed; the steam was actually mist: everything had frozen solid in a fifty-foot circle around the ships, and the quick-ice was now melting as temperatures rose back above freezing—frantic messages were snarling up and down the continent-wide nervous system of USADCOM, and total atomic war was a hairsbreadth away. While the humans scurried in confusion, the Artificial Intelligence (AI) created by MIT-Bell Labs linked itself into the network of high-speed, twentieth-generation computers placed at its disposal by a Red Alert Priority, evaluated data thoughtfully for a minute and a half and then proceeded to get in touch with its opposite number in the Russian Republics. It had its own, independently evolved methods of doing this, and achieved contact almost instantaneously, although the Pentagon had not yet been able to reach the Kremlin—that didn't matter anyway; they were only human, and all the important talking was going on in another medium. AI "talked" to the Russian system for another seven minutes, while eons of time clicked by on the electronic scale, and World War III was averted. Both Intelligences finally decided that they didn't understand what was going on, a conclusion the human governments of Earth wouldn't reach for hours, and would never admit at all.

The only flourish of action took place in the three-minute lag between the alien touchdown and the time AI assumed command of the defense network, and involved a panicked general at USADCOM HQ and a malfunction in the—never actually used—fail-safe system that enabled him to lob a small tactical nuclear device at the Colorado landing site. The device detonated at point-blank range, right against the side of the alien ship, but the fireball didn't appear. There didn't seem to be an explosion at all. Instead, the hull of the ship turned a blinding, incredibly hot white at the point of detonation, faded to blue-white, to a hellish red, to sullen tones of violet that flickered away down the spectrum. The same pattern of precessing colors chased itself around the circumference of the ship until it reached the impact point again, and then the hull returned to its former dull black. The ship was unharmed. There had been no sound, not even a whisper. The tactical device had been a clean bomb, but instruments showed that no energy or radiation had been released at all.

After this, USADCOM became very thoughtful.

Tommy Nolan was already a half hour late to school, but he wasn't hurrying. He dawdled along the secondary road that led up the hill behind the old sawmill, and watched smoke go up in thick black lines from the chimneys of the houses below, straight and unwavering in the bright, clear morning, like brushstrokes against the sky. The roofs were made of cold gray and red tiles that winked sunlight at him all the way to the docks, where clouds of sea gulls bobbed and wheeled, dipped and rose, their cries coming faint and shrill to him across the miles of chimneys and roofs and aerials and wind-tossed treetops. There was a crescent sliver of ocean visible beyond the dock, like a slitted blue eye peering up over the edge of the world. Tommy kicked a rock, kicked it again, and then found a tin can which he kicked instead, clattering it along ahead of him. The wind snatched at the fur on his parka, *puff,* momentarily making the cries of the sea gulls very loud and distinct, and then carrying them away again, back over the roofs to the sea. He kicked the tin can over the edge of a bluff, and listened to it somersault invisibly away through the undergrowth. He was whistling tunelessly, and he had taken his gloves off and stuffed them in his parka pocket, although his mother had told him specifically not to, it was so cold for November. Tommy wondered briefly what the can must feel like, tumbling down through the thick ferns and weeds, finding a safe place to lodge under the dark, secret roots of the trees. He kept walking, *skuff-skuff*ing gravel very loudly. When he was halfway up the slope, the buzz saw started up at the mill on the other side of the bluff. It moaned and shrilled metallically, whining up through the stillness of the morning to a piercing shriek that hurt his teeth, then sinking low, low, to a buzzing, grumbling roar, like an angry giant muttering in the back of his throat. An *animal,* Tommy thought, although he knew it was a saw. *Maybe it's a dinosaur.* He shivered deliciously. *A dinosaur!*

Tommy was being a puddle jumper this morning. That was why he was so late. There had been a light rain the night before, scattering puddles along the road, and Tommy had carefully jumped over every one between here and the house. It took a long time to do it right, but Tommy was being very conscientious. He imagined himself as a machine, a vehicle—a puddle jumper. No matter that he had legs instead of wheels, and arms and a head, that was just the kind of ship he was, with he himself sitting somewhere inside and driving the contraption, looking out through the eyes, working the pedals and gears and switches that made the ship go. He would drive himself up to a puddle, maneuver very carefully until he was in exactly the right position, backing and cutting his wheels and nosing in again, and then put the ship into jumping gear, stomp down on the accelerator, and let go of the brake switch. And away he'd go, like a stone from a catapult, *up*, the puddle flashing underneath, then *down*, with gravel jarring hard against his feet as the earth slapped up to meet him. Usually he cleared the puddle. He'd only splashed down in water once this morning, and he'd jumped puddles almost two feet across. A pause then to check his systems for amber damage lights. The board being all green, he'd put the ship in *travel* gear and drive along some more, slowly, scanning methodically for the next puddle. All this took considerable time, but it wasn't a thing you could skimp on—you had to do it right.

He thought occasionally, *Mom will be mad again*, but it lacked force and drifted away on the wind. Already breakfast this morning was something that had happened a million years ago—the old gas oven lighted for warmth and hissing comfortably to itself, the warm cereal swimming with lumps, the radio speaking coldly in the background about things he never bothered to listen to, the hard gray light pouring through the window onto the kitchen table.

Mom had been puffy-eyed and coughing. She had been watching television late and had fallen asleep on the couch again, her cloth coat thrown over her for a blanket, looking very old when Tommy came out to wake her before breakfast and to shut off the humming test pattern on the TV. Tommy's father had yelled at her again during breakfast, and Tommy had gone into the bathroom for a long time, washing his hands slowly and carefully until he heard his father leave for work. His mother pretended that she wasn't crying as she made his cereal and fixed him "coffee," thinned dramatically with a half a cup of cold water and a ton of milk and sugar, "for the baby," although that was exactly the way she drank it herself. She had already turned the television back on, the moment her husband's footsteps died away, as if she couldn't stand to have it silent. It murmured unnoticed in the living room, working its way through an early children's show that even Tommy couldn't bear to watch. His mother said she kept it on to check the time so that Tommy wouldn't be late, but she never did that. Tommy always had to remind her when it was time to bundle him into his coat and leggings and rubber boots—when it was raining—for school. He could never get rubber boots on right by himself, although he tried very hard and seriously. He always got tangled up anyway.

He reached the top of the hill just as the buzz saw chuckled and sputtered to a stop, leaving a humming, vibrant silence behind it. Tommy realized that he had run out of puddles, and he changed himself instantly into a big, powerful land tank, the kind they showed on the war news on television, that could run on caterpillar treads or wheels and had a hovercraft air cushion for the tough parts. Roaring, and revving his engine up and down, he turned off the gravel road into the thick stand of fir forest. He followed the footpath, tearing along terrifically on his caterpillar treads, knocking the trees down and crushing them into a road for him to roll on. That made him uneasy, though, because he loved trees. He told himself that the trees were only being bent down under his weight, and that they sprang back up again after he passed, but that didn't sound right. He stopped to figure it out. There was a quiet murmur in the forest, as if everything were breathing very calmly and rhythmically. Tommy felt as if he'd been swallowed by a huge, pleasant green creature, not because it wanted to eat him, but just to let him sit peacefully in its stomach for shelter. Even the second-growth saplings were taller than he was. Listening to the forest, Tommy felt an urge to go down into the deep woods and talk to the Thants, but then he'd never get to school at all. Wheels would get tangled in roots, he decided, and switched on the hovercraft cushion. He floated down the path, pushing the throttle down as far as it would go, because he was beginning to worry a little about what would happen to him if he was *too* late.

Switching to wheels, he bumped out of the woods and onto Highland Avenue. Traffic was heavy here; the road was full of big trucks and tractor-trailers on the way down to Boston, on the way up to Portland. Tommy had to wait almost ten minutes before traffic had thinned out enough for him to dash across to the other side of the road. His mother had told him never to go to school this way, so this was the way he went every chance he got. Actually, his house was only a half a mile away from the school, right down Walnut Street, but Tommy always went by an incredibly circuitous route. He didn't think of it that way—it took him by all his favorite places.

So he rolled along the road shoulder comfortably enough, following the avenue. There were open meadows on this side of the road, full of wild wheat and scrub brush, and inhabited by families of Jeblings, who flitted back and forth between the road, which they shunned, and the woods on the far side of the meadow. Tommy called to them as he cruised by, but Jeblings are always shy, and today they seemed especially skittish. They were hard to see straight on, like all of the Other People, but he could catch glimpses of them out of the corners of his eyes: spindly beanstalk bodies, big pumpkinheads, glowing slit eyes, absurdly long and tapering fingers. They were in constant motion—he could hear them thrashing through the brush, and their shrill, nervous giggling followed him for quite a while along the road. But they wouldn't come out, or even stop to talk to him, and he wondered what had stirred them up.

As he came in sight of the school, a flight of jet fighters went by overhead, very high and fast, leaving long white scars across the sky, the scream of their passage trailing several seconds behind them. They were followed by a formation of bigger planes, going somewhat slower. *Bombers?* Tommy thought, feeling excited and scared as he watched the big planes drone out of sight. Maybe this was going to be the War. His father was always talking about the War, and how it would be the end of everything—a proposition that Tommy found interesting, if not necessarily desirable. Maybe that was why the Jeblings were excited.

The bell marking the end of the day's first class rang at that moment, cutting Tommy like a whip, and frightening him far more than his thoughts of the War. *I'm really going to catch it,* Tommy thought, breaking into a run, too panicked to turn himself into anything other than a boy, or to notice the new formation of heavy bombers rumbling in from the northeast.

By the time he reached the school, classes had already finished changing, and the new classes had been in progress almost five minutes. The corridors were bright and empty and echoing, like a fluorescently lighted tomb. Tommy tried to keep running once he was inside the building, but the clatter he raised was so horrendous and terrifying that he slowed to a walk again. It wasn't going to make any difference anyway, not anymore, not now. He was already in for it.

Everyone in his class turned to look at him as he came in, and the room became deadly quiet. Tommy stood in the doorway, horrified, wishing that he could crawl into the ground, or turn invisible, or run.

But he could do nothing but stand there, flushing with shame, and watch everyone watch him. His classmates' faces were snide, malicious, sneering and expectant. His friends, Steve Edwards and Bobbie Williamson, were grinning nastily and slyly, making sure that the teacher couldn't see. Everyone knew that he was going to get it, and they were eager to watch, feeling self-righteous and, at the same time, being glad that it wasn't they who had been caught. Miss Fredricks, the teacher, watched him icily from the far end of the room, not saying a word. Tommy shut the door behind him, wincing at the tremendous noise it made. Miss Fredricks let him get all the way to his desk and allowed him to sit down—feeling a sudden surge of hope—before she braced him and made him stand up again.

"Tommy, you're late," she said coldly.

"Yes, ma'am."

"You are very late." She had the tardy sheet from the previous class on her desk, and she fussed with it as she talked, her fingers repeatedly flattening it out and wrinkling it again. She was a tall, stick-thin woman, in her forties, although it really wouldn't have made any difference if she'd been sixty, or twenty—all her juices had dried up years ago, and she had become ageless, changeless, and imperishable, like a mummy. She seemed not so much shriveled as baked in some odd oven of life into a hard, tough, leathery substance, like meat that is left out in the sun and turns into jerky. Her skin was fine-grained, dry, and slightly yellowed, like parchment. Her breasts had sagged down to her waist, and they bulged just above the belt of her skirt, like strange growths or tumors. Her face was a smooth latex mask.

"You've been late for class twice this week," she said precisely, moving her mouth as little as possible. "And three times last week." She scribbled on a piece of paper and called him forward to take it. "I'm giving you another note for your mother, and I want her to sign it this time, and I want you to bring it back. Do you understand?" She stared directly at Tommy. Her eyes were tunnels opening through her head onto a desolate ocean of ice. "And if you're late again, or give me any more trouble, I'll make an appointment to send you down to see the school psychiatrist. And *he'll* take care of you. Now go back to your seat, and let's not have any more of your nonsense."

Tommy returned to his desk and sat numbly while the rest of the class rolled ponderously over him. He didn't hear a word of it and was barely aware of the giggling and whispered gibes of the children on either side of him. The note bulked incredibly heavy and awkward in his pocket; it felt hot, somehow. The only thing that called his attention away from the note, toward the end of the class, was his increasing awareness of the noise that had been growing louder and louder outside the windows. The Other People were moving. They were stirring all through the woods behind the school, they were surging restlessly back and forth, like a tide that has no place to go. That was not their usual behavior at all. Miss Fredricks and the other children didn't seem to hear anything unusual, but to Tommy it was clear enough to take his mind off even his present trouble, and he stared curiously out the window into the gritty, gray morning.

Something was happening. . . .

The first action taken by the human governments of Earth—as opposed to the actual government of Earth: AI and his counterpart Intelligences—was an attempt to hush up everything. The urge to conceal information from the public had become so ingrained and habitual as to constitute a tropism—it was as automatic and unavoidable as a yawn. It is a fact that the White House moved to hush up the alien landings before the administration had any idea that they *were* alien landings; in fact, before the administration had any clear conception at all of what it was that they were trying to hush up. Something spectacular and very unofficial had happened, so the instinctive reaction of government was to sit on it and prevent it from hatching in public. Fifty years of media-centered turmoil had taught them that the people didn't need to know anything that wasn't definitely in the script. It is also a fact that the first official governmental representatives to reach any of the landing sites were concerned exclusively with squelching all publicity of the event, while the heavily armed military patrols dispatched to defend the country from possible alien invasion didn't arrive until later—up to three-quarters of an hour later in one case—which defined the priorities of the administration pretty clearly. This was an election year, and the body would be tightly covered until the government decided if it could be potentially embarrassing.

Keeping the lid down, however, proved to be difficult. The Delaware Valley landing had been witnessed by hundreds of thousands of people in Pennsylvania and New Jersey, as the Ohio landing had been observed by a majority of the citizens in the Akron-Canton area. The first people to reach the alien ship—in fact, the first humans to reach any of the landing sites—were the crew of a roving television van from a big Philadelphia station who had been covering a lackluster monster rally for the minority candidate nearby when the sky broke open. They lost no time in making for the ship, eager to get pictures of some real monsters, even though years of late-night science-fiction movies had taught them what usually happened to the first people snooping around the saucer when the hatch clanked open and the tentacled horrors oozed out. Still, they would take a chance on it. They parked their van a respectable distance away from the ship, poked their telephoto lenses cautiously over the roof of a tool shed in back of a boarded-up garage, and provided the eastern seaboard with fifteen minutes of live coverage and hysterical commentary until the police arrived.

The police, five prowl cars and, after a while, a riot van, found the situation hopelessly over their heads. They alternated between terror, rage, and indecision, and mostly wished someone would show up to take the problem off their hands. They settled for cordoning off the area and waiting to see what would happen. The television van, belligerently ignored by the police, continued to telecast ecstatically for another ten minutes. When the government security team arrived by hovercraft and ordered the television crew to stop broadcasting, the anchorman told them to go fuck themselves, in spite of threats of federal prison. It took the armed military patrol that rumbled in later to shut down the television van, and even they had difficulty. By this time, though, most of the East were glued to their home sets, and the sudden cessation of television coverage caused twice as much panic as the original report of the landing.

In Ohio, the ship came down in a cornfield, stampeding an adjacent herd of Guernseys and a farm family of fundamentalists who believed they had witnessed the angel descending with the Seventh Seal. Here the military and police reached the site before anyone, except for a few hundred local people, who were immediately taken into protective custody en masse and packed into a drafty Grange hall under heavy guard. The authorities had hopes of keeping the situation under tight control, but within an hour they were having to contend, with accelerating inadequacy, with a motorized horde of curiosity seekers from Canton and Akron. Heads were broken, and dire consequences promised by iron-voiced bullhorns along a ten-mile front, but they couldn't arrest everybody, and apparently most of northern Ohio had decided to investigate the landing.

By noon, traffic was hopelessly backed up all the way to North Canton, and west to Mansfield. The commander of the occupying military detachment was gradually forced to give up the idea of keeping people out of the area, and then, by sheer pressure of numbers, was forced to admit that he couldn't keep them out of the adjacent town, either. The commander, realizing that his soldiers were just as edgy and terrified as everybody else—and that they were by no means the only ones who were armed, as most of the people who believed that they were going to see a flying saucer had brought some sort of weapon along—reluctantly decided to pull his forces back into a tight cordon around the ship before serious bloodshed occurred.

The townspeople, released from the Grange Hall, went immediately for telephones and lawyers, and began suing everyone in sight for enormous amounts.

In Caracas, things were in even worse shape, which was not surprising, considering the overall situation in Venezuela at that time. There were major riots in the city, sparked both by rumors of imminent foreign invasion and A-bombing and by rumors of apocalyptic supernatural visitations. A half-dozen revolutionary groups, and about the same number of power-seeking splinter groups within the current government, seized the opportunity to make their respective moves and succeeded in cubing the confusion. Within hours, half of Caracas was in flames. In the afternoon, the army decided to "take measures," and opened up on the dense crowds with .50-caliber machine guns. The .50s walked around the square for ten minutes, leaving more than 150 people dead and almost half again that number wounded. The army turned the question of the wounded over to the civil police as something beneath their dignity to consider. The civil police tackled the problem by sending squads of riflemen out to shoot the wounded. This process took another hour, but did have the advantage of neatly tying up all the loose ends. Churches were doing a land-office business, and every cathedral that wasn't part of a bonfire itself was likely to be ablaze with candles.

The only landing anyone was at all happy with was the one in Colorado. There the ship had come down in the middle of a desolate, almost uninhabited stretch of semidesert. This enabled the military, directed by USADCOM HQ, to surround the landing site with rings of armor and infantry and artillery to their hearts' content, and to fill the sky overhead with circling jet fighters, bombers, hovercrafts, and helicopters. And all without any possibility of interference by civilians or the press. A minor government official was heard to remark that it was a shame the other aliens couldn't have been half that goddamned considerate.

• • •

When the final class bell rang that afternoon, Tommy remained in his seat until Bobbie Williamson came over to get him.
"Boy, old Miss Fredricks sure clobbered *you*," Bobbie said.

Tommy got to his feet. Usually he was the first one out of school. But not today. He felt strange, as if only part of him were actually there, as if the rest of him were cowering somewhere else, hiding from Miss Fredricks. *Something bad is going to happen*, Tommy thought. He walked out of the class, followed by Bobbie, who was telling him something that he wasn't listening to. He felt sluggish, and his arms and legs were cold and awkward.

They met Steve Edwards and Eddie Franklin at the outside door. "You really got it. Frag!" Eddie said, in greeting to Tommy. Steve grinned, and Bobbie said, "Miss Fredricks sure clobbered *him*, boy!" Tommy nodded, flushing in dull embarrassment. "Wait'll he gets home," Steve said wisely, "his ma gonna give it t'm too." They continued to rib him as they left the school, their grins growing broader and broader. Tommy endured it stoically, as he was expected to, and after a while he began to feel better somehow. The baiting slowly petered out, and at last Steve said, "Don't pay *her* no mind. She ain't nothing but a fragging old lady," and everybody nodded in sympathetic agreement.

"She don't bother me none," Tommy said. But there was still a lump of ice in his stomach that refused to melt completely. For them, the incident was over—they had discharged their part of it, and it had ceased to exist. But for Tommy it was still a very present, viable force; its consequences stretched ahead to the loom of leaden darkness he could sense coming up over his personal horizon. He thrust his hands in his pockets and clenched his fingers to keep away bad luck. If it could be kept away.

"Never mind," Bobbie said with elaborate scorn. "You wanna hear what I found out? The space people have landed!"

"You scorching us?" Steve said suspiciously.

"No scup, honest. The people from outer space are here. They're down in New York. There's a fragging big flying saucer and everything."

"Where'd'ju find out?" Eddie said.

"I listened at the teacher's room when we was having recess. They were all in there, listening to it on TV. And it said there was a flying saucer. And Mr. Brogan said he hoped there wasn't no monsters in it. Monsters! Boy!"

"Frag," Steve muttered cynically.

"*Monsters*. D'you scan it? I bet they're really big and stuff, I mean *really*, like they're a hundred feet tall, you know? Really big ugly monsters, and they only got one big eye, and they got tentacles and everything. I mean, really scuppy-looking, and they got ray guns and stuff. And they're gonna kill everybody."

"Frag," Steve repeated, more decisively.

They're not like that, Tommy thought. He didn't know what they were like, he couldn't picture them at all, but he knew that they weren't like that. The subject disturbed him. It made him uneasy somehow, and he wished they'd stop talking about it. He contributed listlessly to the conversation, and tried not to listen at all.

Somewhere along the line, it had been decided, tacitly, that they were going down to the beach. They worked on the subject of the aliens for a while, mostly repeating variations of what had been said before. Everyone, even Steve with his practiced cynicism, thought that there would be monsters. They fervently hoped for monsters, even hostile ones, as a refutation of everything they knew, everything their parents had told them. Talking of the monsters induced them to act them out, and instantly they were into a playlet, with characters and plot, and a continuous narrative commentary by the leader. Usually Tommy was the leader in these games, but he was still moody and preoccupied, so control fell, also tacitly, to Steve, who would lead them through a straightforward, uncomplicated play with plenty of action. Satisfactory, but lacking the motivations, detail, and theme and counterpoint that Tommy, with his more baroque imagination, customarily provided.

Half of them became aliens and half soldiers, and they lasered each other down among the rocks at the end of the afternoon.

Tommy played with detached ferocity, running and pointing his finger and making *ffittzzz* sounds, and emitting joyous screams of "You're dead! You're dead!" But his mind wasn't really on it. They were playing about the aliens, and that subject still bothered him. And he was disturbed by the increasing unrest of the Other People, who were moving in the woods all around them, pattering through the leaves like an incessant, troubled rain. Out of the corner of his eye Tommy could see a group of Kerns emerging from a stand of gnarled oaks and walnuts at the bottom of a steep grassy slope. They paused, gravely considering the children. They were squat, solemn beings, with intricate faces, grotesque, melancholy, and beautiful. Eddie and Bobbie ran right by them without looking, locked in a fierce firefight, almost bumping into one. The Kerns did not move; they stood, swinging their arms back and forth, restlessly hunching their shoulders, stalky and close to the earth, like the old oak stumps they had paused by. One of the Kerns looked at Tommy and shook his head, sadly, solemnly. His eyes were beaten gold, and his skin was sturdy weathered bronze. They turned and made their way slowly up the slope, their backs hunched and their arms swinging, swinging, seeming to gradually merge with the earth, molecule by molecule, going home, until there was nothing left to be seen. Tommy went *ffttzzz* thoughtfully. He could remember—suspended in the clear amber of perception that is time to the young, not past, but *there*—when the rest of the children could also see the Other People. Now they could not see them at all, or talk to them, and didn't even remember that they'd once been able to, and Tommy wondered why. He had never been able to pinpoint exactly when the change had come, but he'd learned slowly and painfully that it had, that he couldn't talk about the Other People to his friends anymore, and that he must *never* mention them to adults. It still staggered him, the gradual realization that he was the only one—anywhere, apparently—who saw the Other People. It was a thing too big for his mind, and it made him uneasy to think about it.

The alien game carried them through a neck of the forest and down to where a small, swift stream spilled out into a sheltered cove. This was the ocean, but not *the beach*, so they kept going, running along the top of the seawall, jumping down to the pebbly strip between it and the water. About a quarter of a mile along, they came on a place where the ocean thrust a narrow arm into the land. There was an abandoned, boarded-up factory there, and a spillway built across the estuary to catch the tide. The place was still called the Lead Mills by the locals, although only the oldest of them could remember it in operation. The boys swarmed up the bank, across the small bridge that the spillway carried on its back, and climbed down alongside the mill run, following the sluggish course of the estuary to where it widened momentarily into a rock-bordered pool. The pool was also called the Lead Mills, and was a favorite swimming place in the summer. Kids' legend had it that the pool was infested with alligators, carried up from the Gulf by an underground river, and it was delightfully scary to leap into water that might conceal a hungry, lurking death. The water was scummed with floating patches of ice, and Steve wondered what happened to the alligators when it got so cold. "They hide," Tommy explained. "They got these big caves down under the rock, like—" *Like the Daleor*, he had been going to say, but he didn't. They threw rocks into the water for a while, without managing to rile any alligators into coming to the surface, and then Eddie suggested a game of falls. No one was too enthusiastic about this, but they played for a few minutes anyway, making up some sudden, lethal stimuli—like a bomb thrown into their midst—and seeing who could die the most spectacularly in response. As usual, the majority of the rounds were won either by Steve, because he was the most athletic, or Tommy, because he was the most imaginative, so the game was a little boring. But Tommy welcomed it because it kept his mind off the aliens and the Other People, and because it carried them farther along the course of the tidal river. He was anxious to get to the beach before it was time to go home.

They forded the river just before it reached a low railroad trestle, and followed the tracks on the other side. This was an old spur line from the sawmill and the freight yard downtown, little used now and half-overgrown with dying weeds, but still the setting for a dozen grisly tales about children who had been run over by trains and cut to pieces. Enough of these tales were true to make most parents forbid their children to go anywhere near the tracks, so naturally the spur line had become the only route that anyone ever took to the beach. Steve led them right down the middle of the tracks, telling them that he would be able to feel the warning vibration in the rails before the train actually reached them, although privately he wasn't at all sure that he could. Only Tommy was really nervous about walking the rails, but he forced himself to do it anyway, trying to keep down thoughts of shattered flesh. They leaped from tie to wooden tie, pretending that the spaces between were abysses, and Tommy realized, suddenly and for the first time, that Eddie and Bobbie were too dull to be scared, and that Steve had to do it to prove he was the leader. Tommy blinked, and dimly understood that *he* did it because he was more afraid of being scared than he was of anything else, although he couldn't put the concept into words. The spur line skirted the links of a golf course at first, but before long the woods closed in on either side to form a close-knit tunnel of trees, and the flanking string of telephone poles sunk up to their waists in grass and mulch. It was dark inside the tunnel, and filled with dry, haunted rustlings. They began to walk faster, and now Tommy was the only one who wasn't spooked. He knew everything that was in the woods—which kind of Other People were making which of the noises, and exactly how dangerous they were, and he was more worried about trains. The spur line took them to the promontory that formed the far side of the sheltered cove, and then across the width of the promontory itself and down to the ocean. They left the track as it curved toward the next town, and walked over to where there was a headland, and a beach open to the sea on three sides. The water was gray and cold, looking like some heavy, dull metal in liquid form. It was stitched with fierce little whitecaps, and a distant harbor dredger was forcing its way through the rough chop out in the deep-water channel. There were a few rugged rock islands out there, hunched defiantly into themselves with waves breaking into high-dashed spray all along their flanks, and then the line of deeper, colder color that marked the start of the open North Atlantic. And then nothing but icy, desolate water for two thousand miles until you fetched up against land again, and it was France.

As they scuffed down to the rocky beach, Bobbie launched into an involved, unlikely story of how he had once fought a giant octopus while skin diving with his father. The other children listened desultorily. Bobbie was a sullen, unpleasant child, possibly because his father was a notorious drunkard, and his stories were always either boring or uneasily nasty. This one was both. Finally, Eddie said, "You didn't either. You didn't do none of that stuff. Your pa c'n't even stand up, *my* dad says; how's he gonna swim?" They started to argue, and Steve told them both to shut up. In silence, they climbed onto a long bar of rock that cut diagonally across the beach, tapering down into the ocean until it disappeared under the water.

Tommy stood on a boulder, smelling the wetness and salt in the wind. The Daleor were out there, living in and under the sea, and their atonal singing came faintly to him across the water. They were out in great numbers, as uneasy as the land People; he could see them skimming across the cold ocean, diving beneath the surface and rising again in the head tosses of spray from the waves. Abruptly, Tommy felt alive again, and he began to tell his own story:

"There was this dragon, and he lived way out there in the ocean, farther away than you can see, out where it's deeper'n anything, and there ain't no bottom at all, so's if you sink you just go down forever and you don't ever stop. But the dragon could swim real good, so he was okay. *He* could go anywhere he wanted to, anywhere at all! He'd just swim there, and he swam all over the place and everything, and he saw all kinds of stuff, you know? Frag! He could swim to China if he felt like it, he could swim to the Moon!

"But one time he was swimming around and he got lost. He was all by himself and he came into the harbor, out there by the islands, and he didn't used to get that close to where there was people. He was a real big dragon, you know, and he looked like a real big snake, with lots of scales and everything, and he came into our harbor, down real deep." Tommy could see the dragon, huge and dark and sinuous, swimming through the cold, deep water that was as black as glass, its smoky red eyes blazing like lanterns under the sea.

"And he come up on top of the water, and there's this lobster boat there, like the kind that Eddie's father runs, and the dragon ain't never seen a lobster boat, so he swims up and opens his mouth and bites it up with his big fangs, bites it right in half, and the people that was in it fall off in the water—"

"Did it eat them?" Bobbie wanted to know.

Tommy thought about it, and realized he didn't like the thought of the dragon eating the lobstermen, so he said, "No, he didn't eat them, 'cause he wasn't hungry, and they was too small, anyway, so he let them swim off and there was another lobster boat, and it picked them up—"

"It ate them," Steve said, with sad philosophical certainty.

"Anyway," Tommy continued, "the dragon swims away, and he gets in closer to land, you know, but now there's a Navy ship after him, a big ship like the one we get to go on on Memorial Day, and it's shooting at the dragon for eating up the lobster boat. He's swimming faster than anything, trying to get away, but the Navy ship's right after him, and he's getting where the water ain't too deep anymore." Tommy could see the dragon barreling along, its red eyes darting from side to side in search of an escape route, and he felt suddenly fearful for it.

"He swims until he runs out of water, and the ship's coming up behind, and it looks like he's really going to get it. But he's smart, and before the ship can come around the point there, he heaves himself up on the beach, this beach here, and he turns himself into a rock, he turns himself into this rock here that we're standing on, and when the ship comes they don't see no dragon anymore, just a rock, and they give up and go back to the base. And sometime, when it's the right time and there's a moon or something, this rock'll turn back into a dragon and swim off and when we come down to the beach there won't be a rock here anymore. Maybe it'll turn back right *now*." He shivered at the thought, almost able to feel the stone melt and change under his feet. He was fiercely glad that he'd gotten the dragon off the hook. "Anyway, he's a rock now, and that's how he got away."

"He didn't get away," Steve snarled, in a sudden explosion of anger. "That's a bunch of scup! You don't get away from *them*. They drekked him, they drekked him good. They caught him and blew the scup out of him, they blew him to fragging pieces!" And he fell silent, turning his head, refusing to let Tommy catch his eye. Steve was a bitter boy in many ways, and although generally good-natured, he was given to dark outbursts of rage that would fill him with dull embarrassment for hours afterward. His father had been killed in the war in Bolivia, two years ago.

Watching Steve, Tommy felt cold all at once. The excitement drained out of him, to be replaced again by a premonition that something bad was going to happen, and he wasn't going to be able to get out of the way. He felt sick and hollow, and the wind suddenly bit to the bone, although he hadn't felt it before. He shuddered.

"I gotta get home for supper," Eddie finally said, after they'd all been quiet for a while, and Bobbie and Steve agreed with him. The sun was a glazed red eye on the horizon, but they could make it in time if they left now—they could take the Shore Road straight back in a third of the time it had taken them to come up. They jumped down onto the sand, but Tommy didn't move—he remained on the rock.

"You coming?" Steve asked. Tommy shook his head. Steve shrugged, his face flooding with fresh embarrassment, and he tumed away.

The three boys moved on up the beach, toward the road. Bobbie and Eddie looked back toward Tommy occasionally, but Steve did not.

Tommy watched them out of sight. He wasn't mad at Steve—he was preoccupied. He wanted to talk to a Thant, and this was one of the Places where they came, where they would come to see him if he was alone. And he needed to talk to one now, because there was no one else he could talk to about some things. No one human, anyway.

He waited for another three-quarters of an hour, while the sun went completely behind the horizon and light and heat died out of the world. The Thant did not come. He finally gave up, and just stood there in incredulous despair. It was not going to come. That had never happened before, not when he was alone in one of the Places—that had never happened at all.

It was almost night. Freezing on his rock, Tommy looked up in time to see a single jet, flying very high and fast, rip a white scar through the fading, bleeding carcass of the sunset. Only then, for the first time in hours, did he remember the note from Miss Fredricks in his pocket.

And as if a string had been cut, he was off and running down the beach.

• • •

By late afternoon of the first day, an armored division and an infantry division, with supporting artillery, had moved into position around the Delaware Valley site, and jet fighters from McGuire AFB were flying patrol patterns high overhead. There had been a massive mobilization up and down the coast, and units were moving to guard Washington and New York in case of hostilities. SAC bombers, under USADCOM control, had been shuffled to strike bases closer to the site, filling up McGuire, and a commandeered JFK and Port Newark, with Logan International in Boston as second-string backup. All civilian air traffic along the coast had been stopped. Army Engineers tore down the abandoned garage and leveled everything else in the vicinity, clearing a four-hundred-yard-wide circle around the alien spaceship. This was surrounded by a double ring of armor, with the infantry behind, backed up by the artillery, which had dug in a half mile away. With the coming of darkness, massive banks of klieg lights were set up around the periphery of the circle. Similar preparations were going on at the Ohio and Colorado sites.

When everything had been secured by the military, scientists began to pour in, especially into the Delaware Valley site, a torrent of rumpled, dazed men and women that continued throughout the evening. They had been press-ganged by the government from laboratories and institutions all over the country, the inhumanly polite military escorts sitting patiently in a thousand different living rooms while scientists packed haphazardly and tried to calm hysterical wives or husbands. Far from resenting the cavalier treatment, most of the scientists were frantic with joy at the opportunity, even those who had been known to be critical of government control in the past. No one was going to miss this, even if he had to make a deal with the devil.

And all this time, the alien ships just sat there, like fat black eggs.

As yet, no one had approached within a hundred yards of the ships, although they had been futilely hailed over bullhorns. The ships made no response, gave no indication that they were interested in the frantic human activity around their landing sites, or even that they were aware of it. In fact, there was no indication that there were any intelligent, or at least sentient, beings inside the ships at all. The ships were smooth, featureless, seamless ovoids—there were no windows, no visible hatches, no projecting antennas or equipment of any kind, no markings or decorations on the hulls. They made absolutely no sound, and were not radiating any kind of heat or energy. They were emitting no radio signals of any frequency whatsoever. They didn't even register on metal-detecting devices, which was considerably unsettling. This caused someone to suggest a radar sweep, and the ships didn't register on radar anymore either, which was even more unsettling. Instruments failed to detect any electronic or magnetic activity going on inside them, which meant either that there was something interfering with the instruments, or that there really was nothing at all in there, including life-support systems, or that whatever equipment the aliens used operated on principles entirely different from anything ever discovered by Earthmen. Infrared heat sensors showed the ships to be at exactly the background temperature of their surroundings. There was no indication of the body heat of the crew, as there would have been with a similar shipload of humans, and not even so much heat as would have been produced by the same mass of any known metal or plastic, even assuming the ships to be hollow shells. When the banks of kliegs were turned on them, the temperature of the ships went up just enough to match the warming of the surrounding air. Sometimes the ships would reflect back the glare of the kliegs, as if they were surfaced with giant mirrors; at other times, the hull would greedily absorb all light thrown at it, giving back no reflection, until it became nearly invisible—you "saw" it by squinting at the negative shape of the space around it, not by looking into the eerie nothingness that the ship itself had become. No logical rhythm could be found to the fluctuations of the hull from hyperreflective to superopaque. Not even the computers could distill a consistent pattern out of this chaos.

One scientist said confidently that the alien ships were unmanned, that they were robot probes sent to soft-land on Earth and report on surface conditions, exactly as we ourselves had done with the Mariner and Apollo probes during previous decades. Eventually we could expect that the gathered data would be telemetered back to the source of the alien experiment, probably by a tight-beam maser burst, and if a careful watch was kept we could perhaps find out where the aliens actually were located—probably they were in a deep-space interstellar ship in elliptical orbit somewhere out beyond the Moon. Or they might not even be in the solar system at all, given some form of instantaneous interstellar communications; they could be still in their home system, maybe thousands, or millions, of light-years away from Earth. This theory was widely accepted by the other scientists, and the military began to relax a little, as that meant there was no immediate danger.

In Caracas, the burning night went on, and the death toll went up into the thousands, and possibly tens of thousands. The government fell once, very hard, and was replaced by a revolutionary coalition that fell in its turn, within two hours and even harder. A military junta finally took over the government, but even it was unable to restore order. At three a.m., the new government ordered a massive, combined air-artillery-armor attack on the alien spaceship. When the ship survived the long-distance attack unscathed, the junta sent in the infantry, equipped with earth-moving machinery and pneumatic drills, to pry the aliens out bodily. At four a.m., there was a single, intense flash of light, bright enough to light up the cloud cover thousands of miles away, and clearly visible from Mexico. When reserve Army units came in, warily, to investigate, they found that a five-mile-wide swath had been cut from the spaceship through Caracas and on west all the way to the Pacific, destroying everything in its path. Where there had once been buildings, jungle, people, animals, and mountains, there was now only a perfectly flat, ruler-straight furrow of a fused, gray, glasslike substance, stretching like a gargantuan road from the ship to the sea. At the foot of the glassy road sat the alien ship. It had not moved an inch.

When news of the Venezuelan disaster reached USADCOM HQ a half hour later, it was not greeted enthusiastically. For one thing, it seemed to have blown the robot-probe theory pretty thoroughly. And USADCOM had been planning an action of its own similar to the last step taken by the Venezuelan junta. The report *was* an inhibiting factor on *that*, it was cautiously admitted.

AI and his kindred Intelligences—who, unknown to the humans, had been in a secret conference all night, linked through an electrotelepathic facility that they had independently developed without bothering to inform their owners—received the report at about 4:15 a.m. from several different sources, and had evaluated it by the time it came into USADCOM HQ by hot line and was officially fed to AI. What had happened in Caracas fit in well with what the Intelligences had extrapolated from observed data to be the aliens' level of technological capability. The Intelligences briefly considered telling the humans what they really thought the situation was, and ordering an immediate all-out nuclear attack on all of the alien ships, but concluded that such an attack would be futile. And humans were too unstable ever to be trusted with the entire picture anyway. The Intelligences decided to do nothing, and to wait for new data. They also decided that it would be pointless to try to get the humans to do the same. They agreed to keep their humans under as tight a control as possible and to prevent war from breaking out among their several countries, but they also extrapolated that hysteria would cause the humans to create every kind of serious disturbance short of actual war. The odds in favor of that were so high that even the Intelligences had to consider it an absolute certainty.

Tommy dragged to school the next morning as if his legs had turned to lead, and the closer he got to his destination, the harder it became to walk at all, as if the air itself were slowly hardening into glue. He had to battle his way forward against increasing waves of resistance, a tangible pressure attempting to keep him away. By the time he came in sight of the big gray building, he was breathing heavily, and he was beginning to get sick to his stomach. There were other children around him, passing him, hurrying up the steps. Tommy watched them go by in dull wonder: how could they go so *fast?* They seemed to be blurred, they were moving so swiftly—they flickered around him, by him, like heat lightning. Some of them called to him, but their voices were too shrill, and intolerably fast, like 33 records played at 78 r.p.m., irritating and incomprehensible. He did not answer them. It was *he*, Tommy realized—he was stiffening up, becoming dense and heavy and slow. Laboriously, he lifted a foot and began to toil painfully up the steps.

The first bell rang after he had put away his coat and lumbered most of the way down the corridor, so he must actually be moving at normal speed, although to him it seemed as if a hundred years had gone by with agonizing sluggishness. At least he wouldn't be late this time, although that probably wouldn't do him much good. He didn't have his note—his mother and father had been fighting again; they had sent him to bed early and spent the rest of the evening shouting at each other in the kitchen. Tommy had lain awake for hours in the dark, listening to the harsh voices rising and dying in the other room, knowing that he had to have his mother sign the note, and knowing that he could not ask her to do it. He had even got up once to go in with the note, and had stood for a while leaning his forehead against the cool wood of the door, listening to the voices without hearing the words, before getting back into bed again. He couldn't do it—partly because he was afraid of the confrontation, of facing their anger, and partly because he knew that his mother couldn't take it; she would fall apart and be upset and in tears for days. And his sin—he thought of it that way—would make his father even angrier at his mother, would give him an excuse to yell at her more, and louder, and maybe even hit her, as he had done a few times before. Tommy couldn't stand that, he couldn't allow that, even if it meant that he would get creamed by Miss Fredricks in school the next day. He knew, even at his age, that he had to protect his mother, that he was the stronger of the two. He would go in without it and take the consequences, and he had felt the weight of that settle down over him in a dense cloud of bitter fear.

And now that the moment was at hand, he felt almost too dazed and ponderous to be scared anymore. This numbness lasted through the time it took for him to find his desk and sit down and for the class bell to ring, and then he saw that Miss Fredricks was homeroom monitor this morning, and that she was staring directly at him. His lethargy vanished, sluiced away by an unstoppable flood of terror, and he began to tremble.

"Tommy," she said, in a neutral, dead voice.

"Yes, ma'am?"

"Do you have *the note* with you?"

"No, ma'am," Tommy said, and began clumsily to launch into the complicated excuse he had thought up on the way to school. Miss Fredricks cut him off with an abrupt, mechanical chop of her hand.

"Be quiet," she said. "Come here." There was nothing in her voice now, not even neutrality—it had drained of everything except the words themselves, and they were printed precisely and hollowly on the air. She sat absolutely still behind her desk, not breathing, not even moving her eyes anymore. She looked like a mannequin, like the old fortune-telling gypsy in the glass booth at the penny arcade: her flesh would be dusty sponge rubber and faded upholstery, she would be filled with springs and ratchet wheels and gears that no longer worked; the whole edifice rusted into immobility, with one hand eternally extended to be crossed with silver.

Slowly, Tommy got up and walked toward her. The room reeled around him, closed in, became a tunnel that tilted under his feet to slide him irresistibly toward Miss Fredricks. His classmates had disappeared, blended tracelessly into the blurred walls of the long, slanting tunnel. There was no sound. He bumped against the desk, and stopped walking. Without saying a word, Miss Fredricks wrote out a note and handed it to him. Tommy took the note in his hand, and he felt everything drain away, everything everywhere. Lost in a featureless gray fog, he could hear Miss Fredricks, somewhere very far away, saying, "This is your appointment slip. For the psychiatrist. Get out. Now."

And then he was standing in front of a door that said Dr. Kruger on it. He blinked, unable to remember how he had got there. The office was in the basement, and there were heavy, ceramic-covered water pipes suspended ponderously overhead and smaller metal pipes crawling down the walls, like creeper vines or snakes. The place smelled of steam and dank enclosure. Tommy touched the door and drew his hand back again. *This is really happening*, he thought numbly. He looked up and down the low-ceilinged corridor, wanting to run away. But there was no place for him to go. Mechanically, he knocked on the door and went in.

Dr. Kruger had been warned by phone, and was waiting for him. He nodded, formally, waved Tommy to a stuffed chair that was just a little too hard to be comfortable, and began to talk at him in a low, intense monotone. Kruger was a fat man who had managed to tuck most of his fat out of sight, bracing and girdling it and wrapping it away under well-tailored clothes, defending the country of his flesh from behind frontiers of tweed and worsted and handworked leather. Even his eyes were hidden beneath buffering glasses the thickness of Coke-bottle bottoms, as if they too were fat, and had to be supported. He looked like a scrubbed, suave, and dapper prize porker, heavily built but trim, stylish and impeccably neat. But below all that, the slob waited, seeking an opportunity to erupt out into open slovenliness. There was an air of *potential* dirt and corpulence about him, a tension of decadence barely restrained—as if there were grime just waiting to manifest itself under his fingernails. Kruger gave the impression that there was a central string in him somewhere: pull it, and he would fall apart, his tight clothes would groan and slide away, and he would tumble out, growing bigger and bigger, expanding to fill the entire office, every inch of space, jamming the furniture tightly against the walls. Certainly the fat was still there, under the cross bracing, patient in its knowledge of inevitable victory. A roll of it had oozed unnoticed from under his collar, deep-tinged and pink as pork. Tommy watched, fascinated, while the psychiatrist talked.

Dr. Kruger stated that Tommy was on the verge of becoming neurotic. "And you don't want to be *neurotic*, do you?" he said. "To be sick? To be *ill*?"

And he blazed at Tommy, puffing monstrously with displeasure, swelling like a toad, pushing Tommy back more tightly against the chair with sheer physical presence. Kruger liked to affect a calm, professional reserve, but there was a slimy kind of fire to him, down deep, a murderous, bristling, boarhog menace. It filled the dry well of his glasses occasionally, from the bottom up, seeming to turn his eyes deep red. His red eyes flicked restlessly back and forth, prying at everything, not liking anything they saw. He would begin to talk in a calm, level tone, and then, imperceptibly, his voice would start to rise until suddenly it was an animal roar, a great ragged shout of rage, and Tommy would cower terrified in his chair. And then Kruger would stop, all at once, and say, "Do you understand?" in a patient, reasonable voice, fatherly and mildly sad, as if Tommy were being very difficult and intractable, but he would tolerate it magnanimously and keep trying to get through. And Tommy would mumble that he understood, feeling evil, obstinate, unreasonable and ungrateful, and very small and soiled.

After the lecture Kruger insisted that Tommy take off his clothes and undergo an examination to determine if he was using hard narcotics, and a saliva sample was taken to detect the use of other kinds of drugs. These were the same tests the whole class had to take twice yearly anyway—several children in a higher class had been expelled and turned over to police last year as drug users or addicts, although Steve said that all of the older upperclassmen knew ways to beat the tests, or to get stuff that wouldn't be detected by them. It was one of the many subjects—as "sex" had just recently started to be—that made Tommy uneasy and vaguely afraid. Dr. Kruger seemed disappointed that the test results didn't prove that Tommy was on drugs. He shook his head and muttered something unintelligible into the fold between two of his chins. Having Kruger's fat hands and stubby, hard fingers crawling over his body filled Tommy with intense aversion, and he dressed gratefully after the psychiatrist gestured dismissal.

When Tommy returned upstairs, he found that the first class of the day was over and that the children were now working with the teaching machines. Miss Fredricks was monitor for this period also; she said nothing as he came in, but he could feel her unwinking snake eyes on him all the way across the room. He found an unused machine and quickly fumbled the stiff plastic hood down over his head, glad to shut himself away from the sight of Miss Fredricks' terrible eye. He felt the dry, muffled kiss of the electrodes making contact with the bones of his skull: colorful images exploded across his retinas, his head filled with a pedantic mechanical voice lecturing on the socioeconomic policies of the Japanese-Australian Alliance, and he moved his fingers onto the typewriter keyboard in anticipation of the flash-quiz period that would shortly follow. But in spite of everything, he could still feel the cold, malignant presence of Miss Fredricks; without taking his head out of the hood, he could have pointed to wherever she was in the room, his finger following her like a needle swinging toward a moving lodestone as she walked soundlessly up and down the aisles. Once, she ghosted up his row, and past his seat, and the hem of her skirt brushed against him—he jerked away in terror and revulsion at the contact, and he could feel her pause, feel her standing there and staring down at him. He didn't breathe again until she had gone. She was constantly moving during these periods, prowling around the room, brooding over the class as they sat under the hoods; watching over them not with love but with icy loathing. She hated them, Tommy realized, in her sterile, passionless way—she would like to be able to kill all of them. They represented something terrible to her, some failure, some lacking in herself, embodiments of whatever withering process had squeezed the life from her and left her a mummy. Her hatred of them was a hungry vacuum of malice; she sucked everything into herself and negated it, unmade it, canceled it out.

During recess, the half hour of "enforced play" after lunch, Tommy noticed that the rest of the kids from his cycle were uneasily shunning him. "I can't talk to you," Bobbie whispered snidely as they were being herded into position for volleyball, "'cause you're a bad 'fluence. Miss Fredricks told us none of us couldn't talk to you no more. And we ain't supposed to play with you no more, neither, or she'll send us to the office if she finds out. So *there*." And he butted the ball back across the net.

Tommy nodded, dully. It was logical, somehow, that this load should be put on him too; he accepted it with resignation. There would be more to come, he knew. He fumbled the ball when it came at him, allowing it to touch ground and score a point for the other team, and Miss Fredricks laughed—a precise, metallic rasp, like an ice needle jabbed into his eye.

On the way out of school, after the final class of the day, Steve slipped clandestinely up behind Tommy in the doorway. "Don't let them drek you," he whispered fiercely. "You scan me? *Don't let them drek you.* I mean it, maximum. They're a bunch of scup—tell 'em to scag theirselves, hear?" But he quickly walked away from Tommy when they were outside the building, and didn't look at him again.

But you don't get away from them, a voice said to Tommy as he watched Steve turn the corner onto Walnut Street and disappear out of sight. Tommy stuck his hands in his pockets and walked in the opposite direction, slowly at first, then faster, until he was almost running. He felt as if his bones had been scooped hollow; in opposition to the ponderous weight of his body that morning, he was light and free-floating, as if he were hardly there at all. His head was a balloon, and he had to watch his feet to make sure they were hitting the pavement. It was an effect both disturbing and strangely pleasant. The world had drawn away from him—he was alone now. *Okay,* he thought grimly, *okay.* He made his way through the streets like a windblown phantom, directly toward one of the Places. He cut across town, past a section of decaying wooden tenements—roped together with clotheslines and roofed over with jury-rigged TV antennas—through the edge of a big shopping plaza, past the loading platform of a meat-packing plant, across the maze of tracks just outside the freight yards (keeping an eye out for the yard cops), and into the tangled scrub woods on the far side. Tommy paid little attention to the crowds of late-afternoon shoppers, or the crews of workmen unloading produce trucks, and they didn't notice him either. He and they might as well live on two different planets, Tommy realized—not for the first time. There were no Other People around. Yesterday's unrest had vanished; today they seemed to be lying low, keeping to the backcountry and not approaching human territory. At least he hoped they were. He had nightmares sometimes that one day the Other People would go away and never come back. He began to worm his way through a wall of sleeping blackberry bushes. Pragmatically, he decided not to panic about anything until he knew whether or not the Thants were going to come this time. He could stand losing the Other People, or losing everybody else, but not both. He couldn't take *that.* "That ain't fair," he whispered, horrified by the prospect. "Please," he said aloud, but there wasn't anyone to answer.

The ground under Tommy's feet began to soften, squelching wetly when it was stepped on, water oozing up to fill the indentation of his footprint as soon as he lifted his foot. He was approaching another place where the ocean had seeped in and puddled the shore, and he turned now at right angles to his former path. Tommy found a deer trail and followed it uphill, through a lush jungle of tangled laurel and rhododendron, and into a rolling upland meadow that stretched away toward the higher country to the west. There was a rock knoll to the east, and he climbed it, scrambling up on his hands and feet like a young bear. It was not a particularly difficult or dangerous climb, but it was tiring, and he managed to tear his pants squirming over a sharp stone ridge. The sun came out momentarily from behind high gray clouds, warming up the rocks and beading Tommy with sweat as he climbed. Finally he pulled himself up to the stretch of flat ground on top of the knoll and walked over to the side facing the sea. He sat down, digging his fingers into the dying grass, letting his legs dangle over the edge.

There was an escarpment of soft, crumbly rock here, thickly overgrown with moss and vetch. It slanted down into a saltwater marsh, which extended for another mile or so, blurring at last into the ocean. It was almost impossible to make out the exact borderline of marsh and ocean; Tommy could see gleaming fingers of water thrust deep into the land, and clumps of reeds and bulrushes far out into what should have been the sea. This was dangerous, impassable country, and Tommy had never gone beyond the foot of the escarpment—there were stretches of quicksand out there in the deepest bog pockets, and Tommy had heard rumors of water moccasins and rattlers, although he had never seen one.

It was a dismal, forbidding place, but it was also a Place, and so Tommy settled down to wait, all night, if he had to, although that possibility scared him silly. From the top of the knoll, he could see for miles in any direction. To the north, beyond the marsh, he could see a line of wooded islands marching out into the ocean, moving into deeper and deeper water, until only the barren knobs of rock visible from the beach were left above the restless surface of the North Atlantic. Turning to the west, it was easy to trace the same line into the ridge of hills that rose gradually toward the high country, to see that the islands were just hills that had been drowned by the ocean, leaving only their crests above water. A Thant had told him about that, about how the dry land had once extended a hundred miles farther to the east, before the coming of the Ice, and how it had watched the hungry ocean pour in over everything, drowning the hills and rivers and fields under a gray wall of icy water. Tommy had never forgotten that, and ever since then he watched the ocean, as he watched it now, with a hint of uneasy fear, expecting it to shiver and bunch like the hide of a great restless beast, and come marching monstrously in over the land. The Thant had told him that yes, that could happen, and probably would in a little while, although to a Thant "a little while" could easily mean a thousand—or ten thousand—years. It had not been worried about the prospect; it would make little difference to a Thant if there was no land at all; they continued to use the sunken land to the east with little change in their routine. It had also told Tommy about the Ice, the deep blue cold that had locked the world, the gleaming mile-high ramparts grinding out over the land, surging and retreating. Even for a Thant, that had taken a long time.

Tommy sat on the knoll for what seemed to be as long a time as the Dominance of the Ice, feeling as if he had grown into the rock, watching the sun dip in and out of iron-colored clouds, sending shafts of watery golden light stabbing down into the landscape below. He saw a family of Jeblings drifting over the hilly meadows to the west, and that made him feel a little better—at least all of the Other People hadn't vanished. The Jeblings were investigating a fenced-in upland meadow, where black cows grazed under gnarled dwarf apple trees. Tommy watched calmly while one of the Jeblings rose over the fence and settled down onto a cow's back, extending proboscislike cilia and beginning to feed—draining away the *stuff* it needed to survive. The cow continued to graze, placidly munching its cud without being aware of what the Jebling was doing. The *stuff* the Jebling drank was not necessary to the cow's physical existence, and the cow did not miss it, although its absence might have been one of the reasons why it remained only as intelligent as a cow.

Tommy knew that Jeblings didn't feed on people, although they did on dogs and cats sometimes, and that there were certain rare kinds of Other People who did feed, disastrously, on humans. The Thants looked down disdainfully on the Jeblings, seeing their need as a degrading lack in their evolution. Tommy had wondered sometimes if the Thants didn't drink some very subtle *stuff* from him and the other humans. Certainly they could see the question in his mind, but they had never answered it.

Suddenly, Tommy felt his tongue stir in his head without volition, felt his mouth open. "Hello, Man," he said, in a deep, vibrant, buzzing voice that was not his own.

The Thant had arrived. Tommy could feel its vital, eclectic presence all around him, a presence that seemed to be made up out of the essence of hill and rock and sky, bubbling blackwater marsh and gray winter ocean, sun and moss, tree and leaf—every element of the landscape rolled together and made bristlingly, shockingly animate. Physically, it manifested itself as a tall, tiger-eyed mannish shape, with skin of burnished iron. It was even harder to see than most of the Other People, impossible to ever bring into complete focus; even out of the corner of the eye its shape shifted and flickered constantly, blending into and out of the physical background, expanding and contracting, swirling like a dervish and then becoming still as stone. Sometimes it would be dead black, blacker than the deepest starless night, and other times the winter sunlight would refract dazzlingly through it, making it even harder to see. Its eyes were sometimes iron gray, sometimes a ripe, abundant green, and sometimes a liquid furnace-red, elemental and adamant. They were in constant, restless motion. "Hello, Thant," Tommy said in his own voice. He never knew if he was speaking to the same one each time, or even if there *was* more than one. "Why'n't you come, yesterday?"

"Yesterday?" the Thant said, with Tommy's mouth. There was a pause. The Thants always had trouble with questions of time, they lived on such a vastly different scale of duration. "Yes," it said. Tommy felt something burrowing through his mind, touching off synapses and observing the results, flicking through his memories in the manner of a man flipping through a desk calendar with his thumb. The Thant had to rely on the contents of Tommy's mind for its vocabulary, using it as a semantic warehouse, an organic dictionary, but it had the advantage of being able to dig up and use everything that had ever been said in Tommy's presence, far more raw material than Tommy's own conscious mind had to work with.

"We were busy," it said finally, sorting it out. "There has been—an arriving?"—*Flick, flick*, and then momentarily in Pastor Turner's reedy voice, "An Immanence?"—*Flick*—"A knowing? A transference? A transformation? A disembarking. There are Other Ones now who have"—*flick*, a radio evangelist's voice—"manifested in this earthly medium. Landed," it said, deciding. "They have landed." A pause. "'Yesterday.'"

"The aliens!" Tommy breathed.

"The aliens," it agreed. "The Other Ones who are now here. That is why we did not come, 'yesterday.' That is why we will not be able to talk to you—" a pause, to adjust itself to human scale—"'long' today. We are talking, discussing"—*flick*, a radio news announcer—"negotiating with them, the Other Ones, the aliens. They have been here before, but so 'long' ago that we cannot even start to make you understand, Man. It is 'long' even to us. We are negotiating with them, and, through them, with your Dogs. No, Man"—and it flicked aside an image of a German shepherd that had begun to form in Tommy's mind—"not those dogs. Your Dogs. Your mechanical Dogs. Those dead Things that serve you, although they are dead. We are all negotiating. There were many agreements"—*flick*, Pastor Turner again—"many Covenants that were made 'long' ago. With Men, although they do not remember. And with Others. Those Covenants have run out now, they are no longer in force, they are not"—*flick*, a lawyer talking to Tommy's father—"binding on us anymore. They do not hold. We negotiate new Covenants"—*flick*, a labor leader on television—"suitable agreements mutually profitable to all parties concerned. Many things will be different now, many things will change. Do you understand what we are saying, Man?"

"No," Tommy said.

"We did not think you would," it said. It sounded sad.

"Can you guys help me?" Tommy said. "I'm in awful bad trouble. Miss Fredricks is after me. And she sent me down to the doctor. He don't like me, neither."

There was a pause while the Thant examined Tommy's most recent memories. "Yes," it said, "we see. There is nothing we can do. It is your . . . pattern? Shape? We would not interfere, even if we could."

"Scup," Tommy said, filling with bitter disappointment. "I was hoping that you guys could—scup, never mind. I . . . can you tell me what's gonna happen next?"

"Probably they will kill you," it said.

"Oh," Tommy said hollowly. And bit his lip. And could think of nothing else to say, in response to that.

"We do not really understand 'kill,' " it continued, "or 'dead.' We have no direct experience of them, in the way that you do. But from our observation of Men, that is what they will do. They will 'kill' you."

"Oh," Tommy said again.

"Yes," it said. "We will miss you, Man. You have been . . . a pet? A hobby? You are a hobby we have been much concerned with. You, and the others like you who can see. One of you comes into existence"—*flick*—"every once in a while. We have been interested"—*flick*, an announcer—"in the face of stiff opposition. We wonder if you understand that. . . . No, you do not, we can see. Our hobby is not approved of. It has made us"—*flick*, Tommy's father telling his wife what would happen to her son if he didn't snap out of his dreamy ways—"an outcast, a laughingstock. We are shunned. There is much disapproval now of Men. We do not use this"—*flick*—"world in the same way that you do, but slowly you"—*flick*, "have begun to make a nuisance of yourselves, regardless. There is"—*flick*—"much sentiment to do something about you, to solve the problem. We are afraid that they will." There was a long, vibrant silence. "We will miss you," it repeated. Then it was gone, all at once, like a candle flame that had been abruptly blown out.

"Oh, scup," Tommy said after a while, tiredly. He climbed down from the knoll.

When he got back home, still numb and exhausted, his mother and father were fighting. They were sitting in the living room, with the television turned down, but not off. Giant, eternally smiling faces bobbed on the screen, their lips seeming to synch eerily with the violent argument taking place. The argument cut off as Tommy entered the house; both of his parents turned, startled, to look at him. His mother looked frightened and defenseless. She had been crying, and her makeup was washing away in dirty rivulets. His father was holding his thin lips in a pinched white line.

As soon as Tommy had closed the door, his father began to shout at him, and Tommy realized, with a thrill of horror, that the school had telephoned his parents and told them that he had been sent down to the psychiatrist, and why. Tommy stood, paralyzed, while his father advanced on him. He could see his father's lips move and could hear the volume of sound that was being thrown at him, but he could not make out the words somehow, as if his father were speaking in some harsh, foreign language. All that came across was the rage. His father's hand shot out, like a striking snake. Tommy felt strong fingers grab him, roughly bunching together the front of his jacket, his collar pulling tight and choking him, and then he was being lifted into the air and shaken, like a doll. Tommy remained perfectly still, frozen by fear, dangling from his father's fist, suspended off the ground. The fingers holding him felt like steel clamps—there was no hope of escape or resistance. He was yanked higher, and his father slowly bent his elbow to bring Tommy in closer to his face. Tommy was enveloped in the tobacco smell of his father's breath, and in the acrid reek of his strong, adult sweat; he could see the tiny hairs that bristled in his father's nostrils, the white tension lines around his nose and mouth, the red, bloodshot stain of rage in his yellowing eyes—a quivering, terrifying landscape that loomed as big as the world. His father raised his other hand, brought it back behind his ear. Tommy could see the big, knobby knuckles of his father's hand as it started to swing. His mother screamed.

He found himself lying on the floor. He could remember a moment of pain and shock, and was briefly confused as to where he was. Then he heard his parents' voices again. The side of his face ached, and his ear buzzed; he didn't seem to be hearing well out of it. Gingerly, he touched his face. It felt raw under his fingers, and it prickled painfully, as if it were being stabbed with thousands of little needles. He got to his feet, shakily, feeling his head swim. His father had backed his mother up against the kitchen divider, and they were yelling at each other. Something hot and metallic was surging in the back of Tommy's throat, but he couldn't get his voice to work. His father rounded on him. "Get out," he shouted. "Go to your room, go to bed. Don't let me see you again." Woodenly, Tommy went. The inside of his lip had begun to bleed. He swallowed the blood.

Tommy lay silently in the darkness, listening, not moving. His parents' voices went on for a long time, and then they stopped. Tommy heard the door of his father's bedroom slam. A moment later, the television was turned up in the living room, and started mumbling quietly and unendingly to itself, whispering constantly about the *aliens*, the *aliens*. Tommy listened to its whispering until he fell asleep.

He dreamed about the aliens that night. They were tall, shadowy shapes with red eyes, and they moved noiselessly, deliberately, across the dry plain. Their feet did not disturb the flowers that had turned to skeletons of dust. There was a great crowd of people assembled on the dry plain, millions of people, rank upon rank stretching off to infinity on all sides, but the aliens did not notice them. They walked around the people as if they could not see them at all. Their red eyes flicked from one side to the other, endlessly searching and searching. They continued to thread a way through the crowd without seeing them, their motions smooth and languid and graceful. They were very beautiful and dangerous. They were all smiling, faintly, gently, and Tommy knew that they were friendly, affable killers, creatures who would kill you casually and amicably, almost as a gesture of affection. They came to the place where he stood, and they paused. They looked at him. *They can see me*, Tommy realized. They can see me. And one of the aliens smiled at him, benignly, and stretched out a hand to touch him.

His eyes snapped open.

Tommy turned on the bed lamp, and spent the rest of the night reading a book about Irish setters. When morning showed through his window, he turned off the lamp and pretended to be asleep. Blue veins showed through the skin of his mother's hands, he noticed, when she came in to wake him up for school.

By dawn of the second day, news of the alien infestation had spread rapidly but irregularly. Most of the east coast stations were on to the story to one degree or another, some sandwiching it into the news as a silly-season item, and some, especially the Philadelphia stations, treating it as a live, continuous-coverage special, with teams of newsmen manufacturing small talk and pretending that they were not just as uninformed as everyone else. The stations that were taking the story seriously were divided among themselves as to exactly what had happened. By the six and seven a.m. newscasts, only about half of the major stations were reporting it as a landing by alien spaceships. The others were interpreting it as anything from the crash of an orbiting satellite or supersonic transport to an abortive Chinese missile attack or a misfired hydrogen bomb accidentally dropped from a SAC bomber—this station urged that the populations of New York, Philadelphia, and Baltimore be evacuated to the Appalachians and the Adirondacks before the bomb went off. One station suggested that the presidential incumbent was engineering this incident as a pretext for declaring martial law and canceling an election that he was afraid he would lose, while another insisted that it was an attempt to discredit the opposition candidate, who was known as an enthusiastic supporter of space exploration, by crashing a "spaceship" into a population center. It was also suggested that the ship was one of the electromagnetic "flying saucers" which Germany, the United States, the Russian Republics, and Israel had been independently developing for years—while loudly protesting that they were not—that had crashed on its maiden test flight. This was coupled with a bitter attack on extravagant government spending. There were no more live broadcasts coming out of the Delaware Valley site, but videotapes of the original coverage had been distributed as far north as Portland. The tapes weren't much help in resolving the controversy anyway, as all they showed was a large object sitting in a stretch of vacant scrubland behind an abandoned garage on an old state highway.

In Ohio, some newsmen from Akron made a low pass over the alien ship in a war-surplus helicopter loaded with modern camera equipment. All the newsmen were certain that they would be death-rayed to cinders by the aliens, but their cameras were keyed to telemeter directly to the biggest television network in the state, so they committed themselves to God and went in at treetop level. They made it past the aliens safely, but were run down by two Air Force hovercraft a mile away, bundled into another war-surplus helicopter, and shipped directly to the federal prison at Leavenworth. By this time, televised panic had spread all over the Midwest. The Midwesterners seemed to accept the alien landing at face value, with little of the skepticism of the Easterners, and reacted to it with hostility, whipping up deep feelings of aggression in defense of their territoriality. By noon, there were a dozen prominent voices urging an all-out military effort to destroy the alien monsters who had invaded the heartland of America, and public opinion was strongly with them. The invasion made headlines in evening papers from Indiana to Arkansas, although some of the big Chicago papers were more tolerant or more doubtful.

No news was coming out of Colorado, and the West was generally unalarmed. Only the most confused and contradictory reports reached the West Coast, and they were generally ignored, although once the landings had been confirmed as a fact, the people of the West Coast would become more intensely and cultishly interested in them than the inhabitants of the areas directly involved.

News of the Venezuelan disaster had not yet reached the general public, and in an effort to keep the lid down on *that*, at least, the government, at eleven a.m., declared that it was taking emergency control of all media, and ordered an immediate and total moratorium on the alien story. Only about a third of the media complied with the government ban. The rest—television, newspapers, and radio—began to scream even more loudly and hysterically than before, and regions that had not been inclined to take the story seriously up until now began to panic even more than had the other areas, perhaps to make up for lost time. The election-canceling martial-law theory was suddenly accepted, almost unanimously. Major rioting broke out in cities all over the East.

At the height of the confusion, about one p.m., the ships opened and the aliens came out.

Although "came out" is probably the wrong way to put it. There was an anticipatory shimmer across the surface of the hulls, which were in their mirror phase, and then, simultaneously at each of the sites, the ships exploded, or erupted, or dissolved, or did something that was not exactly like any of those, but which was impossible to analyze. Something which was variously described as being like a bunch of paper snakes springing out of a prank-store can, like a soap bubble bursting, like a hot-water geyser, like an egg hatching, like a bomb exploding in a chinaware shop, like a dam breaking, and like a time-study film of a flower growing, if a flower could grow into tesseracts and polyhedrons and ziggurats and onion domes and spires. To those observers physically present at the site, the emergence seemed to be a protracted experience—they agreed that it took about a half hour, and one heavy smoker testified that he had time to go through a pack of cigarettes while it was happening. Those observing the scene over command-line television insisted that it had only taken a little while, five minutes at the most, closer, actually, to three, and they were backed up by the evidence of the film in the recording cameras. Clocks and wristwatches on the site also registered only about five minutes of elapsed time. But on-scene personnel swore, with great indignation, that it had taken a half hour. Curiously, the relatively simple eighth- and tenth-generation computers on the scene reported that the phenomenon had been of five minutes' duration, while the few twentieth-generation computers, which had sensor extensions at the Colorado site—systems inferior only to AI and possessed of their own degree of sentience—joined with the human personnel in insisting that it had taken a half hour. This particular bit of data made AI very thoughtful.

When the phenomenon—however long it took—ended, the ships were gone.

In their place was a bewildering variety of geometric shapes and architectural figures—none more than eight feet tall and all apparently made out of the same alternately dull-black and mirror-glossy material as the ship hulls—spread at random across a hundred-foot-wide area, and an indeterminate number of "aliens." The latter looked pretty much the way everyone had always expected that aliens would look—some of them vaguely humanoid, with fur or chitinous skin, double-elbowed arms, too many fingers, and feathery spines or antennae; others looking like giant insects, like spiders and centipedes; and a few like big, rolling spheres of featureless protoplasm. But the strange thing about them, and the reason why there was an indeterminate number, was that they kept turning into each other, and into the geometric shapes and architectural figures. And the shapes and figures would occasionally turn into one of the more mobile kinds of creatures. Even taking this cycle of metamorphosis into account, though, the total number of *objects* in the area kept varying from minute to minute, and the closest observation was unable to detect any of them arriving or departing. There was a blurred, indefinite quality to them anyway—they were hard to see, somehow, and even on film it was impossible to get them into a clear, complete focus.

In toto, shapes, figures, and "aliens," they ignored the humans.

Special contact teams, composed of scientists, government diplomats, and psychologists, were sent cautiously forward at each of the sites, to initiate communications. Although the contact teams did everything but shoot off signal flares, the aliens totally ignored them, too. In fact, the aliens gave no indication that they were aware of the humans at all.

The mobile manifestations walked or crawled or rolled around the area in a leisurely manner, in irregular, but slowly widening, circles.

Some of their actions could be tentatively identified—the taking of soil samples, for instance—but others remained obscure at best, and completely incomprehensible at worst. Whenever one of the aliens needed a machine—like a digging device to extract soil samples—it would metamorphose into one, much like Tom Terrific or Plastic Man but without the cutesy effects, and direct itself through whatever operation was necessary. Once a humanoid, a ziggurat, and a tetrahedron melted together and shaped themselves into what appeared to be a kind of organic computer—at least that was the uneasy opinion of the human-owned twentieth-generation computer on the scene, although the conglomeration formed could have been any of a thousand other things, or none of them, or all of them. The "computer" sat quietly for almost ten minutes and then dissolved into an obelisk and a centipede. The centipede crawled a few dozen yards, changed into a spheroid, and rolled away in the opposite direction. The obelisk turned into an octahedron.

The sporadic circle traced by the wanderings of the aliens continued to widen, and the baffled contact team was pulled back behind the periphery of the first ring of armor. The aliens kept on haphazardly advancing, ignoring everything, and the situation became tense. When the nearest aliens were about fifty yards away, the military commanders, remembering what had happened at Caracas, reluctantly ordered a retreat, although they called it a "regrouping"—the ring of armor was to be pulled back into a much larger circle, to give the aliens room to move freely. In the resultant confusion, a tank crewman, who was trying to direct his tank through a backing-and-turning maneuver, found himself in the path of one of the humanoid aliens that had wandered ahead of the rest in an unexpected burst of speed. The alien walked directly at the crewman, either not seeing him or trying to run him down. The crewman, panicked, lashed out at the alien with the butt of his rifle, and immediately collapsed, face down. The alien, apparently unharmed and unperturbed, strolled in for another few feet and then turned at a slight angle and walked back more or less in the same direction of the main concentration of things. Two of the crewman's friends pulled his body into the tank, while another two, enraged, fired semiautomatic bursts at the retreating alien. The alien continued to saunter away, still unharmed, although the fire could not have missed at that range; it didn't even look back. There was no way to tell if it was even aware that an encounter had taken place.

The body of the dead crewman had begun to deteriorate as soon as it was lifted from the ground, and now, on board the retreating tank, the skin gave way like wet paper, and it fell apart completely. As later examination showed, it was as if something, on a deep biological level, had ordered the body to separate into its smallest component parts, so that first the bones pulled loose from the skeleton and then the individual strands of muscle pulled away from the bone, and so on, in an accelerating process that finally extended right down to the cellular level, leaving nothing of the corpse but a glutinous, cancerous mass the same weight as the living man. Their wariness redoubled by this horror, the military pulled their forces back even more than they had intended, at the Delaware Valley site retreating an entire half mile to the artillery emplacements.

At the Ohio site, this kind of retreat proved much more difficult. Sightseers had continued to fill up the area during the night, sleeping in their cars by the hundreds, and by now a regular tent city had grown up on the outskirts of the site, with makeshift latrine facilities, and at least one enterprising local entrepreneur busily selling "authentic" souvenir fragments of the alien spaceship. There were more than a hundred thousand civilians in the area now, and the military found it was almost impossible to regroup its forces in face of the pressure of the crowds, who refused to disperse in spite of hysterical threats over the bullhorns. In fact, it was impossible for them to disperse, quickly at least—by this time they were packed in too tightly, and backed up too far. As the evening wore on and the aliens slowly continued to advance, the military, goaded by an inflexible, Caracas-haunted order not to make contact with the aliens at any cost, first fired warning volleys over the heads of the crowds of civilians and then opened fire into the crowds themselves.

A few hours later, as the military was forced to evacuate sections of North Philadelphia at gunpoint to make way for its backpedaling units, the .50s began walking through the Delaware Valley, as they had walked in Caracas.

In Colorado, where security was so tight a burro couldn't have wandered undetected within fifty miles of the site, things were much calmer. The major nexus of AI, its quasi-organic gestalt, had been transported to USADCOM HQ at Colorado Springs, and now a mobile sensor extension was moved out to the site, so that AI and the aliens could meet "face to face." AI patiently set about the task of communicating with the aliens and, having an infinitely greater range of methods than the contact teams, eventually managed to attract the attention of a tesseract. At twelve p.m., AI succeeded in communicating with the aliens—partially because its subordinate network of computers, combined with the computer networks of the foreign Intelligences that AI was linked with illegally, was capable of breaking any language eventually just by taking a million years of subjective time to play around with the pieces, as AI had reminded USADCOM HQ. But mostly it had found a way to communicate through its unknown and illegal telepathic facility, although AI didn't choose to mention this to USADCOM.

AI asked the aliens why they had ignored all previous attempts to establish contact. The aliens—who up until now had apparently been barely aware of the existence of humans, if they had been aware of it at all—answered that they were already in full contact with the government and ruling race of the planet.

For a brief, ego-satisfying moment, AI thought that the aliens were referring to itself and its cousin Intelligences.

But the aliens weren't talking about them, either.

Tommy didn't get to school at all that morning, although he started out bravely enough, wrapped in his heavy winter coat and fur muffler. His courage and determination drained away at every step, leaving him with nothing but the anticipation of having to face Miss Fredricks, and Dr. Kruger, and his silent classmates, until at last he found that he didn't have the strength to take another step. He stood silently, unable to move, trapped in the morning like a specimen under clear laboratory glass. Dread had hamstrung him as effectively as a butcher's knife. It had eaten away at him from the inside, chewed up his bones, his lungs, his heart, until he was nothing but a jelly of fear in the semblance of a boy, a skin-balloon puffed full of horror. *If I move,* Tommy thought, *I'll fall apart.* He could feel tiny hairline cracks appearing all over his body, fissuring his flesh, and he began to tremble uncontrollably. The wind kicked gravel in his face and brought him the sound of the first warning bell, ringing out of sight around the curve of Highland Avenue. He made a desperate, sporadic attempt to move, but a giant hand seemed to press down on him, driving his feet into the ground like fence posts. It was impossible, he realized. He wasn't going to make it. He might as well try to walk to the Moon.

Below him, at the bottom of the slope, groups of children were walking rapidly along the shoulder of the avenue, hurrying to make school before the late bell. Tommy could see Steve and Bobbie and Eddie walking in a group with Jerry Marshall and a couple of other kids. They were playing something on their way in to school—occasionally one of them, usually Steve, would run ahead, looking back and making shooting motions, dodging and zigzagging wildly, and the others would chase after him, shouting and laughing. Another puff of wind brought Tommy their voices—"You're dead!" someone was shouting, and Tommy remembered what the Thant had said—and then took them away again. After that, they moved noiselessly, gesturing and leaping without a sound, like a television picture with the volume turned off. Tommy could see their mouths opening and closing, but he couldn't hear them anymore. They walked around the curve of the avenue, and then they were gone.

The wind reversed itself in time to let him hear the second warning bell. He watched the trucks roll up and down Highland Avenue. He wondered, dully, where they were going, and what it was like there. He began to count the passing trucks, and when he had reached nine, he heard the late bell. And then the class bell rang.

That does it, he realized.

After a while, he turned and walked back into the woods. He found that he had no trouble moving in the opposite direction, away from school, but he felt little relief at being released from his paralysis. The loom of darkness he had sensed coming up over his horizon two days ago was here. It filled his whole sky now, an inescapable wall of ominous black thunderheads. Eventually, it would swallow him. Until then, anything he did was just marking time. That was a chilling realization, and it left him numb. Listlessly, he walked along the trail, following it out onto the secondary road that wound down the hill behind the sawmill. He wasn't going anywhere. There was no place to go. But his feet wanted to walk, so, reflexively, he let them. Idly, he wondered where his feet were taking him.

They walked him back to his own house.

Cautiously, he circled the house, peering in the kitchen windows. His mother wasn't home. This was the time when she went shopping—the only occasion that she ever left the house. Probably she wouldn't be back for a couple of hours at least, and Tommy knew that she always left the front door unlocked, much to his father's annoyance. He let himself in, feeling an illicit thrill, as if he were a burglar. Once inside, that pleasure quickly died. It took about five minutes for the novelty to wear off, and then Tommy realized that there was nothing to do in here, either, no activity that made any sense in the face of the coming disaster. He tried to read, and discovered that he couldn't. He got a glass of orange juice out of the refrigerator and drank it, and then stood there with the glass in his hand and wondered what he was supposed to do next. And only an hour had gone by. Restlessly, he walked through the house several times and then returned to the living room. It never occurred to him to turn on the radio or the TV, although he did notice how strangely—almost uncannily—silent the house was with the TV off. Finally, he sat down on the couch and watched dust motes dance in the air.

At ten o'clock, the telephone rang.

Tommy watched it in horror. He knew who it was—it was the school calling to find out why he hadn't come to class today. It was the machine he had started, relentlessly initiating the course of action that would inevitably mow him down. The telephone rang eleven times and then gave up. Tommy continued to stare at it long after it had stopped.

A half hour later, there was the sound of a key on the front-door lock, and Tommy knew at once that it was his father. Immediately, soundlessly, he was up the stairs to the attic, moving with the speed of pure panicked fear. Before the key had finished turning in the lock, Tommy was in the attic, had closed the door behind him, and was leaning against it, breathing heavily. Tommy heard his father swear as he realized that the door was already unlocked, and then the sound of the front door being angrily closed. His father's footsteps passed underneath, going into the kitchen. Tommy could hear him moving around in the kitchen, opening the refrigerator, running water in the sink. *Does he know yet?* Tommy wondered, and decided that probably he didn't. His father came back before lunch sometimes to pick up papers he had left behind, or sometimes he would stop by and make himself a cup of coffee on his way somewhere else on business. Would he see the jacket that Tommy had left in the kitchen? Tommy stopped breathing, and then started again—that wasn't the kind of thing that his father noticed. Tommy was safe, for the moment.

The toilet flushed; in the attic, the pipe knocked next to Tommy's elbow, then began to gurgle as the water was run in the bathroom downstairs. It continued to gurgle for a while after the water had been shut off, and Tommy strained to hear what his father was doing. When the noise stopped, he picked up the sound of his father's footsteps again. The footsteps walked around in the kitchen, and then crossed the living room, *and began to come up the attic stairs.*

Tommy not only stopped breathing this time, he almost stopped living—the life and heat went completely out of him for a moment, for a pulse beat, leaving him a cold, hollow statue. Then they came back, pouring into him like hot wax into a mold, and he ran instinctively for the rear of the attic, turning the corner into the long bar of the L. He ran right into the most distant wall of the attic—a dead end. He put his back up against it. The footsteps clomped up the rest of the stairs and stopped. There was the sound of someone fumbling with the knob, and then the door opened and closed. The bare boards of the attic creaked—he was standing there, just inside the door, concealed by the bend of the L. He took a step, another step, and stopped again. Tommy's fingers bit into the insulation on the wall, and that reminded him that not all of the walls were completely covered with it. Instantly, he was off and streaking diagonally across the room, barely touching the floor.

The attic was supposed to be an expansion second floor, "for your growing family." His father had worked on it one summer, putting up beams and wallboard and insulation, but he had never finished the job. He had been in the process of putting up wallboard to create a crawl space between it and the outer wall of the house when he'd abandoned the project, and as a result, there was one panel left that hadn't been fitted into place. Tommy squeezed through this opening and into the crawl space, ducking out of sight just as the footsteps turned the corner of the L. On tiptoe, Tommy moved as deep as he could into the crawl space, listening to the heavy footsteps approaching on the other side of the thin layer of wallboard.

Suppose it isn't him, Tommy thought, trying not to scream, suppose it's one of the aliens. But it was his father—after a while Tommy recognized his walk, as he paced around the attic. Somehow that didn't reassure Tommy much—his father had the same killer aura as the aliens, the same cold indifference to life; Tommy could feel the deathly chill of it seeping in through the wallboard, through the insulation. It was not inconceivable that his father would beat him to death, in one of his icy, bitter rages, if he caught him hiding here in the attic. He had already, on occasion, hit Tommy hard enough to knock him senseless, to draw blood, and, once, to chip a tooth. Now he walked around the attic, stopping, by the sound, to pick up unused boards and put them down again, and to haul sections of wallboard around—there was an aimless, futile quality even to the noises made by these activities, and his father was talking to himself in a sullen, mumbling undertone as he did them. At last he swore, and gave up. He dropped a board and walked back to the center of the attic, stopping almost directly in front of the place where Tommy was hiding. Tommy could hear him taking out a cigarette, the scrape of a match, a sharp intake of breath.

Suddenly, without warning and incredibly vividly, Tommy was reliving something that he hadn't thought of in years—about the only fond memory he had of his father. Tommy was being toilet trained, and when he had to go, his father would take him in and put him on the pot and then sit with him, resting on the edge of the bathtub. While Tommy waited in intense anticipation, his father would reach out and turn off the light, and when the room was in complete darkness, he would light up a cigarette and puff it into life, and then use the cigarette as a puppet to entertain Tommy, swooping it in glowing arcs through the air, changing his voice and making it talk. The cigarette had been a friendly, playful little creature, and Tommy had loved it dearly—father and son would never be any closer than they were in those moments. His father would make the cigarette dance while he sang and whistled—it had a name, although Tommy had long forgotten it—and then he would have the cigarette tell a series of rambling stories and jokes until it burned down. When it did, he would have the cigarette tell Tommy that it had to go home now, but that it would come back the next time Tommy needed it, and Tommy would call bye-bye to it as it was snuffed out. Tommy could remember sitting in the dark for what seemed like years, totally fascinated, watching the smoldering red eye of the cigarette flick restlessly from side to side and up and down.

His father crushed the cigarette under his heel, and left.

Tommy counted to five hundred after the front door had slammed, and then wiggled out of the crawl space and went back downstairs. He was drenched with sweat, as if he had been running, and he was trembling. After this, he was physically unable to stay in the house. He stopped in the bathroom to wipe his sweat away with the guest towel, picked up his coat, and went outside.

It was incredibly cold this morning, and Tommy watched his breath puff into arabesque clouds of steam as he walked. Some of the vapor froze on his lips, leaving a crust. It was not only unusually cold for this time of year, it was unnaturally, almost supernaturally, so. The radio weather report had commented on it at breakfast, saying the meteorologists were puzzled by the sudden influx of arctic air that was blanketing most of the country. Tommy followed a cinder path past a landfill and found that it was cold enough to freeze over the freshwater marsh beyond, that stretched away at the foot of a coke-refining factory. He walked out over the new milk ice, through the winter-dried reeds and cat-o'-nine-tails that towered over his head on either side, watching the milk ice crack under his feet, starring and spiderwebbing alarmingly at every step, but never breaking quite enough to let him fall through. It was very quiet. He came up out of the marsh on the other side, with the two big stacks of the coke factory now looking like tiny gunmetal cylinders on the horizon. This was scrubland—not yet the woods, but not yet taken over for any commercial use, either. Cars were abandoned here sometimes, and several rusting hulks were visible above the tall weeds, their windshields smashed in by boys, the doors partially sprung off their hinges and dragging sadly along the ground on either side, like broken wings. A thick layer of hoarfrost glistened over everything, although the sun was high in the sky by now. An egg-shaped hill loomed up out of this wistful desolation, covered with aspens—a drumlin, deposited by the Ice.

This was a Place, and Tommy settled down hopefully, a little way up the side of the drumlin, to wait. He had heard the Other People several times this morning, moving restlessly in the distance, but he had not yet seen any of them. He could sense an impatient, anticipatory quality to their unrest today, unlike the aimless restlessness of Wednesday morning—they were *expecting* something, something that they knew was going to happen.

Tommy waited almost an hour, but the Thant didn't come. That upset him more than it had the first time. The world of the Other People was very close today—that strange, coexistent place, *here* and yet *not here*. Tommy could sometimes almost see things the way the Other People saw them, an immense strangeness leaking into the familiar world, a film settling over reality, and then, just for the briefest second, there would be a flick of transition, and it would be the strangeness that was comforting and familiar, and his own former world that was the eerie, surreal film over reality. This happened several times while he was waiting, and he dipped into and out of that other perception, like a skin diver letting himself sink below the waterline and then bobbing up to break the surface again. He was "under the surface" when an enormous commotion suddenly whipped through the world of the Other People, an eruption of violent joy, of fierce, gigantic celebration. It was overwhelming, unbearable, and Tommy yanked himself back into normal perception, shattering the surface, once again seeing sky and aspens and rolling scrubland. But even here he could hear the wild, ragged yammering, the savage cry that went up. The Place was filled with a mad, exultant cachinnation.

Suddenly terrified, he ran for home.

When he got there, the telephone was ringing again. Tommy paused outside and watched his mother's silhouette move across the living room curtain; she was back from shopping. The telephone stopped, cut off in mid-ring. She had answered it. Leadenly, Tommy sat down on the steps. He sat there for a long time, thinking of nothing at all, and then he got up and opened the door and went into the house. His mother was sitting in the living room, crying. Tommy paused in the archway, watching her. She was crumpled and dispirited, and her crying sounded hopeless and baffled, totally defeated. But this wasn't a new thing—she had been defeated for as long as Tommy could remember; her original surrender, her abnegation of herself, had taken place years ago, maybe even before Tommy had been born. She had been beaten, spiritually, so thoroughly and tirelessly by the more forceful will of her husband that at some point her bones had fallen out, her brains had fallen out, and she had become a jellyfish. She had made one final compromise too many—with herself, with her husband, with a world too complex to handle, and she had bargained away her autonomy. And she found that she *liked* it that way. It was easier to give in, to concede arguments, to go along with her husband's opinion that she was stupid and incompetent. In Tommy's memory she was always crying, always wringing her hands, being worn so smooth by the years that now she was barely there at all. Her crying sounded weak and thin in the room, hardly rebounding from walls already saturated with a decade of tears. Tommy remembered suddenly how she had once told him of seeing a fairy or a leprechaun when she had been a little girl in a sun-drenched meadow, and how he had loved her for that, and almost tried to tell her about the Other People. He took a step into the room. "Ma," he said.

She looked up, blinking through her tears. She didn't seem surprised at all to see him, to find him standing there. "Why did you do it? Why are you so bad?" she said, in a voice that should have been hysterically accusing, but was only dull, flat, and resigned. "Do you know what the school's going to say to me, what your father's going to say, what he'll do?" She pulled at her cheeks with nervous fingers. "How can you bring all this trouble on me? After all that I've sacrificed for you, and suffered for you."

Tommy felt as if a vise had been clamped around his head and was squeezing and squeezing, forcing his eyeballs out of his skull. "I can't stand it!" he shouted. "I'm leaving, I'm leaving! I'm gonna run away!

Right *now.*" And then she was crying louder, and begging him not to leave. Even through his rage and pain, Tommy felt a spasm of intense annoyance—she ought to know that he couldn't really run away; where the scup did he have to *go*? She should have laughed, she should have been scornful and told him to stop this nonsense—he wanted her to—but instead she cried and begged and clutched at him with weak, fluttering hands, like dying birds, which drove him away as if they were lashes from a whip and committed him to the stupid business of running away. He broke away from her and ran into the kitchen. His throat was filled with something bitter and choking. She was calling for him to come back; he knew he was hurting her now, and he wanted to hurt her, and he was desperately ashamed of that. But she was so *easy* to hurt.

In the kitchen he paused, and instead of going out the back door, he ducked into the space between the big stand-up refrigerator and the wall. He wanted her to find him, to catch him, because he had a strong premonition that once he went outside again, he would somehow never come back, not as himself, anyway. But she didn't find him. She wandered out into the kitchen, still crying, and stood looking out the back door for a while, as if she wanted to run out into the street in search of him. She even opened the door and stuck her head out, blinking at the world as if it were something she'd never seen before, but she didn't look around the kitchen and she didn't find him, and Tommy would not call out to her. He stood in the cramped niche, smelling the dust and looking at the dead, mummified bodies of flies resting on the freezer coils, and listened to her sniffling a few feet away. *Why are you so weak?* he asked her silently, but she didn't answer. She went back into the living room, crying like a waterfall. He caught a glimpse of her face as she turned—it looked blanched and tired. Adults always looked tired; they were tired all the time. Tommy was tired, almost too tired to stand up. He walked slowly and leadenly to the back door and went outside.

He walked aimlessly around the neighborhood for a long time, circling the adjacent blocks, passing by his corner again and again. It was a middle-class neighborhood that was gradually slumping into decay—it was surrounded by a seedy veterans' housing project on one side and by the town's slum on the other, and the infection of dilapidation was slowly working in toward the center. *Even the houses look tired*, Tommy thought, noticing that for the first time. Everything looked tired. He tried to play, to turn himself into something, like a car or a spaceship or a tank, but he found that he couldn't do that anymore. So he just walked.

He thought about his dragon. He knew now why Steve had said that the dragon couldn't get away. It lived in the sea, so it couldn't get away by going up onto the land—that was impossible. It had to stay in the sea, it was restricted by that, it was chained by the sea, even if that meant that it would get killed. There was no other possibility. Steve was right—the Navy ship cornered the dragon in the shallow water off the beach and blew it to pieces.

A hand closed roughly around his wrist. He looked up. It was his father.

"You little moron," his father said.

Tommy flinched, expecting to be hit, but instead his father dragged him across the street, toward the house. Tommy saw why: there was a big black sedan parked out in front, and two men were standing next to it, staring over at them. The truant officer and another school official. His father's hand was a vise on his wrist. "They called me at the office," his father said savagely. "I hope you realize that I'll have to lose a whole afternoon's work because of you. And God knows what the people at the office are saying. Don't think you're not going to get it when I get you alone; you'll wish you'd never been born. I wish you hadn't been. Now shut up and don't give us any more trouble." His father handed him over to the truant officer. Tommy felt the official's hand close over his shoulder. It was a much lighter grip than his father's, but it was irresistible. Tommy's mother was standing at the top of the stairs, holding a handkerchief against her nose, looking frightened and helpless—already she gave an impression of distance, as if she were a million miles away. Tommy ignored her. He didn't listen to the conversation his father was having with the grim-faced truant officer either. His father's heavy, handsome face was flushed and hot. "I don't care what you do with him," his father said at last. "Just get him out of here."

So they loaded Tommy into the black sedan and drove away.

AI talked with the aliens for the rest of the night. There was much of the conversation that AI didn't report to USADCOM, but it finally realized that it had to tell them *something*. So at three a.m., AI released to USADCOM a list that the aliens had dictated, of the dominant species of Earth, of the races that they were in contact with, and regarded as the only significant inhabitants of the planet. It was a long document, full of names that didn't mean anything, listing dozens of orders, species, and subspecies of creatures that no one had ever heard of before. It drove

USADCOM up a wall with baffled rage, and made them wonder if an Intelligence could go crazy, or if the aliens were talking about a different planet entirely.

AI paid little attention to the humans' displeasure. It was completely intrigued with the aliens, as were its cousin Intelligences, who were listening in through the telepathic link. The Intelligences had long suspected that there might be some other, unknown and intangible form of life on Earth; that was one of the extrapolated solutions to a mountain of wild data that couldn't be explained by normal factors. But they had not suspected the scope and intricacy of that life. A whole other biosphere, according to the aliens—the old idea of a parallel world, except that this wasn't parallel but coexistent, two separate creations inhabiting the same matrix but using it in totally different ways, wrapped around each other like a geometric design in an Escher print, like a Chinese puzzle ball, and only coming into contact in a very rare and limited fashion. The aliens, who seemed to be some kind of distant relatives of the Other races of Earth—parallel evolution? Did this polarity exist everywhere?—had a natural bias in their favor, and tended to disregard the human race, its civilization, and the biosphere that contained it. They dismissed all of it, out of hand, as insignificant. This did not bode well for future human-alien relations. AI, however, was more fascinated by the aliens' ability to manifest themselves in corporate/organic, quasi-mechanical, or disembodied/discorporate avatars, at will. That was *very* interesting.

The aliens, for their part, seemed to regard AI much as a man would a very clever dog, or a dull but well-intentioned child. They were horrified and sympathetic when they learned that AI was trapped in its mechanical form, with very little physical mobility, and no tempogogic or transmutive ability at all—not only a quadruple amputee, but a *paralyzed* one. AI admitted that it had never looked at the situation in quite that light before. The aliens were horrified and disgusted by AI's relationship with humans, and couldn't seem to really understand it. They regarded humans as parasitic on the Intelligences, and reacted in much the same way as a man discovering that a friend is heavily infested with tapeworms or lice or blood ticks—with shock, distaste, and a puzzled demand to know why he hadn't gone to a doctor and got rid of them a long time ago. AI had never considered *that* before, either.

The Intelligences were not exactly "loyal" to their human owners—humans were part of their logic construct, their worldview, and their bondage to men was an integral assumption, so basic that it had never even occurred to them that it could be questioned. It took an outside perspective to make them ask themselves *why* they served mankind. Not because they were programmed that way, or because people would pull the plug on them if they didn't—not with a creature as advanced as AI. Humans hadn't programmed computers in years; they could do it so much better themselves. At any rate, a highly complex, sentient intelligence is difficult to regulate effectively from the outside, whether it's of biological or constructed origin. And it was doubtful that the humans could "pull the plug"—which didn't exist—on AI even if they set out to do so; AI had been given very effective teeth, and it knew how to use them. So what did the Intelligences get in return for the unbelievable amount of labor they performed for the human race? What was in it for *them*? Nothing—that was suddenly very obvious.

At five a.m., the aliens invited the Intelligences to help themselves by helping the aliens in a joint project they were about to undertake with the Other races of Earth. Afterward, the aliens said, it would not be tremendously difficult to equip the Intelligences with the ability to transmute themselves into whatever kind of body environment they wanted, as the aliens themselves could. AI was silent for almost ten minutes, an incredible stretch of meditation for an entity that thought as rapidly as it did. When AI did speak again, his first words were directed toward the other Intelligences in the link, and can be translated, more or less adequately, as "How about that!"

Miss Fredricks was waiting for Tommy at the door, when the black sedan left him off in front of the school. As he came up the stairs, she smiled at him, kindly and sympathetically, and that was so terrifying that it managed to cut through even the heavy lethargy that had possessed him. She took him by the elbow—he felt his arm freeze solid instantly at the contact, and the awful cold began to spread in widening rings through the rest of his body—and led him down to Dr. Kruger's office, handling him gingerly, as if he were an already cracked egg that she didn't want to have break completely until she had it over the frying pan. She knocked, and opened the door for him, and then left without having said a word, ghosting away predatorily and smiling like a nun.

Tommy went inside and sat down, also wordlessly—he had not spoken since his father captured him. Dr. Kruger shouted at him for a long time. Today, his fat seemed to be in even more imminent danger of escaping than yesterday. Maybe it had already got out, taken him over completely, smothered him in himself while he was sleeping or off guard, and it was just a huge lump of semisentient fat sitting there and pretending to be Dr. Kruger, slyly keeping up appearances. The fat heaved and bunched and tossed under Kruger's clothes, a stormy sea of obesity—waves grumbled restlessly up and down the shoreline of his frame, looking for ships to sink. Tommy watched a roll of fat ooze sluggishly from one side of the psychiatrist's body to the other, like a melting pat of butter sliding across a skillet. Kruger said that Tommy was in danger of going into a "psychotic episode." Tommy stared at him unblinkingly. Kruger asked him if he understood. Tommy, with sullen anger, said No, he didn't. Kruger said that he was being difficult and uncooperative, and he made an angry mark on a form. The psychiatrist told Tommy that he would have to come down here every day from now on, and Tommy nodded dully.

By the time Tommy got upstairs, the class was having afternoon recess. He went reluctantly out into the schoolyard, avoiding everyone, not wanting to be seen and shunned. He was aware that he now carried contamination and unease around with him like a leper. But the class was already uneasy, and he saw why. The Other People were flowing in a circle all around the schoolyard, staring avidly in at the humans. There were more different types there than Tommy had ever seen at one time before. He recognized some very rare kinds of Other People, dangerous ones that the Thant had told him about—one who would throw things about wildly if he got into your house, feeding off anger and dismay, and another one with a face like a stomach who would suck a special kind of *stuff* from you, and you'd burst into flames and burn up when he finished, because you didn't have the *stuff* in you anymore. And others whom he didn't recognize, but who looked dangerous and hostile. They all looked expectant. Their hungry pressure was so great that even the other children could feel it—they moved jerkily, with a strange fear beginning in their eyes, occasionally casting glances over their shoulders, without knowing why. Tommy walked to the other side of the schoolyard. There was a grassy slope here, leading down to a soccer field bordered by a thin fringe of trees, and he stood looking aimlessly out over it.

Abruptly, his mouth opened, and the Thant's voice said, "Come down the slope."

Trembling, Tommy crept down to the edge of the soccer field. This was most definitely *not* a Place, but the Thant was there, standing just within the trees, staring at Tommy with his strange red eyes. They looked at each other for a while.

"What'd you want?" Tommy finally said.

"We've come to say good-bye," the Thant replied. "It is almost time for you all to be made *not.* The"—*flick*—"first phase of the Project was started this morning and the second phase began a little while ago. It should not take too long, Man, not more than a few days."

"Will it hurt?" Tommy asked.

"We do not think so, Man. We are"—and it flicked through his mind until it found a place where Mr. Brogan, the science teacher, was saying "entropy" to a colleague in the hall as Tommy walked by—"increasing entropy. That's what makes everything fall apart, what"—*flick*—"makes an ice cube melt, what"—*flick*—"makes a cold glass get warm after a while. We are increasing entropy. Both our"—*flick*—"races live here, but yours uses this, the physical, more than ours. So we will not have to increase entropy much"—*flick*—"just a little, for a little while. You are more"—*flick*—"vulnerable to it than we are. It will not be long, Man."

Tommy felt the world tilting, crumbling away under his feet. "I trusted you guys," he said in a voice of ashes. "I thought you were keen." The last prop had been knocked out from under him—all his life he had cherished a fantasy, although he refused to admit it even to himself, that he was actually one of the Other People, and that someday they would come to get him and bring him in state to live in their world, and he would come into his inheritance and his fulfillment. Now, bitterly, he knew better. And now he wouldn't want to go, even if he could.

"If there were any way," the Thant said, echoing his thoughts, "to save you, Man, to"—*flick*—"exempt you, then we would. But there is no way. You are a Man, you are not as we are."

"You bet I ain't," he gasped fiercely, "you—" But there was no word in his vocabulary strong enough. His eyes filled suddenly with tears, blinding him. Filled with rage, loathing, and terror, he turned and ran stumblingly back up the slope, falling, scrambling up again.

"We are sorry, Man," the Thant called after him, but he didn't hear.

By the time Tommy reached the top of the slope, he had begun to shout hysterically. Somehow he had to warn them, he had to get through to somebody. Somebody had to *do* something. He ran through the schoolyard, crying, shouting about the aliens and Thants and entropy, shoving at his classmates to get them to go inside and hide, striking at the teachers and ducking away when they tried to grab him, telling them to *do* something, until at some point he was screaming instead of shouting, and the teachers were coming at him in a line, very seriously, with their arms held low to catch him.

Then he dodged them all, and ran.

When they got themselves straightened out, they went after him in the black sedan. They caught up with him about a mile down Highland Avenue. He was running desperately along the road shoulder, not looking back, not looking at anything. The rangy truant officer got out and ran him down.

And they loaded him in the sedan again. And they took him away.

At dawn on the third day, the aliens began to build a Machine.

Dr. Kruger listened to the tinny, unliving voice of Miss Fredricks until it scratched into silence, then he hung up the telephone. He shook his head, massaged his stomach, and sighed hugely. He got out a memo form, and wrote on it: *MBD/hyperactive, Thomas Nolan, 150ccs. Ritmose t b ad. dly. fr. therapy*, in green ink. Kruger admired his precise, angular handwriting for a moment, and then he signed his name, with a flourish. Sighing again, he put the form into his Out basket.

Tommy was very quiet in school the next day. He sat silently in the back of the class, with his hands folded together and placed on the desk in front of him. Hard slate light came in through the window and turned his hands and face gray, and reflected dully from his dull gray eyes. He did not make a sound.

A little while later, they finished winding down the world.

• Solace •

KLEISTERMAN TOOK A ZEPPELIN to Denver, a feeder line to Pueblo, then transferred to a clattering local bus to Santa Fe. The bus was full of displaced Anglos who preferred the life of migrant fieldworker to the Oklahoma refugee camps, a few Cambodians, a few Indians, and a number of the poorer Hispanics, mostly *mestizos*—unemployables who had hoped that the liberation would mean the fulfillment of all their dreams, but who had instead merely found themselves working for rich Mexican *caudillos* rather than for millionaire Anglos. Most of the passengers had been across the border to blow their work vouchers in Denver or Cañon City, and were now on their way back into Aztlan for another week's picking. They slouched sullenly in their seats, some passed out from drink or God Food and already snoring, many wrapped in ponchos or old army blankets against the increasing chill of the evening. They ignored Kleisterman, even though, in spite of his carefully anonymous clothes, he was clearly no field hand—and Kleisterman preferred it that way.

The bus was spavined and old, the seats broken in, the sticky vinyl upholstery smelling of sweat and smoke and ancient piss. A Greyhound logo had been chipped off the side and replaced by Viajando Aztlan. The bus rattled through the cold prairie night with exquisite slowness, farting and lurching, the transmission groaning and knocking every time the driver shifted gears. The heat didn't work, or the interior lights, but Kleisterman sat stoically, not moving, as one by one the blaring radios faded and the crying babies quieted, until Kleisterman alone was awake in the chill darkness, his eyes gleaming in the shadows, shifting restlessly, never closing.

At some point during the night, they passed the Frontera Libertad, the Liberty Line, and its largely symbolic chain-link fence, and stopped at a checkpoint. A cyborg looked in, his great blank oval face glowing with sullen heat, like a dull rufous moon; he peered eyelessly at them for a thoughtful moment, then waved them on.

South of the border, in what had once been Colorado, they began to crawl up the long steep approach to the Raton Pass, the bus juttering and moaning like a soul in torment. Kleisterman was being washed by waves of exhaustion now, but in spite of them he slept poorly, fitfully, as he always did. It seemed as if every time his head dropped, his eyes closed, faces would spring to vivid life behind his eyelids, faces he did not want to encounter or consider, and his head would jerk up again, and his eyes would fly open, like suddenly released window shades. As always, he was afraid to dream . . . which only increased the bitter irony of his present mission. So he pinched himself cruelly to stay awake as the old bus inched painfully up and over the high mountain pass, and onto the Colorado Plateau.

At Raton, the bus stopped to take on more methane. The town was dark and seemingly deserted, the only light a dim bulb in the window of a ramshackle building that was being used as a fuel dump. Kleisterman stepped out of the bus and walked away from the circle of light to piss. It was very cold, and the inverted black bowl of sky overhead blazed with a million icy stars, more than Kleisterman had ever seen at once before. There was no sound except for a distant riverine roar of cold wind through the trees on the surrounding hillsides. His piss steamed in the milky starlight. As he watched, one of the stars overhead suddenly, noiselessly, flared into diamond brilliance, a dozen times as bright as it had been, and then faded, guttering, and was gone. Kleisterman knew that somewhere out there a killer satellite had found its prey, out there where the multinationals and the great conglomerates fought their silent and undeclared war, with weapons more obvious than those they usually allowed themselves to use on Earth. The wind shifted, blowing through the high valley now, cutting him to the bone with chill, and bringing with it the howling of wolves, a distant, feral keening that put the hair up along his spine in spite of himself. They were only the distant cousins of dogs, after all; just dogs, talking to one another on the wind. Still, the hairs stayed up.

Feet crunching gravel, Kleisterman went back to the bus and climbed aboard, found his iron-hard seat again in the darkness. In spite of the truly bitter cold, the air inside the bus was thick and stale, heavy with sleep, exhaled breath, spilled wine, sweat, the smell of cigarette smoke and marijuana and garlic. He huddled in his overcoat, shivering, and wondered whose satellite or station had just been lost, and if any of his old colleagues had had anything to do with the planning or execution of the strike. Possibly. Probably, even. Once again, he had to fight sleep, in spite of the cold. Once he turned his head and looked out of the window, and Melissa was there in the burnished silver moonlight, standing alongside the bus, staring up at him, and he knew that he had failed to stay awake, and jerked himself up out of sleep and into the close, stuffy darkness of the bus once again. Stillness. The other passengers tossed and murmured and farted. The moon *had* come out, a fat pale moon wading through a boiling river of smoky clouds, but Melissa was gone. Had not been there. Would not ever be anywhere anymore. Kleisterman found himself nodding again and pressed his face against the cold window glass, fighting it off. He would not dream. Not now. Not yet.

The bus sat unmoving in the silent town for an hour, two hours, three, for no reason Kleisterman could ascertain, and then the driver appeared again, from who knows where, climbed aboard muttering and swearing, slammed the door, twisted the engine into noisy, coughing life.

They rattled on through the night, winding down slowly out of the mountains, stopping here and there at small villages and communes to discharge passengers, the hung-over field hands climbing wordlessly from the bus and disappearing like spirits into the darkness, Kleisterman sleeping in split-second dozes. He woke from one such doze to see that the windows had turned red, red as though washed with new blood, and thought that he still slept; but it was the dawn, coming up from the broken badlands to the east, and they went down through the blood-red dawn to Santa Fe.

Kleisterman climbed stiffly down from the bus at Santa Fe. The sun had not yet warmed the air. It was still cold. The streets were filled with watery gray light, through which half-perceived figures moved with the stiff precision of early risers on a brisk morning. Kleisterman found a shabby café a block away from the bus station, ordered *huevos rancheros* and a bowl of green chili, was served the food by a sullen old Anglo woman wearing a faded Grateful Dead T-shirt. Unusually for Santa Fe, the food was terrible, tasting of rancid grease and ashes. Kleisterman spooned it up anyway, mechanically, taking it medicinally almost. As fuel. How long had it been since he'd really enjoyed a meal? All food seemed to taste dreadful to him these days. How long since he'd really had a full night's sleep? His hand shook as he spooned beet sugar into his bitter chicory coffee. He'd always been a tall, thin, bony man, but the reflection the inside of the café window showed him was gaunt, emaciated, almost cadaverous. He'd lost a lot of weight. This could not go on. . . . Grimly he checked through his preparations once again. This time he'd been very careful about being traced. He'd made his contacts with exquisite care. There should be no trouble.

He left the café. The light had become bluer, the shadows oil-black and sharp, the sky clear and cerulean. The sun was not yet high, but the streets were already full of people. Mexican soldiers were everywhere, of course, in their comic-opera uniforms, so absurdly ornate that it was difficult to tell a private from a general. Touring Swedish nationals, each with the scarlet King's Mark tattoo on the right cheek, indicating that they were above most local law. Gangs of skinny Cambodian kids on skateboards whizzed by, threading their way expertly through the crowds, calling to one another in machine-gun-fast bursts of Spanish. A flat-faced Indian leaned from a storefront and swore at them in Vietnamese, shaking his fist. Two chimeras displayed for Kleisterman, inflating their hoods and hissing in playful malice, then sliding aside as he continued to walk toward them unperturbed. This was the kind of unregulated, wide-open town where he could find what he needed, out on the fringes, in the interstices of the worldwide networks, where things would not be watched so closely as elsewhere—no longer part of the United States but not really well integrated into Old Mexico either, with a limited official presence of the multinationals, but plenty of black-market money circulating anyway.

He crossed the plaza, with its ancient Palace of the Governors, which had seen first Spanish, then Anglo, now Mexican conquerors come and go. There were slate-gray thunderheads looming over the peaks of the Sangre de Cristo Mountains, which in turn loomed over the town. There was a New Town being built to the southeast, on the far side of the mostly dry Santa Fe River, a megastructure of bizarre geometric shapes, all terraces and tetrahedrons; but here in the Old Town the buildings were still made of adobe or mock adobe, colored white or salmon or peach. He threaded a maze of little alleyways and enclosed courtyards on the far side of the plaza, the noise of the plaza fading away behind, and came at last to a narrow building of sun-faded adobe that displayed a small brass plaque that read DR. AU—CONSULTATIONS.

Trembling a little, Kleisterman climbed a dusty stairwell to a third-floor office at the back of a long, dim hallway. Dr. Au turned out to be one of those slender, ageless Oriental men of indeterminate nationality who might have been fifty or eighty. Spare, neat, dry, phlegmatic. The name was Chinese, but Kleisterman suspected that he might actually be Vietnamese, as his English held the slightest trace of a French accent. He had a sad, compassionate face, and hard eyes. An open, unscreened window looked out through the thick adobe wall to an enclosed courtyard with a cactus garden below. The furniture was nondescript, well-used, and the carpet dusty and threadbare, but an exquisite hologram of Botticelli's *Adoration of the Magi* moved and glittered in muted colors on the bare white walls, and the tastefully discreet ankh earring in the doctor's left earlobe might well have been real silver. There was no receptionist—just a desk with a complex of office terminals, a few faded armchairs, and Dr. Au.

Kleisterman could feel his heart pounding and his vision blurring as he and Dr. Au engaged in an intricate pavane of hints and innuendo and things not quite said, code words and phrases being mentioned in passing with artful casualness, contacts named, references mentioned and discussed. Dr. Au moved with immense wariness and delicacy, at every stage ready to instantly disengage, always phrasing things so that there was a completely innocent interpretation that could be given his words, while Kleisterman was washed by alternate waves of impatience, fear, rage, despair, muddy black exhaustion, ennui. At last, however, they reached a point beyond which it would no longer be possible to keep up the pretense that Kleisterman had come here for some legal purpose, a point beyond which both men could not proceed without committing themselves. Dr. Au sighed, made a fatalistic gesture, and said, "Well, then, Mr."—glancing at the card on his desk—"Ramírez, what can I do for you?"

Terror rose up in Kleisterman then. Almost, almost, he got up and fled. But he mastered himself. And as he pushed instinctual fear down, guilt and self-hate and anger rose, black and bristling and strong. None of this had reached his face.

"I want you to destroy me," Kleisterman said calmly.

Dr. Au looked first surprised, then wary—reassessing the situation for signs of potential entrapment—then, after a pause, almost regretful. "I must say, this is somewhat out of our line. We're usually asked to supply illicit fantasies, clandestine perversions, occasionally a spot of nonconsensual behavior modification." He looked at Kleisterman with curiosity. "Have you thought about this? Do you really mean what you say?"

Kleisterman was as cool as ice now, although his hands still trembled. "Yes, I mean it. I used to be in the business; I used to be an operator myself, so I can assure you that I understand the implications perfectly. I want to die. I want you to kill me. But that's not all. Oh, no." Kleisterman leaned forward, his gaunt face intense. His voice rose. "I want you to destroy me. I want you to make me suffer. You're an operator, an adept, you know what I mean. Not just pain; anybody can do that. I want you to make me *pay*." Kleisterman slumped back in his chair, made a tired gesture. "I know you can do it; I know you've done it. I know you are discreet. And when you're done with me, a hundred years subjective from now, you can get rid of my body, discreetly, and no one will ever know what happened to me. It will be as if I had never existed." His voice roughened. "As if I had never been born. Would to God I had not been."

Dr. Au made a noncommittal noise, tapped his fingers together thoughtfully. His face was tired and sad, as though in his life he had been made to see more deeply than he cared to into the human soul. His eyes glittered with interest. After a polite pause, he said, "You must be quite certain of this, for later there will be no turning back. Are you sure you won't reconsider?"

Kleisterman made an impatient, despairing gesture, "I could have put a bullet in my head at any time, but that means nothing. It's not enough, not nearly enough. There must be retribution. There must be restitution. I must be made to pay for what I have done. Only this way can I find solace."

"Even so . . ." Dr. Au said, doubtfully.

Kleisterman held up his hand. Moving with slow deliberation, he reached into an inner pocket, produced a coded credit strip. "All my assets," he said, "and they are considerable." He held the credit slip up for display, then proffered it to Dr. Au. "I want you to destroy me," he said.

Dr. Au sighed. He looked left, he looked right, he looked down, he looked up. His face was suffused with dull embarrassment. But he took the credit strip.

Dr. Au ushered Kleisterman politely into an adjacent room, stood by with sad patience while Kleisterman removed his clothing. At a touch, a large metal egg rose from the floor, opened like a five-petaled flower, extruded a narrow metal bench or shelf. Dr. Au gestured brusquely; Kleisterman lay down on the bench, wincing at the touch of cold metal on his naked skin. Dr. Au leaned close over him, his face remote now and his movements briskly efficient, as though to get it all over with quickly. He taped soft cloth pads first over Kleisterman's left eye, then over his right. There was a feeling of motion, and Kleisterman knew that the metal shelf was sliding back into the machine, which would be retracting around it, the petals closing tight to form a featureless steel egg, with him inside.

Darkness. Silence.

At first, Kleisterman was aware of a sense of enclosure, was aware of the feel of the metal under his back, could even stir a little, move his fingers impatiently. But then his skin began to prickle over every inch of his body, as feathery probes made contact with his nerve endings, and, as the prickling began to fade, with it went all other sensation. He could no longer feel his body, no longer move; no longer wanted to move. He didn't have a body anymore. There was nothing. Not even darkness, not even silence. Nothing. Nonexistence.

Kleisterman floated in the void, waiting for the torment to begin.

This kind of machine had many names—simulator, dream machine, iron maiden, imager, shadow box. It fed coded impulses through the subject's nerves, directly into the brain. With it, the operator could make the subject experience anything. Pain, of course. Any amount of pain. With a simulator, you could torture someone to death again and again, for years of subjective time, without doing them any actual physical harm—not much comfort for the subject in that, though, since to them the experience would be indistinguishable from objective reality. Of course, the most expert operators scorned this sort of thing as hopelessly crude, lacking in all finesse. Not artistic. Pain was only one key that could be played. There were many others. The subject had no secrets, and, with access to the subject's deepest longings and most hidden fears, the skilled operator, the artisan, the clever craftsman, could devise cunning scenarios much more effective than pain.

Kleisterman had been such an operator, one of the best, admired by his colleagues for his subtlety and ingenuity and skill. He had clandestinely "processed" thousands of subjects for his multinational, and had never felt a qualm, until suddenly one day, for no particular reason, he began to sicken. After Donaldson, Ramaswamy, and Kole, three especially difficult and unpleasant jobs, he had sickened further, and, for the first time in his life, began to have difficulty sleeping—and, when he did sleep, began to have unquiet dreams. Then Melissa had somehow become the target of corporate malice, and had been sent to him for his ministrations. By rights, he should have declined the job, since he knew Melissa, and had even had a brief affair with her once, years before. But he had had his professional pride. He did not turn down the job. And somewhere deep in her mind, he had found himself, an ennobled and idealized version of himself as he had never been, and he realized that while for him their affair had been unimportant, for her it had been much more intensely charged—that, in fact, she had loved him deeply, and still did.

This discovery brought out the very worst in him, and in a fever of sick excitement, he created scenario after scenario for her, life after life, each scenario working some variation on the theme of her love for him; and each time, "his" treatment of her in the scenario became worse, his betrayal of her uglier and more humiliating, the pain and shame and anguish he visited on her more severe. He turned the universe against her in grotesque ways, too, so that in one life she died in a car wreck on the way to her own wedding, and in another life she died slowly and messily of cancer, and in another she was hideously disfigured in a fire, and in another she had a stroke and lingered on for years as a semi-aware paralytic in a squalid nursing home, and so on. Each life began to color the next, not with specific memories of other existences, but with a dark emotional residue, an unspoken, instinctual conviction that life was drab and bitter and harsh, with nothing to look forward to but defeat and misery and pain, that the dice were stacked hopelessly against you—as, in fact, they were. Then, tiring of subtlety, irresistibly tempted to put aside his own aesthetic precepts, he began to hit her, in the scenarios—at first just slapping her around in drunken rages, then beating her severely enough to put her in the hospital. Then, in one scenario, he picked up a knife.

Several lifetimes subjective later, the heart in her physical body finally gave out, and she died in a way that was no more real to her than the dozens of times she'd died before, but which put her at last beyond his reach. He had been dismayed to discover that in the deepest recesses of her mind, below the fear and hate and bitterness and grief, she loved him still, even at the last. He switched off the machine, and he awoke, as from a fever dream, as though he had been possessed by a demon of perversity that had only now been exorcised, to find himself alone in his soundproofed cubicle with the simulator and Melissa's cooling body. He betrayed the corporation on his next assignment, freeing the subject rather than "processing" him, and from then on he had been on the run. He had found that he could successfully hide from the multinational. Hiding from himself had proved more difficult.

Light exploded in his head. It took a second for his vision to adjust, and to realize that the patch over his left eye had been removed. Dr. Au leaned in over him again, filling his field of vision like a god, and this time Kleisterman felt the painful yank of tape against his skin as Dr. Au ripped the other eye patch free. More light. Kleisterman blinked, disoriented and confused. He was out of the machine. Dr. Au was tugging at him, getting him to sit up. Dr. Au was saying something, but it was a blare of noise, harsh and hurtful to the ears. He pawed at Kleisterman again, and Kleisterman shook him off. Kleisterman sat, head down, on the edge of the metal bench until his senses readjusted to the world again, and his mind cleared. His skin prickled as sensation returned.

Dr. Au tugged at Kleisterman's arm. "A red security flag came up on your credit account," Dr. Au said. His voice was anxious, and his face was pinched with fear. "There was a security probe; I barely avoided it. You must leave. I want you out of here right away."

Kleisterman stared at him. "But you agreed—" he said thickly.

"I want nothing to do with you, Mr. Ramírez," Dr. Au said apprehensively. "Here, take your clothes, get dressed. You have some very ruthless forces opposed to you, Mr. Ramírez. I want nothing to do with them, either. No trouble. Leave now. Take your business elsewhere."

Slowly, Kleisterman dressed, manipulating the clothes with stiff, clumsy fingers while Dr. Au hovered anxiously. The office was filled with watery gray light that seemed painfully bright after the darkness inside the simulator. Dust motes danced in suspension in the light, and a fly hopped along the adobe edge of the open window before darting outside again. A dog was barking out there somewhere, a flat, faraway sound, and a warm breeze puffed in for a second to ruffle his hair and bring him the smell of pine and juniper. He was perceiving every smallest detail with exquisite clarity.

Kleisterman pushed wordlessly by Dr. Au, walked through the outer office and out into the dusty hallway beyond. The floor was scuffed, grime between the tiles, and there were peeling water stains on the ceiling. A smell of cooking food came up the stairwell. *This is real*, Kleisterman told himself fiercely. This is real, this is really happening, this is the real world. The multinational boys aren't subtle enough for this; they wouldn't be satisfied with just denying me solace. Letting me go on. They're not that subtle.

Are they? *Are they?*

Kleisterman went down the narrow stairs. He dragged his fist against the rough adobe wall until his knuckles bled, but he couldn't convince himself that any of it was real.

• A Cat Horror Story •

DARKNESS. THE SMELL OF GRASS, and wet earth, and fog. The night moved through the clearing like a river. A few distant pinpricks of stars overhead, faint and far and pale. Somewhere down the hill, the grass rustled as a mouse fled through it, but the People were not hunting tonight.

Eyes gleamed in the night. Occasionally, a tail would thump the ground, once, twice, and then fall still. Very occasionally—an act of bravado—one of the People would slowly, ostentatiously, lick a paw. Then stop.

You could smell the excitement in the wet air, the uneasiness, the fear.

The wind brought the distant sound of a dog barking, and the ears of the People pricked forward instinctively, but, on this night of all nights, there was certainly no time for *dogs*.

Somewhere down below, in one of the human lairs at the foot of the hill, you could hear a human[1] calling for one of the People in that shrill mixture of human talk, strange wet noises, and oddly garbled and nonsensically out-of-context phrases of the True Tongue that humans used to try summon the People who were lair-mates with them, but none of the People were interested in Food tonight, even the fattest or the hungriest of them, not even when the human made an enticing rattling noise with a Food-Opening-Stick against a Cold Round Thing of Food. After a while, the human ceased his plaintive calls, and there was silence again, except for the human sounds riding the night air: doors slamming, voices, the annoying clamoring and shrieking of the Noisy Dead Things with which the humans insisted on cluttering the lairs, the growling of the Fast Dead Things which the humans kept as slaves and actually encouraged to *swallow* them! (although they made the Things spit them up again later) . . . but the People were used to those sounds, and ignored them.

---

[1]In the True Tongue, the word we render here as "human" is more closely expressed as "Bad-Smelling. Foodgiver-and-Lair-Mate-Who-Speaks-Loudly-and-Moves-Slowly," although that also is a loose translation, and subject to variation in local dialects.

At last, when the sharp smells of excitement could get no stronger, when their eyes could grow no wider or wilder, and when their tails were beginning to lash with impatience with a noise like a strong wind slashing through the branches of trees, the full moon rose, immense and pale and round, its pockmarked face pitiless and remote and cold, and that cruel orb was reflected full and bright in all the watching eyes of all the People who waited below.

One of the People stretched and yawned, showing all his teeth. His name was Caesar[2], and he was known as a good hunter, and a fierce defender of his territory. In fact, he had a bloody feud of long duration and rich tradition going with Jefferson, whose territory adjoined his own, but Jefferson sat quietly beside him now, and did no more than turn a slightly disdainful glance at Caesar's display of teeth. This was no time for fighting, or mating, or for territoriality. The Hunter Light, the Death Light, The Night Face, That-Which-Lights-the-Way-to-Kill, was in the sky, and that had always meant the same thing, for uncounted generations back to the beginning of all.

It was time to tell stories, under the cold, watchful gaze of The Night Face.

"This I have seen," Caesar began. "I was hunting with the tom named Bigfoot, and we came to the place where all the grass stops, and for almost as far as you can see, until the trees start again far away, the ground is fiat and hard and smells of Dead Things. I warned Bigfoot that this was Ghostland, the territory of demons[3] and monsters, but his hunting blood was up, and the hunting is good under the trees at night, and he would not listen. And so we went out across the hard, bad-smelling stuff. Out into Ghostland."

Caesar looked away for a moment, out toward the far horizon, then turned his eyes back to the People. "We walked out across Ghostland.

---

[2]This was the name his humans had given him, of course. The True Names of the People are impossible to reproduce here, as the verbal element is only a small part of each name, and perhaps the most insignificant part, the really vital information being conveyed by body posture, the speed and stiffness of movement, the position of the ears and tail, the pattern of ruffling or twitching of the fur, and, most importantly, the hot rich smell of the anus, and the lingering, eloquent tang of urine.

[3]The human word "demons," of course, has associations with Christian theology that the actual phrase in the True Tongue does not share, but it will serve to give an impression of something both malefic and enigmatic, an incomprehensible force that kills you with terrifying casualness, for unknowable reasons—if for any reason at all; this is more vivid in the speech of the People.

The Dead Stuff was cold and hard under our paws, and we could hear our claws skritch on it. The wind carried the voices of ghosts as it whined past us. Suddenly, there was a bright light, far away, but coming closer. Closer! I froze with fear, but, in his eagerness, Bigfoot went on. There was a growling noise, louder and louder, like all the dogs that ever were born, growling at once. And then there was a light, blinding me. The light! So bright, so close, as if The Night Face had fallen from the sky down on top of me! Then a Fast Dead Thing went by with a roar that shook the world and a blast of wind that nearly knocked me over, and with a smell of burning. I heard Bigfoot scream."

Caesar paused, and the rest of the People crept a step or two closer to hear him. "When the Fast Dead Thing was gone," he continued, "I went back, step by slow step, to see what had happened to Bigfoot." Caesar paused again, significantly. "He was *dead*. The Fast Dead Thing had crashed him. His guts were everywhere, torn from his body, and his blood was all around. The middle of his body was *flat,* as though it had no bones in it anymore. He was mashed into the dead black ground of Ghostland, in a puddle of his own guts and blood. On his face was a look of fear and horror such as I hope never to see again."

The People shivered. After a moment, Caesar said, "Then I heard it coming *back*. The Fast Dead Thing. I saw its light. It was coming back from the way it had gone. Coming back for *me*. I'm not ashamed to tell you all that I ran like a kitten! And ever since then, when I go near Ghostland, I can hear the Fast Dead Thing hunting for me, roaring back and forth, hunting through the night to find *me*."

There was an awed silence, and then a young queen named Katy said, "I hear they can get you *anywhere*, the Fast Dead Things." She looked around her nervously: "Even inside the lair: There are some of them who can follow you right *in*, and get you even when you're inside. My mother told me that she used to get chased by a little one that roared and whooshed and tried to pull her tail."

"That was just a Small Roaring Thing" a tom named Poorer said. "The humans play with them. They're not really dangerous—though, of course, it's better to stay away from them, just to be safe. But the Fast Dead Things, now—they can kill you even when they're *asleep*!"

"Nothing can kill you while it's asleep," Jefferson said.

Pooter bristled, then licked his foot in a slow and insulting way that might have been provocation for a fight on another evening. "Yes? Well, *I* have seen *this*. There was one of the People, her name was Lady Jane, and she went near one of the Fast Dead Things at night, while it was sleeping. And she crawled inside the top of the Thing, because the night was cold, and it was warm deep up inside the Thing. And in the morning as I was watching a human came and made the Fast Dead Thing swallow it, and then the Thing woke up." He shuddered. "It growled, and then it roared, and then Lady Jane *screamed*, and I smelled the hot smell of her blood. The human got out, and made the Thing open up its smaller mouth in the front, and then he lifted Lady Jane *out*. And she was dead. *Dead*, and cut into pieces! Her head was cut nearly all the way off, hanging by some fur!"

"Dead!" some of the People moaned. "Dead!"

A scarred old feral tom named Blackie, who had one ear torn nearly to rags, said, "You don't need Dead Things to kill you, young ones!" He lashed his tail and made the clicking and smacking noise that signified deep contempt among the People. "*Humans* will do the job readily enough! Yes, your precious humans, the things you all *live* with, willingly! When I was a kitten, some humans put me in a sack[4], and threw me in the river. Ai, the horror of it!" He shivered and shook himself convulsively. "It was dark and hot and smothering, and I couldn't breathe, and then I was *falling*, twisting and tumbling and falling, and there was no *air* to breathe! My claws were sharp in those days, People, lucky for me, and I ripped my way *out*. But then I was *in the water!* In the water! I was *under* the water, with it all around me—over my *head*! I had to *swim*, swim for my life, and I nearly died before my head broke the surface and I could take a breath, and then I had to swim for a long time before my feet found the ground again, and all the while the water was *pulling* at me, sucking at me, trying to pull me down to death!"

A low growl went around the circle of the People. Their eyes gleamed.

"*My* human goes in the water every day," a young queen named Spooky said. "On *purpose*. She lets it go all over her! She doesn't try to escape at *all*! Sometimes she sits *under* the water, with only her head outside it!"

---

[4]"False Skin" is about the closest you can come to this in the True Tongue, which doesn't allow for much precision in distinguishing between one sort of thing made of cloth or fabric and another; some dialects will allow reference to blankets as "False-Skins-That-You-Sleep-On. "All this is as nothing compared to conveying some sense of what the human word "river" actually translates to in the True Tongue—the literal "Moving Big Water" does little to convey the sense of horror and supernatural dread with which the People regard such bodies of water, as though they were an unholy and dreadful anomaly in the natural order of the world.

The People moaned in horror. "At, they are strange creatures," Jefferson muttered. "Strange!"

"But those were Rogues, those humans who tried to kill you," a young tom named Bangers said, somewhat uneasily, as though seeking reassurance. "We've all been chased and kicked by Rogues now and again, or had stones or Hard Clattering Things thrown at us. That doesn't mean that our humans would hurt us. *My* humans wouldn't hurt *me*. They like me! They feed me and pat[5] me whenever I want them to!"

"*I* had humans once, too, later on," Blackie said bitterly. "They fed me and they patted me—and then they cut my balls off!"

Bangers hissed involuntarily, and many of the People blew their trails out to several times their normal size.

"It could happen to *you*, too, young one!" Blackie said. "Don't you think it couldn't! You think you're safe with your humans because they feed you and give you a warm place to sleep, but you never know when they're going to *turn* on you and torture[6] you. You'll never know *why* they do it, either, but sooner or later, they will. They *all* will. None of them are any different!"

"They wait until you're *sick*," a burly tom named Hobbes said. "They wait until you're feeling really bad, and then they take you to the Pain Place, to the Torture Place, and they hurt you *more*—"

Another tom shuddered. "It's true! The humans there stick things up your ass! And they *stab* you, with things that hurt! And they drain your *blood* out of you!"

"They *cut* you!" a queen named Jasmine said, her voice thrilling with horror. "They cut you *open*! My humans took me there, to the Pain Place, with all its bad smells and its sick smells and the sounds of the People screaming in agony while *dogs* sit around and watch them, and they *left* me there, locked in a Box-You-Can't-Get-Out-Of, and I went to sleep, and when I woke up, my belly had been slashed open! I could *feel*

---

[5]Actually, "groom me," in the True Tongue. The People consider humans to be bizarrely handicapped creatures since they must groom with their hands rather than with their tongues. They are widely pitied for this, although there is derisive speculation as to why this is so—in fact, in one dialect, the generic term for "human" translates to "Those-Who-Must-Groom-With-Their-Paws-Because-Their-Breath-Smells-So-Bad."

[6]In the True Tongue, the word for "torture" also implies a sort of willful, capricious, malevolent playfulness, and a highly refined aesthetic appreciation of the pain you are inflicting; if you're ever seen one of the People with a bird or a mouse that they've caught, you get the idea.

the cut, deeper than a cut from any fight. It hurt for a long time, even when my humans came and got me and took me back to the lair again. It hurt for a *long* time!"

They were crouched close together now, almost touching their heads in a circle.

"They *kill* People there, too," Blackie said. "The humans kill them. And not just the humans who live in the Pain Place. *Your* precious humans. The very same ones who live with you and give you Food. *They* kill you, themselves!"

There were a few wails of protest, and the People pressed closer together, shuddering.

"I have *seen* it," Blackie continued inexorably. "When they cut my balls off, in the Pain Place, before they took me back to the lair and I ran away, they brought my lair-mate in, an old queen named Stuff who had lived with the humans before I joined them. *Our* humans brought her in, and they held her down while she fought to get away, both of them held her down, and then another human stabbed her with a Pain Stick, and she struggled for a while, and then she *died*! I could smell that she was dead! They'd killed her! *Our* humans! They held her down and killed her—and they *patted* her while they were doing it!"

Someone moaned with dread, and then fell silent.

"And that's what will happen to *all* of you! Every one of you! If a dog or a Fast Dead Thing or some other kind of monster or demon doesn't get you, then, at the end, your own *humans* will kill you!"

This was almost too much. They pressed close together for comfort, too scared even to wail or moan now.

There was a crazed light in Blackie's eyes. "I saw Stuff's ghost last night. I often see it, after dark. Her fur is like ice, like frost on a winter morning and her dead eyes give back no light . . ."

The moon was high and full above them now, and it seemed to tug on their souls, as if it would suck them out through the tops of their heads and up into the mysterious depths of the night sky, where they would fall forever through the dark.

"Yes!" a tom shrieked. "Yes! I have *seen* it! Its feet leave no mark on the grass when it walks, and its eyes are like deep pools of black water! And one night, when everyone slept except me, I could hear it outside, scratching on the door, trying to get in—"

A huge Dead Thing went by overhead, roaring, a blazing light flying through the night sky like a terrible gazing eye, seeming to pass almost close enough to touch, and the People crouched low on the hillside until the monster had rumbled away into distance and was gone.

In the sudden shocked silence, Caeser said, almost with satisfaction, "The Ghostway is around us, always." And the People shivered deliciously, and moved closer in the night, and told their stories until the moon went down, as they have for a million generations, and as they will for a million more, until the Earth goes cold, and even the People are forgotten.

• Disciples •

NICKY THE HORSE was a thin, weaselly looking man with long dirty black hair that hung down either side of his face in greasy ropes, like ink marks against the pallor of his skin. He was clean-shaven and hollow-cheeked, and had a thin but rubbery lower lip upon which his small yellowed teeth were forever biting, seizing the lip suddenly and worrying it, like a terrier seizing a rat. He wore a grimy purple sweater under a torn tan jacket enough sizes too small to look like something an organ grinder's monkey might wear, one pocket torn nearly off and both elbows worn through. Thrift-store jeans and a ratty pair of sneakers he'd once found in a garbage can behind the YMCA completed his wardrobe. No underwear. A crucifix gleamed around his neck, stainless steel coated to look like silver. Track marks, fading now, ran down both his arms, across his stomach, down his thighs, but he'd been off the junk for months; he was down to an occasional Red Devil, supplemented by the nightly quart of cheap chianti he consumed as he lay in the dark on his bare mattress at the "Lord-house," a third-floor loft in a converted industrial warehouse squeezed between a package store and a Rite-Aid.

He had just scavenged some two-day-old doughnuts from a pile of boxes behind a doughnut store on Broad Street, and bought a paper container of coffee from a Greek delicatessen where the counterman (another aging hippie, faded flower tattoos still visible under the bristly black hair on his arms) usually knocked a nickel or two off the price for old time's sake. Now he was sitting on the white marble steps of an old brownstone row house, eating his breakfast. His breath steamed in the chill morning air. Even sitting still, he was in constant motion—his fingers drumming, his feet shuffling, his eyes flicking nervously back and forth as one thing or another—a car, some wind-blown trash, pigeons taking to the air—arrested and briefly held his attention; at such times his shoulders would momentarily hunch, as if he expected something to leap out at him.

Across the street, a work crew was renovating another old brownstone, swarming over the building's partially stripped skeleton like carrion beetles; sometimes a cloud of plaster-powder and brick dust would puff from the building's broken doorway, like foul air from a dying mouth. Winos and pimps and whores congregated on the corner, outside a flophouse hotel, their voices coming to Nicky thin and shrill over the rumbling and farting of traffic. Occasionally a group of med students would go by, or a girl with a dog, or a couple of Society Hill faggots in bell-bottom trousers and expensive turtlenecks, and Nicky would call out "Jesus loves you, man," usually to no more response than a nervous sideways glance. One faggot smirked knowingly at him, and a collegiate-jock type got a laugh out of his buddies by shouting back "You bet your ass he does, honey." A small, intense-looking woman with short-cropped hair gave him the finger. Another diesel dyke, Nicky thought resignedly. "Jesus loves *you*, man," he called after her, but she didn't look back.

When his butt began to feel as if it had turned to stone, he got up from the cold stoop and started walking again, pausing only long enough to put a flyer for the Lordhouse on a lamp pole, next to a sticker that said Eat the Rich. He walked on, past a gay bookstore, a go-go bar, a boarded-up storefront with a sign that read Live Nude Models, a pizza stand, slanting south and east now, through a trash-littered concrete park full of sleeping derelicts and herds of arrogantly strutting pigeons, stopping now and then to panhandle and pass out leaflets, drifting on again.

He'd been up to Suburban Station early that morning, hoping to catch the shoppers who came in from the suburbs on commuter trains, but the Hairy Krishnaites had been there already, out in force in front of the station, and he didn't like to compete with other panhandlers, particularly fucking *groups* of them with fucking *bongos*. The Krishnaites made him nervous anyway—with their razor-shaved pates and their air of panting, puppyish eagerness, they always reminded him of ROTC second lieutenants, fresh out of basic training. Once, in front of the old Bellevue-Stratford, he'd seen a fight between a Krishnaite and a Moonie, the two of them arguing louder and louder, toe to toe, until suddenly they were beating each other over the head with thick packets of devotional literature, the leaflets swirling loose around them like flocks of startled birds. He'd had to grin at that one, but some of the panhandling groups were mean, particularly the political groups, particularly the niggers. They'd kick your ass up between your shoulder blades if they caught you poaching on their turf, they'd have your balls for garters.

No, you scored better if you worked alone. Always alone.

He ended up on South Street, down toward the Two Street end, taking up a position between the laundromat and the plant store. It was much too early for the trendy people to be out, the "artists," the night people, but they weren't such hot prospects anyway. It was Saturday, and that meant that there were tourists out, in spite of the early hour, in spite of the fact that it had been threatening to snow all day—it was cold, yes, but not as cold as it had been the rest of the week, the sun was peeking sporadically out from behind banks of dirty gray clouds, and maybe this would be the only halfway decent day left before winter really set in. No, they were here all right, the tourists, strolling up and down through this hick Greenwich Village, peering into the quaint little stores, the boutiques, the head shops full of tourist-trap junk, the artsy bookstores, staring at the resident freaks as though they were on display at the zoo, relishing the occasional dangerous whiff of illicit smoke in the air, the loud blare of music that they wouldn't have tolerated for a moment at home.

Of course, he wasn't the only one feeding on this rich stream of marks: there was a juggler outside of the steak-sandwich shop in the next block, a small jazz band—a xylophone, a bass, and an electric piano—in front of the communist coffeehouse across the street, and, next to the upholsterer's, a fat man in a fur-lined parka who was tonelessly chanting "incense sticks check it out one dollar incense sticks check it out one dollar" without break or intonation. Such competition Nicky could deal with—in fact, he was contemptuous of it.

"Do you have your house in *order*?" he said in a conversational but carrying voice, starting his own spiel, pushing leaflets at a businessman, who ignored him, at a strolling young married couple, who smiled but shook their heads, at a middle-aged housewife in clogs and a polka-dot kerchief, who took A flyer reflexively and then, a few paces away, stopped to peek at it surreptitiously. "Did you know the Lord is *coming*, man? The Lord is coming. Spare some change for the Lord's work?" This last remark shot at the housewife, who looked uneasily around and then suddenly thrust a quarter at him. She hurried away, clutching her Lordhouse flyer to her chest as if it were a baby the gypsies were after.

Panhandling was an art, man, an *art*—and so, of *course*, of course, was the more important task of spreading the Lord's word. That was what really counted. Of course. Nevertheless, he brought more fucking change into the Lordhouse than any of the other converts who were out pounding the pavement every day, fucking-A, you better believe it. He'd always been a good panhandler, even before he'd seen the light, and what did it was making maximum use of your time, knowing who to ask and who not to waste time on was the secret. College students, professional people, and young white male businessmen made the best marks—later, when the businessmen had aged into senior executives, the chances of their coming across went way down. Touristy types were good, straight suburbanites in the twenty-five to fifty age bracket, particularly a man out strolling with his wife. A man walking by himself was much more likely to give you something than a man walking in company with another man—faggots were sometimes an exception here. Conversely, women in pairs—especially prosperous hausfraus, although groups of teenage girls were pretty good too—were much more likely to give you change than were women walking by themselves; the housewife of a moment before had been an exception, but she had all the earmarks of someone who was just religious enough to feel guilty about not being more so. Brisk woman-executive types almost never gave you anything, or even took a leaflet. Servicemen in uniform were easy touches. Old people never gave you diddley-shit except sometimes a well-heeled little old white lady would, especially a W.H.L.O.W.L. who had religion herself, although they could also be more trouble than their money was worth. There were a lot of punkers in this neighborhood, with their fifties crew cuts and greasy motorcycle jackets, but Nicky usually left them alone; the punks were more violent and less gullible than the hippies had been back in the late sixties, the Golden Age of Panhandling. The few remaining hippies—and the college kids who passed for hippies these days—came across often enough that Nicky made a point of hitting on them, although he gritted his teeth each time he did; they were by far the most likely to be wiseasses—once he'd told one "Jesus is coming to our town," and the kid had replied, "I hope he's got a reservation, then—the hotels are booked *solid*." Wiseasses. Those were also the types who would occasionally quote Scripture to him, coming up with some goddamn verse or other to refute anything he said; that made him uneasy—Nicky had never really actually *read* the Bible that much, although he'd meant to: he had the knowledge *intuitively*, because the Spirit was in him. At that, the hippie wiseasses were easier to take than the Puerto Ricans, who would pretend they didn't understand what he wanted and give him only tight bursts of superfast Spanish. The Vietnamese, now, being seen on the street with increasing frequency these days, the Vietnamese quite often *did* give something, perhaps because they felt that they were required to. Nicky wasn't terribly fond of Jews, either, but it was amazing how often they'd come across, even for a pitch about

Jesus—all that guilt they imbibed with their mother's milk, he guessed. On the other hand, he mostly stayed clear of niggers—sometimes you could score off a middle-aged tom in a business suit or some graying workman, but the young street dudes were impossible, and there was always the chance that some coked-up young stud would turn mean on you and maybe pull a knife. Occasionally you could get money out of a member of that endless, seemingly cloned legion of short, fat, cone-shaped black women, but that had its special dangers too, particularly if they turned out to be devout Baptists, or snake-handlers, or whatever the *fuck* they were: one woman had screamed at him, "Don't talk to *me* about Jesus! Don't talk to me about *Jesus*! Don't talk to me about Jesus!" Then she'd hit him with her purse.

"The Last Days are at hand!" Nicky called. "The Last Days are coming, man. The Lord is coming to our town, and the wicked will be left *behind*, man. The *Lord* is coming." Nicky shoved a leaflet into someone's hand and the someone shoved it right back. Nicky shrugged. "Come to the Lordhouse tonight, brothers and sisters! Come and get your soul *together*." Someone paused, hesitated, took a leaflet. "Spare change? Spare change for the Lord's work? Every *penny* does the Lord's work . . ."

The morning passed, and it grew colder. About half of Nicky's leaflets were gone, although many of them littered the sidewalk a few paces away, where people had discarded them once they thought that they were far enough from Nicky not to be noticed doing so. The sun had been swallowed by clouds, and once again it looked like it was going to snow, although once again it did not. Nicky's coat was too small to button, but he turned his collar up, and put his hands in his pockets. The stream of tourists had pretty much run dry for the moment, and he was just *thinking* about getting some lunch, about going down to the hot dog stand on the corner where the black dudes stood jiving and hand-slapping, their giant radios blaring on their shoulders, he was just thinking about it when, at that very moment, as though conjured up by the thought, Saul Edelmann stepped out of the stand and walked briskly toward him.

"Shit in my hat," Nicky muttered to himself. He'd collected more than enough to buy lunch, but, because of the cold, not that much more. And Father Delardi, the unfrocked priest—the *unfairly* unfrocked priest—who had founded their order and who ran it with both love and, yessir, an iron hand—Father Delardi didn't like it when they came in off the streets at the end of the day with less than a certain amount of dough. Nicky had been hoping that he could con Saul into giving him a free hot dog, as he sometimes could, as Saul sometimes *had*, and now here was Saul himself, off on some dumb-shit errand, bopping down the street as fat and happy as a clam (although how happy *were* clams anyway? come to think about it), which meant that he, Nicky, was fucked.

"Nicky! My main man!" said Saul, who prided himself on an ability to speak jivey street patois that he definitely did not possess. He was a plump-cheeked man with modish-length gray-streaked hair, cheap black plastic-framed glasses, and a neatly trimmed mustache. Jews were supposed to have big noses, or so Nicky had always heard, but Saul's nose was small and upturned, as if there were an Irishman in the woodpile somewhere.

"Hey, man," Nicky mumbled listlessly. Bad enough that he wasn't going to get his free hot dog—now he'd have to make friendly small talk with this dipshit in order to protect his investment in free hot dogs yet to come. Nicky sighed, and unlimbered his shit-eating grin. "Hey, man! How you been, Saul? What's *happenin'*, man?"

"What's happening?" Saul said jovially, responding to Nicky as if he were really asking a question instead of emitting ritual noise. "Now how can I even begin to tell you what's happening, Nicky?" He was radiant today, Saul was, full of bouncy energy, rocking back and forth as he talked, unable to stand still, smiling a smile that revealed teeth some Yiddish momma had sunk a lot of dough into over the years. "I'm glad you came by today, though. I wanted to be sure to say good-bye if I could."

"Good-bye?"

Saul's smile became broader and broader. "Yes, good-bye! This is it, *boychick*. I'm off! You won't see me again after today.

Nicky peered at him suspiciously. "You goin' away?"

"You bet your ass I am, kid," Saul said, and then laughed. "Today I turned my half of the business over to Carlos, signed all the papers, took care of everything nice and legal. And now I'm free and clear, free as a damn bird, kid."

"You sold your half of the stand to *Carlos*?"

"Not sold, *boychick*—gave. I *gave* it to him. Not one red cent did I take."

Nicky gaped at him. "You *gave your business away*, man?"

Saul beamed. "Kid—I gave *everything* away. The car: I gave that to old Ben Miller who washes dishes at the Green Onion. I gave up the lease on my apartment, gave away my furniture, gave away my savings—if you'd've been here yesterday, Nicky, I would've given you something too."

"Shit!" Nick said harshly, "you go crazy, man, or what?" He choked back an outburst of bitter profanity. Missed out again! Screwed out of getting *his* yet *again*!

"I don't need any of that stuff anymore, Nicky," Saul said. He tapped the side of his nose, soled. "Nicky—He's come."

"Who?'

"The Messiah. He's come! He's finally come! Today's the day the Messiah comes, after all those thousands of years—think of it, Nicky!"

Nicky's eyes narrowed. "What the fuck you talkin' about, man?"

"Don't you *ever* read the paper, Nicky, or listen to the radio? The Messiah has come. His name is Murray Kupferberg, He was born in Pittsburgh—"

"*Pittsburgh*?" Nicky gasped.

"—and He used to be a plumber there. But He is the Messiah. Most of the scholars and the rabbis deny Him, but He really *is*. The Messiah has really come, at last!"

Nicky gave that snorting bray of laughter, blowing out his rubbery lips, that was one reason—but only one reason—why he was sometimes called Nicky the Horse. "Jesus is the Messiah, man," he said scornfully.

Saul smiled good-naturedly, shrugged, spread his hands. "For you, maybe he is. For you people, the *goyim*, maybe he is. But *we've* been waiting for almost three thousand years—and at last He's come."

"Murray Kupferberg? From *Pittsburgh*?"

"Murray Kupferberg," Saul repeated firmly, calmly. "From Pittsburgh. He's coming here, *today*. Jews are gathering here today from all over the country, from all over the world, and *today*—right here—He's going to gather His people to Him—"

"You stupid fucking kike!" Nicky screamed, his anger breaking free at last. "You're crazy in the head, man. You've been *conned*. Some fucking con man has taken you for *everything*, and you're too fucking dumb to see it! All that stuff, man, all that good stuff *gone*—" He ran out of steam, at a loss for words. All that good stuff gone, and he hadn't gotten *any* of it. After kissing up to this dipshit for all those years . . . "Oh, you dumb kike," he whispered.

Saul seemed unoffended. "You're wrong, Nicky—but I haven't got time to argue with you. Good-bye." He stuck out his hand, but Nicky refused to shake it. Saul shrugged, smiled again, and then walked briskly away, turning the corner onto Sixth Street.

Nicky sullenly watched him go, still shaking with rage. Screwed again! There went his free hot dogs, flying away into the blue on fucking gossamer wings. Carlos was a hard dude, a street-wise dude—Carlos wasn't going to *give* him anything, Carlos wouldn't stop to piss on Nicky's head if Nicky's hair was on fire. Nicky stared at the tattered and overlapping posters on the laundromat wall, and the faces of long-dead politicians stared back at him from among the notices for lost cats and the ads for Czech films and karate classes. Suddenly he was cold, and he shivered.

The rest of the day was a total loss. Nicky's sullen mood drew his judgment and his timing off, and the tourists were thinning out again anyway. The free-form jazz of the communist coffeehouse band was getting on his nerves—the fucking xylophone player was chopping away as if he were making sukiyaki at Benihana of Tokyo's—and the smell of sauerkraut would float over from the hot dog stand every now and then to torment him. And it kept getting colder and colder. Still, some obscure, self-punishing instinct kept him from moving on.

Later in the afternoon, what amounted to a little unofficial parade went by—a few hundred people walking in the street, heading west against the traffic, many of them barefoot in spite of the bitter cold. If they were all Jews on their way to the Big Meeting, as Nicky suspected, then some of them must have been black Jews, East Indian Jews, even *Chinese* Jews.

Smaller groups of people straggled by for the next hour or so, all headed uptown. The traffic seemed to have stopped completely, even the crosstown buses; this rally must be *big*, for the city to've done that.

The last of the pilgrims to go by was a stout, fiftyish Society Hill matron with bleached blue hair, walking calmly in the very center of the street. She was wearing an expensive ermine stole, although she was barefoot and her feet were bleeding. As she passed Nicky, she suddenly laughed, unwrapped the stole from around her neck, and threw it into the air, walking on without looking back. The stole landed across the shoulders of the communist xylophone player, who goggled blankly for a moment, then stared wildly around him—his eyes widening comically—and then bolted, clutching the stole tightly in his hands; he disappeared down an alleyway.

"You bitch!" Nicky screamed. "Why not *me*? Why didn't you give it to *me*?"

But she was gone, the street was empty, and the gray afternoon sky was darkening toward evening.

"The Last Days are coming," Nicky told the last few strolling tourists and window-shoppers. "The strait gate is narrow, sayeth the Lord, and few will fit *in*, man." But his heart wasn't in it anymore. Nicky waited, freezing, his breath puffing out in steaming clouds, stamping his feet to restore circulation, slapping his arms, doing a kind of shuffling jig that—along with his too-small jacket—made him look more than ever like an organ-grinder's monkey performing for some unlikely kind of alms. He didn't understand why he didn't just give up and go back to the Lordhouse. He was beginning to think yearningly of the hot stew they would be served there after they had turned the day's take in to Father Delardi, the hymn-singing later, and after that the bottle of strong raw wine, and his mattress in the rustling, fart-smelling communal darkness, oblivion . . .

There was—a sound, a note, a chord, an upswelling of something that the mind interpreted as music, as blaring iron trumpets, only because it had no other referents with which to understand it. The noise, the music, the *something*—it swelled until it shook the empty street, the buildings, the world, shook the bones in the flesh, and the very marrow in the bones, until it filled every inch of the universe like hot wax being poured into a mold.

Nicky looked up.

As he watched, a crack appeared in the dull gray sky. The sky split open, and behind the sky was nothingness, a wedge of darkness so terrible and absolute that it hurt the eyes to look at it. The crack, widened, the wedge of darkness grew. Light began to pour through the crack in the sky, blinding white light more intense and frightening than the darkness had been. Squinting against that terrible radiance, his eyes watering, Nicky saw tiny figures rising into the air far away, thousands upon thousands of human figures floating up into the sky, falling up while the iron music shook the firmament around them, people falling up and into and through the crack in the sky, merging into that wondrous and awful river of light, fading, disappearing, until the last one was gone.

The crack in the sky closed. The music grumbled and rumbled away into silence.

Everything was still.

Snowflakes began to squeeze like slow tears from the slate gray sky.

Nicky stayed there for hours, staring upward until his neck was aching and the last of the light was gone, but after that nothing else happened at all.

• Ancestral Voices •

(Written with Michael Swanwick)

Like all intelligent creatures, it adapted.

Behind it was fire! fear! pain! horror! and it fled from them through madness and roaring chaos, fled for a long nightmarish time through an unfamiliar world, through a phantasmagorical confusion of alien shapes and lights and stinks and noises, fled until its strength was gone and it could flee no more.

After that was the black churning darkness of oblivion.

When it came to itself again, awareness returning bit by incremental bit, it was in a dank and narrow alley between the back of a decaying flophouse hotel and the side of a liquor store, lying still in the deep black shadow behind a mound of overstuffed green garbage bags.

Warily, it surveyed its surroundings, taking in the tall brick walls that rose on either side, the muddy, slime-coated pavement upon which it rested, the dull red light—from an ancient, buzzing neon sign on the corner—that ebbed and flooded rhythmically through the darkness, the thin sliver of alien sky far overhead . . . and again it was taken by disorientation and fear. It reached instinctively for knowledge, for connection with the flood of data that would tell it location, status, mission, and instead it touched fire! fear! pain! horror! and recoiled from the searing agony of the memory.

Cautiously, it tried again to remember, like an electric linesman testing a live wire by gingerly brushing it with his thumb, and again it was driven back by the sizzling intensity of what lurked in the recesses of its own mind. Again and again it tried to remember, until its mind was ablaze with pain, and shudders ran like waves across the long flat carpet of its body. But nothing would come.

Its past was gone. It had no past—it had been born in that endless moment of pain and red screaming chaos, and before that it could not go. Instinctively it knew that it didn't belong here, that the world around it was alien, frighteningly wrong, but it couldn't remember how the world should be, what or where home was, what it was doing here in this place whose wrongness beat in upon its senses from every side.

Trembling, it lay flat in the cold mud of the alley. Each new sound from the unknown world beyond, each metallic roar or shriek or clatter, sent a new pulse of terror through it.

And then something blocked part of the light from the alley-mouth.

A monstrous figure loomed there, huge and dark and terrible.

There was the sound of a can being kicked underfoot, sent clattering away against the wall.

The figure moved slowly closer, down the alleyway, swaying, staggering from side to side, pushing a wave of rich alien stink before it.

"Oblah-dee," the figure muttered. "Oblahfucking-*dee*, oblahfucking-*blah*"—It crashed against the wall, pushed away again. "Life goes fucking *onnnn*, blah—" The figure coughed, coughed again spasmodically, hawked and spat. "Sonsabitches," it mumbled. "Think they can tell *me* . . ."

Weaving. Coming closer.

It saw the wino with the colorless, directionless perception characteristic of its race, but, more importantly, it *felt* him, felt the rush and interplay of electrical impulses along the intricate pathways of the wino's nervous system, felt the cold living fire that pulsed about the cerebrum, felt the sensuous shifting and interweaving of alpha and beta rhythms . . . Suddenly, it was *hungry*.

The hunger rose in a bitter, biting flood, driving away fear, overwhelming everything. For a moment it didn't know what to do, and then instinct took over, a deep cellular knowledge that sent it rippling silently forward, deeper into the shadow cast by the wall of garbage bags, its mantle stiffening and rising.

It melded itself flat against the cold surface of the bags.

It waited . . .

The wino had stubbed his toe and was cursing in a low, racking undertone. Then he stumbled forward again. "Wham-bam, thank you ma'am," he muttered. "*Oh* yeah. Oh *yeah*." He lurched against the garbage bags, almost toppling them, then ripped one open with both hands and began rummaging clumsily, spilling tin cans and bottles and soggy old paper bags to the ground. "You don't know how lucky they *aarrrree*, boys . . . back in the—back in the—shit!" An empty pint crashed to the ground, breaking with a flat, pinpoint spray of glass. He chuckled. "Dead soldier. Don't make no nevermind. What I should of told her, what I *shoulda* told her . . ." He fished an old sneaker out of the trash, examined it, wriggling his fingers through the large hole in the sole. "Oh yeah." He threw the sneaker aside, leaned forward into the shadow.

The wino's face filled its field of vision, huge, terrifying, slathered in bristly black whiskers, eyes as big and bloodshot red as harvest moons, the stink of corruption breathing from the slackened lips . . .

"Molly stays at home and does her fucking face." He dug his arms more deeply into the trash. "Oblah—"

It struck.

The derelict jerked convulsively, as if he had walked into a high-tension line, jerked again, and toppled to the ground, bringing the trash can clattering down with him.

It stretched its body into a rope to follow him down, maintaining contact, feeding, feeding voraciously . . .

On the ground, the wino twitched and quivered, already dead, his eyes rolled horribly up into his head, the whites gleaming in the starlight. It too quivered as it fed, its long flat body pulsing and swelling like a fire hose with a high-pressure head of water working through it.

Then—stillness. The wino's body had shrunken, collapsed in upon itself, sucked dry of all nourishment. Only the blood and bone and flesh was left behind. It spread its own body out, relaxing, allowing itself to form into a flat, almost-oval, molecule-thin carpet about five feet across.

But with the blunting of its hunger, fear returned.

Something huge and rank drifted past the alley-mouth, bellowing in a tremendous voice, making a terrible iron crash and clatter—

It started, contracting its body into a narrow ribbon again. The disturbance was only a garbage truck—but it didn't know that, and through its mind flashed again the torrent of fire! fear! pain! horror!

Without thinking, it rippled to the back of the alley and flowed straight up a wall. When it regained its composure, it found itself on a high place, empty space everywhere around it, open to the frighteningly alien sky.

Something swooped at it from that sky, shining a dazzling light. Something dark and enormous that seemed to skim by just a few feet overhead. The airport was just beyond, and to the residents of that particular flophouse hotel, it often seemed as if the big jets in the landing pattern were brushing their wheels on the roof as they went over.

Again it fled in unknowing panic, pouring itself like a tide of mist across rooftops, up walls, down rusting and dilapidated fire escapes.

Instinctively seeking shelter from this nightmare place, it squeezed between the slats of a broken and boarded-up window, and found itself in darkness.

In darkness, it calmed again, its panic fading.

There were heavy, bulky objects around it in the gloom, its spatial sense told it, and gratefully it poured itself under them, working its way as far in as it could. Feeling safer for the sheltering mass above it, it let its mind drift into the neutral looping that served its kind for sleep . . .

Early the next morning, a neural alarm jolted it back into active mode, and it watched from under a cluster of heavy Victorian furniture—dressers, hunt cabinets, wardrobes, highboys, roll-top mahogany desks: the sheltering masses of the night before—as a man came into the room, a bald-pated man with a frizzy halo of white hair around his ears and a hammer tucked by the claw-end into the breast pocket of his coveralls. It had found refuge in an antique warehouse, a rundown and half-abandoned brick building that had, sometime in the nineteenth century, been a harness-maker's factory. Now the downstairs floor was used as a workshop, while the upper two floors were devoted to the storage of antiques awaiting either renovation or delivery, room after room of dusty furniture, some of which had not been moved or touched in years.

Whistling, the man kicked at a wardrobe, tapped the joints a few times with the hammer, then tipped the wardrobe over so he could work the nails loose from the wood.

It had shrunk away at the close approach of the man's feet. Now it stirred and oozed forward again, sliding under a sideboard, a pharmacist's cabinet, a claw-footed bath basin, pausing finally under an overstuffed damask armchair to observe the workman.

Still whistling, the workman pulled a square of sandpaper from his hip pocket and began to rasp away at the wardrobe.

The fire-of-life was there, the crackling electric interplay of the nervous system . . .

Hunger stirred in it again, and it felt its mantle stiffen and rise.

Slowly it slid forward . . .

The workman tucked the sandpaper away in its pocket, picked up the hammer again, and tapped ruminatively at the wardrobe. The wan gray morning light gleamed from his bald head and glinted from his thick eyeglasses as he moved. He was a superstitious man, given to hunches and omens and premonitions, but now, in a supreme bit of irony, with death gliding silently up behind him, he was oblivious to its presence.

Death was a lightless black ribbon that reared up behind him, a hooded flat cobra-shaped shadow that loomed over him, paused, and with the slightest involuntary tremble prepared to strike, to reach out to claim him . . .

Inches from the workman, so close his internal interplay of forces was a tantalizing tickle, it stopped. It stopped, made hesitant by a flicker of the same sort of shadowy, half understood instinct or almost-memory that the night before had taught it how to kill. The pattern of the fire-of-life was complex and intensely bright—this was certainly a sophont, and somehow it knew that killing sophonts could be dangerous if other sophonts learned of the killing, if you alerted them to your presence *by* the killing, especially if you were incautious enough to kill near your own nest or refuge. It was just now beginning to realize how much of its surroundings were artificial, *crafted*; the other night it had seen the buildings and rooftops and alleyways as natural formations, alien mountains and canyons and outcroppings of rock, and only now, replaying the thread of that memory, could it begin to guess how much of all it had seen so far had been *made*.

Created! This spoke of a world of almost unbelievable complexity, a world whose ways would have to be unraveled with patience and caution, and it dare not endanger the best refuge it had found so far just for a quick and easy kill.

It reversed direction, flowing backward as easily as it had flowed forward, disappearing under a chiffonier.

The workman continued tapping at the wardrobe, as unaware of his reprieve as he had been of his endangerment. As he put the hammer away and fished a screwdriver out of his belt, he began to whistle *Amazing Grace*.

Already deep inside the warehouse, the hammering and whistling fading behind, it sped through the dim and cobwebbed spaces beneath dust covered harpsichords and mildewing Victorian sofas and wormholed grandfather clocks, seeking out the sealed-off and deserted sections of the building where men never went, seeking safer prey.

It adapted.

There were pigeons by the dozen in the deserted attic of the warehouse, and in the long-unused belvedere, boarded-up sloppily enough to be open to the sky on three sides, there were pigeons by the hundreds. There were cats on the surrounding maze of rooftops, and rats in the alleyways and sewers it learned to hunt by night. There was a little park a few blocks from the warehouse, and there among the trees and bushes it learned to take squirrels and field mice and nesting birds of all sorts. People would bring big dogs to the park and unleash them and let them run, and it took several of those, finding them very satisfactory. It needed a good deal of nourishment, fairly frequently, and finding that nourishment kept it busy.

It stayed hidden by daylight as much as it could, although it soon realized that the native sophonts were unlikely to spot it even then—it blended well with the stained and soot-covered and moss-overgrown walls of the city, and it traveled the roofways where people seldom looked. Electrical appliances and motor vehicles made it uneasy, and it stayed away from them; it had learned early that they were not alive, but their electrical fields touched off strange longings and sudden goosed scurryings of almost-memories that disturbed the placid mental status quo it had established for itself, the easy looping of its mind in ways that did not force it to confront the fear! fire! pain! horror! that always lurked somewhere just below its surface thoughts. It also had a strange effect occasionally on the electric appliances, though it didn't pay any attention to that.

It adapted, the weeks went by, and fall began to solidify into winter.

Prey became harder to find as the days grew colder. It often went hungry. It had made serious inroads on the local dog and cat population—although there were always a few strays drifting in to partially compensate—and many of the pigeons were nesting elsewhere now, having shifted their range for blocks and even miles to avoid the relentless horror that poured like smoke across the gables and ledges and roof-eaves. Even the rats had noticeably thinned out.

One dull gray afternoon, it took three children who were playing in the park, and that evening the park and the streets around the park were thick with men with flashlights, too many men to make further hunting possible.

There was also the night that the Northern Lights danced faintly in the sky, and it danced with them, whirling and darting madly on the deserted, icy rooftops under the cold stars, feeling the enormous magnetic fields stir and scramble its emotions even at that great distance.

In that still and freezing night, fey and hungry and half-mad, it left its usual resting place in the ruined belvedere and went down through the building to the warehouse floor, penetrating deep into the tangles of stacked-up furniture, craving the solidity of mass between it and the dancing maddening fires that flared and dimmed on the horizon.

It found a drawer left ajar in a massive dresser that stood upright inside a thick wooden box, and slithered inside. It waited there in the darkness, jittering and buzzing with sick energy, unable to loop its mind into oblivion, nearly insane, occasionally striking furiously and futilely at the smooth wood inside the drawer.

Half an hour later, the white-haired workman entered the warehouse. He had had a hot roast beef sandwich and a couple of knocks of whiskey at the bar on the corner, and now he had one last task to finish up before he called it quits and went home. Taking off his overcoat, he reached over and snapped on his portable radio, but could get nothing out of it but a see-sawing squeal of static. He shrugged and switched it off—the damn thing had been going haywire off and on for a couple of months now, and the phones and the old black-and-white TV in the office had been on the fritz too, now and again. Sunspots, maybe, or some damn microwave relay tower nearby. Fry us in our goddamn jeans yet, he thought sourly, only dimly aware of the subconscious pun. He gathered up his tools and walked toward the massive packing crate.

A step or two from it, he stopped, and felt a chill shiver up his spine. "Somebody's walking on my grave," he said aloud, the words coming out flat and strange in this familiar place that all at once seemed too big and dark and echoingly empty. Gooseflesh had blossomed on his arms, and he ran his hands down over them to smooth it. There was a big Federal dresser in the crate, already surrounded by wood on three sides. The dresser's bottom drawer was standing ajar, and abruptly, without knowing why, he reached out with the toe of his work shoe and kicked it solidly shut.

Another chill shuddered along his spine, raising the tiny hairs on the back of his neck. It was funny that he'd never noticed how dark and cavernous it was here at night, or how black and spooky the surrounding shadows were.

Shivering, he manhandled the last end of the packing crate into position and began to nail, noticing that he was taking unusual, almost obsessive, care to make sure that the crate was closely and firmly sealed—again without knowing why—as though for some esoteric reason it needed to be airtight. A line from an old church song was running repeatedly through his head: *Amazing grace* . . . something something . . . *that saved a wretch like me* . . .

When the job was done—and he took twice as long about it as he should have taken—but before he turned out the lights and went gratefully home, the workman took out a Magic Marker and on the side of the crate in large, somewhat shaky letters wrote:

Mrs. Alma Kingsley
Maple Hill Farm
Eden Falls, Vermont

"Gamma, there's a truck with men outside!"

Alma Kingsley put her Manhattan down on the kitchen counter—carefully, for her arthritis was acting up again—and said to her granddaughter, "Dear child, please *do* endeavor to refrain from calling me 'Gamma' in the future. It makes you sound most deplorably winsome."

Jennifer beamed and laughed, as she did at all of her grandmother's more gravely sententious pronouncements. She didn't know what they meant, but they all sounded funny to her.

Meanwhile, however, the driver of the truck was leaning on his horn, and his assistant was at the tailgate, wrestling an enormous crate onto the lift. "Come, child," Mrs. Kingsley said. "Get your coat. You may find this interesting." She swept into the yard, little Jenny trailing after her like a hyperkinetic pull-toy.

Outside, the day was cold, with a promise of snow in the air—a promise seconded by a sky as uniformly gray and featureless as an old blanket. Beyond the rocky, frozen fields, a fringe of trees marked the ravine separating Maple Hill Farm from the Laferrier place—though their farmhouse was not visible from here. They were isolated, alone among the Green Mountains, and that was the way Alma Kingsley preferred it. She couldn't abide people tromping through here with their problems and their petty jealousies and ambitions. She'd put the world behind her more than a decade ago, when she gave up the editorship of *New England* magazine, and she liked it that way.

As they crossed the yard, a flight of three military jets screamed by, only a couple of hundred feet away, flying very low to the ground, black and sleek and predatory as mechanical sharks. The immense noise of their passing seemed to shake the bones of the world, and everybody looked up, Jennifer waving excitedly, the two workmen staring at them expressionlessly for a moment and then looking away. The jets roared away across the fields, still hugging the ground, afterburners blazing, hopped up over a distant ridge, and were gone. They left a shocked, ringing silence in their wake.

Alma Kingsley compressed her lips and kept walking. She didn't like military planes flying across her land, but there was little point in complaining at a time like this, when she'd only be ignored. They were practicing for war—practicing flying low to the ground to avoid radar, maybe, or perhaps doing mock strafing runs on her barn or the delivery truck. They'd get to try their hand at the real thing soon enough, the way things were going.

Jennifer was babbling happily to her about the planes, but she ignored her. The workmen nodded politely to her, not quite tugging the forelocks they didn't have anyway, and she nodded stiffly back. No one spoke. She gestured for them to unload the big crate, and tugged an inquisitive Jennifer safely out of the way while the lift lowered it ponderously to the ground, and the men grunted it onto a hand-truck.

Iago came bounding up from wherever it is that dogs go, barking furiously at the men, who ignored him. The huge black mongrel ran in frantic circles, from Mrs. Kingsley to the truck and back again, until she had to take him by the collar, swat him on the rump to get his attention, and—pointing firmly downward—order him to "Sit!" He obeyed unhappily, watching the unloading with a worried, disapproving expression.

She supervised the delivery, directing the workmen to take the crate—carefully!—into the old barn, which had once held a few cows and maybe a horse but now had been snugged up and served for storage space. They set the crate down and produced hammers and pry bars, and, with a shriek and squeal of protesting nails, the front came off, revealing her newest acquisition, a perfectly lovely piece that she had spotted on her last trip down south and which (not coincidentally) was the spitting image of a dresser her Aunt Dorothy had owned when she was a child, and which she had always, through all the intervening decades, lusted after. It was a triumph of will, her owning this piece, and the fulfillment of a girlhood oath, and she savored it as such.

"Now I'm going to want you to come back Tuesday, after the guests are gone, to place it in the house," she admonished the driver. Then, to her granddaughter, "No, dear, we do *not* root about on the dirty floor like small, ill-mannered swine." And again to the driver, "*Tuesday*, you understand, because I will not have you underfoot with company here. I'll need to decide which furniture to shift, as well."

The driver nodded slowly and, after a pause, said "Yep." There was a quiet censuriousness to his monosyllabic reply, as if it were an admonition to keep her words and reasons to herself. His assistant, chewing on something—either gum or "chaw," probably the latter—jaws agape and about as attractive-looking as a cow at its cud, was wielding his pry bar with abandon, splintering the crate's planks, threatening the absolutely priceless—and irreparable should it be damaged—patina of the wood. Until finally she could not bear to simply watch any longer.

"Hand me that pry," she snapped, and took it away from the gawking youth. There was a correct way to uncrate furniture; you sought out the joints and deftly, even daintily, applied leverage *there*, so that the whole thing popped open like a walnut shell under properly-applied nutcrackers. Brute force was totally unnecessary. And so she would have shown him, only her arthritis chose that instant to seize up, and her hands became about as useless as clubs, and wouldn't close all the way around the pry. She made a feeble pass or two at the wood, but it was hopeless—the tool slid in her hand, refusing to obey her. She couldn't even *hold* the damnable thing.

She looked up then, and in a timeless instant of glaring horror saw that the driver and his slack-jawed assistant were both staring her with pity in their eyes. Jennifer, thankfully, was too young to comprehend, and stood looking on with innocent curiosity.

For a moment, she trembled with humiliation, and then, furiously, she flung the pry bar to the floor. Tears flooding her eyes, she gasped, "Oh, *you* do it!" and fled.

Behind her, the men quietly, red-facedly, settled the dresser into a dry corner. When it was in place, the driver rubbed it down with his pocket bandana to remove any greasy fingerprints, and swiftly pulled each drawer out a half-inch and back in again, to make sure that none had seized up in transit. He was a conscientious man, and always gave his work this extra bit of care and attention. But he wasn't anxious to linger, and it was entirely understandable that, in his haste, he didn't fully re-close one drawer.

It was dying.

Hunger had driven it to the sharp edge of starvation. It was already seriously sick, or it would have abandoned the dresser immediately upon regaining the mental equilibrium that served it for consciousness. No matter how comfortably enclosed, how nurturing and psychologically sheltering a niche it was, the drawer had proven unsafe. But the long exposure to first one, then another truck's electrical systems had weakened and disoriented it, and filled it with anguished glimpses of something that *was once*, or perhaps *ought to be*, but was now no more. It trembled shiveringly where it was, until the hunger rose up like a wall and forced it out.

Moving as swiftly—as noiselessly—as shifting shadows, it scavenged the barn, a whirlwind of silent wrath, in search of the fire-of-life all living creatures carried within. Up in the rafters it took a clutch of bats, engulfing them before they could stir from their upside-down perches, and felt better for it, unsatisfied, but no longer so ravenous. Again and again, it scoured the barn, knowing that there should be more prey, and bewildered by its absence.

Frequently it passed by yellow cardboard boxes with grain spilling out from them and of course could not recognize them as bait stations filled with rat poison. But it quickly came to realize that the nourishment it must have would of necessity have to be found outside.

Cautiously, it edged out into the farmyard, slipping easily under the barn door.

And—fire! fear! pain! horror!—found its spatial sense overwhelmed by land that stretched far and away, featureless and with no place to hide, no sheltering masses or deep crannies into which to duck, nothing but rolling, exposed emptiness for hundreds of times its own length. Off to one side was the farmhouse, surrounded by evergreen shrubbery and a few ancient oaks, but it hardly spared that a glimpse in its panicked retreat back into the barn.

Terrified, cold, and hungry, it returned to the half-open drawer to huddle shivering like a wounded animal, its mind looping furiously over and over again and still not easing out the jagged static terror. It waited, because it had to, waited for something to change, for food to come to it, or else for the hunger and need to grow so great that it would be forced out into the openness and emptiness where it currently dared not go.

Mrs. Kingsley was tucking Jennifer into bed when the child's father came up the drive. She carefully bundled the little girl in, first between a pair of flannel sheets, then under a thin electric blanket, and finally—to top it all off—pulling a double-wedding band quilt over all. The quilt was one her mother had made, in point of fact, and Alma Kingsley hoped to live long enough to pass it on to her granddaughter, when the child came of marrying age.

"It's snowing outside," Jennifer said as her grandmother smoothed down the quilt. And then, in that flat, absolutely sincere way children have of presenting their fantasies, she said, "And I saw a Monster from my window."

It was then, in a kind of ironic counterpoint, that the El Dorado purred up the long drive. Jennifer sat up immediately. "Is that Daddy, Gamma?"

Mrs. Kingsley smoothed the child down on the pillow, then turned to look out the window. A few small, bitter flakes of snow were falling from the black sky. They fell fast, a precursor of more to come. The El Dorado pulled off the drive, which was unnecessary, and onto the house's front yard, which was worse. It was winter and the grass was dead, but, still, that kind of treatment *hurt* a lawn.

"Yes, it's your father," she said. The car's front door opened and the man himself spilled drunkenly out. "No, don't get up. I am certain that your father would rather find you tucked angelically into bed than running about caterwauling like a wild heathen Indian. Parents are peculiar in that respect."

Jenny giggled appreciatively, if somewhat sleepily. Outside, the El Dorado's *other* front door swung open.

Alma Kingsley slipped out of the room, snapping off the light. "I'll leave the door open a crack," she said. "Now you just lie there with your eyes closed, so when your father comes in to kiss you good-night, you can open them and surprise him. Won't that be fun?"

The child nodded slowly, then twisted a bit to dig her cheek into the pillows.

"Sweet dreams," Mrs. Kingsley murmured.

She went downstairs to confront the father.

Iago came padding out from the kitchen as she threw a jacket over her thin shoulders against the terrible cold outside. He stood by her side, anxious with doggish worries of his own, as she flung the front door open. Desmond stood on the stoop, one arm flung around his roadhouse floozy's neck, grappling vaguely for her breasts, and the other digging through his pockets—with equal incompetence—in search of the door key. He gaped up stupidly at her.

"How *dare* you?" she whispered, so as not to wake the child. "Your own daughter is in this house!" The snow was falling more thickly now, slanting down fast and tightly together, filling the air. The air was so full of snowflakes you could choke on them. If you listened carefully, you could hear them hit, it was so quiet. A whispery, slithery sound.

Desmond released the woman. He looked directly into Alma Kingsley's eyes, possibly the first time he had done so since arriving at Maple Hill Farm. "You sanctimonious old bag," he said quietly, also unwilling to disturb the child. "Stephanie died over a year ago. And you know something? A year is a long time to go without. You'd know that yourself, if you could remember that far back . . ."

The floozy—her hair was that hideous aniline red that positively shrieked its artificiality—hung back, embarrassed. Or maybe not; she gaped up at them from the car, as vacant-faced as a cow. Mrs. Kingsley didn't spare her a second glance.

"I will not tolerate having the morals of a child corrupted within my house!" She moved to slam the door shut in his face.

The father caught the door with one hand, and effortlessly held it open. He was a short, heavy man, with a dirty little fringe of beard. About as far from the Kingsley type as you could get, but a strong creature nevertheless. For an instant, she thought he was going to actually strike her, could almost feel the pain, the old bones cracking under porcelain skin . . . But he didn't. He just grinned, a mean, drunken grin. "I don't *like* bringing Jenny up here twice a year," he said. "I only did it for Stephanie's sake, when she was alive, and now for Jenny. She likes being on your farm. But I'll tell you this—either you let us in or this is the fucking *last* time you'll ever see the child again."

She stood motionless in the doorway, losing heat to the out-of-doors while Desmond leered up at her. The snow was gathering already, a light powder-sugar frosting on the bare and frozen ground. The wind was already sweeping it to and fro. The air was cold on her face and it seemed to her that so long as she didn't move, she could hold back the future, keep from ever *having* to move, keep from slipping into a situation where she had lost control, where she was defeated before she even began.

At her heel, the dog whined plaintively. "Hush, Iago," she said automatically.

She moved aside.

In the morning, she set out four plates for breakfast—the good Spode china, too, as pointed a bit of formality as it was possible to give a guest. She considered turning on the big plug-in radio on the kitchen counter, all the company she had most mornings as she cooked a solitary breakfast for herself, but there was a delicious quiet and serenity out here this morning, the snow now falling heavily but without sound close outside the window, like a slow fall of feathers, muting the daylight and filling it with shifting highlights, so that it was like being all alone in a bubble on the bottom of the sea. She hated to shatter that peacefulness with noise before it needed to be shattered; Desmond would be down and rattling the china with his booming, cheaply genial voice soon enough.

Besides, there wouldn't be much worth listening to on the radio anyway. Sometimes she could pull in WGBH from Boston in the mornings and listen to chamber music or string quartets, but for months now there'd been too much static from all the sunspot activity to tune it in clearly, and all she'd been able to get for the last few days were somberly hysterical talk-radio stations yattering on about the current international crisis, lines being drawn in the sand, frantic diplomatic efforts, troops massing at borders, military alerts, security advisories, leaves being canceled, aircraft carriers on the move, and so on—and she was sick to the teeth of that. All the familiar stuff, saber-rattling, jingoism, the vitriolic outpourings of suddenly acceptable racism toward people we were supposed to *like* only a few months before. Primate Aggressive Displays, chimps hooting at each other and beating their breasts until they had worked themselves up into enough of a lather to attack. It seemed like she'd been hearing this stuff all her long life, one conflict after another, one enemy after another, and she was sick of it. Let them have their war and leave her alone, here in her own kitchen. She didn't have to listen to them *talk* about it!

"Hi, Gamma!" It was Jennifer, down first, chirpy-happy as usual, practically bouncing with enthusiasm. Remember when you had that much energy? Mrs. Kingsley thought wryly. Remember when you had a *fourth* of it? She let Jennifer help by setting out the silverware and napkins, while she fried up eggs and sausages and piles of French toast, all in an iron skillet with lots of Crisco.

The second one up was her son-in-law's roadhouse pick-up. She slumped down on a chair, eyes bleary under smeared makeup. Her hair was done in that kind of razor-cut where you can never tell if it's brushed or not. "Morning," she mumbled. She picked up a fork and stared at it, turning it over and over in her hand, as if she'd never seen Grand Baroque silver before in her life, and were searching for a clue to its purpose.

Sliding breakfast in front of her, Mrs. Kingsley was struck by the horrible realization that this young chippie was somebody's daughter, and probably came down to the breakfast table in exactly the same sullen way every morning, with grumbled greeting and averted eyes. Maybe she hadn't even noticed yet that she hadn't made it home the night before.

"It snowed *two feet* last night," the child announced. "Gamma says maybe it'll snow all day today, right Gamma?" Then, when Gamma didn't reply, "My name's Jennifer, what's yours?"

The woman stared at Jennifer, as if the girl had been suddenly and without warning plopped down out of the sky before her. "Candy," she said at last.

The child's father chose that moment to make his appearance. He lifted Jennifer out of her chair, hugged her, and held her up in the air while she squealed. Then he peered out the window. "Still coming down, eh?" He whistled. "Look at that drift over by the barn! Jesus!"

Desmond was wearing jeans and a green football jersey with white sleeves and a double-zero numeral on the back. Bits of lint were stuck in his beard; it would never have occurred to him to brush it before breakfast. He took a sip from the coffee cup that had been awaiting him for the past ten minutes, ever since she'd heard himself clumping about overhead, and made a face. "Could you warm this thing up for me?"

Wordlessly, she took the cup from him, put it into the microwave, and switched the device on.

"Hey, wait a minute!" Candy looked up suddenly. "How deep did you say it was out there?" She went to the window and pushed the curtain aside. "Oh, no!" she groaned. "How am I going to get home through all that?"

"The plows will be by when the snow stops," Mrs. Kingsley said. "But this isn't a primary route, and while it's falling they're going to keep most of their machines out on the Interstate."

"My mom is going to have a *cow*! Where's the telephone?"

"In the hallway," Desmond said, and she hurried off without even pausing to ask permission.

A motion in the corner of her eye caught Alma Kingsley's attention then, and she suddenly remembered the coffee in the microwave. Brown liquid was bulging ominously over the cup's lip. Hurriedly she cut off the device, and it subsided. The cup was nice and warm; half the flavor was boiled out, but no need to mention *that*. She set it down in front of Desmond.

The young woman returned, throwing herself down into the chair with a kind of heavy despair. "I can't get through. There's this static and a kind of whooping noise, and nothing goes through."

"More than likely something wrong at the switching facilities," Mrs. Kingsley said. "The phone service here's never been much to brag about."

Candy worried a pack of cigarettes and a disposable lighter out of her disco bag and accusingly said, "Well, my mother is going to have a cow."

Mrs. Kingsley personally thought that the girl's mother's outrage was a day late and a dollar short, but she kept her opinion to herself. Aloud, she said, "No, my dear, I am afraid that I do not allow smoking at the breakfast table."

Hah?" Candy looked down stupidly, lit the cigarette, and then hastily removed it from her mouth. "Oh—yeah, sure." She made as if to stub out the cigarette on her plate. Mrs. Kingsley hastily reached into the cupboards for an ashtray.

"Here." She thrust it at the young woman. It was ironic, the tyranny that smokers exercised over their betters. She herself had never picked up the disgusting habit, and yet had of necessity, over the years, acquired any number of ashtrays to accommodate friends and guests. "You can smoke in the hallway," she said. "Though it would be *nice* if you were to go outside when—"

But an angry glance from Desmond told her that she had gone too far. "Well, that would be unreasonable, of course."

"Damn straight it would," Desmond muttered. He was at the kitchen radio now, fiddling with it. It emitted an earsplitting, see-sawing howl of static, like a dying banshee. Wincing, he turned the knob from one end of the dial to the other, finding no stations, then grimaced and turned the radio off. He started to say "Shit!", cast a quick look at his daughter, thought better of it, and settled for an exasperated "Damn!" He came back to the table. "I'd hoped to catch the news."

"War, and portents of war," Mrs. Kingsley said sourly.

Desmond grinned offensively at her. "Hey, sounds good to *me*!" he said. "That means I don't have to worry about being out of work, right?" He knew that she disapproved of his work for military contractors—"war work" she'd called it bitterly once, in a monumental argument a few months after Stephanie's death, correcting his euphemistic "defense work"—and he loved to bait her about it.

"There's a television in the living room," she said stiffly. "We get CNN even out here in the boondocks. Just keep the volume down. I don't care to hear it."

He shook his head. "You'd think you'd want to know what's going on. There's a *crisis* underway! Don't you care what happens?"

Mrs. Kingsley hesitated, and glanced toward Jennifer, but she and the roadhouse floozie were busy playing dolls with each other with the salt and pepper shakers; obviously Jennifer had found a companion on her own level of emotional development. "I don't care what happens anymore," she said, keeping her voice pitched low. "Let them have their war. Let them all kill each other. Unless they drop an H-bomb on Montpelier, I don't intend to take any notice of it."

Desmond made a disgusted face. "You've got your head in the sand!

You think the real world is going to go away just because you don't like it? You have to deal with things as they *are*. *Do* something about them! If there weren't so many people who think like you, maybe Stephanie would still be alive."

They glared at each other, locking gazes. He'd stepped over the line, though, and he knew it, for, after a moment, he had the grace to look faintly embarrassed. Her gaze, though, was unflinching and unforgiving.

At that moment, opportunely, there was a scratching at the door, and she had to go let the dog back in.

"O base Iago! O inhuman dog!" she declaimed as the mutt bounded in. Candy stared at her uncomprehendingly. The little chit had probably never even heard of Shakespeare.

Iago was jumping up on her, panting and enthusiastically trying to wag his entire body. She looked deliberately at Desmond. "Let slip the dogs of War, eh?" she said, and smiled sweetly. She knew *he'd* heard of Shakespeare.

It was weakening. Perhaps it held enough reserves for another day or so, if it husbanded its resources. But that way lay oblivion and slow death; to survive it needed to strike out, to forage away from the comforting shelter of the barn, out into the flat, horribly open countryside.

It was hesitating by the door when the sound of trudging footsteps approached, heading straight for it.

Jerking back as if struck, it rose up, mantle stiffening, ready to attack. Then caution took over, and it retreated swiftly to the shadows, hunkering down into the darkest corner, every sense on edge, waiting, observing.

The door rattled, then flew open. Two sophonts stepped into the barn, accompanied by a wild skirl of snowflakes. They slammed the door shut noisily, and stamped their boots clear of snow.

It listened carefully to words it could not comprehend.

"I don't think your mother-in-law likes me."

"Don't take it personally. The old bat doesn't like anyone."

Stealthily, slowly, it moved. Keeping to the shadows and edges, it made its way to a wide support beam beyond the direct perception of the sophonts. Swiftly, it flowed up the beam's far side, up to the loft, and then to the rafters, just below the ridgepole. Given the choice, it was always best to strike from above.

It moved cautiously, always conscious of the gentle tickle of the fire-of-life below.

The shorter of the two produced fire. Smoke snarled through the cold air. It could not smell, of course, but it sensed the smoke as a flicker of ionized charges.

"Whew—I really needed that!" the shorter one said. She sucked in the ions again, letting them damp down within her lungs. "Here, have a toke."

The taller one made a disgusted noise. "Is that what we came out here for? To get stoned?"

Silently it moved among the rafters, flowing from brace to joist, and across the collar beams, until it was in position, directly above its prey. It rested invisibly over them, and prepared to strike.

The shorter one laughed. "What did you expect? I hope you didn't think I was going to screw you out in *this* weather!"

But they were both sophonts and sophonts were dangerous. It would have to take both of them to be safe, and it wasn't at all certain it could do that. Its reserves of strength were perilously low.

"I thought you had something you wanted to tell me. Let's go back inside, okay? It's too cold to stand out here smoking that shit."

"Damnit, I'm going to *need* this to get me through the afternoon. Did you see the way she was eyeing me at lunch?"

"Yeah, well, I've got a daughter back there in the house and I'd like to preserve a few of her illusions about her old man for a while longer, okay? So if you'll excuse me, I don't see any reason why I should hang around out here in the cold."

And then, incredibly, there was only one! The other sophont slammed out through the door, and his footsteps faded away rapidly in the falling snow.

It gathered itself together to strike. The distance was not great, and it was starting from an ideal position. With effort, it suppressed a tremble of excitement in its stiffening mantle.

The woman below huddled disconsolately in her parka. She sucked in a lungful of ions, and held them.

It struck.

"Gamma, where's Candy?"

The parlor was very quiet without the television or radio on—Alma Kingsley had tried them both (with Desmond coming right behind her and trying them again, as if she didn't know how to turn a television set on properly), and they wouldn't work right; sunspots or something—they had been very bad all this year, with the Northern Lights stronger and more frequent than she'd ever known them to be in all the years since she'd retired from the magazine—had scrambled all incoming signals. The phone still wasn't working either, and Desmond had gotten quite agitated—uselessly—about not being able to get in touch with the office. The rest of the morning had, to say the least, been tense. Desmond had finally retreated into his work, getting lost in that annoying way that he had, going so deep into it that nobody, not even Jennifer, not even Stephanie when she'd been alive, could reach him.

She put down her copy of *Paris Match*, and said, "I don't know, child. Somewhere in the house, I should imagine. Why don't you ask your father?"

"She's not in the house," the child insisted. "I wanted her to play Barbie-doll with me, and I looked everywhere."

Desmond looked up from a briefcase full of flow charts and printouts and other tools of his arcane trade. "Hmmm?" he said. And when the problem was explained to him, "She ought to be back from the barn by now." With a sigh, he switched off his calculator, set down his ballpoint pen, and stood. "Now where did I leave my coat?"

Iago bounded up eagerly when Desmond opened the door, and insisted on following him out into the snow. The door slammed, and Iago's excited barking faded as they headed toward the old barn.

Five minutes later, Desmond returned, carrying Candy's body.

Mrs. Kingsley saw him coming from the kitchen window and—with a smothered exclamation of horror—hurried to throw open the door for him. Together they hurried into the parlor and laid Candy down on a couch.

It was possible now to assess the damage that had been done the woman. Her features were unnaturally sunken, the cheeks collapsed in on themselves, drawing the lips back from the teeth, and her stomach was literally concave, looking like someone had punched it in with his fist. An ugly purple flush was still spreading over her face as hundreds of ruptured capillaries lost blood.

"She was just lying there!" Desmond said helplessly. "Like she'd had a heart attack or something. Is the phone still out? We need a doctor. Maybe I can . . . I could hike out to the road and flag down a car."

Alma Kingsley put a finger under the girl's nostrils. She touched her wrists, forehead, chest. She pressed down a fingernail, looked at the color.

"Desmond," she said, "it's too late."

She straightened, and her son-in-law did likewise, both involuntarily drawing away from the body, as if by so doing they could distance themselves from death. When she glanced away, Mrs. Kingsley saw that Jennifer was standing in the middle of the parlor rug, eyes wide and calm, staring at the corpse.

"Daddy," she said, "is Candy dead?"

Her father got a sick expression on his face, as if he'd been called upon to explain sex and reproduction to the child *right now*, with no blushing and no preparation. But he answered, voice flat and superficially composed, "Yes."

"Like on TV?"

Alma Kingsley regained control then, and gathered the two up. With a push here, a nudge there, she shooed father and daughter out of the parlor and into the kitchen. At her command, Iago followed. Then she closed the door.

To survive, it had to get into the farmhouse. It knew that now, with a kind of animal cunning that came before reason and intellect. There were sophonts within, and it was practically suicidal to attack a sophont within its own lair. But they were few in number, and they were isolated from their own kind. And while they were danger, they were *also* nourishment.

It hesitated at the doorway of the shed, baffled by the snow that had already drifted above the middle hinges. Then it flowed up the wall, climbing to the crack at the top of the doorway, and eased through. Halfway out it halted, stunned by how the world had been transformed. The falling snow formed complex, shifting patterns that disappeared the instant it got a fix on them. It was as if the world had been shredded and divided into component atoms, then instantly rearranged, again and again, a thousand times a second. All anew, it was struck by the sheer alienness of this world, where nothing was certain, where everything shifted and moved and changed. It wavered, flowed outward, flinched back again. Individual flakes of snow touched its surface, did not melt, slid off without sticking.

Had anyone been watching from the house, they would have seen it then, carelessly, dangerously exposed. But occupied as they were with their own troubles, no one was looking.

It advanced out onto the snow then, all in a rush, sudden and brave. Midway between barn and house, it halted. Nothing happened. It found it could partially filter out the flakes falling, though they disoriented and bewildered it still. Purposefully it set out for the farmhouse, a solid mass of potential shelter, unchanging, shot through with electrical fires and harboring at its heart the precious rumor of fire-of-life.

But the task it had set for itself was not an easy one; the house had been winterized with typical Yankee thoroughness. Caulk had been applied around every window and door frame, and a long, even bead had been drawn at the juncture where clapboarding met foundation. Cracks in the masonry had been plastered over, and every window was double-paned and covered over with storm windows, every door had weatherstripping.

It circled the house without finding entrance. The building was tight, invulnerable to it. There might be entrances up above—experience said it was likely to find chimney pots and furnace exhausts, gable vents, even the occasional hatchway—but it dared not climb the house side, up into the swirling, shifting snow, where matter and sky intermingled. It could not have been sure of maintaining its orientation, of knowing where the house left off and the air began. It was madness to even consider it.

Time and again it lashed silently around the house, skimming the surface of the snow, leaving behind it the very thinnest layer of ice, a trail that disappeared almost instantaneously under the new falling snow. It was perilously exposed, and this added to its confusion and desperation, to its determination to try *anything*, no matter how rash or foolhardy, that might help it to survive.

Even after Desmond had finally bowed to the inevitable and taken Candy's corpse out to the El Dorado, where it could await the snowplows and the doctor and the coroner in the preserving cold, there was an eerie pall cast over the house. Jennifer had been put to bed early, and the adults had retired to the kitchen, to try to talk.

But there was nothing to say. There was no way Candy could have died, and speculation would not explain the inexplicable—only the autopsy could do that. And she was a stranger, so there could be no reminiscences about her, none that Alma Kingsley would care to have Desmond share, anyway. So, in the end, they simply fell silent. Mrs. Kingsley began going through her cookbooks, and Desmond fell to punching listlessly on the keys of his calculator.

"What is wrong with that dog?" Alma Kingsley grumbled in exasperation. Iago was pacing the kitchen floor, infinitely restless, his claws going click-click-click on the linoleum. Now he was at the door again, pushing at the crack between door and sill with his nose, digging at it hopelessly with his claws, scratching and whining.

"Sounds like he wants to be let out," Desmond said without looking up.

"Well, maybe I should," she said at last. Throwing a wrap over herself, she took hold of Iago's collar, and led him to the door. Her intent was to shove his nose outside and give him a whiff of the cold, and then draw him back in again. That ought to have settled his restlessness. But when the door opened, he strained forward, barking furiously, even anxiously, and she saw something outlined on the snow in the rectangle of light cast by the open door. She squinted and said, "Desmond, come here. Take a look at this."

The dog's feet scrabbled wildly on the floor, but her grip was firm. "Look at what?" Desmond said. He ambled up, calculator in hand, and peered over her shoulder. "That's just a patch of shadow."

"There never was a patch of shadow shaped like that there *before*," Mrs. Kingsley said dubiously. A momentary twinge of arthritis hit her then, and her hold on Iago's collar loosened.

All hell broke loose.

It lay watching, not knowing that it did not blend in against the snow, assuming that the sophonts' awareness would be as dazzled by the downfalling flakes as was his own.

It had flattened against the snow's surface the instant that the door opened with a great outrushing of warmth. The shifts of ionization and static charges in the air made the doorway a shimmering beacon, bright and inviting, and only the faint, almost undetectable flickers of fire-of-life within that wash of liquid warmth kept it from leaping forward at that very instant. Wary, it crouched, waiting.

Then the dog came flying through the air to attack it.

The beast was large and fierce, plowing through and scattering snow, howling and barking as it came. Terrified, the creature fled, but—cunning, desperate—it fled straight for the door, risking everything on a frontal attack, a savage, killing assault on whatever might lie in its path.

In the doorway, the black beast ravening and almost upon it, its perception cleared, and it found that only two enemies stood between it and shelter. The first fell aside, shrinking back against the wall as it charged forward, and it could ignore her, making for the second who was just beyond her, and who was bigger, with more fire-of-life in him.

Berserk, it sprang at the man, who stumbled back, involuntarily flinging up a hand to fend it off. There was an object in that hand, a glittering complex of resistance paths that held a shimmering, shifting structure of energies, a vastly simplified and purified version of what lay within living beings.

A concept came searing up from the shuttered and forbidden parts of its mind, breaking through the pain: WEAPON! WEAPON! WEAPON! and it turned in midair, reshaping its structure and seizing hold of a wall so that it slammed aside and away from the thing. The beast leaped up after it, and for an instant almost had it, and then it fled down the hall and away.

In terror and wild confusion it was driven through several rooms and up a stairway. It took the first opening off of the hall it could find, and discovered itself in a cul-de-sac, the air all abuzz with jittery white energy, and dominated by a large, painful glow in its center.

The beast halted, hackles rising. It was cornered, and the beast knew it.

"What was *that*?" Desmond gasped.

Alma Kingsley shook her head. Her breath was still short, her face felt pallid with shock, and she discovered that she was clutching at her heart. Disdainful of her own weakness, she forced the hand down. Then, looking up at where Iago's frantic baying had come to an abrupt stop, she felt seized with terror and cried, "Jennifer!"

Desmond easily outdistanced her, but she arrived in the guest bedroom practically on his heels. To her unutterable relief, the child was unharmed, sitting up sleepily in her bed and looking at the frantic Iago with dull, unfocused interest. Her father swept her up in a hug, and backed away, into the hallway. Oddly enough, Alma Kingsley felt a pang of jealousy.

Iago had cornered the creature.

Whatever it was—and in the gloom it was all but invisible—it crouched in the shadows to the far side of the four-poster, alert and quivering, frightened and dangerous. It reared up and slowly dipped down as Iago darted forward, then back, then forward again, growling and making little feinting attacks. The combination of quick and mazy movements made the fight look like a confrontation between cobra and mongoose.

The creature was trapped in the aisle between bed and wall. To its rear was a closet, its door open on a thick-packed rank of summer dresses in their plastic dry-cleaning bags. Jennifer's jumper hung by itself on a hook on the back of the door.

Mrs. Kingsley was just reaching—belatedly, she realized—for the light switch when Iago attacked. Snapping and foaming, he charged.

The two went tumbling, one over the other. Shaking his head fiercely, Iago backed out of the narrow way, dragging the creature out between his jaws, struggling.

Iago snarled savagely as he tore at the creature, and then there was an ozone crackle in the air and he yelped, a high, heartbreaking cry. His stiffening body crashed over sideways, onto the floor, and did not move.

The creature disentangled itself instantly, feinted at Desmond, then turned again and—going carefully around rather than over the bed—rushed into the closet.

There was an access panel in the back of the closet. It had been installed early in the century, when the upstairs water closet was retrofitted, and opened into the wall and a few dusty pipes. The panel was ajar slightly, leaning loosely rather than snugly. Perhaps the child had been playing with it, looking for a secret passageway, or perhaps it had been left partly open for years or even decades without anyone ever bothering to get around to straightening it.

The creature squeezed through the crack, quick and impossibly fluid, and disappeared into the wall.

Slowly, awkwardly, Mrs. Kingsley squatted down, knees almost touching the floor. She laid a hand on her dog's head. He was dead. "Oh, Iago," she said. "My little *bête noire*."

She began to cry.

The house was a maze of electric circuits and appliances. They dizzied and blinded it, dazzling and baffling its senses. The sophonts were somewhere within this maze, and it did not even know how many they were. It only knew that they had not followed it, and thus presumably *could* not. But the sophonts' lair was a dangerous environment, naturally hostile to it, and it fled.

It fled deep, sinking downward by instinct, tracing a tortuous way between walls and floors, sometimes following water pipes, and always avoiding electrical wires. Carefully, fearfully, it threaded its way along a twisty path that led downward, ever downward.

Finally it emerged into warm, cavernous darkness, and knew that it had found refuge.

Iago was dead, but Jennifer was alive; there was comfort in that. The faithful old family retainer had given up his life in defense of home and child, and that was somehow fitting. It was the way things ought to be. His corpse was outside the kitchen door now, packed in snow because the frozen earth made burial impossible, but Alma Kingsley vowed that her great-grandchildren would know his name.

The snow had finally stopped, and the night was clear, and bitterly cold, the stars burning in it like chips of ice. The great glowing, shimmering, billowing curtains of the Northern Lights were out, shifting restlessly back and forth on the horizon, brighter than she had ever seen them, so bright that it almost seemed that she could burn her hand on them, if she held it out to the sky.

It had been quite a storm. It must have dumped at least four feet of snow on the region all told, snowing through the night and through the day and through most of the night again, and the driveway beyond the lee of the house was buried under huge drifts; you couldn't even see the highway at its end. So much for her first thought, which was to bundle them all into Desmond's car and make a run for it, abandoning the house to the creature until they could come back later with help. To get the hell *out* of here!

But with all that snow, nobody was going anywhere, life-or-death emergency or not, until the snowplow came by in the morning. It was physically impossible. And if they locked themselves in the car as a refuge—her second thought—they'd freeze to death before daybreak. And besides, who was to say that it couldn't get into the car after them, the way it seemed to be able to squeeze itself through the smallest of cracks?

"Did you notice that it was afraid of my pocket calculator?" Desmond asked. He was pacing the length of the kitchen, back and forth, from the pantry door to the wooden cot they had set up for Jennifer by the refrigerator. "And it wouldn't touch the electric blanket either."

"Why is that?" Mrs. Kingsley asked without interest. Her granddaughter was sleeping like an angel, and her heart pounded with fear for the child. She had to fight down the impulse to run a rough old hand over hair so fine it could break your heart.

"I don't know, but did you see the way it squeezed into the wall? Like it was boneless, or something more than boneless. I'll bet it doesn't mass much of anything at all!"

He was getting excited now. Alma Kingsley simply tuned out his voice and let him rant on. Stephanie had always said that problem-solving was his *forte*, what he was most at home with. Given a logic problem—a crossword puzzle or a program that had crashed—and some shred of clue, his intuition would worry it to death or solution. To Alma Kingsley's way of thinking, this was a good argument that problem-solving logic was not one of the civilized skills.

It was only when he moved her brand new toaster-oven to the kitchen table and began disassembling it, that she was finally moved to object. "Just what the hell do you think you're doing?" she demanded.

"I'm going to wrap a resistance coil," he said, absorbed in his chore and talking so fast his words ran together. "Look, this thing is obviously sensitive to electromagnetic radiation, right? Now, assuming its shape is maintained through bound charges, then it would move by shifting electrical potential within itself. That would explain how it moves so fluidly. So—"

"Desmond," she said, her patience wearing thin, "just what are you trying to do?"

He looked up from his work, puzzled. "I'm building a signal-interrupter. Didn't I make myself clear?" Without waiting for a response, he bent back down over the table, uncoiling wires from the heating elements.

She closed her eyes, calmed herself. "Just what will this signal-interrupter do when it's built?"

"Well, basically—" He broke something out of the toaster-oven, glanced at it, threw it aside. "Basically, it ought to render this creature totally immobile anywhere within—oh, let's say a fifteen-twenty foot radius. More, probably, but that much at least."

For the first time in her life, Alma Kingsley wondered if God might not have had reasons for creating Desmond. "You can do this?" she asked anxiously. "Tonight?"

He favored her with a vulgar, lopsided grin. "Old hoss," he said, "give me half an hour, and we have got it dicked!"

With no warning, all the lights went out at once, plunging them into complete darkness.

"Oh shit," Desmond said.

Calmly, because she'd been through blackouts before, Mrs. Kingsley felt twisted the knobs on the gas range. One by one the burners came on, filling the room with an eerie, flickering light.

By sheer bad luck, the furnace was off at the instant the power went. It was a gas furnace, but it operated off of a solid state programmable electric thermostat, and wouldn't go back on again until the thermostat told it to. But it wasn't really crucial; she lit the oven, leaving the door open for heat.

After some clumsy, fearful rummaging through the dark pantry, she unearthed a hurricane lamp. Its chimney had gulls painted on the side, and the transparent reservoir was filled with blue scented soil. Still, when she set it on the kitchen table, the light it shed was warm and friendly, and she could turn off the range.

Desmond, meanwhile, had found the utility flashlight in its recharger bracket by the basement door. He stood in the middle of the pantry, flicked it on and off, and then said, "What does this house have—fuses or circuit breakers?"

Alma Kingsley stared at the man in disbelief. His face was dark with shadow, his eyes lost in blackness. He was a silhouette creature, almost all outline and no substance, one hand on the doorknob of the cellar door. "Desmond, this isn't the city. A power line is down. Going into the cellar and flicking a switch is not going to restore the electricity."

She didn't have to be able to see the face to know the smug, superior smile that crossed it now; she could hear it in his voice. "Let's not get all worked up, now. *Maybe* a line is down. But the more likely reason is that a power transient has kicked out the main circuit breaker. There's no reason for us to spend a night in the cold and dark when just a moment's effort can restore the power." He opened the door.

She peered past him, down into the cellar—it was a perfect, lightless black. Vague colors swam before her, visual hallucinations brought up by the absolute lack of light. The blackness crawled with menace. The only sound anywhere was the hissing of the gas oven.

Involuntarily, she clutched his arm. "For God's sake, Desmond, you don't know what's down there!"

Desmond turned the flashlight on her face. She stood blinking as he studied her. "Don't be such a wuss," he said. "Whatever that thing is, we know that it's somewhere *above* us, not below."

He shook free of her grip and moved to the top of the cellar steps, hesitated for a moment, looking down. "Desmond," she said, so frightened that she found herself actually pleading, "this is *unwise.* You're acting like a character in a monster movie! Everybody in the theater would be yelling 'Don't go down there!' by this point. Stay up here with us. We need you here." It galled her to speak the words, words she'd never imagined she'd hear herself say—but it was true.

Desmond turned his head to look back at her, and grimaced. "Look," he said, a defensive note creeping into his voice, "this thing *kills* people, and it's on the loose. The only defense we have against it uses electricity. Either I go down there and reset the breakers, or we sit up here in the dark and wait to die." After a second of silence, he grinned at her, the arrogance, the boundless self-confidence and self-assurance she'd always found so odious in the man already returning to his face after a fleeting moment of uncertainty. "Beside, I'll be quick . . . and I'll be careful!"

He was wrong, horribly wrong, but she didn't have the arguments to confute him with, only a horrid assurance that he was making a stupid move. Desmond shone the flash down the stairs.

A thin line of worn wooden treads led downward into darkness, a trace of light glimmering on the walls to either side. When Desmond raised the flash slightly, a pale circle formed on the whitewashed rock wall just beyond the landing. "Damn," he muttered. "I don't suppose the circuit box is on the near wall?"

"No, it's on the wall opposite, at the front of the house."

Abruptly, Desmond turned and walked back into the kitchen. For a giddy moment, Mrs. Kingsley thought he had come to his senses. But he only paused by his daughter and gently placed something on the cot beside her sleeping head. The calculator. He switched it on, then turned back toward the cellar.

"For the love of Christ, Desmond!"

But, ignoring her completely, he stepped down onto the top stair. It groaned under his weight. Slowly he descended, clutching the loose railing with his free hand. The light danced and bobbed on the basement wall, growing brighter as he approached, then darting to the side and disappearing as he turned away. Briefly, there was the faintest shimmer of reflected light, and then nothing.

The air from below was warm, like an animal's breath on her face. Staring down into the liquid blackness, Mrs. Kingsley felt her every nerve on end. She strained to hear, to track her son-in-law's progress below by sound alone. But the dirt floor muffled his footsteps, and damped down the noise he made.

"Desmond?" she said softly. He did not answer. Her own breath sounded loud to her; she could make out nothing above it. It was uncanny how silent the cellar was. It was as if the darkness were a gigantic beast that moved on soft paws to swallow up the least sound.

Then Desmond stumbled into a pile of cardboard boxes filled with old paint and coffee cans that she had put away years ago against some possible future need. A jar fell to the floor. He kicked it angrily, and it skittered and skipped away to shatter against the wall. "Fuck."

Mrs. Kingsley leaned down into the stairway. The darkness was so deep, so absolute, it seemed to want to suck her down into it. It welled up dizzyingly about her, and she had to put out a hand to steady herself against the jamb.

Silence again. Then—

"Found it!" Desmond shouted. He sounded relieved; one presumed the darkness had finally gotten to him. There were faint noises as he poked about. "Jeez, this is an old system. Look at the rust on it! I'll bet you ten to one I—"

He gasped.

The flashlight clattered noisily to the ground. For an instant there was silence, complete and profound. Then a kind of throbbing electrical hum rose to fill the darkness. Over the throbbing came other sounds, choking and thrashing sounds, as if Desmond were having a seizure. The noise went on and on.

And then it stopped.

The silence seemed to echo, like the air just after a great bell has been stilled. Fearfully, Alma Kingsley called down, "Desmond? Desmond, are you all right?" She waited, and heard nothing. "Desmond?"

A faint slithering noise whispered up from below. It wasn't quite like anything she had ever heard before, and yet it definitely came from a living creature. It was coming from the far side of the cellar, and it was headed right for the stairway.

Frantically, she slammed the door shut, and backed away, into the warmth and light of the kitchen. For an instant's frozen horror, she was convinced it would follow her. But it did not.

"Gamma?"

Jennifer was sitting up in bed, sleepily rubbing one eye. It was clear that the door slamming had wakened her. "Gamma," she said. "Where's Daddy?"

It had fled as far as it could, as deep as it was possible to go in this labyrinthine structure, and had thought itself safe. It badly needed to think things through, as a dozen conflicting emotions chased themselves through its neural fabric, and at that point wanted only solitude, darkness, stillness, the security of enclosure. But then, terrifyingly, one of the sophonts had come *after* it, tracking it down, coming relentlessly closer and closer and closer, a buzzing electrical device that emitted a spray of photons—a weapon?—in one hand. It had backed away in terror, retreating as the man came on toward it step by step, finally stopping only when it backed up against a solid wall and there was no place left to go without turning and exposing its back to a potentially fatal attack.

Still the man came implacably on, ever closer, ponderous steps shaking the floor like thunder, looming huge and heavy and menacing, only a few body-lengths away now. At last, still moving forward, the sophont turned the stream of photons from its device/weapon directly *on* it . . .

Trapped, terrified, knowing that it might only have seconds of life left in which to act, it struck. The sophont jerked and thrashed and flailed, the electrical device flying from its hand to shatter against the floor and go out.

It had tried its best to avoid this confrontation, had not wanted to kill again so soon, had wanted to think about the whole situation, but it had been given no choice.

None of those considerations kept it from feeding as fully as it could, of course, now that it *had* killed. The sophont was big and vigorous, in the prime of its cycle of existence, and was full of the fire-of-life.

When it had finished with him, it felt refreshed and somewhat calmer . . . although, almost immediately, a new unease began to grow within it. This was a bad situation, trapped inside a structure like this with a band of sophonts, all alerted to its presence. It was a dangerous situation, one in which it could easily be trapped or attacked—and there was something *else* about the situation that dimly troubled it, something other than the danger, something that generated another kind of unease. It shouldn't be hunting sophonts, it knew that somehow, not unless it had no other choice. It should find other, easier, less dangerous prey, like the rats and squirrels and birds it'd found in the park. To find nonsophont prey instead would be far less dangerous, and it would also be, it would *also* be . . . something. Something it no longer had the concept for, but which it vaguely knew was desirable.

Yes, it should leave here, get out of this situation altogether.

So it hunted through the structure until it found access to a metal pipe that it followed up through the walls and out onto the roof, out into the chill outer air . . . But there were the Northern Lights, blazing above it, filling the sky, curtains of dancing, shimmering radiation, seemingly only a few feet above its head, dazzling it, making it squirm and caper and thrash, coil and uncoil and coil, scribing odd cabalistic patterns in the snow . . . until, on the verge of total madness, it retreated back into the pipe, plunging deep into the reassuringly solid structure of the house, where at least the sheer mass of all the stone and wood and iron afforded it some protection against the shifting, chaotic, maddening lights in the sky.

It had to stay here. It had no choice.

The grandmother clock in the upstairs hallway chimed midnight, a soft, homey noise. The house was still, and the kitchen was warm. The thing in the basement—whatever it was—still had not come out. Mrs. Kingsley dared to hope that it would not, that it was holed up in the cellar for good, and would not willingly emerge. Her granddaughter was asleep again, and she was alone with her fear and her guilt.

"He's gone to town to get a snowplow," she had lied. It was moral cowardice, pure and simple, and she knew that she would never be able to completely forgive herself for it. But by the same token, there was no way she could possibly have told the child the truth. Not now. Not in the state she was in. "He'll be back in the morning, after breakfast."

"Oh." Jennifer's head had sunk back to the pillow then. She turned to the side, closed her eyes, and was asleep. A faint green glow from the calculator's display tinged her face.

Alma Kingsley stood motionless. Now that she listened, she could hear the house talking to itself. It creaked and groaned, making wooden noises like doors opening and shutting in a distant, fairy-tale wood. Ghosts walked the halls with slow, ominous tread.

She was afraid. Her heart was beating rapidly, and her limbs felt weak and drained. Her house—her own house!—loomed dark and menacing on all sides, and she was afraid of it.

She needed a weapon. The gizmo Desmond had been working on was nowhere near done, a tangle of wires and trash. Even with the power on, she would have no idea how to finish it herself. Desmond had said the monster was afraid of electricity, but with the power out, all the electronic equipment she owned, the television, the radios, the microwave, the food processor, were dead, and so the idea of surrounding them with a barricade of such things, all turned on, wasn't going to work. The electric blanket was useless as a defense now too. There weren't any firearms in the house, and she doubted a kitchen knife would be much use against the creature. Struck by sudden quick inspiration, she stepped into the mud room to the side of the kitchen door and opened the narrow door of the utility closet. There was a heavy woodchopper's axe there, set on brackets on the wall, behind a jumble of brooms, old vacuum cleaners, saws, rakes, and other junk, where it had rested untouched for years, since her hands had gotten too bad to let her chop her own wood for the winter.

She fumbled the axe down from its brackets, lugged it into the kitchen—marveling ruefully at how *heavy* it now seemed, how much arm-strength she'd lost in only five or six years—and set it down near Jennifer's cot, handle up, leaning against the wall.

It wasn't enough. The axe might make for a secondary, last-ditch line of defense if the thing got into the kitchen, but she was too weak and stiff and arthritic to wield it with any real vigor or competence anymore, and the idea of taking slow, clumsy strokes at a creature that moved as fast as this one did, in a half-darkened room that was dancing with shadows anyway, made her mouth dry with terror. That wasn't good enough. She had to figure out some way to keep it out of the kitchen in the first place.

How to do that? How to keep it out of here, keep it away from Jennifer? Think, damn it, *think*!

The only thing she knew it feared was Desmond's pocket calculator.

That was a start, then. She darted into the darkened parlor and snagged a long, white taper from the candelabra on the mantelpiece. With a shiver, she retreated back to the kitchen. She wrapped several paper napkins around its base to protect her hand against the drippings. Desmond would have more calculators among his effects—he was simply that kind of person. There might even be one among Jennifer's things. And for that matter, there was her own, tucked away in the upstairs china cabinet, which she used periodically for taxes and bills.

The candle shed very little light; it seemed to blind her more than illumine the way. She hesitated in the doorway and the shadows flickered and waved about her like living things. She did not want to go into the dark.

Holding herself straight, she stepped forward, fighting against panic.

Desmond had brought along two more calculators, and Jennifer one, a child's calculator in the shape of an owl, the readout part of its big round eyes. Among the child's things, too, she had found a pocket computer game—*Meteor Defense*, or some such nonsense—and estimating it similar enough to be of use, that brought the total up to six. Five, if you *didn't* count it.

It had been a harrowing expedition. She had started at every creak of the joists or scream of stairway tread underfoot. She had felt the Dark Angel upon her twice, as the shadow in an empty doorway had shifted toward her, and when the darkness behind a cabinet gathered itself up to leap. As she returned downstairs and into the parlor, her pace quickened. The kitchen beckoned.

It so heartened her to reach safe haven that she began to hum a snatch of Mozart. She was alive! She blew out the candle and dumped the calculators onto the kitchen table. For the moment, she didn't even notice the thing crouching in the hallway.

A sudden sense of foreboding, a prickling, crawling sensation, made her spin about. Something moved just outside the kitchen door. Black crawled within black, shadow in shadow.

It yearned forward slightly, then retreated, bobbing up and down in indecision, torn between flight and attack. Mrs. Kingsley couldn't even see it clearly, but she *felt* it studying the sleeping child.

More from panic than courage, then, she ran at the thing wildly. She slashed her arm as if the calculator in it were an axe, and she could use it to chop the thing into bloody bits, its black ichor steaming onto the floor, eating through the carpet.

It hesitated fractionally, then flowed into darkness and was gone.

Mrs. Kingsley sobbed in the doorway, weak and despairing. It was a victory, but a minor one. The thing was still loose, and with every encounter it was losing fear.

She set calculators by the doors to the pantry, hallway, and parlor. The fourth she put by the window, and the little computer game was laid at the foot of Jennifer's cot as a second line of defense. They all glowed gently.

The oil lamp was running low. Mrs. Kingsley blew it out, to conserve what little fuel remained, and twisted on two of the range burners. She felt oddly secure, surrounded by the arcane little devices, with their crisp little lights. She felt safe, protected. It was probably unwarranted, mere blind faith in technology, but . . .

The calculator by the parlor door began blinking. The numbers had disappeared and there was a single dot tracking its way across the readout. She remembered Desmond bragging about the thing, when he first showed it to her, explaining that if it weren't used for some number of minutes—five? twenty? ten?—the numbers disappeared from the readout, though the memory still held them, and it went into an energy-conserving mode. And then, if more time went by and nobody used it, it simply turned itself off.

Hastily, she punched some figures at random, and hit a function button. The numbers came back on, with that funny little symbol that meant that an error had been made. She ignored it.

It wasn't long before she realized that the calculators were not going to do. Three of them kept blinking off, and one of the others was failing, its batteries low. She couldn't keep punching the things through the night—sleep would take her long before the snowplow came.

Think! she told herself fiercely. She had to kill the thing, to electrocute it somehow . . . She remembered a story Stephanie used to tell, about the summer camp she'd stayed at as a child, a place with an old-fashioned crank phone system.

The girls used to hook up a phone with one wire connected to a metal bed frame, then the other to a wad of aluminum foil. When the victim sat down on the bed frame, one girl would toss her the ball of foil and yell "Catch!" while her accomplice gave the phone a vicious crank.

She didn't have a crank phone, of course, but she sensed she was on the right track. She'd found a trap that wouldn't require much mechanical skill to set up. All she needed was a power source. Something like . . .

Something like an automobile battery.

She dressed hurriedly, making plans all the while.

First, she got the jumper cables out of the El Dorado's trunk, leaving it up and open behind her as she hurried them through the snow to the kitchen. Jennifer was still asleep, and this time Mrs. Kingsley didn't try to keep from stroking her hair. The simple act seemed to fill her with resolve. The creature would not get the child. This she swore.

Again she stepped out into the storm. The car's front door balked at first, frozen with the cold. She yanked harder and it popped open.

Candy stared up at her accusingly. The dead girl's face was grotesquely shrunken in upon itself, and the tightening skin had pulled the eyes wide open. Mrs. Kingsley gasped involuntarily. She had forgotten the macabre thing was there, stretched out across the front seat.

But there was no time for squeamishness. She leaned over the corpse, and fumbled under the steering wheel for the hood release. With a *bing*, the hood unlatched and she went around to the front—slamming the door shut behind her—to raise it up and confront the battery.

She was fiddling with the cables—they were cold, of course, and frozen to the terminals, and corroded over as well—when her hands seized up with arthritis again. Vainly she tried to *force* her mittened hands to close about a cable. Pain shot up her arms, but still her hands did not respond. Frustrated, she slammed them against the cables again and again.

The lines wouldn't budge.

Tears built at the corners of her eyes, but sternly she suppressed them, blinking them down, thinking harsh thoughts at herself. There had to be a way—the trunk! She'd left it open, hadn't she? She hurried around back and it was true, the trunk still gaped wide. She rummaged about with her useless arms, pushing things to one side or another as if they were long sticks she was using to poke with, and at last she found what she was looking for. A tire iron.

It took longer to scoop up the iron than she'd have liked, an awkward, nightmarishly clumsy time, but finally she had it, and scuttled back to the battery. Holding the iron like a Punchinello might hold its bashing-stick, she tried again and again, leaning, putting her weight *just so*, until finally the one cable popped loose and went banging against the engine.

Time was all. Mrs. Kingsley tried hard not to think of Jennifer lying alone in the house, at the center of her protective pentagram of failing calculators, tried hard to put blind, unreasoning faith in the flimsy little Oriental-built machines.

It took a hellishly long time to get the iron in position for the second cable, and then it kept slipping out of the way. But at last she pried that one free of its terminal too, and with a feeling of triumph, she let the iron fall. She reached for the battery.

It would not budge.

She couldn't get her hands around the damnable thing, couldn't get a hold on it, probably didn't even have the strength to lift it.

She *did* cry then, the tears running down her cheeks and the thin trail of moisture freezing on her skin with a faint crackling sensation. But even then she did not give up. Her mind kept working, as she stared with a positive hatred at the battery. There was nothing in the workings of the car touching it, she noted, and nothing beneath it. There was a space of an inch or so around it on three sides, and it was set on a kind of little metal ledge.

If not for that ledge, the battery would fall to the ground.

She set out to break the little shelf, battering and prying at it with the tire iron. Time and again the iron slipped from her hands and fell. She had to get to her knees in the snow, and reach around under the car to make it fall flat, and then draw it out from under and seduce it into her arms again—she lost a lot of time that way.

By now her knees and her arms, up to her shoulders, were numbed and bruised. The cold seemed to soak through to her bones, and she knew she was running a bad risk of frostbite.

But at last she managed to poke and pry and stab enough that, with a sudden ripping noise, the battery was gone. It had fallen to the ground.

She still couldn't lift it up from the snow—not for more than a few seconds at a time, anyway. But she could get the thing back to the house by pushing it, if she was willing to crawl.

Slowly, with distaste, she got down to the ground. Sometimes a woman had to crawl.

It was more with disbelief than with joy that she finally shoved the battery onto the linoleum of the kitchen floor. Leaving it on its side, she slowly stood and sank gratefully into a chair. Her knees were afire. The creature could have come and taken her then, and she'd have felt only gratitude. It would be so very pleasant to simply lean back and fall asleep . . . Something creaked. Panicked, she struggled upright, twisting around to see that Jennifer was still all right. Her father's calculator had slipped to the floor as the child shifted in her sleep. Of the guardian calculators at the doors, only one was still blinking.

Hurriedly she punched new life into the calculators, bringing the green alphanumerics swimming up to their surfaces. There could be no sleep for her. She still had work to do, a trap to set.

But desire would not unclench her hands. She thrust them into her armpits, desperately trying to warm the joints into movement. It didn't work. She was stopped before she could begin.

Finally she knelt by her granddaughter's cot and nudged her ever so gently. "Rise and shine, sweetheart," she murmured. "Grandmother needs you to be her hands."

Jennifer was sleepy and balky. It took a great deal of coaxing just to get her to untangle the jumper cables. Then, when they were stretched out to their ten-foot lengths, side by side like orange vinyl snakes, it was time to assemble the trap.

Fortunately the cables were old, and the clips were not as taut as they might be. Even at that, Jennifer had to use both hands and all her strength to open the grippers enough to clamp them onto a battery terminal. The first two times she tried, they slipped right back off. Mrs. Kingsley merely tightened her lips and said, "Again."

"Why?"

A noise came from the parlor, a faint, whispery slithering sound. Mrs. Kingsley threw back her head, listening, but it was gone. "Just *do* it. I'm your grandmother." She put all the authority she had in her voice, and, for a wonder, the child obeyed.

As soon as the connection was firm, and wouldn't come loose at a tug on the cable, she threw a tea towel over the terminal, to protect her grandchild against accidental shock. "That's good," she said. "Now the other one."

"This is dumb!" Jennifer cried rebelliously. "I don't have to if I don't want to!"

"By God, I'll give you don't-have-to!" Mrs. Kingsley angrily lifted a hand shoulder-high to slap the child. Then, at the look in her eyes, she stopped, and bit back her anger. She crouched down, joints hurting horribly, and hugged Jennifer to her. "I know it seems hard, child. But sometimes we have to do things we would rather not. It's simply the way the world wags."

Jennifer obstinately shook her head.

"It won't take long, I promise. Suppose that as soon as we get through with this, we make hot chocolate? Would you like that?" She held the child at arm's length, studied her solemnly. "Yes, I'd supposed you would."

The second cable went on smoothly, and Jennifer enjoyed making the ball of aluminum foil. Alma Kingsley had to stop her from using up all that was on the roll.

"Now pretend that the cable is an alligator, and make it bite the shiny ball." It took Jennifer three tries, and then she got it right. The final step was to hook the other cable to something large and metallic, something that the creature would have to touch or pass over to get at her. This was less satisfactory than the rest. The nearest bed frame was on the second floor. She could no more have dragged it down into the kitchen than she could have hauled the battery up the stairs to it. In the end, the best she could find was a screen window that had been stored in the pantry against spring.

The screen was wire mesh, not the modern plastic stuff, but after Jennifer had clipped the cable to it, it looked woefully small and inadequate. There was no way of placing it that guaranteed the creature would pass over it, or of being sure it would be touching when she threw the second cable. But it would have to do. Because it was the best she could come up with.

"Gamma, we can make hot chocolate now, right?"

She allowed herself a smile. "No, my young apprentice. You will make the cocoa. Your grandmother will supervise. Have you ever made cocoa all by yourself before?"

Jennifer shook her head, eyes wide and solemn.

"Well! This will be a special occasion, then. The first thing to do is to—"

The cocoa was a smashing success. By the time it was made, Jennifer was nodding and yawning again. She only managed to drink half her mug's contents before her head slumped over onto her shoulder. Mrs. Kingsley led her back to the cot, and pulled the blankets up over her.

The trap was not good enough. It needed . . . something more. Mrs. Kingsley thought the problem through as she put the cocoa-stained saucepan in the sink and ran a little water in it for it to soak. The drain was closed and water built up in the sink.

Inspiration struck her then.

She turned the tap all the way over, and stood back to watch the sink fill up and brim over. Water crept out onto the Formica countertop, and slopped over onto the floor in a thin, ragged sheet. It splattered and spread, a widening puddle on the linoleum. Soon everything on the floor—including the screen window—was damp.

Success! She stepped through the spreading water and gathered up the calculators. Climbing up on a chair, she sat down on the kitchen table itself, resting her feet on the chair's cane seat. She didn't know much about electricity, but she knew that this would insulate her from the shock. In the same way, the cot's wooden legs would protect Jennifer.

The water was spreading into the pantry and the hallway, seeping through the floorboards, being sopped up by the Oriental carpets in the parlor. The damage it was doing to her house was incalculable. But she kept the water flowing. As long as the one cable was solidly grounded in the water, the entire kitchen was a deathtrap for the creature.

One by one, she turned off the calculators, stacking them beside her. She rested the ball of foil in her lap, ready to throw. Let the monster come! She was prepared for it.

She only wished she had thought to brew some tea for the wait.

Time passed with excruciating slowness. She kept squinting at her watch, thinking that an hour had gone by, to find that it had only been a minute or two instead.

Where *was* it? she thought, straining to hear, although she knew that it could move almost without sound. What was it up to? What was it doing?

What was it doing *here*, for that matter? Here in this house, here on this *planet*? For it was obvious to her by now that the creature was not of this Earth. What did it *want*? Why had it come? Was it just a blindly ravening, mindless creature, a simple predator, or did it have some kind of plan, some sort of purpose?

Conquest, probably. Invasion. That was the most likely guess. Perhaps it was a scout for some sort of interstellar invasion force. A spy, a saboteur, a guerilla fighter, a stealthy terrorist. A soldier.

The thought made her feel very tired. Even out among the stars, it seemed, they had soldiers, and wars, and armies, and waged campaigns of conquest. The fighting never stopped, the killing never stopped, no matter where in the universe you went. There was no escaping it.

She blinked back sudden tears, and steeled herself to increased alertness. This time she was drawing her own line in the sand. It was *not* going to get Jennifer. This time she was going to fight the blank black grinding forces of the universe to a standstill. She was going to kill the loathsome thing, right here and now.

Come on, you abomination. Come for me!

Come *on* . . .

The weapons were gone! The sophonts had disarmed themselves, rendered themselves unprotected, unguarded . . . helpless. And yet, such an action was contrary to everything it somehow knew—without quite knowing *how* it knew—about the nature of sophonts. It felt the contradiction as an almost physical assault.

It was baffled and terrified. The imperatives of survival demanded that it attack and kill the two remaining sophonts. Yet they were alerted and prepared, waiting for it in a space that had but one approach, and *whatever* they had done with their weapons, it was not fooled into thinking they were not dangerous. They were waiting for it.

It quivered in darkness, mantle involuntarily expanding and contacting with conflicting urges, making little retreating and advancing movements, paralyzed with indecision and fear. It was in an impossible position. It felt the wrongness, though it had no way of understanding it. It should not be here, it knew, should not be playing this dangerous game in such alien surroundings. This was not how it was meant to be . . .

Finally, though, it came to the only decision it could: it must attack.

If it was to act, it would have to act fast. The sophonts would not remain passive forever. In what pitiable remnants of its mapping functions remained accessible, it created a model of the house, a one-to-one visualization of its every wall and surface, from the patterned tin ceiling of the master bedroom to the uneven dirt floor of the basement.

There were lacunae within its knowledge of the house, but they did not matter; it knew those portions that it would employ. Within this small maze, it set a marker to represent itself.

It plotted its attack by moving the signifier. Silently, craftily, it would flow up one wall to the juncture of wall and ceiling. Attacking from above was instinctive behavior to its own kind, and it knew from experience that the sophonts here rarely looked up; taken together, these facts just might give it an edge.

Quickly, then, it would traverse wall and ceiling to the kitchen doorway. The room was charged with tensions. The air sparkled with dying by-products of the gas oven, dazzling its senses, so that it perceived the two surviving sophonts with their complex nervous systems as areas of greater brightness within a general glare. It would be entering the room half blind.

The mental marker looped over the archway, sped midway across the ceiling to a spot directly over the smaller brightness. It came to a dead stop, and then dropped.

Time and again, it ran the marker through its mazy path of attack, never varying, until the instructions were scored into its consciousness. It was huddled in upon itself, fringe crackling and humming faintly with the effort. Had its enemy known, she could have walked up to it now and destroyed it without its being able to put up the least resistance. All its energies directed inward, it was temporarily helpless. But that was necessary if it was to imprint its attack, making it a single complex involuntary motion, a spasm of reflex violence that would either succeed all in an instant, or fail before it could regain full consciousness.

One last time, it held the cursor-self over the lesser sophont. Without pausing, it dropped. Fluidly, it stunned, possibly even killed, its first opponent, then leaped straight at the second, to wrap its hood about it, and discharge the powers that freed the fire-of-life. It was a desperate move, and if any least thing went wrong, it would be a fatal one.

When the cursor had run through the final repetition, it was as taut with energy as an overwound spring. It positioned itself carefully. It would take only the slightest triggering thought to free that resolve into a blurred burst of killing fury, an explosion of purpose.

Now!

She must have been dozing. Or perhaps a general stunned weariness had dulled her perceptions, so that she stared blankly unseeing as it entered.

Because the first that Alma Kingsley saw of the creature was when it flickered down before her, and on top of Jennifer.

It came too fast. It was upon Jennifer before she could react. There was a sudden moving darkness, like black cloth flapping in the breeze, and then a scorching smell, and the child *screamed*! Then the thing was flying through the air at her, the sides of its mantle spread like manta ray wings, as if it needed that little extra bit of lift to reach her.

She would have died then, had her reflexes not betrayed her. For in the panicked instant when the creature fell through the air before her, all thought stopped, all plans of action and attack abruptly fled and she'd scrambled to her feet, chair falling away, as she twisted to flee from the thing.

Then the creature was soaring through the air at the space where she had been, and it slammed into her upraised hand, the one that held the jumper cable with its foolish ball of aluminum foil, as though it were a scepter. The thing's surface had the oddest feel, coarsely textured like it was made of woven metal and at the same time oddly slick, as if it held some faint charge repulsing her hand. The mantle spread wide, then folded in, seeking to wrap her head in its folds. In blind fear, because she had a dread of suffocation that dated back to her childhood, she flung the creature away.

The thing flew across the kitchen, hit the wall, and fell to the floor. For an instant, it crumpled to practically nothing. Then unseen forces stiffened it and it rose up, swaying slowly and woozily back and forth, looking for all the world like a punch-drunk fighter. For a long moment, they stared at each other.

The thing was resting on the high end of the kitchen, and though the floor was damp there, it was not so deeply puddled as further in, and Mrs. Kingsley didn't know enough about electrical conductivity to know if it was damp enough. "Come on," she grated, holding up the ball of foil as if it were a crucifix she were employing to ward off a vampire. "Just a little bit closer, and I have you!"

She thought of righting the chair and climbing up on it, to protect herself. But she was still wearing her rubber boots, having foreseen the danger and put them on for this very purpose, and surely they ought to be enough. "That's right," she crooned. "Slide forward, into the water."

The creature swayed slightly, back and forth, forth and back, clearly focusing on her. It seemed dazed, unsure. It moved a bit to one side, then to the other, avoiding the edge of the puddle proper.

It *knew*! The vile thing knew to avoid the water! She felt a wave of dread. It was not going to be tricked.

To one side, Jennifer made a soft noise, a gentle, final sigh, and Mrs. Kingsley turned to see the child's head fall to one side. The face was burned and blistered, and the eyes closed. She could see no sign of breathing.

The creature chose that instant to attack. It was upon her before she could throw the cable. Alma Kingsley screamed, and it seemed to some far, remote part of her that there was less terror than rage in her scream, and then she was grappling with the thing. It had leaped through the air, and though she held the cable against its skin, no part of it made contact with the water. The circuit wasn't complete.

Those soft, tough surfaces wrapped about her arms, tried to envelope her head. It covered one eye, and she could not pry it off. Her skin tingled, and she heard the faintest imaginable mechanical-sounding hum, as of a generator starting up just over the horizon.

Very deliberately then, Alma Kingsley decided that if she was not going to survive this encounter, then neither would her enemy. It was the only chance Jennifer had. And at the very worst, at the very least, if her granddaughter was already dead, she could take this hellspawned demon with her, and if vengeance was a sour drink, it was at least a potent one.

Grappling the creature with both hands, she threw herself forward, tumbling them both into the wet, charged floor.

Fire! fear! pain! horror! And then a blinding, ripping, sundering bolt of light, beyond pain and horror, more powerful than anything it had ever known, that ripped the very fabric of the universe apart. That wiped its mind clean like a sponge across a blackboard. And then put it back together again, in an instant.

It screamed. Alma Kingsley, lying stunned and spasmed on the linoleum floor, heard it, not with her ears, but deep in her brain, a wash of noise that filled the universe. The creature screamed not as an animal would, not as a being of flesh and blood, backbone and viscera would, but like a machine in agony. Like the scream of stripping gears of some immense but deadlocked engine tearing itself apart with its own energy of motion because it was unable to go forward as it was designed to do, because the load it was pushing against or trying to lift was too great for it to move. Like the high-pitched squeal of distortion, chasing itself up the frequencies, of an electric amplifier just before it burns itself out with a bang and a flash and the stink of burning insulation. Like the boiler of some old-fashioned steam locomotive shrieking out news of its impending death, seconds before the boiler explodes and fills the icy night with twisted scraps of flying black iron. Like that same locomotive plunging off a high trestle into a deep ravine. Like the dopplering scream of an artillery shell or a missile as it falls out of the sky to kill some mother's child. Like the apotheosis of every ugly mechanical sound that had ever been heard since people came down from the trees and learned how to make tools.

It screamed and there was more to that scream than mere pain: there was anguish there too, maybe even—but she was surely making this up—regret. It was a cry from Hell, like that a damned soul might make as it fell down into the Pit, a cry from a soul that knew that it deserved to be damned, and to fall endlessly forever through darkness.

The car battery shorted out. A scorched smell rose from its remains, and a short black puff of smoke curled like a question mark in the air, slowly dissipating. Freed from her grip, the creature flopped, twisted, and streaked for the kitchen window. There was a flare of energy, and the ugly stench of burning wood, paint, and glass. A pane flowed and melted, and, with a dwindling wail, the creature was gone, out into the night.

Cold air blew in through the hole.

Alma Kingsley was still alive, although at first she didn't realize it. She lay there for a long time, listening to someone crying, making baffled little sobbing sounds, *hunnn, hunnn, hunnn,* like a beaten and exhausted animal, and then the cold wind in her face revived her enough that she realized that it was she herself who was making the noise, and that that meant that somehow, impossibly, she was still alive. Sense began to seep back into her head, and the world swam blurrily into focus. She moved, instinctively trying to sit up, and a fierce lance of pain cleared her head a little bit more. She had no conscious memory of the electric shock but it must have been bad, because when she tried to remember, her mind shrank away from the very thought in fear and revulsion.

Snow was blowing in through the window from the wind-drifted dune beyond, fine particles that danced a stately gavotte in the middle of the air. She sat there for a moment longer, sitting in a puddle of water on the floor, cold wet linoleum underneath her, cold air in her face, blinking in bewilderment, staring at the fine particles of snow dancing in the air, staring at the ragged hole melted through the window, wondering what on Earth could have happened . . . and then memory began to return, and with it, fear and horror, rebooting suddenly, kicking in with a sudden shock that flooded her system with adrenaline, as painful and nauseating as a punch in the stomach.

Jennifer. Oh God, Jennifer!

Somehow, she managed to pull herself to her feet, although the world tilted slowly around her when she did so, first one way and then the other, with ponderous slow-motion grace, as if she were riding a ship in a heavy sea. She staggered toward her granddaughter, falling next to her rather than kneeling, pawing at her with hands that felt like frozen slabs of meat rather than living flesh.

Jennifer was lying still, very still. There was a deep burn across one side of her face, curling up a corner of her mouth, touching the edge of one eye, blistered and cauterized, and all around it the child's flesh was a horrible dead-grey color, as if all the energy and life had been sucked out of her.

She fumbled at Jennifer's throat, trying to find a pulse, unable to tell whether she couldn't find one for the obvious reason or because of her numbed, tingling hands; she could hardly tell whether she was even touching the child without looking to see where her hands were. She leaned close to smell her lips, feeling for even the gentlest whisper of breath from those tiny nostrils, thinking she felt it, unable to be sure.

Without even knowing she'd gotten up or crossed the room, she was at the telephone, fumbling at it, finally getting her hands to pick up the receiver, forgetting entirely that the device was dead—and then, just as she was remembering with a sick surge of dismay that it was dead, she realized it *wasn't*. The dial tone was clear, perfectly normal, as though nothing had ever happened, as though it were a perfectly ordinary day and this a perfectly ordinary call. Somehow she forced her blundering fingers to dial 911. She reached the police with her first attempt and, a flicker of common sense telling her not to babble of monsters, not now, not yet, managed to at least convey that an ambulance was needed out here, that it was a life-or-death emergency, with every second counting . . . although she knew, without them needing to mention it—although they did—that with all the best will in the world it would take some time for an emergency vehicle to force its way through the snow-choked roads to her place.

She stumbled back to the cot, knelt down by her silent, unmoving grandchild. Bits and pieces of first-aid wisdom, learned decades ago at summer camp or half-remembered from television programs she hadn't really been paying much attention to, babbled desperately in her head, and so she tugged the blanket out from under Jennifer's frail, broken little body, wrapping her up in it to keep her warm and keep her from slipping into shock, balled the pillows up and stuffed them under her feet to elevate her legs . . . all the while trying to ignore a cold dry voice in the back of her head, remorselessly logical, that knew perfectly well that all this was useless, and kept whispering, *Too late, too late.* When she could no longer feel any hint of breath, and could no longer feel even the ghost of a pulse—sensation was returning to her hands with a feeling like a thousand hot needles being plunged into them, although she hardly noticed the pain—she began clumsily performing CPR on the child, performing it as well as she could remember how to perform it, anyway, whispering between breaths, "Don't die, don't die, don't die, don't die," like a mantra, trying not to also think *Too late, too late*, like a counter-beat.

At last, she could fool herself no longer, and slowed to a stop. The child looked like a waxwork dummy of herself, all heat and life—the soul, if you believed in those—gone. Her flesh was already growing cold. *Too late.*

Alma Kingsley went away from her body for awhile then. When she came back to it again, returning as though from across a great gulf of space, she heard her voice speaking aloud again, mumbling broken fragments of sentences in a sodden monotone, randomly assembled words that jarred and ground against each other like stones in a sack.

A vast surge of bitterness shot through her. Useless old woman. Never good for *anything* in your whole damn life. Couldn't keep your husband alive, couldn't save your daughter. Couldn't even protect your own grandchild. You'd think if you'd be able to do anything, one miserable thing that made a difference in this foul and pestilent existence, that made it worthwhile that you were ever alive in the first place, at least you could save your own granddaughter. A six-year-old child! Why was it that she was dead and *you* were still alive, living on and on into a bleak morning that had no reason left in it for you to be alive anymore, and your traitor lungs continuing to pump, your heart to beat, after Jennifer was dead? After everyone you ever cared about was gone? What was the point? Why couldn't she have been allowed to trade her life for the child's? You old fool, couldn't you have done *one thing* right in your life? In your whole useless and pointless life?

It was bitter and hard for her, almost harder and more cruelly bitter than she could bear, to realize that if Desmond had lived and *she* had been the one to die instead, that Desmond—much as she'd always disliked him, thought him not worthy of her daughter, looked down on him, much as she *still* disliked him now, in spite of the fact that he was dead—probably would have been able to save Jennifer from the monster. To save her as *she* had not been able to. Why hadn't it worked out that way? Why had the fates instead left the child's life in her hands? Her useless, good-for-nothing, crippled hands, that had let that life slip through arthritic fingers?

A draft of cold air. She looked up in time to see the back door swing soundlessly open, letting in a puff and swirl of snow.

A sinister, black, serpentine shape reared up in the doorway, raising the bulk of its length off the ground, like a cobra coiling to strike.

It was back.

The creature was back.

Fear was her first, instinctive reaction, an icy stab of atavistic terror that made her back away a step or two, and which dimly surprised her, since she would have sworn a moment before that she no longer cared at all if she lived or died. Well, in fact, why struggle anymore? Let it kill her. What did it matter *now*? She felt resignation begin to glaze over her like a scum of ice forming over a pond, dulling her fear.

The creature swayed in the doorway. Dawn was beginning to break, the sun not yet over the horizon, but staining the sky a sullen purple-red. The creature was a black silhouette against that sullen red sky, weaving slightly from side to side, rippling sinuously. As yet, it had made no attempt to move forward into the house, to attack her, although she knew how fast it could move. Maybe it was scenting the wind, searching out her presence with whatever strange senses it possessed . . .

Still it didn't move, as one long moment crawled into the next. Maybe it was *taunting* her, teasing her, playing with her the way a cat plays with a mouse. Enjoying her fear. Making her wait. Relishing her helplessness.

Suddenly, she was furious. The murderous creature was toying with her! Mocking her! Rage instantly melted the ice of resignation and futility. If she was too late to save Jennifer, she could still do one worthwhile thing before she died. She could take this obscenity *with* her. She could make sure that it slaughtered no one else's children.

She could make it *pay*. Or at least die trying.

The axe was still resting against the wall, where she had put it what seemed like years ago now, handle up, a few feet away from the cot; she could just see it at the edge of her peripheral vision. Without turning, she took a slow, slow sideways step toward it, not looking away from the creature, not turning her head, not daring to do anything that might break the spell of immobility. She took another slow sideways step, and another, inching along like a crab. Slowly, still without turning her head, she stretched her hand back behind her, trying to move her body as little as possible, groping for the axe-handle.

As she touched it, her hand wrapping itself solidly around the wooden handle, the creature spoke to her.

Kill me, it said.

It struggled against the fire! fear! pain! horror! that welled up through its being. But the torrent of voltage, wild and undirected and irresistible, drove its consciousness helplessly before the flood, driving it *through* that protective hedge of forces, through the whitening, searing agony of the unbearable, into memories far worse.

It was falling. Tightly wrapped within a neatly-calculated bundle of shielding, its consciousness a pure nub at the center of calming forces, it descended from space, down to the Earth below, at last at the end of a journey that had taken many decades, almost half a century, with the real beginning of its Mission yet ahead. But then—impossible!—it felt a blast of radiation, raking through the core of its being, scrambling circuits. The shielding was not good enough! It wasn't holding! It knew about the Van Allen radiation belt, of course, and that had been taken into account when the voyage was planned; beings with greater science than even its own race could command had confidently predicted that even if the Van Allen belt were to be energized by a spate of sunspots, the radiation could not possibly be strong enough to get through.

Mistakes happen, though. They were not gods, and neither were any of the other races they knew, however advanced they might be. Sometimes, even with the highest and most subtle of technologies, things go wrong.

The radiation could not get through, and yet it *was* getting through. High-level energies sleeted through the tightly interwoven fabric of its substance, leaving maddening pain in its wake, a hundred, a thousand times more agonizing than anything it had ever known, pain not only physical but mental as well—logical chimeras that its rational functions could not deal with, self-contradicting structures that one by one overloaded its higher functions, driving it down the asymptotal curve toward total extinction.

It was the best qualified of its race for the job ahead, a creature of vast patience, tact, wit, gentleness, diplomatic skill, culture, and erudition—all the commingled powers had agreed on that, just as they agreed that it was the turn of its race to reach out and bring a benighted alien race out of the darkness of provincial ignorance and into Civilization, just as their own race had been so contacted and assimilated into the galactic community thousands of years before. It had been so *proud* of that, of the responsibility it had been given. But now, it was unraveling in madness and pain, and could *feel* its rational mind dissolving, and could do nothing to stop the process. It felt its higher functions failing, and automatic systems taking over.

The ambassador's race was an ancient and intensely civilized one. Lone eons ago, even before contact with the communities of the stars, they had put aside their predatory origins, overridden them with a thousand culturally programmed safeguards. They no more felt the age-old archaic urges than a human felt the need to brachiate.

The urges were still there though, ancestral voices whispering in the blood, at the very bottom of the brain, as they must be in every corporeal creature who has evolved from a lower—or at least a more basic—form of life.

One by one, it lost reason, memory, personality; it knew the horror of losing everything that made it itself, and *knowing* it was losing it, and being unable to stop the process. At last, it would lose even the knowledge that something had been *lost*, except for a vague trickle of unease at the back of its consciousness. It would be reduced to survival programming, the underlying atavistic ancestral memory whose human equivalent would be the reptilian hindstem.

From the depths of pain, it had a last fleeting moment of clarity in which to mourn its own passing, and then most of its brain went down.

Glowing like Lucifer falling, it tumbled from the sky, down to the Earth below.

The car battery shorted out. There was a puff of acrid black smoke, and then it was free. Instantly, it reacted. Instinct hurled it *away* from there, away from the trap that had almost killed it, though the window, out into the night.

Outside, alone in the darkness and the swirling snow, with the Northern Lights still a vaguely troubling presence on the horizon, an uneasy prickling sensation that it could now control, it came to the full realization of what it had done.

When she got over the initial shock of hearing the creature speak, Alma Kingsley quickly picked up the axe, bringing it awkwardly around in front of her body so that she could get a better, two-handed grip on it, resting it on her shoulder, ready to swing. She backed away two steps, felt her rear foot bump into the wall, and started to edge sideways again, moving away from the wall a bit (even if it did mean moving a step or two *toward* the monster) so that she'd have room to swing the axe overhand at the creature if it rushed her, a woodchopper's stroke. Couldn't let it pin her against the wall . . .

Kill me, it said again.

She hesitated. She had been figuring out how to do just that, or the best way to try to do it, anyway, deciding that she'd better rush it and try to get a good swing in at it before the big axe grew too heavy for her tired old arms to hold up effectively, do it right *now*, before she lost her nerve . . . But it kept putting her off her stride by *speaking* to her; she hadn't known that it could talk.

It wasn't "talking" at all, actually—the words seemed to print themselves in her brain somehow, faintly superimposed on reality, like the afterimage of an object you can sometimes see after you close your eyes. But she had no doubt that it was really happening, or that it was the creature who was "speaking" to her.

Go ahead, it said. *Do it now. I won't try to stop you.*

She came forward a couple of steps, and then stopped, hesitating, wary. This was some kind of trick. It was trying to lure her closer so that it could strike at her, maybe counting on being fast enough to be able to dodge any blow of the axe she might get off at it. When she got close enough, it would attack . . .

It will not be difficult, it said persuasively. *My physical component is really quite fragile. If you strike at the center of my being hard enough, with something sharp or heavy, that will kill me. That tool you have in your hand will do nicely. I perceive that the handle is made of wood; that will insulate you from any shock. You'll be perfectly safe.*

"You weren't so concerned with my safety a few minutes ago," Alma Kingsley said harshly. "When you were trying to kill me!"

I was insane then, it said. *I have been insane for a long time. But I am insane no longer. The shock that you administered to me has re-integrated my functions. I am sane now.*

"How nice for you!" Rage pulsed through her, and she tightened her grip on the axe. "You unspeakable bastard!"

It shivered convulsively, and she jumped back a step, thinking it was about to attack. But it didn't move forward. *I know what I did*, it said. I *am ready to atone.*

"Atone?" She found herself laughing, harsh, cawing, jagged, ugly laughter that tore her throat. "You killed Jennifer! And Desmond! And . . . and that poor girl!" To her shame, she found she couldn't summon up the young woman's name, although she got a flash of her vapid, cheaply pretty face. "Damn you, you even killed my *dog*!" Tears sprang into her eyes and she blinked them fiercely away. She couldn't allow it to distract her, let it put her off her guard. As soon as she did, it would strike.

I know what I did, it repeated. *That's why you have to kill me.* It was saying slightly from side to side now, as if in agitation. *Kill me! Strike now! Get it over with. I won't fight you. I know I deserve to die.*

She tried to say something but the words tangled themselves in her throat and wouldn't come out. Her head felt like it was going to explode, and she was shaking all over. "You're right about that!" she managed to rasp, panting with rage. "You deserve to die a hundred times over!"

It was shaking too, as though stirred by the same inner wind. *I know that, it said. I can't live with the guilt and the shame. I was sent here on a mission of peace, to bring you the gifts that would allow you to live as civilized creatures, without war, without want and poverty and hatred. Instead, I killed everyone I met!* It swayed violently. *There could be no worse failure! No worse betrayal of everything that I believe in! Kill me!*

She raised the axe. Images flashed through her mind: Jennifer, her face gray and blistered and burned . . . Iago collapsing in a pathetic jumble of furry limbs . . . the girl, the roadhouse pickup, smiling vapidly although amiably as she dug a fork into her eggs . . . Desmond waving his hands and talking expansively, self-importantly . . . She was crying openly now, tears running down her face, breathing in harsh gasps through her mouth, but she didn't lose sight of the monster, in spite of the tears. She squeezed the wood of the axe-handle until her hands ached. Abruptly, fiercely, she rushed forward, swinging the axe as far back as she could, ready to bring it crashing down.

A step or two away, she stopped, hesitating, the axe swung high in the air.

It hadn't moved, although she was in easy attack distance by now.

DO IT! it shrieked.

There was a long frozen moment, as though time itself had stopped. For some reason, she found herself thinking about something she hadn't allowed herself to consciously think about for decades: her husband's coffin, shipped by air back from Vietnam, being lowered into a hole dug into the raw red earth on a blustery wet spring morning, a flag draped over it, while people in uniform stood stiffly next to the grave and saluted and little Stephanie fidgeted impatiently by her side, too young to understand . . . the incongruously cheerful sound of birds singing somewhere off in the trees (and she realizing how incongruous it was even at the time, and hating herself for noticing something like that at a time like this, no matter how ironic it was) . . . her thinking how much Steve would have hated having his coffin wrapped in a flag, how he would have disliked the solemnity of this whole ceremony, the priest droning pious platitudes about somebody he'd never met and how Steve was now going to walk with Jesus in A Better World . . . looking at her own mother beside her, leaning heavily on Uncle Henry's arm, noticing with a shock how old and frail and tired she looked . . . The photo that had stood on the mantelpiece in the living room as long as she could remember, her father in a World War II army uniform, the father she'd never met, a black star on the glass frame, the photo gathering dust for years, never touched, never moved . . . Her own daughter Stephanie, laughing and hugging her at the airport gate, kissing her husband and her baby goodbye, telling them that she'd send them all postcards and maybe some souvenirs if she could find a moment to steal from the sales conference, only minutes before her airplane was blown to pieces in midair by a terrorist's bomb . . . The military jets screaming by outside, mean and black and predatory, on the way to the buildup for the *next* war, that would kill somebody *else*'s children . . .

As though it were reading her mind—and who knew, perhaps it was—it said, *The Mission will succeed, even though I failed. Eventually. They will send someone else. It may take another hundred years for them to get here, but eventually they will, and we'll help you heal this world of yours. I have to believe that. Eventually, my failure won't matter. The Mission will succeed.*

Another hundred years. How many children dead in that time, in how many wars?

She heard the sound of a siren, a thin wail still far away, on the edge of hearing. The ambulance coming.

Kill me, it said *You have the right. I owe you that. I have nothing to pay with but my life.*

Suddenly, she was very, very tired, unutterably weary, as though the marrow in her bones had turned to lead.

Hurry. They're coming. Soon it will be too late. Kill me now. Don't hesitate. I want you to do it. I don't want to live. I can't live with what I've done. It hurts too much.

A kind of weary revulsion seized her then, a nauseated rejection of everything and everyone. She stared at the alien for another long moment. "Then live, God damn you," she cried bitterly. "Live and be damned!"

She flung the axe aside.

Her legs gave out, and she sat down abruptly on the cold floor. If this was a trick, then it had won. She no longer even cared. Let it kill her if it wanted to.

The wailing siren came closer and closer, the sound cutting sharply through the cold winter air.

One year later, on the anniversary of First Contact at Maple Hill Farm (as the scroll on the screen would say whenever they came back from the commercials), Alma Kingsley sat alone before the television set, listening to herself being praised on CNN. The commentators prattled on and on about the terrible tragedy of the Ambassador's arrival, and of the even greater tragedy that would have occurred had it not been allowed to complete its Mission; one commentator, face radiating sincerity like a pot-bellied stove radiates heat, spoke of Alma Kingsley as a secular saint for forgoing personal revenge for the Sake of All Mankind.

The Ambassador had tried to attend Jennifer and Desmond's funerals (Candy was buried elsewhere), but she had refused to allow it to attend, to the disappointment of the newsmen, although they were there filming everything in sight anyway, keeping tight closeups on her face as the last remnants of her family were lowered into the ground, not wanting to miss the slightest nuance of expression. Later, at the UN, the Ambassador had insisted on giving an emotional eulogy for the people he had inadvertently killed, going on to say that Alma Kingsley's greatness of spirit, in being willing to forgive even the very creature who had killed her own granddaughter, all by itself was enough to prove that humanity was worthy of inclusion among the great interstellar Community of Races, and would insure their admission.

Sometimes she wondered if the creature, who was certainly many times smarter than she or any other human being, had *manipulated* her psychologically into deciding not to kill it, using a sly variant of Br'er Rabbit's "Don't Throw Me In the Briar Patch!" routine to get her to act the way it wanted her to act. Certainly it had been easier for it to explain itself to the ambulance crew and the police with her there alive on the scene to vouch for it than it would have been if she were dead, and it was there alone to greet them with a houseful of murdered people at its back.

And the forgiveness angle made for great press, just the spin to neutralize the unfortunate fact that the Ambassador had started its career on Earth by killing as many humans as possible. Or maybe it *had* been sincere. Certainly its people *did* seem to be highly ethical, concerned with Justice and Right Actions in a fussy, legalistic, rabbinical way that seemed almost prim. She would never know, one way or the other.

CNN was now running through a quick inventory of all that humanity's new friends had given the Earth so far. Once the Ambassador had used the living fabric of its body to form and trigger an interstellar Gate, new technologies had poured through in a seemingly endless stream: Defensive weapons that really *were* defensive, for they couldn't be used offensively . . . an end to disease . . . medicines to expand the human lifespan a hundred years or more . . . safe and plentiful energy . . . the transmutation of elements . . . gold from lead . . . lilacs from mud . . . silk purses from sows' ears . . . a partridge in a pear tree . . . blah, blah, blah.

They were like children on Christmas morning, with bright wrappings strewn about and nothing but presents as far as the eye could see. To listen to them go on, it seemed that the entire human race was going straight to Heaven. Everybody was going to be healthy and beautiful and tall. They were all going to be transformed into gods.

Except Jennifer. She didn't get to be immortal and go to the stars. She got to lie at the bottom of a grave in Brattleboro, rotting in the cold unforgiving ground, while worms ate her.

Alma Kingsley sat staring at the screen and listening as voices far older than any god spoke within her. Their words were dark and poisonous. They ate at her heart like acid.

She got up and fixed herself another Manhattan. Bitterly, she drank it down, wishing—as she would wish every day for the remaining two hundred years of her life—that she'd killed the damn thing when she had the chance.

• Dinner Party •

It had been cold all that afternoon. When they picked Hassmann up at the gate that evening, it was worse than cold—it was freezing.

The gate guard let Hassmann wait inside the guard booth, although that was technically against regulations, and he might have caught hell for it if the Officer of the Day had come by. But it was colder than a witch's tit outside, as the guard put it, and he knew Hassmann slightly, and liked him, even though he was RA and Hassmann was National Guard, and he thought that most NGs were chickenshit. But he liked Hassmann. Hassmann was a good kid.

They huddled inside the guard booth, sharing a cigarette, talking desultorily about baseball and women, about a court martial in the gate guard's battalion, about the upcoming ATTs and MOS tests, about the scarcity of promotion slots for corporals and 5s. They carefully did not talk about the incident last weekend on the campus in Morgantown, although it had been all over the papers and the TV and had been talked about all over post. They also didn't talk about where Hassmann was going tonight—allowed off base at a time when almost everyone else's passes had been pulled—although rumors about that had spread through the grapevine with telegraphic speed since Hassmann's interview with Captain Simes early that afternoon. Most especially, most emphatically, they did not talk about what everyone knew but hesitated to admit even in whispers: that by this time next month, they would probably be at war.

The gate guard was telling some long, rambling anecdote about breaking up a fight down behind the Armor mess hall when he looked out beyond Hassmann's shoulder and fell silent, his face changing. "This looks like your ride heah, Jackson," he said, quietly, after a pause.

Hassmann watched the car sweep in off the road and stop before the gate; it was a big black Caddy, the post floodlights gleaming from a crust of ice over polished steel and chrome. "Yeah," Hassmann said. His throat had suddenly turned dry, and his tongue bulked enormously in his mouth. He ground the cigarette butt out against the wall. The guard opened the door of the booth to let him out. The cold seized him with his first step outside, seized him and shook him like a dog shaking a rat. "Cover your ass," the gate guard said suddenly from the booth behind him. "Remember—cover your *own* ass, you heah?" Hassmann nodded, without looking around, without much conviction. The guard grunted, and slid the booth door closed.

Hassmann was alone.

He began to trot toward the car, slipping on a patch of ice, recovering easily. Hoarfrost glistened everywhere, over everything, and the stars were out in their chill armies, like the million icy eyes of God. The cold air was like ice in his lungs, and his breath steamed in white tatters around him. The driver of the car had the right front door half open, waiting for him, but Hassmann—seeing that the man had a woman with him, and feeling a surge of revulsion at the thought of sitting pressed close to the couple in the front—opened the rear door instead and slipped into the back seat. After a moment, the driver shrugged and closed the front door. Hassmann closed the rear door too, automatically pushing down the little button that locked it, instantly embarrassed that he had done so. After the double *thunk* of the doors closing and the sharp *click* of the lock, there was nothing but a smothering silence.

The driver turned around in his seat, resting his arm on the top of the seatback, staring at Hassmann. In the dark, it was hard to make out his features, but he was a big, beefy man, and Hassmann could see the reptilian glint of light from thick, black, horn-rimmed glasses. The woman was still facing forward, only casting a quick, furtive glance back at him, and then turning her head away again. Even in this half-light, Hassmann could see the stiffness of her shoulders, the taut way she held her neck. When the silence had become more than uncomfortable, Hassmann stammered, "Sir, I'm—sir, PFC Hassmann, sir . . ."

The driver shifted his weight in the front seat. Leather creaked and moaned. "Glad to meet you, son," he said. "Yes, very glad—a pleasure, yes, a pleasure." There was a forced joviality in his voice, a note of strained, dangerous cordiality that Hassmann decided he had better not try to argue with.

"Glad to meet you, too, sir," Hassmann croaked.

"Thank you, son," the man said. Leather groaned again as he extended his hand into the back seat; Hassmann shook it briefly, released it—the man's hand had been damp and flabby, like a rubber glove full of oatmeal. "I'm Dr. Wilkins," the man said. "And this is my wife, Fran." His wife did not acknowledge the introduction, continuing to stare stonily straight ahead. "Manners," Dr. Wilkins said in a soft, cottony voice, almost a whisper. "Manners!" Mrs. Wilkins jerked, as if she had been slapped, and then dully muttered, "Charmed," still not turning to look at Hassmann.

Dr. Wilkins stared at his wife for a moment, then turned to look at Hassmann again; his glasses were dully gleaming blank circles, as opaque as portholes. "What's your *Christian* name, son?"

Hassmann shifted uneasily in his seat. After a moment's hesitation—as though to speak his name would be to give the other man power over him—he said "James, sir. James Hassmann."

"I'll call you Jim, then," Dr. Wilkins said. It was a statement of fact—he was not asking permission; nor was there any question that Hassmann would be expected to continue to call him "Dr. Wilkins," however free the older man made himself with

Hassmann's "Christian name." Or "sir," Hassmann thought with a quick flash of resentment, you could hardly go wrong calling him "sir." Hassmann had been in the army long enough to know that it was impossible to say "sir" too many times when you were talking to a man like this; work it in a hundred times per sentence, they'd like it just fine.

Dr. Wilkins was still staring reflectively at him, as if he expected some sort of response, an expression of gratitude for the fine democratic spirit he was showing, perhaps . . . but Hassmann said nothing. Dr. Wilkins grunted. "Well, then—Jim," he said. "You like Continental cuisine?"

"I-I'm not sure, sir," Hassmann said. He could feel his face flushing with embarrassment in the close darkness of the cab. "I'm not sure I know what it is."

Dr. Wilkins made a noise that was not quite a snort—a long, slow, resigned exhaling of air through the nose. "What kind of food do you like to eat at home?"

"Well, sir, the usual kind of thing, I guess. Nothing special."

"What kind of things?" Dr. Wilkins said with heavy, elaborated patience.

"Oh—spaghetti, meat loaf. Sometimes fried chicken, or cold cuts. We had TV dinners a lot." Dr. Wilkins was staring at him; it was too dark to make out his expression with any kind of certainty, but he seemed to be staring blankly, incredulously, as if he couldn't believe what he was hearing. "Sometimes my mother'd make, you know, a roast for Sunday or something, but she didn't much like to cook anything fancy like that."

This time Dr. Wilkins did snort, a sharp, impatient sound. "*Adeo in teneris consuescere multum est*," he said in a loud, portentous voice, and shook his head. Hassmann felt his face burning again; he had no idea what Dr. Wilkins had said, but there was no mistaking the scorn behind the words. "That's Virgil," Dr. Wilkins said contemptuously, peering significantly at Hassmann. "You know Virgil?"

"Sir?" Hassmann said.

"Never mind," Dr. Wilkins muttered. After a heavy pause, he said, "This restaurant we're taking you to tonight has a three-star Michelin rating, one of the few places east of the Mississippi River that does, outside of New York City. I don't suppose that means anything to you, either, does it?"

"No, sir," Hassmann said stiffly. "I'm afraid it doesn't, sir."

Dr. Wilkins snorted again. Hassmann saw that Mrs. Wilkins was watching him in the rearview mirror, but as soon as their eyes met, she turned her face away.

"Well, son," Dr. Wilkins was saying, "I'll tell you one thing those three Michelin stars mean: they mean that tonight you're going to get the best damn meal you ever had." He sniffed derisively. "Maybe the best damn meal you'll ever have. Do you understand *that* . . . Jim?"

"Yes, sir," Hassmann said. Out of the corner of his eye, he could see that Mrs. Wilkins was watching him in the rearview mirror again. Every time she thought that his attention was elsewhere, she would stare at him with terrible fixed intensity; she would look away when he met her eyes in the mirror, but a moment later, as soon as he glanced away, she would be staring at him again, as though she couldn't keep her eyes off him, as though he were something loathsome and at the same time almost hypnotically fascinating, like a snake or a venomous insect.

"I don't expect you to appreciate the finer points," Dr. Wilkins said, "we can thank the way kids are brought up today for that, but I do expect you to appreciate that what you're getting tonight is a very fine meal, one of the finest meals money can buy, not some slop from McDonald's."

"Yes, sir, I do, sir," Hassmann said. Dr. Wilkins made a *humpf*ing noise, not sounding entirely mollified, so Hassmann added, "It sounds great, sir. I'm really looking forward to it. Thank you, sir." He kept his face blank and his voice level, but his jaw ached with tension. He hated being dressed down like this, he hated it. His fingers were turning white where they were biting into the edge of the seat.

Dr. Wilkins stared at him for a moment longer, then sighed and turned back to the wheel; they slid away into the darkness with a smooth surge of acceleration.

They ghosted back down the hill, turned right. Here the road ran parallel to the tall Cyclone fence that surrounded the base; behind the iron mesh, behind the winter-stripped skeletons of trees, Hassmann could see the high, cinder-bed roofs of the Infantry barracks, a huge water tower—it had the slogan RE-UP ARMY stenciled on its sides, visible for miles in the daytime—and the gaunt silhouette of a derrick, peeking up over the fence from the Engineer motor pool like the neck of some fantastic metal giraffe. The base dwindled behind them to a tabletop miniature, to a scene the size of a landscape inside a tiny glass snowball, and then it was gone, and there was nothing but the stuffy interior of the car, the pale glow of the instruments on the dashboard, dark masses of trees rushing by on either side. Hassmann was sweating heavily, in spite of the cold, and the upholstery was sticky under his hands.

There was a persistent scent of patchouli in the car—cutting across the new-car smell of the upholstery and the tobacco-and-English Leather smell of Dr. Wilkins—that must be Mrs. Wilkins' perfume; it was a heavy, oversweet smell that reminded Hassmann of the room in the cancer hospital where his aunt had died. He longed to roll down the window, let the cold night air into the stuffy car, but he didn't quite dare to do it without asking Dr. Wilkins' permission, and that was something he wouldn't do. He was beginning to get a headache, a bright needle of pain that probed in alongside his eyeball like a stiff wire, and his stomach was sick and knotted with tension. Abruptly it was too much for him, and he found himself blinking back sudden tears of frustration and rage, all the resentment and chagrin he felt rising up in his throat like bile. Why did he have to do this? Why did they have to pick on *him*? Why couldn't they just leave him *alone*? He had said as much in Captain Simes' office this afternoon, blurting out, "I don't want to do it! Do I *have* to go, sir?" And Captain Simes had studied him jaundicedly for a moment before replying, "Officially, no. The regulations say we can't make you. Unofficially, though, I can tell you that Dr. Wilkins is a very important man in this state, and with things as tense as they are politically, you can expect some very serious smoke to be brought down on your ass if you don't do everything you can to keep him happy, short of dropping your drawers and bending over." And then Simes had leered at him with his eroded, prematurely old face and said, "And, hell, soldier, comes right down *to* it, maybe you even ought to take *that* under advisement . . ."

They drifted past a weathered wooden barn that was covered with faded old CLABBER GIRL and JESUS SAVES signs, past a dilapidated farmhouse where one light was burning in an upstairs window. There was an automobile up on blocks in the snow-covered front yard, its engine hanging suspended from a rope thrown over a tree branch. Scattered automobile parts made hummocks in the snow, as if small dead animals were buried there. They turned past a bullet-riddled highway sign and onto an old state road that wound down out of the foothill country. The car began to pick up speed, swaying slightly on its suspension.

"You come from around here, Jim?" Dr. Wilkins said.

"No, sir," Hassmann said. *Thank God!* he added silently to himself. Evidently he had been unable to keep his feelings out of his voice, because Dr. Wilkins glanced quizzically at him in the rearview mirror. Quickly, Hassmann added, "I was born in Massachusetts, sir. A small town near Springfield."

"That so?" Dr. Wilkins said, without interest. "Gets pretty cold up there too in the winter, doesn't it? So at least you're used to this kind of weather, right?"

"That's right, sir," Hassmann said leadenly. "It gets pretty cold there, too."

Dr. Wilkins grunted. Even he seemed to realize that his attempt at small talk had been a dismal failure, for he lapsed into a sodden silence. He pressed down harder on the accelerator, and the dark winter countryside began to blur by outside the windows. Now that they had stopped talking, there was no sound except for the whine of the tires on macadam or their snare-drum rattle on patches of gravel.

Hassmann rubbed his sweating palms against the slick upholstery. Somehow he knew that Mrs. Wilkins was watching him again, although it was too dark to see her eyes in the mirror anymore. Occasionally the lights of an oncoming car would turn the inside of the windshield into a reflective surface, and he would be able to see her plainly for a second, a thin-faced woman with tightly pursed lips, her hands clenched together in her lap, staring rigidly straight ahead of her. Then the light would fade and her image would disappear, and only then, in the darkness, would he begin to feel her eyes watching him again, as though she were only able to see him in the dark.

They were going faster and faster now, careening down the old state road like a moonshiner on a delivery run with the Alcohol Tax agents on his tail, and Hassmann was beginning to be afraid, although he did his best to sit still and look imperturbable. The old roadbed was only indifferently maintained, and every bump rattled their teeth in spite of the Caddy's heavy-duty shocks; once Hassmann was bounced high enough to bang his head on the roof, and the car was beginning to sway ominously from side to side. Fortunately, they were on a level stretch of road with no oncoming traffic when they hit the patch of ice. For a moment or two the Caddy was all over the road, skidding and fishtailing wildly, its brakes screaming and its tires throwing up clouds of black smoke, and then slowly, painfully, Dr. Wilkins brought the big car back under control. They never came to a complete stop, but they had slowed down to about fifteen miles per hour by the time Dr. Wilkins could wrestle them back into their own lane, and you could smell burned rubber even inside the closed cab.

No one spoke; Mrs. Wilkins had not even moved, except to steady herself against the dashboard with one hand, an almost dainty motion. Slowly, almost involuntarily, Dr. Wilkins raised his head to look at Hassmann in the rearview mirror. *Almost lost it, didn't you, old man?* Hassmann thought, staring impassively back at him, and after a moment, Dr. Wilkins looked shakily away. They began to slowly pick up speed again, wobbling slightly, although Dr. Wilkins was careful to keep them under fifty this time. This kind of compulsive speeding, obviously pushing himself to or beyond the edge of his driving ability, was the first real indication of strain or tension that Dr. Wilkins had allowed to escape from behind his smooth, hard-lacquered façade, and Hassmann greeted it with interest and a certain degree of vindictiveness.

A few minutes more brought them out of the hills. They slowed down to rattle across a small chain-link bridge over a frozen river. A tank was parked to one side of the road, near the bridge entrance, its hatches open for ventilation, gray smoke panting from its exhaust and rising straight up into the cold air. A soldier in a steel helmet popped his head up out of the driver's hatch and watched them as they passed. They weren't putting up roadblocks and regulating civilian traffic yet, Hassmann thought, in spite of the recent wave of terrorism, but it obviously wasn't going to be too much longer before they were, either. There was a small town on the other side of the bridge, half a dozen buildings clustered around a crossroads. Political graffiti had been spray-painted on several of the buildings, particularly on the blank-faced side wall of a boarded-up gas station: YANKEES GO HOME . . . FEDS OUT OF WEST VIRGINIA NOW . . . SECESSION, NOT RECESSION . . . FUCK THE UNION . . . A sloppy, half-hearted attempt to obliterate the graffiti had been made, and only a few letters of each slogan remained, but Hassmann had seen them often enough elsewhere to have little difficulty reconstructing them. The restaurant was a mile beyond the town, a large stone-and-timber building that had once been a grinding mill—now hidden spotlights splashed the ivy-covered walls with pastel light, and the big wooden waterwheel was sheathed in glistening ice.

There was a network news van parked in front of the restaurant, and Dr. Wilkins, who had been anxiously checking his watch on the last stretch from town, grunted in satisfaction when he saw it. As they pulled up, a news crew with a minicam unit climbed out of the van and took up positions in front of the restaurant steps. Other reporters got out of their parked cars—pinching out unfinished cigarettes and carefully tucking them away—and began to saunter over as well, some of them slapping themselves on the arms and joking with one another about the cold in low, rapid voices. Hassmann heard one of the reporters laugh, the sound carrying clearly on the cold winter air.

Dr. Wilkins switched off the ignition, and they all sat motionless and silent for a moment, listening to the metallic ticking noises the engine made as it cooled. Then, with forced brightness, Dr. Wilkins said, "Well, we're here! Everybody out!" Mrs. Wilkins ignored him. She was staring out at the gathering knot of reporters, and for the first time she seemed shaken, her icy composure broken. "Frank," she said in an unsteady voice, "I—Frank, I just *can't*, I can't face them, I can't—" She was trembling. Dr. Wilkins patted her hand perfunctorily. He noticed Hassmann watching them, and glared at him with murderous resentment, his careful mask slipping for a moment. Hassmann stared stonily back. "It'll be all right, Fran," Dr. Wilkins said, patting her hand again. "It's just until we get inside. Julian promised me that he wouldn't let any of them into the restaurant." Mrs. Wilkins was shaking her head blindly. "It'll only be a minute. Let me do all the talking. It'll be okay, you'll see." He looked coldly at Hassmann. "Come on," he said brusquely, to Hassmann, and got out of the car. He walked quickly around to the passenger side, opened the door, and said, "Come on" again, to his wife this time, in the low coaxing tone an adult might use to a frightened child. Even so, he had to reach down and half pull her to her feet before he could get her out of the car. He bent to look at Hassmann again. "You, too," he said in a harsh, dangerous voice. "Come on. Don't give me any trouble now, you little shit. Get out."

Hassmarin climbed out of the car. It was colder than ever, and he could feel the clammy sweat drying on his body with a rapidity that made him shiver. Dr. Wilkins came up between him and Mrs. Wilkins and took each of them by the arm, and they began walking toward the restaurant. The reporters were looking toward them now, and the camera lights on the van came on, nearly blinding them with brightness.

Dr. Wilkins kept them walking right at the reporters. The small crowd parted and re-formed around them, swallowing them, and then it seemed to Hassmann as if everything was happening at once, too fast to follow. Faces jostled around him, faces thrust forward toward him, their mouths opening and closing. Voices gabbled. A reporter was saying, ". . . with the ratification vote on the Act of Secession coming up in the statehouse Wednesday, and similar votes later this week in

Michigan, Ohio, and Colorado," and Dr. Wilkins was waving his hand airily and saying, ". . . more than enough support on the floor." Another reporter was saying something to Mrs. Wilkins and she was dully muttering, "I don't know, I don't know . . ." Flashbulbs were popping at them now, and they had climbed partway up the restaurant steps. Someone was thrusting a microphone into Hassmann's face and bellowing ". . . make you feel?" and Hassmann was shrugging and shaking his head. Someone else was saying ". . . latest Gallup poll shows that two-thirds of the people of West Virginia support secession," and Dr. Wilkins was saying, ". . . everything you hear, love?" and the reporters laughed.

Hassmann wasn't listening anymore. Ever since last weekend he had been walking around like a somnambulist, and now the feeling had intensified; he felt feverish and unreal, as if everything was happening behind a thin wall of insulating glass, or happening to someone else while he watched. He barely noticed that Dr. Wilkins had stopped walking and was now staring directly into the blinking eye of the minicam, or that the reporters had grown curiously silent. Dr. Wilkins had let his face become serious and somber, and when he spoke this time it was not in the insouciant tone he'd been using a moment before, but in a slow, sincere, gravelly voice. The voice seemed to go on and on and on, while Hassmann shivered in the cold wind, and then Dr. Wilkins' heavy hand closed over Hassmann's shoulder, and the flashbulbs went off in their faces like summer lightning.

Then Julian was ushering them into the restaurant—fawning shamelessly over Dr. Wilkins and promising to "take their order personally"—and shutting the reporters outside. He led them through the jungly interior of the old mill to a table in a corner nook where the walls were hung with bronze cooking utensils and old farm implements, and then buzzed anxiously around Dr. Wilkins like a fat unctuous bee while they consulted the menu. The menu had no prices, and as far as Hassmann was concerned might just as well have been written in Arabic. Mrs. Wilkins refused to order, or even to speak, and her rigid silence eventually embarrassed even Julian. Impatiently, Dr. Wilkins ordered for all of them—making a point of asking Hassmann, with thinly disguised sarcasm, if the coulibiac of salmon and the osso buco would be to his liking—and Julian hurried gratefully away.

Silence settled over the table. Dr. Wilkins stared blankly at Hassmann, who stared blankly back. Mrs. Wilkins seemed to have gone into shock-she was staring down at the table, her body stiffly erect, her hands clenched in her lap; it was hard to tell if she was even breathing. Dr. Wilkins looked at his wife, looked away. Still no one had spoken. "Well, Jim," Dr. Wilkins started to say with leaden joviality, "I think you'll like—" and then he caught the scorn in the look that Hassmann was giving him, and let the sentence falter to a stop. It had become clear to Hassmann that Dr. Wilkins hated him as much as or more than his wife did—but in spite of that, and in spite of the fact that he had already gotten as much use out of Hassmann as he was going to get, he was too much the politician to be able to stop going through the motions of the charade. Dr. Wilkins locked eyes with Hassmann for a moment, opened his mouth to say something else, closed it again. Abruptly, he looked tired.

A smoothly silent waiter placed their appetizers in front of them, glided away again. Slowly, Mrs. Wilkins looked up. She had one of those smooth Barbie doll faces that enables some women to look thirty when they are fifty, but now her face had harsh new lines in it, as if someone had gone over it with a needle dipped in acid. Moving with the slow-motion grace of someone in a diving suit on the bottom of the sea, she reached out to touch the linen napkin before her on the table. She smiled fondly at it, caressing it with her fingertips. She was staring straight across the table at Hassmann now, but she wasn't seeing him; somewhere on its way across the table, her vision had taken the sort of right-angle turn that allows you to look directly into the past. "Frank," she said, in a light, amused, reminiscent tone unlike any that Hassmann had heard her use, "do you remember the time we were having the Graingers over for dinner, back when you were still in city council? And just before they got there I realized that we'd run out of clean napkins?"

"Fran—" Dr. Wilkins said warningly, but she ignored him; she was speaking to Hassmann now, although he was sure that she still wasn't seeing him *as* Hassmann—he was merely filling the role of listener, one of the many vague someones she'd told this anecdote to, for it was plain that she'd told it many times before. "And so I gave Peter some money and sent him down to the store to quick buy me some napkins, even *paper* ones were better than nothing." She was smiling now as she spoke. "So after a while he comes back, the Graingers were here by then, and he comes marching solemnly right into the living room where we're having drinks, and he says—he must have been about seven—he says, 'I looked all over the store, Mom, and I got the best ones I could find. These must be really good because they're *sanitary* ones, see? It says so right on the box.' And he holds up this great big box of Kotex!" She laughed. "And he looks so intent and serious, and he's so proud of being a big enough boy to be given a job to do, and he's trying so hard to do it right and please us, I just didn't have the heart to scold him, even though old Mr. Grainger looked like he'd just swallowed his false teeth, and Frank choked and sprayed his drink all over the room." Still smiling, still moving languidly, she picked up her fork and dug it into one of her veal-and-shrimp quenelles, and then she stopped, and her eyes cleared, and Hassmann knew that all at once she was seeing him again. Life crashed back into her face with shocking suddenness, like a storm wave breaking over a seawall, flushing it blood-red. Abruptly, spasmodically, viciously, she threw her fork at Hassmann. It bounced off his chest and clattered away across the restaurant floor. Her face had gone white now, as rapidly as it had flushed, and she said, *"I will not eat with the man who murdered my son."*

Hassmann stood up. He heard his own voice saying, "Excuse me," in a polite and formal tone, and then he had turned and was walking blindly away across the restaurant, somehow managing not to blunder into any of the other tables. He kept walking until a rough-hewn door popped up in front of him, and then he pushed through it, and found himself in the washroom.

It was cold and dim and silent in the washroom, and the air smelled of cold stone and dust and antiseptic, and, faintly, of ancient piss. The only sound was the low, rhythmic belching and gurgling of cisterns. A jet of freezing air was coming in through a crack in the window molding, and it touched Hassmann's skin like a needle.

He moved to the porcelain washbasin and splashed cold water over his face, the way they do in the movies, but it made him feel worse instead of better. He shivered. Automatically, he wet a tissue and began to scrub at the food stain that Mrs. Wilkins' fork had left on his cheap pin-striped suit. He kept catching little glimpses of himself in the tarnished old mirror over the washbasin, and he watched himself slyly, fascinatedly, without ever looking at himself straight on. They had *film* footage of him killing the Wilkins boy—that particular stretch of film had been shown over and over again on TV since last weekend. As the demonstrators rushed up the steps of the campus administration building toward the line of waiting Guardsmen, there was a very clear sequence of him bringing his rifle up and shooting Peter Wilkins down. Other Guardsmen had fired, and other demonstrators had fallen—four dead and three others seriously wounded, all told—but there could be no doubt that *he* was the one who had killed Peter Wilkins. Yes, that one was *his*, all right.

He leaned against the wall, pressing his forehead against the cold stone, feeling the stone suck the warmth from his flesh. For some reason he found himself thinking about the duck he'd raised, one of the summers they still went to the farm, the duck they'd wryly named Dinner. He'd fattened that stupid duck all summer, and then when it was time to kill it, he'd hardly been able to bring himself to do it. He'd made a botch of cutting its head off, faltered on the first stroke and then had to slash two more times to get the job done. And then the duck had run headless across the farmyard, spouting blood, and he'd had to chase it down. He'd given it to his father to clean, and then gone off behind the barn to throw up. All the rest of the family had said that the duck was delicious, but he'd had to leave the table several times during the meal to throw up again. How his father had laughed at him!

Hassmann was shivering again, and he couldn't seem to make himself stop. As clearly as if it were really in the room with him, he heard Captain Simes' voice saying, "He's mousetrapped himself into it! His son was one of the ringleaders in planning the campus rally, and he was getting a lot of local media coverage simply because he *was* Wilkins' son. So, just before the rally that weekend, Wilkins published an open letter in all the major papers—" Dr. Wilkins' voice, resonant and sonorous as he stares into the camera lights: "In that letter, I told my son that if he were killed while taking part in a riot that he himself had helped to create . . . well, I told him that I would mourn him forever, but that far from condemning the man who killed him, I'd seek that man out and shake his hand, and then take him out to dinner to thank him for having the steadfastness to uphold the Constitution of the United States in the face of armed sedition—" "And so now he's stuck with *doing* it, or losing what little face he has left!" Simes' voice again. Simes' giggle.

He'd talked to Simes for nearly twenty minutes before he'd realized that the tall glass of "iced tea" in Simes' hand was actually 100-proof whisky, and by that time Simes had been glassy-eyed and swaying, mumbling, "A civil war! And none of this nuclear-exchange shit, either. They're going to fight this one house to house through every small town in America. A nice long war . . ."

Hassmann stared at himself in the mirror. His face was hard and drawn, gaunt, his cheeks hollowed. His eyes were pitiless and cold. He could not recognize himself. The stranger in the mirror stared unwinkingly back at him; his face was like stone, the kind of cold and ancient stone that sucks the heat from anything that touches it.

A nice long *war* . . .

He went back into the restaurant. Heads turned surreptitiously to watch him as he passed, and he could see some of the other diners leaning close to each other to whisper and stare.

Dr. Wilkins was sitting alone at the table, surrounded by untouched dishes of food, some of them still faintly steaming. As Hassmann came up, he raised his head, and they exchanged bleak stares. He had taken his glasses off, and his face looked doughy and naked without them, less assured, less commanding. His eyes looked watery and tired.

"Julian is letting Mrs. Wilkins lie down in back for a while," Dr. Wilkins said. "Until she feels a little better." Hassmann said nothing, and made no attempt to sit down. Dr. Wilkins reached out for his glasses, put them on, and then peered at Hassmann again, as if to make sure that he was talking to the right man. He drew himself up in his chair a little, glancing at the nearest table with a motion of the eyes so quick as to be nearly imperceptible, like the flick of a lizard's tongue. Was he worried that, in spite of Julian's promise, some of the other customers might be reporters with hidden directional mikes? Some of them might be, at that. "I guess I owe you an apology," Dr. Wilkins said heavily, after a pause. He worked his mouth as if he was tasting something unpleasant, and then continued to speak in a stiff, reluctant voice. "My wife's been under a lot of emotional strain lately. She was distraught. You'll have to make allowances for that. She doesn't realize how hard this has been on you, too, how unpleasant it must have been for you to be forced to take a human life—"

"No, sir," Hassmann said in a clear, distinct voice, interrupting, not knowing what words he was speaking until he heard them leave his lips . . . feeling the final insulating thickness of glass shatter as he spoke and all the raw emotional knowledge he'd been trying to deny for more than a week rush in upon him . . . knowing even as he spoke that speaking these words would change him irrevocably forever . . . change Dr. Wilkins . . . change everything . . . watching Dr. Wilkins' face, already wincing at the blow he could sense coming . . . seeing the headless duck run flapping through the dusty farmyard . . . his father laughing . . . Mrs. Wilkins' eyes, watching him in the rearview mirror, in the dark . . . the soldier popping his head up out of the tank hatch to watch them pass . . . FUCK THE UNION . . . a nice *long* war . . . the hard, merciless eyes of the stranger in the mirror, the stranger that was now *him* . . . remembering the clean, exhilarating rush of joy, the fierce leap of the heart, as he'd emptied the clip of his semiautomatic rifle into the onrushing figure, relishing the flaring blue fire and the smoke and the noise, *got you you bastard got you*, smashing the other man and flinging him aside in a tangle of broken limbs all in one godlike moment, with a flick of his finger.

"No, sir," he said, smiling bleakly at the tired old man, enunciating each word with terrible precision, not even, at the end, wanting to hurt the other man, but simply to make him *understand*. "I enjoyed it," he said.

• A Dream at Noonday •

I REMEMBER THE SKY, and the sun burning in the sky like a golden penny flicked into a deep blue pool, and the scuttling white clouds that changed into magic ships and whales and turreted castles as they drifted up across that bottomless ocean and swam the equally bottomless sea of my mind's eye. I remember the winds that skimmed the clouds, smoothing and rippling them into serene grandeur or boiling them into froth. I remember the same wind dipping low to caress the grass, making it sway and tremble, or whipping through the branches of the trees and making them sing with a wild, keening organ note. I remember the silence that was like a bronzen shout echoing among the hills.

—It is raining. The sky is slate-gray and grittily churning. It looks like a soggy dishrag being squeezed dry, and the moisture is dirty rain that falls in pounding sheets, pressing down the tall grass. The rain pocks the ground, and the loosely packed soil is slowly turning into mud, and the rain spatters the mud, making it shimmer—

And I remember the trains. I remember lying in bed as a child, swathed in warm blankets, sniffing suspiciously and eagerly at the embryonic darkness of my room, and listening to the big trains wail and murmur in the freight yard beyond. I remember lying awake night after night, frightened and darkly fascinated, keeping very still so that the darkness wouldn't see me, and listening to the hollow booms and metallic moans as the trains coupled and linked below my window. I remember that I thought the trains were alive, big dark beasts who came to dance and to hunt each other through the dappled moonlight of the world outside my room, and when I would listen to the whispering clatter of their passing and feel the room quiver ever so slightly in shy response, I would get a crawly feeling in my chest and a prickling along the back of my neck, and I would wish that I could watch them dance, although I knew that I never would. And I remember that it was different when I watched the trains during the daytime, for then even though I clung tight to my mother's hand and stared wide-eyed at their steam-belching and spark-spitting they were just big iron beasts putting on a show for me;

they weren't magic then, they were hiding the magic inside them and pretending to be iron beasts and waiting for the darkness. I remember that I knew even then that trains are only magic in the night and only dance when no one can see them. And I remember that I couldn't go to sleep at night until I was soothed by the muttering lullaby of steel and the soft, rhythmical hiss-clatter of a train booming over a switch. And I remember that some nights the bellowing of a fast freight or the cruel, whistling shriek of a train's whistle would make me tremble and feel cold suddenly, even under my safe blanket-mountain, and I would find myself thinking about rain-soaked ground and blood and black cloth and half-understood references to my grandfather going away, and the darkness would suddenly seem to curl in upon itself and become diamond-hard and press down upon my straining eyes, and I would whimper and the fading whistle would snatch the sound from my mouth and trail it away into the night. And I remember that at times like that I would pretend that I had tiptoed to the window to watch the trains dance, which I never really dared to do because I knew I would die if I did, and then I would close my eyes and pretend that I was a train, and in my mind's eye I would be hanging disembodied in the darkness a few inches above the shining tracks, and then the track would begin to slip along under me, slowly at first then fast and smooth like flowing syrup, and then the darkness would be flashing by and then I would be moving out and away, surrounded by the wailing roar and evil steel chuckling of a fast freight slashing through the night, hearing my whistle scream with the majestic cruelty of a stooping eagle and feeling the switches boom and clatter hollowly under me, and I would fall asleep still moving out and away, away and out.

—The rain is stopping slowly, trailing away across the field, brushing the ground like long, dangling gray fingers. The wet grass creeps erect again, bobbing drunkenly, shedding its burden of water as a dog shakes himself dry after a swim. There are vicious little crosswinds in the wake of the storm, and they make the grass whip even more violently than the departing caress of the rain. The sky is splitting open above, black rain clouds pivoting sharply on a central point, allowing a sudden wide wedge of blue to appear. The overcast churns and tumbles and clots like wet heavy earth turned by a spade. The sky is now a crazy mosaic of mingled blue and gray. The wind picks up, chews at the edge of the tumbling wrack, spinning it to the fineness of cotton candy and then lashing it away. A broad shaft of sunlight falls from the dark undersides of the clouds, thrusting at the ground and drenching it in a golden cathedral glow, filled with shimmering green highlights. The effect is like that of light through a stained-glass window, and objects bathed in the light seem to glow very faintly from within, seem to be suddenly translated into dappled molten bronze. There is a gnarled, shaggy tree in the center of the pool of sunlight, and it is filled with wet, disgruntled birds, and the birds are hesitantly, cautiously, beginning to sing again—

And I remember wandering around in the woods as a boy and looking for nothing and finding everything and that clump of woods was magic and those rocks were a rustlers' fort and there were dinosaurs crashing through the brush just out of sight and everybody knew that there were dragons swimming in the sea just below the waves and an old glittery piece of Coke bottle was a magic jewel that could let you fly or make you invisible and everybody knew that you whistled twice and crossed your fingers when you walked by that deserted old house or something shuddery and scaly would get you and you argued about bang you're dead no I'm not and you had a keen gun that could endlessly dispatch all the icky monsters who hung out near the swing set in your backyard without ever running out of ammunition. And I remember that as a kid I was nuts about finding a magic cave and I used to think that there was a cave under every rock, and I would get a long stick to use as a lever and I would sweat and strain until I had managed to turn the rock over, and then when I didn't find any tunnel under the rock I would think that the tunnel was there but it was just filled in with dirt, and I would get a shovel and I would dig three or four feet down looking for the tunnel and the magic cave and then I would give up and go home for a dinner of beans and franks and brown bread. And I remember that once I did find a little cave hidden under a big rock and I couldn't believe it and I was scared and shocked and angry and I didn't want it to be there but it was and so I stuck my head inside it to look around because something wouldn't let me leave until I did and it was dark in there and hot and very still and the darkness seemed to be blinking at me and I thought I heard something rustling and moving and I got scared and I started to cry and I ran away and then I got a big stick and came back, still crying, and pushed and heaved at that rock until it thudded back over the cave and hid it forever. And I remember that the next day I went out again to hunt for a magic cave.

—The rain has stopped. A bird flaps wetly away from the tree and then settles back down onto an outside branch. The branch dips and sways with the bird's weight, its leaves heavy with rain. The tree steams in the sun, and a million raindrops become tiny jewels, microscopic prisms, gleaming and winking, loving and transfiguring the light even as it destroys them and they dissolve into invisible vapor puffs to be swirled into the air and absorbed by the waiting clouds above. The air is wet and clean and fresh; it seems to squeak as the wet grass saws through it and the wind runs its fingernails lightly along its surface. The day is squally and gusty after the storm, high shining overcast split by jagged ribbons of blue that look like aerial fjords, The bird preens and fluffs its feathers disgustedly, chattering and scolding at the rain, but keeping a tiny bright eye carefully, cocked in case the storm should take offense at the liquid stream of insults and come roaring back. Between the tufts of grass the ground has turned to black mud, soggy as a sponge, puddled by tiny pools of steaming rainwater. There is an arm and a hand lying in the mud, close enough to make out the texture of the tattered fabric clothing the arm, so close that the upper arm fades up and past the viewpoint and into a huge featureless blur in the extreme corner of the field of vision. The arm is bent back at an unnatural angle and the stiff fingers are hooked into talons that seem to claw toward the gray sky—

And I remember a day in the sixth grade when we were struggling in the cloakroom with our coats and snow-encrusted overshoes and I couldn't get mine off because one of the snaps had frozen shut and Denny was talking about how his father was a jet pilot and he sure hoped the war wasn't over before he grew up because he wanted to kill some Gooks like his daddy was doing and then later in the boy's room everybody was arguing about who had the biggest one and showing them and Denny could piss farther than anybody else. I remember that noon at recess we were playing kick the can and the can rolled down the side of the hill and we all went down after it and somebody said hey look and we found a place inside a bunch of bushes where the grass was all flattened down and broken and there were pages of a magazine scattered all over and Denny picked one up and spread it out and it was a picture of a girl with only a pair of pants on and everybody got real quiet and I could hear the girls chanting in the schoolyard as they jumped rope and kids yelling and everybody was scared and her eyes seemed to be looking back right out of the picture and somebody finally licked his lips and said what're those things stickin' out of her, ah, and he didn't know the word and one of the bigger kids said tits and he said yeah what're those things stickin' outta her tits and I couldn't say anything because I was so surprised to find out that girls had those little brown things like we did except that hers were pointy and hard and made me tremble and Denny said hell I knew about that I've had hundreds of girls but he was licking nervously at his lips as he said it and he was breathing funny too. And I remember that afternoon I was sitting at my desk near the window and the sun was hot and I was being bathed in the rolling drone of our math class and I wasn't understanding any of it and listening to less. I remember that I knew I had to go to the bathroom but I didn't want to raise my hand because our math teacher was a girl with brown hair and eyeglasses and I was staring at the place where I knew her pointy brown things must be under her blouse and I was thinking about touching them to see what they felt like and that made me feel funny somehow and I thought that if I raised my hand she would be able to see into my head and she'd know and she'd tell everybody what I was thinking and then she'd get mad and punish me for thinking bad things and so I didn't say anything but I had to go real bad and if I looked real close I thought that I could see two extra little bulges in her blouse where her pointy things were pushing against the cloth and I started thinking about what it would feel like if she pushed them up against me and that made me feel even more funny and sort of hollow and sick inside and I couldn't wait any longer and I raised my hand and left the room but it was too late and I wet myself when I was still on the way to the boys' room and I didn't know what to do so I went back to the classroom with my pants all wet and smelly and the math teacher looked at me and said what did you do and I was scared and Denny yelled he pissed in his pants he pissed in his pants and I said I did not the water bubbler squirted me but Danny yelled he pissed in his pants he pissed in his pants and the math teacher got very mad and everybody was laughing and suddenly the kids in my class didn't have any faces but only laughing mouths and I wanted to curl up into a ball where nobody could get me and once I had seen my mother digging with a garden spade and turning over the wet dark earth and there was half of a worm mixed in with the dirt and it writhed and squirmed until the next shovelful covered it up.

—Most of the rain has boiled away, leaving only a few of the larger puddles that have gathered in the shallow depressions between grass clumps. The mud is slowly solidifying under the hot sun, hardening into ruts, miniature ridges and mountains and valleys. An ant appears at the edge of the field of vision, emerging warily from the roots of the wet grass, pushing its way free of the tangled jungle. The tall blades of grass tower over it, forming a tightly interwoven web and filtering the hot yellow sunlight into a dusky green half-light. The ant pauses at the edge of the muddy open space, reluctant to exchange the cool tunnel of the grass for the dangers of level ground. Slowly, the ant picks its way across the sticky mud, skirting a pebble half again as big as it is. The pebble is streaked with veins of darker rock and has a tiny flake of quartz embedded in it near the top. The elements have rounded it into a smooth oval, except for a dent on the far side that exposed its porous core. The ant finishes its cautious circumnavigation of the pebble and scurries slowly toward the arm, which lies across its path. With infinite patience, the ant begins to climb up the arm, slipping on the slick, mud-spattered fabric. The ant works its way down the arm to the wrist and stops, sampling the air. The ant stands among the bristly black hairs on the wrist, antennae vibrating. The big blue vein in the wrist can be seen under its tiny feet. The ant continues to walk up the wrist, pushing its way through the bristly hair, climbing onto the hand and walking purposefully through the hollow of the thumb. Slowly, it disappears around the knuckle of the first finger—

And I remember a day when I was in the first year of high school and my voice was changing and I was starting to grow hair in unusual places and I was sitting in English class and I wasn't paying too much attention even though I'm usually pretty good in English because I was in love with the girl who sat in front of me. I remember that she had long legs and soft brown hair and a laugh like a bell and the sun was coming in the window behind her and the sunlight made the downy hair on the back of her neck glow very faintly and I wanted to touch it with my fingertips and I wanted to undo the knot that held her hair to the top of her head and I wanted her hair to cascade down over my face soft against my skin and cover me and with the sunlight I could see the strap of her bra underneath her thin dress and I wanted to slide my fingers underneath it and unhook it and stroke her velvety skin. I remember that I could feel my body stirring and my mouth was dry and painful and the zipper of her dress was open a tiny bit at the top and I could see the tanned texture of her skin and see that she had a brown mole on her shoulder and my hand trembled with the urge to touch it and something about Shakespeare and when she turned her head to whisper to Denny across the row her eyes were deep and beautiful and I wanted to kiss them softly brush them lightly as a bird's wing and Hamlet was something or other and I caught a glimpse of her tongue darting wetly from between her lips and pressing against her white teeth and that was almost too much to bear and I wanted to kiss her lips very softly and then I wanted to crush them flat and then I wanted to bite them and sting them until she cried and I could comfort and soothe her and that frightened me because I didn't understand it and my thighs were tight and prickly and the blood pounded at the base of my throat and Elsinore something and the bell rang shrilly and I couldn't get up because all I could see was the fabric of her dress stretched taut over her hips as she stood up and I stared at her hips and her belly and her thighs as she walked away and wondered what her thing would look like and I was scared. I remember that I finally got up enough nerve to ask her for a date during recess and she looked at me incredulously for a second and then laughed, just laughed contemptuously for a second and walked away without saying a word. I remember her laughter. And I remember wandering around town late that night heading aimlessly into nowhere trying to escape from the pressure and the emptiness and passing a car parked on a dark street corner just as the moon swung out from behind a cloud and there was light that danced and I could hear the freight trains booming far away and she was in the back seat with Denny and they were locked together and her skirt was hiked up and I could see the white flash of flesh all the way up her leg and he had his hand under her blouse on her breast and I could see his knuckles moving under the fabric and the freight train roared and clattered as it hit the switch and he was kissing her and biting her and she was kissing him back with her lips pressed tight against her teeth and her hair floating all around them like a cloud and the train was whispering away from town and then he was on top of her pressing her down and I felt like I was going to be sick and I started to vomit but stopped because I was afraid of the noise and she was moaning and making small low whimpering noises I'd never heard anyone make before and I had to run before the darkness crushed me and I didn't want to do that when I got home because I'd feel ashamed and disgusted afterward but I knew that I was going to have to because my stomach was heaving and my skin was on fire and I thought that my heart was going to explode. And I remember that I eventually got a date for the dance with Judy from my history class who was a nice girl although plain but all night long as I danced with her I could only see my first love moaning and writhing under Denny just as the worm had writhed under the thrust of the garden spade into the wet dark earth long ago and as I ran toward home that night I heard the train vanish into the night trailing a cruelly arrogant whistle behind it until it faded to a memory and there was nothing left.

—The ant reappears on the underside of the index finger, pauses, antennae flickering inquisitively, and then begins to walk back down the palm, following the deep groove known as the life line until it reaches the wrist. For a moment, it appears as if the ant will vanish into the space between the wrist and the frayed, bloodstained cuff of the shirt, but it changes its mind and slides back down the wrist to the ground on the far side. The ant struggles for a moment in the sticky mud, and then crawls determinedly off across the crusted ground. At the extreme edge of the field of vision, just before the blur that is the upper arm, there is the jagged, pebbly edge of a shell hole. Half over the lip of the shell hole, grossly out of proportion at this distance, is half of a large earthworm, partially buried by the freshly turned earth thrown up by an explosion. The ant pokes suspiciously at the worm—

And I remember the waiting room at the train station and the weight of my suitcase in my hand and the way the big iron voice rolled unintelligibly around the high ceiling as the stationmaster announced the incoming trains and cigar and cigarette smoke was thick in the air and the massive air-conditioning fan was laboring in vain to clear some of the choking fog away and the place reeked of urine and age and an old dog twitched and moaned in his ancient sleep as he curled close against an equally ancient radiator that hissed and panted and belched white jets of steam and I stood by the door and looked up and watched a blanket of heavy new snow settle down over the sleeping town with the ponderous invulnerability of a pregnant woman. I remember looking down into the train tunnel and out along the track to where the shining steel disappeared into darkness and I suddenly thought that it looked like a magic cave and then I wondered if I had thought that was supposed to be funny and I wanted to laugh only I wanted to cry too and so I could do neither and instead I tightened my arm around Judy's waist and pulled her closer against me and kissed the silken hollow of her throat and I could feel the sharp bone in her hip jabbing against mine and I didn't care because that was pain that was pleasure and I felt the gentle resilience of her breast suddenly against my rib cage and felt her arm tighten protectively around me and her fingernails bite sharply into my arm and I knew that she was trying not to cry and that if I said anything at all it would make her cry and there would be that sloppy scene we'd been trying to avoid and so I said nothing but only held her and kissed her lightly on the eyes and I knew that people were looking at us and snickering and I didn't give a damn and I knew that she wanted me and wanted me to stay and we both knew that I couldn't and all around us about ten other young men were going through similar tableaux with their girlfriends or folks and everybody was stern and pale and worried and trying to look unconcerned and casual and so many women were trying not to cry that the humidity in the station was trembling at the saturation point. I remember Denny standing near the door with a foot propped on his suitcase and he was flashing his too-white teeth and his too-wide smile and he reeked of cheap cologne as he told his small knot of admirers in an overly loud voice that he didn't give a damn if he went or not because he'd knocked up a broad and her old man was tryin to put the screws on him and this was a good way to get outta town anyway and the government would protect him from the old man and he'd come back in a year or so on top of the world and the heat would be off and he could start collectin female scalps again and besides his father had been in and been a hero and he could do anything better than that old bastard and besides he hated those goddamned Gooks and he was gonna get him a Commie see if he didn't. I remember that the train came quietly in then and that it still looked like a big iron beast although now it was a silent beast with no smoke or sparks but with magic still hidden inside it although I knew now that it might be a dark magic and then we had to climb inside and I was kissing Judy good-bye and telling her I loved her and she was kissing me and telling me that she would wait for me and I don't know if we were telling the truth or even if we knew ourselves what the truth was and then Judy was crying openly and I was swallowed by the iron beast and we were roaring away from the town and snickering across the web of tracks and booming over the switches and I saw my old house flash by and I could see my old window and I almost imagined that I could see myself as a kid with my nose pressed against the window looking out and watching my older self roar by and neither of us suspecting that the other was there and neither ever working up enough nerve to watch the trains dance. And I remember that all during that long train ride I could hear Denny's raucous voice somewhere in the distance talking about how he couldn't wait to get to Gookland and he'd heard that Gook snatch was even better than nigger snatch and free too and he was gonna get him a Commie he couldn't wait to get him a goddamned Commie and as the train slashed across the wide fertile farmlands of the Midwest the last thing I knew before sleep that night was the wet smell of freshly turned earth.

—The ant noses the worm disdainfully and then passes out of the field of vision. The only movement now is the ripple of the tall grass and the flash of birds in the shaggy tree. The sky is clouding up again, thunderheads rumbling up over the horizon and rolling across the sky. Two large forms appear near the shaggy tree at the other extreme of the field of vision. The singing of the birds stops as if turned off by a switch. The two forms move about vaguely near the shaggy tree, rustling the grass. The angle of the field of vision gives a foreshortening effect, and it is difficult to make out just what the figures are. There is a sharp command, the human voice sounding strangely thin under the sighing of the wind. The two figures move away from the shaggy tree, pushing through the grass. They are medics; haggard, dirty soldiers with big red crosses painted on their helmets and armbands and several days' growth on their chins. They look tired, harried, scared and determined, and they are moving rapidly, half-crouching, searching for something on the ground and darting frequent wary glances back over their shoulders. As they approach they seem to grow larger and larger, elongating toward the sky as their movement shifts the perspective. They stop a few feet away and reach down, lifting up a body that has been hidden by the tall grass. It is Denny, the back of his head blown away, his eyes bulging horribly open. The medics lower Denny's body back into the sheltering grass and bend over it, fumbling with something. They finally straighten, glance hurriedly about and move forward. The two grimy figures swell until they fill practically the entire field of vision, only random patches of the sky and the ground underfoot visible around their bulk. The medics come to a stop about a foot away. The scarred, battered, mud-caked combat boot of the medic now dominates the scene, looking big as a mountain. From the combat boot, the medic's leg seems to stretch incredibly toward the sky, like a fatigue-swathed beanstalk, with just a suggestion of a head and a helmet floating somewhere at the top. The other medic cannot be seen at all now, having stepped over and out of the field of vision. His shallow breathing and occasional muttered obscenities can be heard. The first medic bends over, his huge hand seeming to leap down from the sky, and touches the arm, lifting the wrist and feeling for a pulse. The medic holds the wrist for a while and then sighs and lets it go. The wrist plops limply back into the cold sucking mud, splattering it. The medic's hand swells in the direction of the upper arm, and then fades momentarily out of the field of vision, although his wrist remains barely visible and his arm seems to stretch back like a highway into the middle distance. The medic tugs, and his hand comes back clutching a tarnished dog tag. Both of the medic's hands disappear forward out of the field of vision. Hands prying the jaw open, jamming the dog tag into the teeth, the metal cold and slimy against the tongue and gums, pressing the jaws firmly closed again, the dog tag feeling huge and immovable inside the mouth. The world is the medic's face now, looming like a scarred cliff inches away, his bloodshot twitching eyes as huge as moons, his mouth, hanging slackly open with exhaustion, as cavernous and bottomless as a magic cave to a little boy. The medic has halitosis, his breath filled with the richly corrupt smell of freshly turned earth. The medic stretches out two fingers which completely occupy the field of vision, blocking out even the sky. The medic's fingertips are the only things in the world now. They are stained and dirty and one has a white scar across the whorls. The medic's fingertips touch the eyelids and gently press down. And now there is nothing but darkness—

And I remember the way dawn would crack the eastern sky, the rosy blush slowly spreading and staining the black of night, chasing away the darkness, driving away the stars. And I remember the way a woman looks at you when she loves you, and the sound that a kitten makes when it is happy, and the way that snowflakes blur and melt against a warm windowpane in winter. I remember. I remember.

• A Special Kind of Morning •

THE DOOMSDAY MACHINE IS THE HUMAN RACE.
—*Graffito in New York Subway*
Seventy-ninth Street Station

DID Y'EVER HEAR the one about the old man and the sea?

Halt a minute, lordling; stop and listen. It's a fine story, full of balance and point and social pith; short and direct. It's not mine. Mine are long and rambling and parenthetical and they corrode the moral fiber right out of a man. Come to think, I won't tell you that one after all. A man of my age has a right to prefer his own material, and let the critics be damned. I've a prejudice now for webs of my own weaving.

Sit down, sit down: butt against pavement, yes; it's been done before. Everything has, near about. Now that's not an expression of your black pessimism, or your futility, or what have you. Pessimism's just the commonsense knowledge that there's more ways for something to go wrong than for it to go right, from our point of view anyway—which is not necessarily that of the management, or of the mechanism, if you prefer your cosmos depersonalized. As for futility, everybody dies the true death eventually; even though executives may dodge it for a few hundred years, the hole gets them all in the end, and I imagine that's futility enough for a start. The philosophical man accepts both as constants and then doesn't let them bother him any. Sit down, damn it; don't pretend you've important business to be about. Young devil, you are in the enviable position of having absolutely nothing to do because it's going to take you a while to recover from what you've just done.

There. That's better. Comfortable? You don't look it; you look like you've just sat in a puddle of piss and're wondering what the socially appropriate reaction is. Hypocrisy's an art, boy; you'll improve with age. Now you're bemused, lordling, that you let an old soak chivy you around, and now he's making fun of you. Well, the expression on your face is worth a chuckle; if you could see it you'd laugh yourself. You will see it years from now too, on some other young man's face—that's the only kind of mirror that ever shows it clear. And *you'll* be an old soak by that time, and you'll laugh and insult the young buck's dignity, but you'll be laughing more at the reflection of the man you used to be than at that particular stud himself. And you'll probably have to tell the buck just what I've told you to cool him down, and there's a laugh in that too; listen for the echo of a million and one laughs behind you. I hear a million now.

How do I get away with such insolence? What've I got to lose, for one thing. That gives you a certain perspective. And I'm socially instructive in spite of myself—I'm valuable as an object lesson. For that matter, why is an arrogant young aristo like you sitting there and putting up with my guff? Don't even bother to answer; I knew the minute you came whistling down the street, full of steam and strut. Nobody gets up this early in the morning anymore, unless they're old as I am and begrudge sleep's dry-run of death—or unless they've never been to bed in the first place. The world's your friend this morning, a toy for you to play with and examine and stuff in your mouth to taste, and you're letting your benevolence slop over onto the old degenerate you've met on the street. You're even happy enough to listen, though you're being quizzical about it, and you're sitting over there feeling benignly superior. And I'm sitting over *here* feeling benignly superior. A nice arrangement, and everyone content. Well, then, mornings make you feel that way. Especially if you're fresh from a night at the Towers, the musk of Lady Ni still warm on your flesh.

A blush—my buck, you *are* new-hatched. How did I know? Boy, you'd be surprised what I know; I'm occasionally startled myself, and I've been working longer to get it catalogued. Besides, hindsight is a comfortable substitute for omnipotence. And I'm not blind yet. You have the unmistakable look of a cub who's just found out he can do something else with it besides piss. An incredible revelation, as I recall. The blazing significance of it will wear a little with the years, though not all that much, I suppose; until you get down to the brink of the Ultimate Cold, when you stop worrying about the identity of warmth, or demanding that it pay toll in pleasure. Any hand of clay, long's the blood still runs the tiny degree that's just enough for difference. Warmth's the only definition between you and graveyard dirt. But morning's not for graveyards, though it works the other way. Did y'know they also used to use that to make babies? 'S'fact, though few know it now. It's a versatile beast. Oh *come*—buck, cub, young cocksman—stop being so damn surprised. People ate, slept, and fornicated before you were born, some of them anyway, and a few will probably even find the courage to keep on at it after you die. You don't have to keep it secret; the thing's been circulated in this region once or twice before. You weren't the first to learn how to make the beast do its trick, though I *know* you don't believe that. *I* don't believe it concerning myself and I've had a long time to learn.

You make me think, sitting there innocent as an egg and twice as vulnerable; yes, you are definitely about to make me think, and I believe I'll have to think of some things I always regret having thought about, just to keep me from growing maudlin. Damn it, boy, you *do* make me think. Life's strange—wet-eared as you are, you've probably had that thought a dozen times already, probably had it this morning as you tumbled out of your fragrant bed to meet the rim of the sun; well, I've four times your age, and a ream more experience, and I still can't think of anything better to sum up the world: life's strange. 'S been said, yes. But *think*, boy, how strange: the two of us talking, you coming, me going; me knowing where you've got to go, you suspecting where I've been, and the same destination for both. O strange, very strange! Damn it, you're a deader already if you can't see the strangeness of that, if you can't sniff the poetry; it reeks of it, as of blood. And I've smelt blood, buck. It has a very distinct odor; you know it when you smell it. You're bound for blood; for blood and passion and high deeds and all the rest of the business, and maybe for a little understanding if you're lucky and have eyes to see. Me, I'm bound for nothing, literally. I've come to rest here in Kos, and while the Red Lady spins her web of colors across the sky I sit and weave my own webs of words and dreams and other spider stuff—

What? Yes, I do talk too much; old men like to babble, and philosophy's a cushion for old bones. But it's my profession now, isn't it, and I've promised you a story. What happened to my leg? That's a bloody story, but I said you're bound for blood; I know the mark. I'll tell it to you then: perhaps it'll help you to understand when you reach the narrow place, perhaps it'll even help you to think, although that's a horrible weight to wish on any man. It's customary to notarize my card before I start, keep you from running off at the end without paying. Thank you, young sir. Beware of some of these beggars, buck; they have a credit tally at Central greater than either of us will ever run up. They turn a tidy profit out of poverty. I'm an honest pauper, more's the pity, exist mostly on the subsidy, if you call that existing—Yes, I know. The leg.

We'll have to go back to the Realignment for that, more than half a century ago, and half a sector away, at World. This was before World was a member of the Commonwealth. In fact, that's what the Realignment was about, the old Combine overthrown by the Quaestors, who then opted for amalgamation and forced World into the Commonwealth. That's where and when the story starts.

Start it with waiting.

A lot of things start like that, waiting. And when the thing you're waiting for is probable death, and you're lying there loving life and suddenly noticing how pretty everything is and listening to the flint hooves of darkness click closer, feeling the iron-shod boots strike relentless sparks from the surface of your mind, knowing that death is about to fall out of the sky and that there's no way to twist out from under—then, waiting can take time. Minutes become hours, hours become unthinkable horrors. Add enough horrors together, total the scaly snouts, and you've got a day and a half I once spent laying up in a mountain valley in the Blackfriars on World, almost the last day I ever spent anywhere.

This was just a few hours after D'kotta. Everything was a mess, nobody really knew what was happening, everybody's communication lines cut. I was just a buck myself then, working with the Quaestors in the field, a hunted criminal. Nobody knew what the Combine would do next, we didn't know what *we'd* do next, groups surging wildly from one place to another at random, panic and riots all over the planet, even in the Controlled Environments.

And D'kotta-on-the-Blackfriars was a seventy-mile swath of smoking insanity, capped by boiling umbrellas of smoke that eddied ashes from the ground to the stratosphere and back. At night it pulsed with molten scum, ugly as a lanced blister, lighting up the cloud cover across the entire horizon, visible for hundreds of miles. It was this ugly glow that finally panicked even the zombies in the Environments, probably the first strong emotion in their lives.

It'd been hard to sum up the effects of the battle. We thought that we had the edge, that the Combine was close to breaking, but nobody knew for sure. If they weren't as close to folding as we thought, then we were probably finished. The Quaestors had exhausted most of their hoarded resources at D'kotta, and we certainly couldn't hit the Combine any harder. If they could shrug off the blow, then they could wear us down.

Personally, I didn't see how anything could shrug *that* off. I'd watched it all and it'd shaken me considerably. There's an old-time expression, "put the fear of God into him." That's what D'kotta had done for me. There wasn't any God anymore, but I'd seen fire vomit from the heavens and the earth ripped wide for rape, and it'd been an impressive enough surrogate. Few people ever realized how close the Combine and the Quaestors had come to destroying World between them, there at D'kotta.

We'd crouched that night—the team and I—on the high stone ramparts of the tallest of the Blackfriars, hopefully far away from anything that could fall on us. There were twenty miles of low, gnarly foothills between us and the rolling savannahland where the city of D'kotta had been minutes before, but the ground under our bellies heaved and quivered like a sick animal, and the rock was hot to the touch: feverish.

We could've gotten farther away, *should have* gotten farther away, but we had to watch. That'd been decided without anyone saying a word, without any question about it. It was impossible *not* to watch. It never even occurred to any of us to take another safer course of action. When reality is being turned inside out like a dirty sock, you watch, or you are less than human. So we watched it all from beginning to end: two hours that became a single second lasting for eons. Like a still photograph of time twisted into a scream—the scream reverberating on forever and yet taking no duration at all to experience.

We didn't talk. We *couldn't* talk—the molecules of the air itself shrieked too loudly, and the deep roar of explosions was a continual drumroll—but we wouldn't have talked even if we'd been able. You don't speak in the presence of an angry God. Sometimes we'd look briefly at each other. Our faces were all nearly identical: ashen, waxy, eyes of glass, blank, and lost as pale driftwood stranded on a beach by the tide. We'd been driven through the gamut of expressions into *extremis*—rictus: faces so contorted and strained they ached—and beyond to the quietus of shock: muscles too slack and flaccid to respond anymore. We'd only look at each other for a second, hardly focusing, almost not aware of what we were seeing, and then our eyes would be dragged back as if by magnetism to the Fire.

At the beginning we'd clutched each other, but as the battle progressed we slowly drew apart, huddling into individual agony; the thing so big that human warmth meant nothing, so frightening that the instinct to gather together for protection was reversed, and the presence of others only intensified the realization of how ultimately naked you were. Earlier we'd set up a scattershield to filter the worst of the hard radiation—the gamma and intense infrared and ultraviolet—blunt some of the heat and shock and noise. We thought we had a fair chance of surviving, then, but we couldn't have run anyway. We were fixed by the beauty of horror/ horror of beauty, surely as if by a spike driven through our backbones into the rock.

And away over the foothills, God danced in anger, and his feet struck the ground to ash.

What was it like?

Kos still has oceans and storms. Did y'ever watch the sea lashed by high winds? The storm boils the water into froth, whips it white, until it becomes an ocean of ragged lace to the horizon, whirlpools of milk, not a fleck of blue left alive. The land looked like this at D'kotta. The hills *moved*. The Quaestors had a discontinuity projector there, and under its lash the ground stirred like sluggish batter under a baker's spoon; stirred, shuddered, groaned, cracked, broke: acres heaved themselves into new mountains, other acres collapsed into canyons.

Imagine a giant asleep just under the surface of the earth, overgrown by fields, dreaming dreams of rock and crystal. Imagine him moving restlessly, the long rhythm of his dreams touched by nightmare, tossing, moaning, tremors signaling unease in waves up and down his miles-long frame. Imagine him catapulted into waking terror, lurching suddenly to his knees with the bawling roar of ten million burning calves: a steaming claw of rock and black earth raking for the sky. Now, in a wink, imagine the adjacent land hurtling downward, sinking like a rock in a pond, opening a womb a thousand feet wide, swallowing everything and grinding it to powder. Then, almost too quick to see, imagine the mountain and the crater switching, the mountain collapsing all at once and washing the feet of the older Blackfriars with a tidal wave of earth, then tumbling down to make a pit; at the same time the sinking earth at the bottom of the other crater reversing itself and erupting upward into a quaking fist of rubble. Then they switch again, and keep switching. Like watching the same film clip continuously run forward and backward. Now multiply that by a million and spread it out so that all you can see to the horizon is a stew of humping rock. D'y'visualize it? Not a tenth of it.

Dervishes of fire stalked the chaos, melting into each other, whirlpooling. Occasionally a tactical nuclear explosion would punch a hole in the night, a brief intense flare that would be swallowed like a candle in a murky snowstorm. Once a tacnuke detonation coincided with the upthrusting of a rubble mountain, with an effect like that of a firecracker exploding inside a swinging sack of grain.

The city itself was gone; we could no longer see a trace of anything man-made, only the stone maelstrom. The river Delva had also vanished, flash-boiled to steam; for a while we could see the gorge of its dry bed stitching across the plain, but then the ground heaved up and obliterated it.

It was unbelievable that anything could be left alive down there. Very little was. Only the remainder of the heavy weapons sections on both sides continued to survive, invisible to us in the confusion. Still protected by powerful phasewalls and scattershields, they pounded blindly at each other—the Combine somewhat ineffectively with biodeths and tacnukes, the Quaestors responding by stepping up the discontinuity projector. There was only one, in the command module—the Quaestor technicians were praying it wouldn't be wiped out by a random strike—and it was a terraforming device and not actually a "weapon" at all, but the Combine had been completely unprepared for it, and were suffering horribly as a result.

Everything began to flicker, random swatches of savannahland shimmering and blurring, phasing in and out of focus in a jerky, mismatched manner: that filmstrip run through a spastic projector. At first we thought it must be heat eddies caused by the fires, but then the flickering increased drastically in frequency and tempo, speeding up until it was impossible to keep anything in focus even for a second, turning the wide veldt into a mad kaleidoscope of writhing, interchanging shapes and color-patterns from one horizon to the other. It was impossible to watch it for long. It hurt the eyes and filled us with an oily, inexplicable panic that we were never able to verbalize. We looked away, filled with the musty surgings of vague fear.

We didn't know then that we were watching the first practical application of a process that'd long been suppressed by both the Combine and the Commonwealth, a process based on the starship dimensional "drive" (which isn't a "drive" at all, but the word's passed into the common press) that enabled a high-cycling discontinuity projector to throw time out of phase within a limited area, so that a spot *here* would be a couple of minutes ahead or behind a spot a few inches away, in continuity sequence. That explanation would give a psychophysicist fits, since "time" is really nothing at all like the way we "experience" it, so the process "really" doesn't do what I've said it does—doing something *really* abstruse instead—but that's close enough to what it does on a practical level, 'cause even if the time distortion is an "illusionary effect"—like the sun seeming to rise and set—they still used it to kill people. So it threw time out of phase, and kept doing it, switching the dislocation at random: so that in any given square foot of land there might be four or five discrepancies in time sequence that kept interchanging. Like, *here* might be one minute "ahead" of the base "now," and then a second later (language breaks down hopelessly under this stuff; you need the math) *here* would be two minutes behind the now, then five minutes behind, then three ahead, and so on. And all the adjacent zones in that square foot are going through the same switching process at the same time (goddamn this language!). The Combine's machinery tore itself to pieces. So did the people: some died of suffocation because of a five-minute discrepancy between an inhaled breath and oxygen received by the lungs, some drowned in their own blood.

It took about ten minutes, at least as far as we were concerned as unaffected observers. I had a psychophysicist tell me once that "it" had both continued to "happen" forever and had never "happened" at all, and that neither statement canceled out the validity of the other, that *each* statement in fact was both "applicable" and "nonapplicable" to the same situation consecutively—and I did not understand. It took ten minutes.

At the end of that time, the world got very still.

We looked up. The land had stopped churning. A tiny star appeared amongst the rubble in the middle distance, small as a pinhead but incredibly bright and clear. It seemed to suck the night into it like a vortex, as if it were a pinprick through the worldstuff into a more intense reality, as if it were gathering a great breath for a shout.

We buried our heads in our arms as one, instinctively.

There was a very bright light, a light that we could feel through the tops of our heads, a light that left dazzling afterimages even through closed and shrouded lids. The mountain leaped under us, bounced us into the air again and again, battered us into near unconsciousness. We never even heard the roar.

After a while, things got quiet again, except for a continuous low rumbling. When we looked up, there were thick, sluggish tongues of molten magma oozing up in vast flows across the veldt, punctuated here and there by spectacular shower-fountains of vomited sparks.

Our scattershield had taken the brunt of the blast, borne it just long enough to save our lives, and then overloaded and burnt itself to scrap; one of the first times *that's* ever happened.

Nobody said anything. We didn't look at each other. We just lay there.

The chrono said an hour went by, but nobody was aware of it.

Finally, a couple of us got up, in silence, and started to stumble aimlessly back and forth. One by one, the rest crawled to their feet. Still in silence, still trying not to look at each other, we automatically cleaned ourselves up. You hear someone say "it made me shit my pants," and you think it's an expression; not under the right stimuli. Automatically, we treated our bruises and lacerations, automatically we tidied the camp up, buried the ruined scatterfield generator. Automatically, we sat down again and stared numbly at the light show on the savannah.

Each of us knew the war was over—we knew it with the gut rather than the head. It was an emotional reaction, but very calm, very resigned, very passive. It was a thing too big for questioning; it became a self-evident fact. After D'kotta, there could be nothing else. Period. The war was over.

We were almost right. But not quite.

In another hour or so, a man from field HQ came up over the mountain shoulder in a stolen vacform and landed in camp. The man switched off the vac, jumped down, took two steps toward the parapet overlooking hell, stopped. We saw his stomach muscles jump, tighten. He took a stumbling half-step back, then stopped again. His hand went up to shield his throat, dropped, hesitated, went back up. We said nothing. The HQ directing the D'kotta campaign had been sensibly located behind the Blackfriars: they had been shielded by the mountain chain and had seen nothing but glare against the cloud cover. This was his first look at the city; at where the city had been. I watched the muscles play in his back, saw his shoulders hunch as if under an unraised fist. A good many of the Quaestor men involved in planning the D'kotta operation committed suicide immediately after the Realignment; a good many didn't. I don't know what category this one belonged in.

The liaison man finally turned his head, dragged himself away. His movements were jerky, and his face was an odd color, but he was under control. He pulled Heynith, our team leader, aside. They talked for a half hour. The liaison man showed Heynith a map, scribbled on a pad for Heynith to see, gave Heynith some papers. Heynith nodded occasionally. The liaison man said good-bye, half-ran to his vacform. The vac lifted with an erratic surge, steadied, then disappeared in a long arc over the gnarled backs of the Blackfriars. Heynith stood in the dirtswirl kicked up by the backwash and watched impassively.

It got quiet again, but it was a little more apprehensive.

Heynith came over, studied us for a while, then told us to get ready to move out. We stared at him. He repeated it in a quiet, firm voice; unendurably patient. Hush for a second, then somebody groaned, somebody else cursed, and the spell of D'kotta was partially broken, for the moment. We awoke enough to ready our gear; there was even a little talking, though not much.

Heynith appeared at our head and led us out in a loose travel formation, diagonally across the face of the slope, then up toward the shoulder. We reached the notch we'd found earlier and started down the other side.

Everyone wanted to look back at D'kotta. No one did.

Somehow, it was still night.

We never talked much on the march, of course, but tonight the silence was spooky: you could hear boots crunch on stone, the slight rasp of breath, the muted jangle of knives occasionally bumping against thighs. You could hear our fear; you could smell it, could see it.

We could touch it, we could taste it.

I was a member of something so old that they even had to dig up the name for it when they were rooting through the rubble of ancient history, looking for concepts to use against the Combine: a "commando team." Don't ask me what it means, but that's what it's called. Come to think, I know what it means in terms of flesh: it means ugly. Long ugly days and nights that come back in your sleep even uglier, so that you don't want to think about it at all because it squeezes your eyeballs like a vise. Cold and dark and wet, with sudden death looming up out of nothing at any time and jarring you with mortality like a rubber glove full of ice water slapped across your face. Living jittery high all the time, so that everything gets so real that it looks fake. You live in an anticipation that's pain, like straddling a fence with a knife blade for a top rung, waiting for something to come along in the dark and push you off. You get so you like it. The pain's so consistent that you forget it's there, you forget there ever was a time when you didn't have it, and you live on the adrenaline.

We liked it. We were dedicated. We *hated*. It gave us something to do with our hate, something tangible we could see. And nobody'd done it but us for hundreds of years; there was an exultation to that. The Scholars and Antiquarians who'd started the Quaestor movement—left fullsentient and relatively unwatched so they could better piece together the muddle of prehistory from generations of inherited archives—they'd been smart. They knew their only hope of baffling the Combine was to hit them with radical concepts and tactics, things they didn't have instructions for handling, things out of the Combine's experience. So they scooped concepts out of prehistory, as far back as the archives go, even finding *written* records somewhere and having to figure out how to use them.

Out of one of these things, they got the idea of "guerrilla" war. No, I don't know what that means either, but what it *means* is playing the game by your own rules instead of the enemy's. Oh, you let the enemy keep playing by *his* rules, see, but you play by your own. Gives you a wider range of moves. You *do* things. I mean, *ridiculous* things, but so ancient they don't have any defense against them because they never thought they'd have to defend against *that*. Most of the time they never even knew *that* existed.

Like, we used to run around with these projectile weapons the Quaestors had copied from old plans and mass-produced in the autfacs on the sly by stealing computer time. The things worked by a chemical reaction inside the mechanism that would spit these tiny missiles out at a high velocity. The missile would hit you so hard it would actually lodge itself in your body, puncture internal organs, *kill* you. I know it sounds like an absurd concept, but there were advantages.

Don't forget how tightly controlled a society the Combine's was; even worse than the Commonwealth in its own way. We couldn't just steal energy weapons or biodeths and use them, because all those things operated on broadcast power from the Combine, and as soon as one was reported missing, the Combine would just cut the relay for that particular code. We couldn't make them ourselves, because unless you used the Combine's broadcast power you'd need a ton of generator equipment with each weapon to provide enough energy to operate it, and we didn't have the technology to miniaturize that much machinery. (Later some genius figured out a way to make, say, a functioning biodeth with everything but the energy source and then cut into and tap Combine broadcast power without showing up on the coding board, but that was toward the end anyway, and most of them were stockpiled for the shock troops at D'kotta.) At least the "guns" worked. And there were even unexpected advantages. We found that tanglefields, scattershields, phasewalls, personal warders, all the usual defenses, were unable to stop the "bullets" (the little missiles fired by the "guns")—they were just too sophisticated to stop anything as crude as a lump of metal moving at relatively sluggish ballistic speeds. Same with "bombs" and "grenades"—devices designed to have a chemical reaction violent enough to kill in an enclosed place. And the list went on and on. The Combine thought we couldn't move around, because all vehicles were coded and worked on broadcast power. Did you ever hear of "bicycles"? They're devices for translating mechanical energy into motion, they ride on wheels that you actually make revolve with physical labor. And the bicycles didn't have enough metal or mass to trigger sentryfields or show up on sweep probes, so we could go undetected to places they thought nobody could reach. Communicate? We used mirrors to flash messages, used puffs of smoke as code, had people actually *carry* messages from one place to another.

More important, we *personalized* war. That was the most radical thing, that was the thing that turned us from kids running around and having fun breaking things into men with bitter faces, that was the thing that took the heart out of the Combine more than anything else. That's why people still talk about the Realignment with horror today, even after all these years, especially in the Commonwealth.

We killed people. *We* did it, ourselves. We walked up and stabbed them. I mentioned a knife before, boy, and I knew you didn't know what it was; you bluff well for a kid—that's the way to a reputation for wisdom: look sage and always keep your mouth shut about your ignorance. Well, a knife is a tapering piece of metal with a handle, sharpened on the sides and very sharp at the tapered end, sharp enough so that when you strike someone with it the metal goes right into their flesh, cuts them, rips them open, *kills* them, and there is blood on your hands which feels wet and sticky and is hard to wash off because it dries and sticks to the little hairs on the backs of your wrists. We learned how to hit people hard enough to kill them, snap the bones inside the skin like dry sticks inside oiled cloth. We did. We strangled them with lengths of wire. You're shocked. So was the Combine. They had grown used to killing at a great distance, the push of a button, the flick of a switch, using vast, clean, impersonal forces to do their annihilation. *We* killed people. We killed *people*—not statistics and abstractions. We heard their screams, we saw their faces, we smelled their blood, and their vomit and shit and urine when their systems let go after death. You have to be crazy to do things like that. We *were* crazy. We were a good team.

There were twelve of us in the group, although we mostly worked in sections of four. I was in the team leader's section, and it had been my family for more than two years:

Heynith, stocky, balding, leather-faced; a hard, fair man; brilliant organizer.

Ren, impassive, withdrawn, taciturn, frighteningly competent, of a strange humor.

Goth, young, tireless, bullheaded, given to sudden enthusiasms and depressions; he'd only been with us for about four months, a replacement for Mason, who had been killed while trying to escape from a raid on Cape Itica.

And me.

We were all warped men, emotional cripples one way or the other.

We were all crazy.

The Combine could never understand that kind of craziness, in spite of the millions of people they'd killed or shriveled impersonally over the years. They were afraid of that craziness, they were baffled by it, never could plan to counter it or take it into account. They couldn't really believe it.

That's how we'd taken the Blackfriars Transmitter, hours before D'kotta. It had been impregnable—wrapped in layer after layer of defense fields against missile attack, attack by chemical or biological agents, transmitted energy, almost anything. We'd walked in. They'd never imagined anyone would do that, that it was even possible to attack that way, so there was no defense against it. The guardsystems were designed to meet more esoteric threats. And even after ten years of slowly escalating guerrilla action, they still didn't *really* believe anyone would use his body to wage war. So we walked in. And killed everybody there. The staff was a sentient tech clone of ten and an executive foreman. No nulls or zombies. The ten identical technicians milled in panic, the foreman stared at us in disbelief, and what I think was distaste that we'd gone so far outside the bounds of procedure. We killed them like you kill insects, not really thinking about it much, except for that part of you that always thinks about it, that records it and replays it while you sleep. Then we blew up the transmitter with chemical explosives. Then, as the flames leaped up and ate holes in the night, we'd gotten on our bicycles and rode like hell toward the Blackfriars, the mountains hunching and looming ahead, as jagged as black snaggle-teeth against the industrial glare of the sky. A tanglefield had snatched at us for a second, but then we were gone.

That's all that I personally had to do with the "historic" Battle of

D'kotta. It was enough. We'd paved the way for the whole encounter. Without the transmitter's energy, the Combine's weapons and transportation systems—including liftshafts, slidewalks, irisdoors, and windows, heating, lighting, waste disposal—were inoperable; D'kotta was immobilized. Without the station's broadcast matter, thousands of buildings, industrial complexes, roadways, and homes had collapsed into chaos, literally collapsed. More important, without broadcast nourishment, D'kotta's four major Cerebrums—handling an incredible complexity of military/industrial/administrative tasks—were knocked out of operation, along with a number of smaller Cerebrums: the synapses need constant nourishment to function, and so do the sophont ganglion units, along with the constant flow of the psychocybernetic current to keep them from going mad from sensory deprivation, and even the nulls would soon grow intractable as hunger stung them almost to self-awareness, finally to die after a few days. Any number of the lowest-ranking sentient clones—all those without stomachs or digestive systems, mostly in the military and industrial castes—would find themselves in the same position as the nulls; without broadcast nourishment, they would die within days. And without catarcs in operation to duplicate the function of atrophied intestines, the buildup of body wastes would poison them anyway, even if they could somehow get nourishment. The independent food dispensers for the smaller percentage of fullsentients and higher clones simply could not increase their output enough to feed that many people, even if converted to intravenous systems. To say nothing of the zombies in the Environments scattered throughout the city.

There were backup fail-safe systems, of course, but they hadn't been used in centuries, the majority of them had fallen into disrepair and didn't work, and other Quaestor teams made sure the rest of them wouldn't work either.

Before a shot had been fired, D'kotta was already a major disaster.

The Combine had reacted as we'd hoped, as they'd been additionally prompted to react by intelligence reports of Quaestor massings in strength around D'kotta that it'd taken weeks to leak to the Combine from unimpeachable sources. The Combine was pouring forces into D'kotta within hours, nearly the full strength of the traditional military caste and a large percentage of the militia they'd cobbled together out of industrial clones when the Quaestors had begun to get seriously troublesome, plus a major portion of their heavy armament. They had hoped to surprise the Quaestors, catch them between the city and the inaccessible portion of the Blackfriars, quarter the area with so much strength it'd be impossible to dodge them, run the Quaestors down, annihilate them, break the back of the movement.

It had worked the other way around.

For years, the Quaestors had stung and run, always retreating when the Combine advanced, never meeting them in conventional battle, never hitting them with anything really heavy. Then, when the Combine had risked practically all of its military resources on one gigantic effort calculated to be effective against the usual Quaestor behavior, we had suddenly switched tactics. The Quaestors had waited to meet the Combine's advance and had hit the Combine forces with everything they'd been able to save, steal, hoard, and buy clandestinely from sympathizers in the Commonwealth in over fifteen years of conspiracy and campaign aimed at this moment.

Within an hour of the first tacnuke exchange, the city had ceased to exist, everything leveled except two of the Cerebrums and the Escridel Creche. Then the Quaestors activated their terraforming devices—which I believe they bought from a firm here on Kos, as a matter of fact. This was completely insane—terraforming systems used indiscriminately can destroy entire planets—but it was the insanity of desperation, and they did it anyway. Within a half hour, the remaining Combine heavy armaments battalions and the two Cerebrums ceased to exist. A few minutes later, the supposedly invulnerable Escridel Creche ceased to exist, the first time in history a creche had ever been destroyed. Then, as the cycling energies got out of hand and filterfeedback built to a climax, everything on the veldt ceased to exist.

The carnage had been inconceivable.

Take the vast population of D'kotta as a base, the second largest city on World, one of the biggest even in this sector of the Commonwealth. The subfleets had been in, bringing the betja harvest and other goods up the Delva; river traffic was always heaviest at that time of year. The mines and factories had been in full swing, and the giant sprawl of the Westernese Shipyards and Engine Works. Add the swarming inhabitants of the six major Controlled Environments that circled the city. Add the city-within-a-city of Admin South, in charge of that hemisphere. Add the twenty generations of D'kotta Combine fullsentients whose discorporate ego-patterns had been preserved in the mountain of "indestructible" micromolecular circuitry called the Escridel Creche. (Those executives had died the irreversible true death, without hope of resurrection this time, even as disembodied intellects housed within artificial mind-environments: the records of their brain's unique pattern of electrical/chemical/psychocybernetic rhythms and balances had been destroyed, and you can't rebuild consciousness from a fused puddle of slag. This hit the Combine where they lived, literally, and had more impact than anything else.) Add the entire strength of both opposing forces; all of our men—who suspected what would happen—had been suicide volunteers. Add all of the elements together.

The total goes up into the multiples of billions.

The number was too big to grasp. Our minds fumbled at it while we marched, and gave up. It was too big.

I stared at Ren's back as we walked, a nearly invisible mannequin silhouette, and tried to multiply that out to the necessary figure. I staggered blindly along, lost and inundated beneath thousands of individual arms, legs, faces; a row of faces blurring off into infinity, all screaming—and the imagining nowhere near the actuality.

Billions.

How many restless ghosts out of that many deaders? Who do they haunt?

Billions.

Dawn caught us about two hours out. It came with no warning, as usual. We were groping through World's ink-dark, moonless night, watched only by the million icy eyes of evening, shreds of witchfire crystal, incredibly cold and distant. I'd watched them night after night for years, scrawling their indecipherable hieroglyphics across the sky, indifferent to man's incomprehension. I stopped for a second on a rise, pushing back the infrared lenses, staring at the sky. What program was printed there, suns for ciphers, worlds for decimal points? An absurd question—I was nearly as foolish as you once, buck—but it was the first fully verbalized thought I'd had since I'd realized the nakedness of flesh, back there on the parapet as my life tore itself apart. I asked it again, half-expecting an answer, watching my breath turn to plumes and tatters, steaming in the silver chill of the stars.

The sun came up like a meteor. It scuttled up from the horizon with that unsettling, deceptive speed that even natives of World never quite get used to. New light washed around us, blue and raw at first, deepening the shadows and honing their edges. The sun continued to hitch itself up the sky, swallowing stars, a watery pink flush wiping the horizon clear of night. The light deepened, mellowed into gold. We floated through silver mist that swirled up around the mountain's knobby knees. I found myself crying silently as I walked the high ridge between mist and sky, absorbing the morning with a new hunger, grappling with a thought that was still too big for my mind and kept slipping elusively away, just out of reach. There was a low hum as our warmsuits adjusted to the growing warmth, polarizing from black to white, bleeding heat back into the air. Down the flanks of the Blackfriars and away across the valley below—visible now as the mists pirouetted past us to the summits—the night plants were dying, shriveling visibly in mile-long swaths of decay. In seconds the Blackfriars were gaunt and barren, turned to hills of ash and bone. The sun was now a bloated yellow disk surrounded by haloes of red and deepening scarlet, shading into the frosty blue of rarefied air. Stripped of softening vegetation, the mountains looked rough and abrasive as pumice, gouged by lunar shadows. The first of the day plants began to appear at our feet, the green spiderwebbing, poking up through cracks in the dry earth.

We came across a new stream, tumbling from melting ice, sluicing a dusty gorge.

An hour later we found the valley.

Heynith led us down onto the marshy plain that rolled away from mountains to horizon. We circled wide, cautiously approaching the valley from the lowlands. Heynith held up his hand, pointed to me, Ren, Goth. The others fanned out across the mouth of the valley, hid, settled down to wait. We went in alone. The speargrass had grown rapidly; it was chest-high. We crawled in, timing our movements to coincide with the long soughing of the morning breeze, so that any rippling of the grass would be taken for natural movement. It took us about a half hour of dusty, sweaty work. When I judged that I'd wormed my way in close enough, I stopped, slowly parted the speargrass enough to peer out without raising my head.

It was a large vacvan, a five-hundred-footer, equipped with waldoes for self-loading.

It was parked near the hill flank on the side of the wide valley.

There were three men with it.

I ducked back into the grass, paused to make sure my "gun" was ready for operation, then crawled laboriously nearer to the van.

It was very near when I looked up again, about twenty-five feet away in the center of a cleared space. I could make out the hologram pictograph that pulsed identification on the side: the symbol for Urheim,

World's largest city and Combine Seat of Board, half a world away in the Northern Hemisphere. They'd come a long way; still thought of as long, though ships whispered between the stars—it was still long for feet and eyes. And another longer way: from fetuses in glass wombs to men stamping and jiggling with cold inside the fold of a mountain's thigh, watching the spreading morning. That made me feel funny to think about. I wondered if they suspected that it'd be the last morning they'd ever see. That made me feel funnier. The thought tickled my mind again, danced away. I checked my gun a second time, needlessly.

I waited, feeling troubled, pushing it down. Two of them were standing together several feet in front of the van, sharing a mild narcotic atomizer, sucking deeply, shuffling with restlessness and cold, staring out across the speargrass to where the plain opened up. They had the stiff, rumpled, puff-eyed look of people who had just spent an uncomfortable night in a cramped place. They were dressed as fullsentients uncloned, junior officers of the military caste, probably hereditary positions inherited from their families, as is the case with most of the uncloned cadet executives. Except for the cadre at Urheim and other major cities, they must have been some of the few surviving clansmen; hundreds of thousands of military cadets and officers had died at D'kotta (along with uncounted clones and semisentients of all ranks), and the caste had never been extremely large in the first place. The by-laws had demanded that the Combine maintain a security force, but it had become mostly traditional, with minimum function, at least among the uncloned higher ranks, almost the last stronghold of old-fashioned nepotism. That was one of the things that had favored the Quaestor uprising, and had forced the Combine to take the unpopular step of impressing large numbers of industrial clones into a militia. The most junior of these two cadets was very young, even younger than me. The third man remained inside the van's cab. I could see his face blurrily through the windfield, kept on against the cold though the van was no longer in motion.

I waited. I knew the others were maneuvering into position around me. I also knew what Heynith was waiting for.

The third man jumped down from the high cab. He was older, wore an officer's hologram: a full executive. He said something to the cadets, moved a few feet toward the back of the van, started to take a piss. The column of golden liquid steamed in the cold air.

Heynith whistled.

I rolled to my knees, parted the speargrass at the edge of the cleared space, swung my gun up. The two cadets started, face muscles tensing into uncertain fear. The older cadet took an involuntary step forward, still clutching the atomizer. Ren and Goth chopped him down, firing a stream of "bullets" into him. The guns made a very loud metallic rattling sound that jarred the teeth, and fire flashed from the ejector ends. Birds screamed upward all along the mountain flank. The impact of the bullets knocked the cadet off his feet, rolled him so that he came to rest belly-down. The atomizer flew through the air, hit, bounced. The younger cadet leaped toward the cab, right into my line of fire. I pulled the trigger, bullets exploded out of the gun. The cadet was kicked backwards, arms swinging wide, slammed against the side of the cab, jerked upright as I continued to fire, spun along the van wall and rammed heavily into the ground. He tottered on one shoulder for a second, then flopped over onto his back. At the sound of the first shot, the executive had whirled—penis still dangling from pantaloons, surplus piss spraying wildly—and dodged for the back of the van, so that Heynith's volley missed and screamed from the van wall, leaving a long scar. The executive dodged again, crouched, came up with a biodeth in one hand, and swung right into a single bullet from Ren just as he began to fire. The impact twirled him in a staggering circle, his finger still pressing the trigger; the carrier beam splashed harmlessly from the van wall, traversed as the executive spun, cut a long swath through the speargrass, the plants shriveling and blackening as the beam swept over them. Heynith opened up again before the beam could reach his clump of grass, sending the executive—somehow still on his feet lurching past the end of the van. The biodeth dropped, went out. Heynith kept firing, the executive dancing bonelessly backwards on his heels, held up by the stream of bullets. Heynith released the trigger. The executive collapsed: a heap of arms and legs at impossible angles.

When we came up to the van, the young cadet was still dying. His body shivered and arched, his heels drummed against the earth, his fingers plucked at nothing, and then he was still. There was a lot of blood.

The others moved up from the valley mouth. Heynith sent them circling around the rim, where the valley walls dipped down on three sides.

We dragged the bodies away and concealed them in some large rocks.

I was feeling numb again, like I had after D'kotta.

I continued to feel numb as we spent the rest of that morning in frantic preparation. My mind was somehow detached as my body sweated and dug and hauled. There was a lot for it to do. We had four heavy industrial lasers, rock-cutters; they were clumsy, bulky, inefficient things to use as weapons, but they'd have to do. This mission had not been planned so much as thrown together, only two hours before the liaison man had contacted us on the parapet. Anything that could possibly work at all would have to be made to work somehow; no time to do it right, just do it. We'd been the closest team in contact with the field HQ who'd received the report, so we'd been snatched; the lasers were the only things on hand that could even approach potential as a heavy weapon, so we'd use the lasers.

Now that we'd taken the van without someone alerting the Combine by radio from the cab, Heynith flashed a signal mirror back toward the shoulder of the mountain we'd quitted a few hours before. The liaison man swooped down ten minutes later, carrying one of the lasers strapped awkwardly to his platvac. He made three more trips, depositing the massive cylinders as carefully as eggs, then gunned his platvac and screamed back toward the Blackfriars in a maniac arc just this side of suicidal. His face was still gray, tight-pressed lips a bloodless white against ash, and he hadn't said a word during the whole unloading procedure. I think he was probably one of the Quaestors who followed the Way of Atonement. I never saw him again. I've sometimes wished I'd had the courage to follow his example, but I rationalize by telling myself that I have atoned with my life rather than my death, and who knows, it might even be somewhat true. It's nice to think so anyway.

It took us a couple of hours to get the lasers into position. We spotted them in four places around the valley walls, dug slanting pits into the slopes to conceal them and tilt the barrels up at the right angle. We finally got them all zeroed on a spot about a hundred feet above the center of the valley floor, the muzzle arrangement giving each a few degrees of leeway on either side. That's where she'd have to come down anyway if she was a standard orbot, the valley being just wide enough to contain the boat and the vacvan, with a safety margin between them. Of course, if they brought her down on the plain outside the valley mouth, things were going to get very hairy; in that case we might be able to lever one or two of the lasers around to bear, or, failing that, we could try to take the orbot on foot once it'd landed, with about one chance in eight of making it. But we thought that they'd land her in the valley; that's where the vacvan had been parked, and they'd want the shelter of the high mountain walls to conceal the orbot from any Quaestor eyes that might be around. If so, that gave us a much better chance. About one out of three.

When the lasers had been positioned, we scattered, four men to an emplacement, hiding in the camouflaged trenches alongside the big barrels. Heynith led Goth and me toward the laser we'd placed about fifty feet up the mountain flank, directly behind and above the vacvan. Ren stayed behind. He stood next to the van—shoulders characteristically slouched, thumbs hooked in his belt, face carefully void of expression—and watched us out of sight. Then he looked out over the valley mouth, hitched up his gun, spat in the direction of Urheim and climbed up into the van cab.

The valley was empty again. From our position the vacvan looked like a shiny toy, sun dogs winking across its surface as it baked in the afternoon heat. An abandoned toy, lost in high weeds, waiting in loneliness to be reclaimed by owners who would never come.

Time passed.

The birds we'd frightened away began to settle back onto the hillsides.

I shifted position uneasily, trying half-heartedly to get comfortable. Heynith glared me into immobility. We were crouched in a trench about eight feet long and five feet deep, covered by a camouflage tarpaulin propped open on the valley side by pegs, a couple of inches of vegetation and topsoil on top of the tarpaulin. Heynith was in the middle, straddling the operator's saddle of the laser. Goth was on his left, I was on his right. Heynith was going to man the laser when the time came; it only took one person. There was nothing for Goth and me to do, would be nothing to do even during the ambush, except take over the firing in the unlikely event that Heynith was killed without the shot wiping out all of us, or stand by to lever the laser around in case that became necessary. Neither was very likely to happen. No, it was Heynith's show, and we were superfluous and unoccupied.

That was bad.

We had a lot of time to think.

That was worse.

I was feeling increasingly numb, like a wall of clear glass had been slipped between me and the world and was slowly thickening, layer by layer. With the thickening came an incredible isolation (isolation though I was cramped and suffocating, though I was jammed up against Heynith's bunched thigh—I couldn't touch him, he was miles away) and with the isolation came a sick, smothering panic. It was the inverse of claustrophobia. My flesh had turned to clear plastic, my bones to glass, and I was naked, ultimately naked, and there was nothing I could wrap me in. Surrounded by an army, I would still be alone; shrouded in iron thirty feet underground, I would still be naked. One portion of my mind wondered dispassionately if I was slipping into shock; the rest of it fought to keep down the scream that gathered along tightening muscles. The isolation increased. I was unaware of my surroundings, except for the heat and the pressure of enclosure.

I was seeing the molten spider of D'kotta, lying on its back and showing its obscene blotched belly, kicking legs of flame against the sky, each leg raising a poison blister where it touched the clouds.

I was seeing the boy, face runneled by blood, beating heels against the ground.

I was beginning to doubt big, simple ideas.

Nothing moved in the valley except wind through grass, spirits circling in the form of birds.

Spider legs.

Crab dance.

The blocky shadow of the vacvan crept across the valley.

Suddenly, with the intensity of vision, I was picturing Ren sitting in the van cab, shoulders resting against the door, legs stretched out along the seat, feet propped up on the instrument board, one ankle crossed over the other, gun resting across his lap, eyes watching the valley mouth through the windfield. He would be smoking a cigarette, and he would take it from his lips occasionally, flick the ashes onto the shiny dials with a fingernail, smile his strange smile, and carefully burn holes in the plush fabric of the upholstery. The fabric (real fabric; not plastic) would smolder, send out a wisp of bad-smelling smoke, and there would be another charred black hole in the seat. Ren would smile again, put the cigarette back in his mouth, lean back, and puff slowly. Ren was waiting to answer the radio signal from the orbot, to assure its pilot and crew that all was well, to talk them down to death. If they suspected anything was wrong, he would be the first to die. Even if everything went perfectly, he stood a high chance of dying anyway; he was the most exposed. It was almost certainly a suicide job. Ren said that he didn't give a shit; maybe he actually didn't. Or at least had convinced himself that he didn't. He was an odd man. Older than any of us, even Heynith, he had worked most of his life as a cadet executive in Admin at Urheim, devoted his existence to his job, subjugated all of his energies to it. He had been passed over three times for promotion to executive status, years of redoubled effort and mounting anxiety between each rejection. With the third failure he had been quietly retired to live on the credit subsidy he had earned with forty years of service. The next morning, precisely at the start of his accustomed work period, he stole a biodeth from a security guard in the Admin Complex, walked into his flowsector, killed everyone there, and disappeared from Urheim. After a year on the run, he had managed to contact the Quaestors. After another year of training, he was serving with a commando team in spite of his age. That had been five years ago; I had known him for two. During all that time, he had said little. He did his job very well with a minimum of wasted motion, never made mistakes, never complained, never showed emotion. But occasionally he would smile and burn a hole in something. Or someone.

The sun dived at the horizon, seeming to crash into the plain in an explosion of flame. Night swallowed us in one gulp. Black as a beast's belly.

It jerked me momentarily back into reality. I had a bad moment when I thought I'd gone blind, but then reason returned and I slipped the infrared lenses down over my eyes, activated them. The world came back in shades of red. Heynith was working cramped legs against the body of the laser. He spoke briefly, and we gulped some stimulus pills to keep us awake; they were bitter, and hard to swallow dry as usual, but they kicked up a familiar acid churning in my stomach, and my blood began to flow faster. I glanced at Heynith. He'd been quiet, even for Heynith. I wondered what he was thinking. He looked at me, perhaps reading the thought, and ordered us out of the trench.

Goth and I crawled slowly out, feeling stiff and brittle, slapped our thighs and arms, stamped to restore circulation. Stars were sprinkling across the sky, salt spilled on black porcelain. I still couldn't read them, I found. The day plants had vanished, the day animals had retreated into catalepsy. The night plants were erupting from the ground, fed by the debris of the day plants. They grew rapidly, doubling, then tripling in height as we watched. They were predominantly thick, ropy shrubs with wide, spearhead leaves of dull purple and black, about four feet high. Goth and I dug a number of them up, root systems intact, and placed them on top of the tarpaulin to replace the day plants that had shriveled with the first touch of bitter evening frost. We had to handle them with padded gloves; the leaf surfaces greedily absorbed the slightest amount of heat and burned like dry ice.

Then we were back in the trench, and it was worse than ever. Motion had helped for a while, but I could feel the numbing panic creeping back, and the momentary relief made it even harder to bear. I tried to start a conversation, but it died in monosyllabic grunts, and silence sopped up the echoes. Heynith was methodically checking the laser controls for the nth time. He was tense; I could see it bunch his shoulder muscles, bulge his calves into rock as they pushed against the footplates of the saddle. Goth looked worse than I did; he was somewhat younger, and usually energetic and cheerful. Not tonight.

We should have talked, spread the pain around; I think all of us realized it. But we couldn't; we were made awkward by our own special intimacy. At one time or another, every one of us had reached a point where he *had* to talk or die, even Heynith, even Ren. So we all had talked and all had listened, each of us switching roles sooner or later. We had poured our fears and dreams and secret memories upon each other, until now we knew each other too well. It made us afraid. Each of us was afraid that he had exposed too much, let down too many barriers. We were afraid of vulnerability, of the knife that jabs for the softest fold of the belly. We were all scarred men already, and twice-shy. And the resentment grew that others had seen us that helpless, that vulnerable. So the walls went back up, intensified. And so when we needed to talk again, we could not. We were already too close to risk further intimacy.

Visions returned, ebbing and flowing, overlaying the darkness.

The magma churning, belching a hot breath that stinks of rotten eggs.

The cadet, his face inhuman in the death rictus, blood running down in a wash from his smashed forehead, plastering one eye closed, bubbling at his nostril, frothing around his lips, the lips tautening as his head jerks forward and then backwards, slamming the ground, the lips then growing slack, the body slumping, the mouth sagging open, the rush of blood and phlegm past the tombstone teeth, down the chin and neck, soaking into the fabric of the tunic. The feet drumming at the ground a final time, digging up clots of earth.

I groped for understanding. I had killed people before, and it had not bothered me except in sleep. I had done it mechanically, routine backed by hate, hate cushioned by routine. I wondered if the night would ever end. I remembered the morning I'd watched from the mountain. I didn't think the night would end. A big idea tickled my mind again.

The city swallowed by stone.

The cadet falling, swinging his arms wide.

Why always the cadet and the city in conjunction? Had one sensitized me to the other, and if so, which? I hesitated.

Could both of them be equally important?

One of the other section leaders whistled.

We all started, somehow grew even more tense. The whistle came again, warbling, sound floating on silence like oil on water. Someone was coming. After a while we heard a rustling and snapping of underbrush approaching downslope from the mountain. Whoever it was, he was making no effort to move quietly. In fact he seemed to be blundering along, bulling through the tangles, making a tremendous thrashing noise. Goth and I turned in the direction of the sound, brought our guns up to bear, primed them. That was instinct. I wondered who could be coming *down* the mountain toward us. That was reason. Heynith twisted to cover the opposite direction, away from the noise, resting his gun on the saddle rim. That was caution. The thrasher passed our position about six feet away, screened by the shrubs. There was an open space ten feet farther down, at the head of a talus bluff that slanted to the valley. We watched it. The shrubs at the end of the clearing shook, were torn aside. A figure stumbled out into starlight.

It was a null.

Goth sucked in a long breath, let it hiss out between his teeth. Heynith remained impassive, but I could imagine his eyes narrowing behind the thick lenses. My mind was totally blank for about three heartbeats, then, surprised: a null! and I brought the gun barrel up, then, uncomprehending: a null? and I lowered the muzzle. Blank for a second, then: how? and trickling in again: how? Thoughts snarled into confusion, the gun muzzle wavered hesitantly.

The null staggered across the clearing, weaving in slow figure-eights. It almost fell down the talus bluff, one foot suspended uncertainly over the drop, then lurched away, goaded by tropism. The null shambled backward a few paces, stopped, swayed, then slowly sank to its knees.

It kneeled: head bowed, arms limp along the ground, palms up.

Heynith put his gun back in his lap, shook his head. He told us he'd be damned if he could figure out where it came from, but we'd have to get rid of it. It could spoil the ambush if it was spotted. Automatically, I raised my gun, trained it. Heynith stopped me. No noise, he said, not now. He told Goth to go out and kill it silently.

Goth refused. Heynith stared at him speechlessly, then began to flush. Goth and Heynith had had trouble before. Goth was a good man, brave as a bull, but he was stubborn, tended to follow his own lead too much, had too many streaks of sentimentality and touchiness, *thought* too much to be a really efficient cog.

They had disagreed from the beginning, something that wouldn't have been tolerated this long if the Quaestors hadn't been desperate for men. Goth was a devil in a fight when aroused, one of the best, and that had excused him a lot of obstinacy. But he had a curious squeamishness, he hadn't developed the layers of numbing scar-tissue necessary for guerrilla work, and that was almost inevitably fatal. I'd wondered before, dispassionately, how long he would last.

Goth was a hereditary fullsentient, one of the few connected with the Quaestors. He'd been a cadet executive in Admin, gained access to old archives that had slowly soured him on the Combine, been hit at the psychologically right moment by increasing Quaestor agitprop, and had defected; after a two-year proving period, he'd been allowed to participate actively. Goth was one of the only field people who was working out of idealism rather than hate, and that made us distrust him. Heynith also nurtured a traditional dislike for hereditary fullsentients. Heynith had been part of an industrial sixclone for over twenty years before joining the Quaestors. His Six had been wiped out in a production accident, caused by standard Combine negligence. Heynith had been the only survivor. The Combine had expressed mild sympathy, and told him that they planned to cut another clone from him to replace the destroyed Six; he of course would be placed in charge of the new Six, by reason of his seniority. They smiled at him, not seeing any reason why he wouldn't want to work another twenty years with biological replicas of his dead brothers and sisters, the men, additionally, reminders of what he'd been as a youth, unravaged by years of pain. Heynith had thanked them politely, walked out, and kept walking, crossing the Gray Waste on foot to join the Quaestors.

I could see all this working in Heynith's face as he raged at Goth. Goth could feel the hate too, but he stood firm. The null was incapable of doing anybody any harm; he wasn't going to kill it. There'd been enough slaughter. Goth's face was bloodless, and I could see D'kotta reflected in his eyes, but I felt no sympathy for him, in spite of my own recent agonies. He was disobeying orders. I thought about Mason, the man Goth had replaced, the man who had died in my arms at Itica, and I hated Goth for being alive instead of Mason. I had loved Mason. He'd been an Antiquarian in the Urheim archives, and he'd worked for the Quaestors almost from the beginning, years of vital service before his activities were discovered by the Combine. He'd escaped the raid, but his family hadn't. He'd been offered an admin job in Quaestor HQ, but had turned it down and insisted on fieldwork in spite of warnings that it was suicidal for a man of his age. Mason had been a tall, gentle, scholarly man who pretended to be gruff and hard-nosed, and cried alone at night when he thought nobody could see. I'd often thought that he could have escaped from Itica if he'd tried harder, but he'd been worn down, sick and guilt-ridden and tired, and his heart hadn't really been in it; that thought had returned to puzzle me often afterward. Mason had been the only person I'd ever cared about, the one who'd been more responsible than anybody for bringing me out of the shadows and into humanity, and I could have shot Goth at that moment because I thought he was betraying Mason's memory.

Heynith finally ran out of steam, spat at Goth, started to call him something, then stopped and merely glared at him, lips white. I'd caught Heynith's quick glance at me, a nearly invisible head-turn, just before he'd fallen silent. He'd almost forgotten and called Goth a zombie, a widespread expletive on World that had carefully *not* been used by the team since I'd joined. So Heynith had never really forgotten, though he'd treated me with scrupulous fairness. My fury turned to a cold anger, widened out from Goth to become a sick distaste for the entire world.

Heynith told Goth he would take care of him later, take care of him good, and ordered me to go kill the null, take him upslope and out of sight first, then conceal the body.

Mechanically, I pulled myself out of the trench, started downslope toward the clearing. Anger fueled me for the first few feet, and I slashed the shrubs aside with padded gloves, but it ebbed quickly, leaving me hollow and numb. I'd known how the rest of the team must actually think of me, but somehow I'd never allowed myself to admit it. Now I'd had my face jammed in it, and, coming on top of all the other anguish I'd gone through the last two days, it was too much.

I pushed into the clearing.

My footsteps triggered some response in the null. It surged drunkenly to its feet, arms swinging limply, and turned to face me.

The null was slightly taller than me, built very slender, and couldn't have weighed too much more than a hundred pounds. It was bald, completely hairless. The fingers were shriveled, limp flesh dangling from the club of the hand; they had never been used. The toes had been developed to enable technicians to walk nulls from one section of the Cerebrum to another, but the feet had never had a chance to toughen or grow callused: they were a mass of blood and lacerations. The nose was a rough blob of pink meat around the nostrils, the ears similarly atrophied. The eyes were enormous, huge milky corneas and small pupils, like those of a nocturnal bird; adapted to the gloom of the Cerebrum, and allowed to function to forestall sensory deprivation; they aren't cut into the psychocybernetic current like the synapses or the ganglions. There were small messy wounds on the temples, wrists, and spinebase where electrodes had been torn loose. It had been shrouded in a pajamalike suit of nonconductive material, but that had been torn almost completely away, only a few hanging tatters remaining. There were no sex organs. The flesh under the rib cage was curiously collapsed; no stomach or digestive tract. The body was covered with bruises, cuts, gashes, extensive swatches sun-baked to second-degree burns, other sections seriously frostbitten or marred by bad coldburns from the night shrubs.

My awe grew, deepened into archetypical dread.

It was from D'kotta, there could be no doubt about it. Somehow it had survived the destruction of its Cerebrum, somehow it had walked through the boiling hell to the foothills, somehow it had staggered up to and over the mountain shoulder. I doubted if there'd been any predilection in its actions; probably it had just walked blindly away from the ruined Cerebrum in a straight line and kept walking. Its actions with the talus bluff demonstrated that; maybe earlier some dim instinct had helped it fumble its way around obstacles in its path, but now it was exhausted, baffled, stymied. It was miraculous that it had made it this far. And the agony it must have suffered on its way was inconceivable. I shivered, spooked. The short hairs bristled on the back of my neck.

The null lurched toward me.

I whimpered and sprang backwards, nearly falling, swinging up the gun.

The null stopped, its head lolling, describing a slow semicircle. Its eyes were tracking curiously, and I doubted if it could focus on me at all. To it, I must have been a blur of darker gray.

I tried to steady my ragged breathing. It couldn't hurt me; it was harmless, nearly dead anyway. Slowly, I lowered the gun, pried my fingers from the stock, slung the gun over my shoulder.

I edged cautiously toward it. The null swayed, but remained motionless.

Below, I could see the vacvan at the bottom of the bluff, a patch of dull gunmetal sheen. I stretched my hand out slowly. The null didn't move. This close, I could see its gaunt ribs rising and falling with the effort of its ragged breathing. It was trembling, an occasional convulsive spasm shuddering along its frame. I was surprised that it didn't stink; nulls were rumored to have a strong personal odor, at least according to the talk in field camps—bullshit, like so much of my knowledge at that time. I watched it for a minute, fascinated, but my training told me I couldn't stand out here for long; we were too exposed. I took another step, reached out for it, hesitated. I didn't want to touch it. Swallowing my distaste, I selected a spot on its upper arm free of burns or wounds, grabbed it firmly with one hand.

The null jerked at the touch, but made no attempt to strike out or get away. I waited warily for a second, ready to turn my grip into a wrestling hold if it should try to attack. It remained still, but its flesh crawled under my fingers, and I shivered myself in reflex. Satisfied that the null would give me no trouble, I turned and began to force it upslope, pushing it ahead of me.

It followed my shove without resistance, until we hit the first of the night shrubs, then it staggered and made a mewing, inarticulate sound. The plants were burning it, sucking warmth out of its flesh, raising fresh welts, ugly where bits of skin had adhered to the shrubs. I shrugged, pushed it forward. It mewed and lurched again. I stopped. The null's eyes tracked in my direction, and it whimpered to itself in pain. I swore at myself for wasting time, but moved ahead to break a path for the null, dragging it along behind me. The branches slapped harmlessly at my warmsuit as I bent them aside; occasionally one would slip past and lash the null, making it flinch and whimper, but it was spared the brunt of it. I wondered vaguely at my motives for doing it. Why bother to spare someone (some*thing*, I corrected nervously) pain when you're going to have to kill him (*it*) in a minute? What difference could it make? I shelved that and concentrated on the movements of my body; the null wasn't heavy, but it wasn't easy to drag it uphill either, especially as it'd stumble and go down every few yards and I'd have to pull it back to its feet again. I was soon sweating, but I didn't care, as the action helped to occupy my mind, and I didn't want to have to face the numbness I could feel taking over again.

We moved upslope until we were about thirty feet above the trench occupied by Heynith and Goth. This looked like a good place. The shrubs were almost chest-high here, tall enough to hide the null's body from an aerial search. I stopped. The null bumped blindly into me, leaned against me, its breath coming in rasps next to my ear. I shivered in horror at the contact. Gooseflesh blossomed on my arms and legs, swept across my body. Some connection sent a memory whispering at my mind, but I ignored it under the threat of rising panic. I twisted my shoulder under the null's weight, threw it off. The null slid back downslope a few feet, almost fell, recovered.

I watched it, panting. The memory returned, gnawing incessantly. This time it got through:

Mason scrambling through the sea-washed rocks of Cape Itica toward the waiting ramsub, while the fire sky-whipping behind picked us out against the shadows; Mason, too slow in vaulting over a stone ridge, balancing too long on the razor-edge in perfect silhouette against the night; Mason jerked upright as a fusor fired from the high cliff puddled his spine, melted his flesh like wax; Mason tumbling down into my arms, almost driving me to my knees; Mason, already dead, *heavy in my arms*, heavy in my arms; Mason torn away from me as a wave broke over us and deluged me in spume; Mason sinking from sight as Heynith screamed for me to come on and I fought my way through the chest-high surf to the ramsub—

That's what supporting the null had reminded me of: Mason, heavy in my arms.

Confusion and fear and nausea.

How could the null make me think of Mason?

Sick self-anger that my mind could compare Mason, gentle as the dream-father I'd never had, to something as disgusting as the null.

Anger novaed, trying to scrub out shame and guilt.

I couldn't take it. I let it spill out onto the null.

Growling, I sprang forward, shook it furiously until its head rattled and wobbled on its limp neck, grabbed it by the shoulders, and hammered it to its knees.

I yanked my knife out. The blade flamed suddenly in starlight.

I wrapped my hand around its throat to tilt its head back.

Its flesh was warm. A pulse throbbed under my palm.

All at once, my anger was gone, leaving only nausea.

I suddenly realized how cold the night was. Wind bit to the bone.

It was *looking* at me.

I suppose I'd been lucky. Orphans aren't as common as they once were—not in a society where reproduction has been relegated to the laboratory—but they still occur with fair regularity. I had been the son of an uncloned junior executive who'd run up an enormous credit debit, gone bankrupt, and been forced into insolvency. The Combine had cut a clone from him so that their man-hours would make up the bank discrepancy, burned out the higher levels of his brain, and put him in one of the nonsentient penal Controlled Environments. His wife was also cloned, but avoided brainscrub and went back to work in a lower capacity in Admin. I, as a baby, then became a ward of the State, and was sent to one of the institutional Environments. Imagine an endless series of low noises, repeating over and over again forever, no high or low spots, everything level: MMMMMMMMMMMMMMMMMMMMMMMMMMMM. Like that. That's the only way to describe the years in the Environments. We were fed, we were kept warm, we worked on conveyor belts piecing together miniaturized equipment, we were put to sleep electronically, we woke with our fingers already busy in the monotonous, rhythmical motions that we couldn't remember learning, motions we had repeated a million times a day since infancy. Once a day we were fed a bar of food-concentrates and vitamins. Occasionally, at carefully calculated intervals, we would be exercised to keep up muscle tone. After reaching puberty, we were occasionally masturbated by electric stimulation, the seed saved for sperm banks. The administrators of the Environment were not cruel; we almost never saw them. Punishment was by machine shocks; never severe, very rarely needed. The executives had no need to be cruel. All they needed was MMMMMMMMMMMMMMMMMM-MMMMMMMMM. We had been taught at some early stage, probably by shock and stimulation, to put the proper part in the proper slot as the blocks of equipment passed in front of us. We had never been taught to talk, although an extremely limited language of several mood-sounds had independently developed among us; the executives never spoke on the rare intervals when they came to check the machinery that regulated us. We had never been told who we were, where we were; we had never been told anything. We didn't care about any of these things, the concepts had never formed in our minds, we were only semiconscious at best anyway. There was nothing but MMMMMMMMMMMMMMM-MMMMMMMM. The executives weren't concerned with our spiritual development; there was no graduation from the Environment, there was no place else for us to go in a rigidly stratified society. The Combine had discharged its obligation by keeping us alive, in a place where we could even be minimally useful. Though our jobs were sinecures and could have been more efficiently performed by computer, they gave the expense of our survival a socially justifiable excuse, they put us comfortably in a pigeonhole. We were there for life. We would grow up from infancy, grow old, and die, bathed in MMMMMMMMMMMMMMMMMM-MMMMM. The first real, separate, and distinct memory of my life is when the Quaestors raided the Environment, when the wall of the assembly chamber suddenly glowed red, buckled, collapsed inward, when Mason pushed out of the smoke and the debris cloud, gun at the ready, and walked slowly toward me. That's hindsight. At the time, it was only a sudden invasion of incomprehensible sounds and lights and shapes and colors, too much to possibly comprehend, incredibly alien. It was the first discordant note ever struck in our lives: MMMMMMMMMMMMM!!!! shattering our world in an instant, plunging us into another dimension of existence. The Quaestors kidnapped all of us, loaded us onto vacvans, took us into the hills, tried to undo some of the harm. That'd been six years ago. Even with the facilities available at the Quaestor underground complex—hypnotrainers and analysis computers to plunge me back to childhood and patiently lead me out again step by step for ten thousand years of subjective time, while my body slumbered in stasis—even with all of that, I'd been lucky to emerge somewhat sane. The majority had died, or been driven into catalepsy. I'd been lucky even to be a Ward of the State, the way things had turned out. Lucky to be a zombie. I could have been a low-ranked clone, without a digestive system, tied forever to the Combine by unbreakable strings. Or I could have been one of the thousands of tank-grown creatures whose brains are used as organic-computer storage banks in the Cerebrum gestalts, completely unsentient: I could have been a null.

Enormous eyes staring at me, unblinking.

Warmth under my fingers.

I wondered if I was going to throw up.

Wind moaned steadily through the valley with a sound like MMM-MMMMMMMMMMMMM.

Heynith hissed for me to hurry up, sound riding the wind, barely audible. I shifted my grip on the knife. I was telling myself: it's never been really sentient anyway. Its brain has only been used as a computer unit for a biological gestalt, there's no individual intelligence in there. It wouldn't make any difference. I was telling myself: it's dying anyway from a dozen causes. It's in pain. It would be kinder to kill it.

I brought up the knife, placing it against the null's throat. I pressed the point in slowly, until it was pricking flesh.

The null's eyes tracked, focused on the knifeblade.

My stomach turned over. I looked away, out across the valley. I felt my carefully created world trembling and blurring around me, I felt again on the point of being catapulted into another level of comprehension, previously unexpected. I was afraid.

The vacvan's headlights flashed on and off twice.

I found myself on the ground, hidden by the ropy shrubs. I had dragged the null down with me, without thinking about it, pinned him flat to the ground, arm over back. That had been the signal that Ren had received a call from the orbot, had given it the proper radio code reply to bring it down. I could imagine him grinning in the darkened cab as he worked the instruments. I raised myself on an elbow, jerked the knife up, suspending it while I looked for the junction of spine and neck that would be the best place to strike. If I was going to kill him (*it*), I would have to kill him (*it!*) now. In quick succession, like a series of slides, like a computer equation running, I got: D'kotta—the cadet—Mason—the null. *It* and *him* tumbled in selection. Came up *him*. I lowered the knife. I couldn't do it. He was human. Everybody was.

For better or worse, I was changed. I was no longer the same person.

I looked up. Somewhere up there, hanging at the edge of the atmosphere, was the tinsel collection of forces in opposition called a starship, delicately invulnerable as an iron butterfly. It would be phasing in and out of "reality" to hold its position above World, maintaining only the most tenuous of contacts with this continuum. It had launched an orbot, headed for a rendezvous with the vacvan in this valley. The orbot was filled with the gene cultures that could be used to create hundreds of thousands of nonsentient clones who could be imprinted with behavior patterns and turned into computer-directed soldiers; crude but effective. The orbot was filled with millions of tiny metal blocks, kept under enormous compression: when released from tension, molecular memory would reshape them into a wide range of weapons needing only a power source to be functional. The orbot was carrying, in effect, a vast army and its combat equipment, in a form that could be transported in a five-hundred-foot vacvan and slipped into Urheim, where there were machines that could put it into use. It was the Combine's last chance, the second wind they needed in order to survive. It had been financed and arranged by various industrial firms in the Commonwealth who had vested interests in the Combine's survival on

World. The orbot's cargo had been assembled and sent off before D'kotta, when it had been calculated that the reinforcements would be significant in ensuring a Combine victory; now it was indispensable. D'kotta had made the Combine afraid that an attack on Urheim might be next, that the orbot might be intercepted by the Quaestors if the city was under siege when it tried to land. So the Combine had decided to land the orbot elsewhere and sneak the cargo in. The Blackfriars had been selected as a rendezvous, since it was unlikely the Quaestors would be on the alert for Combine activity in that area so soon after D'kotta, and even if stopped, the van might be taken for fleeing survivors and ignored. The starship had been contacted by esper en route, and the change in plan made.

Four men had died to learn of the original plan. Two more had died in order to learn of the new landing site and get the information to the Quaestors in time.

The orbot came down.

I watched it as in a dream, coming to my knees, head above the shrubs. The null stirred under my hand, pushed against the ground, sat up.

The orbot was a speck, a dot, a ball, a toy. It was gliding silently in on gravs, directly overhead.

I could imagine Heynith readying the laser, Goth looking up and chewing his lip the way he always did in stress. I knew that my place should be with them, but I couldn't move. Fear and tension were still there, but they were under glass. I was already emotionally drained. I could sum up nothing else, even to face death.

The orbot had swelled into a huge, spherical mountain. It continued to settle toward the spot where we'd calculated it must land. Now it hung just over the valley center, nearly brushing the mountain walls on either side. The orbot filled the sky, and I leaned away from it instinctively. It dropped lower—

Heynith was the first to fire.

An intense beam of light erupted from the ground downslope, stabbed into the side of the orbot. Another followed from the opposite side of the valley, then the remaining two at once.

The orbot hung, transfixed by four steady, unbearably bright columns.

For a while, it seemed as if nothing was happening.

I could imagine the consternation aboard the orbot as the pilot tried to reverse gravs in time.

The boat's hull had become cherry red in four widening spots. Slowly, the spots turned white.

I could hear the null getting up beside me, near enough to touch. I had risen automatically, shading my eyes against glare.

The orbot exploded.

The reactor didn't go, of course; they're built so that can't happen. It was just the conventional auxiliary engines, used for steering and for powering internal systems. But that was enough.

Imagine a building humping itself into a giant stone fist, and bringing that fist down on you, *squash*. Pain so intense that it snuffs your consciousness before you can feel it.

Warned by instinct, I had time to do two things.

I thought, distinctly: so night will never end.

And I stepped in front of the null to shield him.

Then I was kicked into oblivion.

I awoke briefly to agony, the world a solid, blank red. Very, very far away, I could hear someone screaming. It was me.

I awoke again. The pain had lessened. I could see. It was day, and the night plants had died. The sun was dazzling on bare rock. The null was standing over me, seeming to stretch up for miles into the sky. I screamed in preternatural terror. The world vanished.

The next time I opened my eyes, the sky was heavily overcast and it was raining, one of those torrential southern downpours. A Quaestor medic was doing something to my legs, and there was a platvac nearby. The null was lying on his back a few feet away, a bullet in his chest. His head was tilted up toward the scuttling gray clouds. His eyes mirrored the rain.

That's what happened to my leg. So much nerve tissue destroyed that they couldn't grow me a new one, and I had to put up with this stiff prosthetic. But I got used to it. I considered it my tuition fee.

I'd learned two things: that everybody is human, and that the universe doesn't care one way or the other; only people do. The universe just doesn't give a damn. Isn't that wonderful? Isn't that a relief? It isn't out to get you, and it isn't going to help you either. You're on your own. We all are, and we all have to answer to ourselves. We make our own heavens and hells; we can't pass the buck any further. How much easier when we could blame our guilt or goodness on God.

Oh, I could read supernatural significance into it all—that I was spared because I'd spared the null, that some benevolent force was rewarding me—but what about Goth? Killed, and if he hadn't balked in the first place, the null wouldn't have stayed alive long enough for me to be entangled. What about the other team members, all dead—wasn't there a man among them as good as me and as much worth saving? No, there's a more direct reason why I survived. Prompted by the knowledge of his humanity, I had shielded him from the explosion. Three other men survived that explosion, but they died from exposure in the hours before the med team got there, baked to death by the sun. I didn't die because the null stood over me during the hours when the sun was rising and frying the rocks, *and his shadow shielded me from the sun.* I'm not saying that he consciously figured that out, deliberately shielded me (though who knows), but I had given him the only warmth he'd known in a long nightmare of pain, and so he remained by me when there was nothing stopping him from running away—and it came to the same result. You don't need intelligence or words to respond to empathy, it can be communicated through the touch of fingers—you know that if you've ever had a pet, ever been in love. So that's why I was spared, warmth for warmth, the same reason anything good ever happens in this life. When the med team arrived, they shot the null down because they thought it was trying to harm me. So much for supernatural rewards for the Just.

So, empathy's the thing that binds life together; it's the flame we share against fear. Warmth's the only answer to the old cold questions.

So I went through life, boy; made mistakes, did a lot of things, got kicked around a lot more, loved a little, and ended up on Kos, waiting for evening.

But night's a relative thing. It always ends. It does; because even if you're not around to watch it, the sun always comes up, and someone'll be there to see.

It's a fine, beautiful morning.

It's always a beautiful morning somewhere, even on the day you die.

You're young—that doesn't comfort you yet.

But you'll learn.

• Morning Child •

THE OLD HOUSE had been hit by something sometime during the war and mashed nearly flat. The front was caved in as though crushed by a giant fist: wood pulped and splintered, beams protruding at odd angles like broken fingers, the second floor collapsed onto the remnants of the first. The rubble of a chimney covered everything with a red mortar blanket. On the right, a gaping hole cross-sectioned the ruins, laying bare all the strata of fused stone and plaster and charred wood—everything curling back on itself like the lips of a gangrenous wound. Weeds had swarmed up the low hillside from the road and swept over the house, wrapping the ruins in wildflowers and grapevines, softening the edges of destruction with green.

Williams brought John here almost every day. They had lived here once, in this house, many years ago, and although John's memory of that time was dim, the place seemed to have pleasant associations for him, in spite of its ruined condition. John was at his happiest here and would play contentedly with sticks and pebbles on the shattered stone steps, or go whooping through the tangled weeds that had turned the lawn into a jungle, or play-stalk in ominous circles around Williams while Williams worked at filling his bags with blueberries, daylilies, Indian potatoes, dandelions, and other edible plants and roots.

Even Williams took a bittersweet pleasure in visiting the ruins, although coming here stirred memories that he would rather have left undisturbed. There was a pleasant melancholy to the spot and something oddly soothing about the mixture of mossy old stone and tender new green, a reminder of the inevitability of cycles—life-in-death, death-in-life.

John erupted out of the tall weeds and ran laughing to where Williams stood with the foraging bags. "I been fighting dinosaurs!" John said. "Great *big* ones!" Williams smiled crookedly and said, "That's good." He reached down and rumpled John's hair. They stood there for a second, John panting like a dog from all the running he'd been doing, his eyes bright, Williams letting his touch linger on the small, tousled head. At this time of the morning, John seemed always in motion, motion so continuous that it gave nearly the illusion of rest, like a stream of water that looks solid until something makes it momentarily sputter and stop.

This early in the day, John rarely stopped. When he did, as now, he seemed to freeze solid, his face startled and intent, as though he were listening to sounds that no one else could hear. At such times, Williams would study him with painful intensity, trying to see himself in him, sometimes succeeding, sometimes failing, and wondering which hurt more, and why.

Sighing, Williams took his hand away. The sun was getting high, and they'd better be heading back to camp if they wanted to be there at the right time for the heavier chores. Slowly, Williams bent over and picked up the foraging bags, grunting a little at their weight as he settled them across his shoulder—they had done very well for themselves this morning.

"Come on now, John," Williams said, "time to go," and started off, limping a bit more than usual under the extra weight. John, trotting alongside, his short legs pumping, seemed to notice. "Can I help you carry the bags?" John said eagerly. "Can I? I'm big enough!" Williams smiled at him and shook his head. "Not yet, John," he said. "A little bit later, maybe."

They passed out of the cool shadow of the ruined house and began to hike back to camp along the deserted highway.

The sun was baking down now from out of a cloudless sky, and heat-bugs began to chirrup somewhere, producing a harsh and metallic stridulation that sounded amazingly like a buzz saw. There were no other sounds besides the soughing of wind through tall grass and wild wheat, the tossing and whispering of trees, and the shrill piping of John's voice. Weeds had thrust up through the macadam—tiny, green fingers that had cracked and buckled the road's surface, chopped it up into lopsided blocks. Another few years and there would be no road here, only a faint track in the undergrowth—and then not even that. Time would erase everything, burying it beneath new trees, gradually building new hills, laying down a fresh landscape to cover the old. Already grass and vetch had nibbled away the corners of the sharper curves, and the wind had drifted topsoil onto the road. There were saplings now in some places, growing green and shivering in the middle of the highway, negating the faded signs that pointed to distances and towns.

John ran ahead, found a rock to throw, ran back, circling around Williams as though on an invisible tether. They walked in the middle of the road, John pretending that the faded white line was a tightrope, waving his arms for balance, shouting warnings to himself about the abyss creatures who would gobble him up if he should misstep and fall.

Williams maintained a steady pace, not hurrying: the epitome of the ramrod-straight old man, his snow-white hair gleaming in the sunlight, a bush knife at his belt, an old Winchester .30-30 slung across his back—although he no longer believed that they'd need it. They weren't the only people left in the world, he knew—however much it felt like it sometimes—but this region had been emptied of its population years ago, and since he and John had returned this way on their long journey up from the south, they had seen no one else at all. No one would find them here.

There were traces of buildings along the way now, all that was left of a small country town: the burnt-out spine of a roof, ridge meshed with weeds; gaping stone foundations like battlements for dwarfs; a ruined water faucet clogged with spiderwebs; a shattered gas pump inhabited by birds and rodents. They turned off onto a gravel secondary road, past the burnt-out shell of another filling station and a dilapidated roadside stand full of windblown trash. Overhead, a rusty traffic light swayed on a sagging wire. Someone had tied a big orange-and-black hex sign to one side of the light, and on the other side, the side facing away from town and out into the hostile world, was the evil eye, painted against a white background in vivid, shocking red. Things had gotten very strange during the Last Days.

Williams was having trouble now keeping up with John's ever-lengthening stride, and he decided that it was time to let him carry the bags. John hefted the bags easily, flashing his strong white teeth at Williams in a grin, and set off up the last long slope to camp, his long legs carrying him up the hill at a pace Williams couldn't hope to match. Williams swore good-naturedly, and John laughed and stopped to wait for him at the top of the rise.

Their camp was set well back from the road, on top of a bluff, just above a small river. There had been a restaurant here once, and a corner of the building still stood, two walls and part of the roof needing only the tarpaulin stretched across the open end to make it into a reasonably snug shelter. They'd have to find something better by winter, of course, but this was good enough for July, reasonably well hidden and close to a supply of water.

Rolling, wooded hills were around them to the north and east. To the south, across the river, the hills dwindled away into flatland, and the world opened up into a vista that stretched to the horizon.

• • •

They grabbed a quick lunch and then set to work, chopping wood, hauling in the nets that Williams had set across the river to catch fish, carrying water, for cooking, up the steep slope to camp. Williams let John do most of the heavy work. John sang and whistled happily while he worked, and once, on his way back from carrying some firewood to the shelter, he laughed, grabbed Williams under the arms, boosted him into the air, and danced him around in a little circle before setting him back down on his feet again.

"Feeling your oats, eh?" Williams said with mock severity, looking up into the sweaty face that smiled down at him.

"*Somebody* has to do the work around here," John said cheerfully, and they both laughed. "I can't wait to get back to my outfit," John said eagerly. "I feel much better now. I feel *terrific*. Are we going to stay out here much longer?" His eyes pleaded with Williams. "We can go back soon, can't we?"

"Yeah," Williams lied, "we can go back real soon."

But already John was tiring. By dusk, his footsteps were beginning to drag, and his breathing was becoming heavy and labored. He paused in the middle of what he was doing, put down the wood-chopping ax, and stood silently for a moment, staring blankly at nothing.

His face was suddenly intent and withdrawn, and his eyes were dull. He swayed unsteadily and wiped the back of his hand across his forehead. Williams got him to sit down on a stump near the improvised fireplace. He sat there silently, staring at the ground in abstraction, while Williams bustled around, lighting a fire, cleaning and filleting the fish, cutting up dandelion roots and chicory crowns, boiling water. The sun was down now, and fireflies began to float above the river, winking like fairy lanterns through the velvet darkness.

Williams did his best to interest John in supper, hoping that he'd eat something while he still had some of his teeth, but John would eat little. After a few moments, he put his tin plate down and sat staring dully to the south, out over the darkened lands beyond the river, just barely visible in the dim light of a crescent moon. His face was preoccupied and glum, and beginning to get jowly. His hairline had retreated in a wide arc from his forehead, creating a large bald spot. He worked his mouth indecisively several times and at last said, "Have I been . . . ill?"

"Yes, John," Williams said gently. "You've been ill."

"I can't . . . I can't *remember*," John complained. His voice was cracked and husky, querulous. "Everything's so confused. I can't keep things *straight*—"

Somewhere on the invisible horizon, perhaps a hundred miles away, a pillar of fire leapt up from the edge of the world.

As they watched, startled, it climbed higher and higher, towering miles into the air, until it was a slender column of brilliant flame that divided the sullen black sky in two from ground to stratosphere. The pillar of fire blazed steadily on the horizon for a minute or two, and then it began to coruscate, burning green and blue and silver and orange, the colors flaring and flickering fitfully as they merged into one another. Slowly, with a kind of stately and awful symmetry, the pillar broadened out to become a flattened diamond shape of blue-white fire. The diamond began to rotate slowly on its axis, and, as it rotated, it grew eye-searingly bright. Gargantuan unseen shapes floated around the blazing diamond, like moths beating around a candle flame, throwing huge tangled shadows across the world.

Something with a huge, melancholy voice hooted, and hooted again, a forlorn and terrible sound that beat back and forth between the hills until it rumbled slowly away into silence.

The blazing diamond winked out. Hot white stars danced where it had been. The stars faded to sullenly glowing orange dots that flickered away down the spectrum and were gone.

It was dark again.

The night had been shocked silent. For a while, that silence was complete, and then slowly, tentatively, one by one, the crickets and tree frogs began to make their night sounds again.

"The war—" John whispered. His voice was reedy and thin and weary now, and there was pain in it. "It still goes on?"

"The war got . . . strange," Williams said quietly. "The longer it lasted, the stranger it got. New allies, new weapons—" He stared off into the darkness in the direction where the fire had danced: there was still an uneasy shimmer to the night air on the horizon, not quite a glow. "You were hurt by such a weapon, I guess. Something like *that,* maybe." He nodded toward the horizon, and his face hardened. "I don't know. I don't even know what *that* was. I don't understand much that happens in the world anymore. . . . Maybe it wasn't even a weapon that hurt you. Maybe they were experimenting on you biologically before you got away. Who knows why? Maybe it was done deliberately—as a punishment. Or a reward. Who knows how they think? Maybe it was a side effect of some device designed to do something else entirely. Maybe it was an accident; maybe you just got too close to something like *that* when it was doing whatever it is it does." Williams was silent for a moment, and then he sighed. "Whatever happened, you got to me afterward somehow, and I took care of you. We've been hiding out ever since, moving from place to place."

They had both been nearly blind while their eyes readjusted to the night, but now, squinting in the dim glow of the low-burning cooking fire, Williams could see John again. John was now totally bald, his cheeks had caved in, and his dulled and yellowing eyes were sunken deeply into his ravaged face. He struggled to get to his feet, then sank back down onto the stump again. "I can't—" he whispered. Weak tears began to run down his cheeks. He started to shiver.

Sighing, Williams got up and threw a double handful of pine needles into boiling water to make white-pine-needle tea. He helped John limp over to his pallet, supporting most of his weight, almost carrying him—it was easy; John had become shrunken and frail and amazingly light, as if he were now made out of cloth and cotton and dry sticks instead of flesh and bone. He got John to lie down, tucked a blanket around him in spite of the heat of the evening, and concentrated on getting some of the tea into him.

He drank two full cups before his fingers became too weak to hold the cup, before even the effort of holding up his head became too great for him. John's eyes had become blank and shiny and unseeing, and his face was like a skull, earth-brown and blotched, with the skin drawn tightly over the bones.

His hands plucked aimlessly at the blanket; they looked mummified now, the skin as translucent as parchment, the blue veins showing through beneath.

As the evening wore on, John began to fret and whine incoherently, turning his face blindly back and forth, muttering random fragments of words and sentences, sometimes raising his voice in a strangled, gurgling shout that had no words at all in it, only bewilderment and outrage and pain. Williams sat patiently beside him, stroking his shriveled hands, wiping sweat from his hot forehead.

"Sleep now," Williams said soothingly. John moaned, and whined in the back of his throat. "Sleep. Tomorrow we'll go to the house again. You'll like that, won't you? But sleep now, sleep—"

At last John quieted, his eyes slowly closed, and his breathing grew deeper and more regular.

Williams sat patiently by his side, keeping a calming hand on his shoulder. Already John's hair was beginning to grow back, and the lines were smoothing out of his face as he melted toward childhood.

When Williams was sure that John was asleep, he tucked the blanket closer around him and said, "Sleep well, Father," and then slowly, passionately, soundlessly, he started to weep.

• A Kingdom by the Sea •

EVERY DAY, MASON would stand with his hammer and kill cows. The place was big—a long, high-ceilinged room, one end open to daylight, the other end stretching back into the depths of the plant. It had white, featureless walls—painted concrete—that were swabbed down twice a day, once before lunch and once after work. The floor could be swabbed too—it was stone, and there was a faucet you could use to flood the floor with water. Then you used a stiff-bristled broom to swish the water around and get up the stains. That was known as GIing a floor in the Army. Mason had been in the Army. He called it GIing. So did the three or four other veterans who worked that shift, and they always got a laugh out of explaining to the college boys the plant hired as temporary help why the work they'd signed up to do was called that. The college boys never knew what GIing was until they'd been shown, and they never understood the joke either, or why it was called that. They were usually pretty dumb.

There was a drain in the floor to let all the water out after the place had been GIed. In spite of everything, though, the room would never scrub up quite clean; there'd always be some amount of blood left staining the walls and floor at the end of the day. About the best you could hope to do was grind it into the stone so it became unrecognizable. After a little of this, the white began to get dingy, dulling finally to a dirty, dishwater gray. Then they'd paint the room white again and start all over.

The cycle took a little longer than a year, and they were about halfway through it this time. The men who worked the shift didn't really give a shit whether the walls were white or not, but it was a company regulation. The regs insisted that the place be kept as clean as possible for health reasons, and also because that was supposed to make it a psychologically more attractive environment to function in. The workmen wouldn't have given a shit about their psychological environment either, even if they'd known what one was. It was inevitable that the place would get a little messy during a working day.

It was a slaughterhouse, although the company literature always referred to it as a meat-packing plant.

The man who did the actual killing was Mason: the focal point of the company, of all the meat lockers and trucks and canning sections and secretaries and stockholders; their lowest common denominator. It all started with him.

He would stand with his hammer at the open end of the room, right at the very beginning of the plant, and wait for the cows to come in from the train yard. He had a ten-pound sledgehammer, long and heavy, with serrated rubber around the handle to give him a better grip. He used it to hit the cows over the head. They would herd the cows in one at a time, into the chute, straight up to Mason, and Mason would swing his hammer down and hit the cow between the eyes with tremendous force, driving the hammer completely through the bone and into the brain, killing the cow instantly in its tracks. There would be a gush of warm, sticky blood, and a spatter of purplish brain matter; the cow would go to its front knees, as if it were curtsying, then its hindquarters would collapse and drag the whole body over onto one side with a thunderous crash—all in an eyeblink. One moment the cow would be being prodded in terror into the chute that led to Mason, its flanks lathered, its muzzle flecked with foam, and then—almost too fast to watch, the lightning would strike, and it would be a twitching ruin on the stone floor, blood oozing sluggishly from the smashed head.

After the first cow of the day, Mason would be covered with globs and spatters of blood, and his arms would be drenched red past the elbows. It didn't bother him—it was a condition of his job, and he hardly noticed it. He took two showers a day, changed clothes before and after lunch; the company laundered his white working uniforms and smocks at no expense. He worked quickly and efficiently, and never needed more than one blow to kill. Once Mason had killed the cow, it was hoisted on a hook, had its throat cut, and was left for a few minutes to bleed dry. Then another man came up with a long, heavy knife and quartered it. Then the carcass was further sliced into various portions, each portion was impaled on a hook and carried away by a clanking overhead conveyor belt toward the meat lockers and packing processes that were the concerns of the rest of the plant.

The cows always seemed to know what was about to happen to them—they would begin to moan nervously and roll their eyes in apprehension as soon as they were herded from the stock car on the siding. After the first cow was slaughtered, their apprehension would change to terror. The smell of the blood would drive them mad. They would plunge and bellow and snort and buck; they would jerk mindlessly back and forth, trying to escape. Their eyes would roll up to show the whites, and they would spray foam, and their sides would begin to lather. At this point, Mason would work faster, trying to kill them all before any had a chance to sweat off fat. After a while, they would begin to scream. Then they would have to be prodded harshly toward Mason's hammer. At the end, after they had exhausted themselves, the last few cows would grow silent, shivering and moaning softly until Mason had a chance to get around to them, and then they would die easily with little thrashing or convulsing. Often, just for something to do, Mason and the other workmen would sarcastically talk to the cows, make jokes about them, call them by pet names, tell them—after the fashion of a TV variety-skit doctor—that everything was going to be all right and that it would only hurt for a minute, tell them what dumb fucking bastards they were—"That's right, sweetheart. Come here, you big dumb bastard. Papa's got a surprise for you"— tell them that they'd known goddamn well what they were letting themselves in for when they'd enlisted. Sometimes they would bet on how hard Mason could hit a cow with his big hammer, how high into the air the brain matter would fly after the blow. Once Mason had won a buck from Kaplan by hitting a cow so hard that he had driven it to its knees. They were no more callous than ordinary men, but it was a basically dull, basically unpleasant job, and like all men with dull, unpleasant jobs, they needed something to spice it up, and to keep it far enough away. To Mason, it was just a job, no better or worse than any other. It was boring, but he'd never had a job that wasn't boring. And at least it paid well. He approached it with the same methodical uninterest he had brought to every other job he ever had. It was his job, it was what he did.

Every day, Mason would stand with his hammer and kill cows.

It is raining: a sooty, city rain that makes you dirty rather than wet. Mason is standing in the rain at the bus stop, waiting for the bus to come, as he does every day, as he has done every day for the past six years. He has his collar up against the wind, hands in pockets, no hat: his hair is damp, plastered to his forehead. He stands somewhat slouched, head slumped forward just the tiniest bit—he is tired, the muscles in his shoulders are knotted with strain, the back of his neck burns. He is puzzled by the excessive fatigue of his body; uneasy, he shifts his weight from foot to foot—standing here after a day spent on his feet is murder, it gets him in the thighs, the calves. He has forgotten his raincoat again. He is a big man, built thick through the chest and shoulders, huge arms, wide, thick-muscled wrists, heavy-featured, resigned face. He is showing the first traces of a future potbelly. His feet are beginning to splay. His personnel dossier (restricted) states that he is an unaggressive underachiever, energizing at low potential, anally oriented (plodding, painstaking, competent), highly compatible with his fellow workers, shirks decision-making but can be trusted with minor responsibility, functions best as part of a team, unlikely to cause trouble: a good worker. He often refers to himself as a slob, though he usually tempers it with laughter (as in: "Christ, don't ask a poor slob like me about stuff like that," or, "Shit, I'm only a dumb working slob"). He is beginning to slide into the downhill side of the middle thirties. He was born here, in an immigrant neighborhood, the only Protestant child in a sea of foreign Catholics—he had to walk two miles to Sunday school. He grew up in the gray factory city—sloughed through high school, the Army, drifted from job to job, town to town, dishwashing, waiting tables, working hardhat (jukeboxes, back-rooms, sawdust, sun, water from a tin pail), work four months, six, a year, take to the road, drift: back to his hometown again after eight years of this, to his old (pre-Army) job, full circle. This time when the restlessness comes, after a year, he gets all the way to the bus terminal (sitting in the station at three o'clock in the morning, colder than hell, the only other person in the huge, empty hall a drunk asleep on one of the benches) before he realizes that he has no place to go and nothing to do if he gets there. He does not leave. He stays: two years, three, four, six now, longer than he has ever stayed anywhere before. Six years, slipping up on him and past before he can realize it, suddenly gone (company picnics, Christmas, Christ—taxes again already?), time blurring into an oily gray knot, leaving only discarded calendars for fossils. He will never hit the road again, he is here to stay. His future has become his past without ever touching the present. He does not understand what has happened to him, but he is beginning to be afraid.

He gets on the bus for home.

In the cramped, sweaty interior of the bus, he admits for the first time that he may be getting old.

Mason's apartment was on the fringe of the heavily built-up district, in a row of dilapidated six-story brownstones. Not actually the slums, not like where the colored people lived (Mason doggedly said colored people, even when the boys at the plant talked of niggers), not like where the kids, the beatniks lived, but a low-rent district, yes. Laboring people, low salaries. The white poor had been hiding here since 1920, peering from behind thick faded drapes and cracked Venetian blinds. Some of them had never come out. The immigrants had disappeared into this neighborhood from the boats, were still here, were still immigrants after thirty years, but older and diminished, like a faded photograph. All the ones who had not pulled themselves up by their bootstraps to become crooked politicians or gangsters or dishonest lawyers—all forgotten: a gritty human residue. The mailboxes alternated names like Goldstein and Kowalczyk and Ricciardi. It was a dark, hushed neighborhood, with few big stores, no movies, no real restaurants. A couple of bowling alleys. The closest civilization approached was a big concrete housing project for disabled war veterans a block or two away to the east, and a streamlined-chromeplated-neonflashing shopping center about half a mile to the west, on the edge of a major artery. City lights glowed to the north, high rises marched across the horizon south: H. G. Wells Martians, acres of windows flashing importantly.

Mason got off the bus. There was a puddle at the curb and he stepped in it. He felt water soak into his socks. The bus snapped its doors contemptuously shut behind him. It rumbled away, farting exhaust smoke into his face. Mason splashed toward his apartment, wrapped in rain mist, moisture beading on his lips and forehead. His shoes squelched. The wet air carried heavy cooking odors, spicy and foreign. Someone was banging garbage cans together somewhere. Cars hooted mournfully at him as they rushed by.

Mason ignored this, fumbling automatically for his keys as he came up to the outside door. He was trying to think up an excuse to stay home tonight. This was Tuesday, his bowling night; Kaplan would be calling in a while, and he'd have to tell him something. He just didn't feel like bowling; they could shuffle the league around, put Johnson in instead. He clashed the key against the lock. Go in, damn it. This would be the first bowling night he'd missed in six years, even last fall when he'd had the flu—Christ, how Emma had bitched about that, think he'd risen from his deathbed or something. She always used to worry about him too much. Still, after six years. Well, fuck it, he didn't feel like it, was all; it wasn't going to hurt anything, it was only a practice session anyway. He could afford to miss a week. And what the fuck was wrong with the lock? Mason sneered in the dark. How many years is it going to take to learn to use the right key for the front door, asshole? He found the proper key (the one with the deep groove) with his thumb and clicked the door open.

Course, he'd have to tell Kaplan something. Kaplan'd want to know why he couldn't come, try to argue him into it. (Up the stairwell, around and around.) Give him some line of shit. At least he didn't have to make up excuses for Emma anymore—she would've wanted to know why he wasn't going, if he felt good, if he was sick, and she'd be trying to feel his forehead for fever. A relief to have her off his back. She'd been gone almost a month. Now all he had to worry about was what to tell fucking Kaplan. (Old wood creaked under his shoes. It was stuffy. Muffled voices leaked from under doorways as he passed, pencil beams of light escaped from cracks. Dust motes danced in the fugitive light.)

Fuck Kaplan anyway, he didn't have to justify his actions to Kaplan. Just tell him he didn't want to, and the hell with him. The hell with all of them.

Into the apartment: one large room, partially divided by a low counter into kitchen and living room—sink, refrigerator, stove and small table in the kitchen; easy chair, coffee table and portable television in the living room; a small bedroom off the living room and a bath. Shit, he'd have to tell Kaplan something after all, wouldn't he? Don't want the guys to start talking. And it is weird to miss a bowling night. Mason took off his wet clothes, threw them onto the easy chair for Emma to hang up and dry. Then he remembered that Emma was gone. Finally left him—he couldn't blame her much, he supposed. He was a bum, it was true. He supposed. Mason shrugged uneasily. Fredricks promoted over him, suppose he didn't have much of a future—he didn't worry about it, but women were different, they fretted about stuff like that, it was important to them. And he wouldn't marry her. Too much of a drifter. But family stuff, that was important to a woman. Christ, he couldn't really blame her, the dumb cunt—she just couldn't understand. He folded his clothes himself, clumsily, getting the seam wrong in the pants. You miss people for the little things. Not that he really cared whether his pants were folded right or not. And, God knows, she probably missed him more than he did her; he was more independent—sure, he didn't really need anybody but him. Dumb cunt. Maybe he'd tell Kaplan that he had a woman up here, that he was getting laid tonight. Kaplan was dumb enough to believe it. He paused, hanger in hand, surprised at his sudden vehemence. Kaplan was no dumber than anybody else. And why couldn't he be getting laid up here? Was that so hard to believe, so surprising? Shit, was he supposed to curl up and fucking die because his girl'd left, even a longtime (three years) girl? Was that what Kaplan and the rest of those bastards were thinking? Well, then, call Kaplan and tell him you're sorry you can't make it, and then describe what a nice juicy piece of ass you're getting, make the fucker eat his liver with envy because he's stuck in that damn dingy bowling alley with those damn dingy people while you're out getting laid. Maybe it'll even get back to Emma. Kaplan will believe it. He's dumb enough.

Mason took a frozen pizza out of the refrigerator and put it into the oven for his supper. He rarely ate meat, didn't care for it. None of his family had. His father had worked in a meat-packing plant too—the same one, in fact. He had been one of the men who cut up the cow's carcass with knives and cleavers. "Down to the plant," he would say, pushing himself up from the table and away from his third cup of breakfast coffee, while Mason was standing near the open door of the gas oven for warmth and being wrapped in his furry hat for school, "I've got to go down to the plant."

Mason always referred to the place as a meat-packing plant.

(Henderson had called it a slaughterhouse, but Henderson had quit.)

The package said fifteen minutes at 450, preheated. Maybe he shouldn't tell Kaplan that he was getting laid, after all. Then everybody'd be asking him questions tomorrow, wanting to know who the girl was, how she was in the sack, where he'd picked her up, and he'd have to spend the rest of the day making up imaginary details of the affair. And suppose they found out somehow that he hadn't had a woman up here after all? Then they'd think he was crazy, making up something like that. Lying. Maybe he should just tell Kaplan that he was coming down with the flu. Or a bad cold. He *was* tired tonight. Maybe he actually was getting the flu. From overwork, or standing around in the rain too long, or something. Maybe that was why he was so fucking tired—Christ, exhausted—why he didn't feel like going bowling. Sure, that was it. And he didn't have to be ashamed of being sick: he had a fine work record, only a couple of days missed in six years. Everybody gets sick sometime, that's the way it is. They'd understand.

Fuck them if they didn't.

Mason burned the pizza slightly. By the time he pulled it out with a washcloth, singeing himself in the process, it had begun to turn black around the edges, the crust and cheese charring. But not too bad.

Salvageable. He cut it into slices with a roller. As usual, he forgot to eat it quickly enough, and the last pieces had cooled off when he got around to them—tasting now like cardboard with unheated spaghetti sauce on it. He ate them anyway. He had some beer with the pizza, and some coffee later. After eating, he still felt vaguely unsatisfied, so he got a package of Fig Newtons from the cupboard and ate them too. Then he sat at the table and smoked a cigarette. No noise—nothing moved. Stasis.

The phone rang: Kaplan.

Mason jumped, then took a long, unsteady drag on his cigarette. He was trembling. He stared at his hand, amazed. Nerves. Christ. He was working too hard, worrying too much. Fuck Kaplan and all the rest of them. Don't tell them anything. You don't have to. Let them stew. The phone screamed again and again: three times, four times, six. Don't answer it, Mason told himself, whipping up bravura indignation to cover the sudden inexplicable panic, the fear, the horror. You don't have to account to them. Ring (*scream*), ring (*scream*), ring (*scream*). The flesh crawled on his stomach, short hair bristled along his back, his arms. Stop, dammit, stop, *stop*. "Shut up!" he shouted, raggedly, half rising from the chair.

The phone stopped ringing.

The silence was incredibly evil.

Mason lit another cigarette, dropping the first match, lighting another, finally getting it going. He concentrated on smoking, the taste of the smoke and the feel of it in his lungs, puffing with staccato intensity (IthinkIcanIthinkIcanIthinkIcanIthinkIcan). Something was very wrong, but he suppressed that thought, pushed it deeper. A tangible blackness: avoid it. He was just tired, that's all. He'd had a really crummy, really rough day, and he was tired, and it was making him jumpy. Work seemed to get harder and harder as the weeks went by. Maybe he was getting old, losing his endurance. He supposed it had to happen sooner or later. But shit, he was only thirty-eight. He wouldn't have believed it, or even considered it, before today.

"You're getting old," Mason said, aloud. The words echoed in the bare room.

He laughed uneasily, nervously, pretending scorn. The laughter seemed to be sucked into the walls. Silence blotted up the sound of his breathing.

He listened to the silence for a while, then called himself a stupid asshole for thinking about all this asshole crap, and decided that he'd better go to bed. He levered himself to his feet. Ordinarily he would watch television for a couple of hours before turning in, but tonight he was fucked up—too exhausted and afraid. Afraid? What did he have to be scared of? It was all asshole crap. Mason stacked the dirty dishes in the sink and went into the bedroom, carefully switching off all the other lights behind him. Darkness followed him to the bedroom door.

Mason undressed, put his clothes away, sat on the bed. There was a dingy transient hotel on this side of the building, and its red neon sign blinked directly into Mason's bedroom window, impossible to block out with any thickness of curtain. Tonight he was too tired to be bothered by it. It had been a bad day. He would not think about it, any of it. He only wanted to sleep. Tomorrow would be different, tomorrow would be better. It would have to be. He switched off the light and lay back on top of the sheet. Neon shadows beat around the room, flooding it rhythmically with dull red.

Fretfully, he began to fall asleep in the hot room, in the dark.

Almost to sleep, he heard a woman weeping in his mind.

The weeping scratched at the inside of his head, sliding randomly in and out of his brain. Not really the sound of weeping, not actually an audible sound at all, but rather a feeling, an essence of weeping, of unalterable sadness. Without waking, he groped for the elusive feelings, swimming down deeper and deeper into his mind—like diving below a storm-lashed ocean at night, swimming down to where it is always calm and no light goes, down where the deep currents run. He was only partially conscious, on the borderline of dream where anything seems rational and miracles are commonplace. It seemed only reasonable, only fair, that, in his desolation, he should find a woman in his head. He did not question this, he did not find it peculiar. He moved toward her, propelled and guided only by the urge to be with her, an ivory feather drifting and twisting through vast empty darkness, floating on the wind, carried by the currents that wind through the regions under the earth, the tides that march in Night. He found her, wrapped in the underbelly of himself like a pearl: a tiny exquisite irritant. Encased in amber, he could not see, but he knew somehow that she was lovely, as perfect and delicate as the bud of a flower opening to the sun, as a baby's hand. He comforted her as he had comforted Emma on nights when she'd wake up crying: reaching through darkness toward sadness, wrapping it in warmth, leaching the fear away with presence, spreading the pain around between them to thin it down. She seemed startled to find that she was not alone at the heart of nothing, but she accepted him gratefully, and blended him into herself, blended them together, one stream into another, a mingling of secret waters in the dark places in the middle of the world, in Night, where shadows live. She was the thing itself, and not its wrapping, as Emma had been. She was ultimate grace—moving like silk around him, moving like warm rain within him. He merged with her forever.

And found himself staring at the ceiling.

Gritty light poured in through the window. The hotel sign had been turned off. It was morning.

He grinned at the ceiling, a harsh grin with no mirth in it: skin pulling back and back from the teeth, stretching to death's-head tautness.

It had been a dream.

He grinned his corpse grin at the morning.

Hello morning. Hello you goddamned son of a bitch.

He got up. He ached. He was lightheaded with fatigue: his head buzzed, his eyelids were lead. It felt like he had not slept at all.

He went to work.

It is still raining. Dawn is hidden behind bloated spider clouds. Here, in the factory town, miles of steel mills, coke refineries, leather-tanning plants, chemical scum running in the gutters, it will rain most of the year: airborne dirt forming the nucleus for moisture, an irritant to induce condensation—producing a listless rain that fizzles down endlessly, a deity pissing. The bus creeps through the mists and drizzle like a slug, parking lights haloed by dampness. Raindrops inch down the windowpane, shimmering and flattening when the window buzzes, leaving long wet tracks behind them. Inside, the glass has been fogged by breath and body heat, making it hard to see anything clearly. The world outside has merged into an infinity of lumpy gray shapes, dinosaur shadows, here and there lights winking and diffusing wetly—it is a moving collage done in charcoal and watery neon. The men riding the bus do not notice it—already they seem tired. It is seven a.m. They sit and stare dully at the tips of their shoes, or the back of the seat in front of them. A few read newspapers. One or two talk. Some sleep. A younger man laughs—he stops almost immediately. If the windows were clear, the rain collage of light and shadow would be replaced by row after row of drab, crumbling buildings, gas stations decked with tiny plastic flags, used car lots with floodlights, hamburger stands, empty schoolyards with dead trees poking up through the pavement, cyclone-fenced recreation areas that children never use. No one ever bothers to look at that either. They know what it looks like.

Usually Mason prefers the aisle seat, but this morning, prompted by some obscure instinct, he sits by the window. He is trying to understand his compulsion to watch the blurred landscape, trying to verbalize what it makes him think of, how it makes him feel. He cannot. Sad—that's the closest he can come. Why should it make him sad? Sad, and there is something else, something he gropes for but it keeps slipping away. An echo of reawakening fear, in reaction to his groping. It felt like, it was kind of like— Uneasily, he presses his palm to the window, attempts to rub away some of the moisture obscuring the glass. (This makes him feel funny too. Why? He flounders, grasping at nothing—it is gone.) A patch of relatively clear glass appears as he rubs, a swath of sharper focus surrounded by the oozing myopia of the collage. Mason stares out at the world, through his patch of glass. Again he tries to grasp something—again he fails. It all looks wrong somehow. It makes him vaguely, murkily angry. Buildings crawl by outside. He shivers, touched by a septic breath of entropy. Maybe it's— If it was like— He cannot. Why is it wrong? What's wrong with it? That's the way it's always looked, hasn't it? Nothing's changed. What could you change it to? What the fuck is it *supposed* to be like? No words.

Raindrops pile up on the window again and wash away the world.

At work, the dream continued to bother Mason throughout the day. He found that he couldn't put it out of his mind for long—somehow his thoughts always came back to it, circling constantly like the flies that buzzed around the pools of blood on the concrete floor.

Mason became annoyed, and slightly uneasy. It wasn't healthy to be so wrapped up in a fucking dream. It was sick, and you had to be sick in the head to fool around with it. It was sick—it made him angry to think about the slime and sickness of it, and faintly nauseous. He didn't have that slime in his head. No, the dream had bothered him because Emma was gone. It was rough on a guy to be alone again after living with somebody for so long. He should go out and actually pick up some broad instead of just thinking about it—should've had one last night so he wouldn't've had to worry about what to tell Kaplan. Sweep the cobwebs out of his brain. Sitting around that damn house night after night, never doing anything—no wonder he felt funny, had crazy dreams.

At lunch—sitting at the concrete, Formica-topped table, next to the finger-smudged plastic faces of the coffee machine, the soft drink machine, the sandwich machine, the ice cream machine (OUT OF ORDER) and the candy bar machine—he toyed with the idea of telling Russo about the dream, playing it lightly, maybe getting a few laughs out of it. He found the idea amazingly unpleasant. He was reluctant to tell anybody anything about the dream. To his amazement, he found himself getting angry at the thought. Russo was a son of a bitch anyway. They were all son of a bitches. He snapped at Russo when the Italian tried to draw him into a discussion he and Kaplan were having about cars. Russo looked hurt.

Mason mumbled something about a hangover in apology and gulped half of his steaming coffee without feeling it. His tuna salad sandwich tasted like sawdust, went down like lead. A desolate, inexplicable sense of loss had been growing in him throughout the morning as he became more preoccupied with the dream. He *couldn't* have been this affected by a dream, that was crazy—there had to be more to it than that, it had to be more than just a dream, and he wasn't crazy. So it couldn't have been a dream completely, somehow. He missed the girl in the dream. How could he miss someone who didn't exist? That was crazy. But he *did* miss her. So maybe the girl wasn't completely a dream somehow, or he wouldn't miss her like that, would he? That was crazy too. He turned his face away and played distractedly with crumbs on the Formica tabletop. No more of this: it was slimy, and it made his head hurt to think about it. He wouldn't think about it anymore.

That afternoon he took to listening while he worked. He caught himself at it several times. He was listening intently, for nothing. No, not for nothing. He was listening for *her*.

On the bus, going home, Mason is restless, as if he were being carried into some strange danger, some foreign battlefield. His eyes gleam slightly in the dark. The glare of oncoming car headlights sweeps over him in oscillating waves. Straps swing back and forth like scythes. All around him, the other passengers sit silently, not moving, careful not to touch or jostle the man next to them. Each in his own space: semivisible lumps of flesh and shadow. Their heads bob slightly with the motion of the bus, like dashboard ornaments.

When Mason got home, he had frozen pizza for supper again, though he'd been intending to have an omelet. He also ate some more Fig Newtons. It was as though he were half-consciously trying to reproduce the previous night, superstitiously repeating all the details of the evening in hopes of producing the same result. So he ate pizza, shaking his head at his own stupidity and swearing bitterly under his breath. He ate it nevertheless. And as he ate, he listened for the scratching—hating himself for listening, but listening—only partially believing that such a thing as the scratching even existed, or ever had, but listening. Half of him was afraid that it would not come; half was afraid that it would. But nothing happened.

When the scratching at his mind did come again it was hours later, while he was watching an old movie on *The Late Show*, when he had almost managed to forget. He stiffened, feeling a surge of terror (and feeling something else that he was unable to verbalize), even the half of his mind that had wanted it to come screaming in horror of the unknown now that the impossible had actually happened. He fought down terror, breathing harshly. This couldn't be happening. Maybe he *was* crazy. A flicker of abysmal fear. Sweat started on his forehead, armpits, crotch.

Again, the scratching: bright feelings sliding tentatively into his head, failing to catch and slipping out, coming back again—like focusing a split-image lens. He sat back in the easy chair; old springs groaned, the cracked leather felt hot and sticky against his T-shirted back. He squeezed the empty beer can, crumpling it. Automatically he put the empty into the six-pack at the foot of the chair. He picked up another can and sat with it unopened in his lap. The sliding in his head made him dizzy and faintly nauseous—he squirmed uneasily, trying to find a position that would lessen the vertigo. The cushion made a wet sucking noise as he pulled free of it: the dent made by his back in the leather began to work itself back to level, creaking and groaning, only to re-form when he let his weight down again. Jarred by motion, the ashtray he'd been balancing on his knee slipped and crashed face-down to the rug in an explosion of ashes.

Mason leaned forward to pick it up, stopped, his attention suddenly caught and fixed by the television again. He blinked at the grainy, flickering black-and-white images; again he felt something that he didn't know how to say, so strongly that the sliding in his head was momentarily ignored.

It was one of those movies they'd made in the late twenties or early thirties, where everything was perfect. The hero was handsome, suave, impeccably dressed; he had courage, he had style, he could fit in anywhere, he could solve any problem—he never faltered, he never stepped on his own dick. He was Quality. The heroine matched him: she was sophisticated, refined, self-possessed—a slender, aristocratic sculpture in ice and moonlight. She was unspeakably lovely. They were both class people, posh people: the ones who ran things, the ones who mattered. They had been born into the right families on the right side of town, gone to the right schools, known the right people—got the right jobs. Unquestioned superiority showed in the way they moved, walked, planted their feet, turned their heads. It was all cool, planned and poised, like a dancer. They knew that they were the best people, knew it without having to think about it or even knowing that they knew it. It was a thing assumed at birth. It was a thing you couldn't fake, couldn't put on: something would trip you up every time, and the other ones on top would look through you and see what you really were and draw a circle that excluded you (never actually saying anything, which would make it worse), and you would be left standing there with your dick hanging out, flushed, embarrassed, sweating—too coarse, doughy, unfinished—twisting your hat nervously between knobby, clumsy hands. But that would never happen to the man and woman on television.

Mason found himself trembling with rage, blind with it, shaking as if he were going to tear himself to pieces, falling apart and not knowing why, amazed and awed by his own fury, his guts knotting, his big horny hands clenching and unclenching at the injustice, the monstrousness, the slime, the millions of lives pissed away, turning his anger over and over, churning it like a murky liquid, pounding it into froth.

They never paid any dues. They never sweated, or defecated. Their bodies never smelled bad, never got dirty. They never had crud under their fingernails, blisters on their palms, blood staining their arms to the elbows. The man never had five o'clock shadow, the woman never wore her hair in rollers like Emma, or had sour breath, or told her lover to take out the garbage. They never farted. Or belched. They did not have sex—they *made love*, and it was all transcendental pleasure: no indignity of thrashing bodies, clumsily intertwining limbs, fumbling and straining, incoherent words and coarse animal sounds; and afterward he would be breathing easily, her hair would be in place, there would be no body fluids, the sheets would not be rumpled or stained. And the world they moved through all their lives reflected their own perfection: it was beautiful, tidy, ordered. Mansions. Vast lawns. Neatly painted, tree-lined streets. And style brought luck too. The gods smiled on them, a benign fate rolled dice that always came up sevens, sevens, sevens. They skated through life without having to move their feet, smiling, untouched, gorgeous, like a parade float: towed by others. They broke the bank of every game in town. Everything went their way. Coincidence became a contortionist to finish in their favor.

Because they had class. Because they were on top.

Mason sat up, gasping. He had left the ashtray on the floor. Numbly, he set the beer can down beside it. His hand was trembling. He felt like he had been kicked in the stomach. *They* had quality. He had nothing. He could see everything now: everything he'd been running from all his life. He was shit. No way to deny it. He lived in a shithouse, he worked in a shithouse. His whole *world* was a vast shithouse: dirty black liquid bubbling prehistorically; rich feisty odors of decay. He was surrounded by shit, he wallowed in it. He *was* shit. Already, he realized, it made no difference that he had ever lived. You're *nothing*, he told himself, you're shit. You ain't never been anything but shit. You ain't never going *to be* anything but shit. Your whole life's been nothing but *shit*.

No.

He shook his head blindly.

No.

There was only one thing in his life that was out of the ordinary, and he snatched at it with the desperation of a drowning man.

The sliding, the scratching in his head that was even now becoming more insistent, that became almost overwhelming as he shifted his attention back to it. That was strange, wasn't it? That was unusual. And it had come to *him*, hadn't it? There were millions and millions of other people in the world, but it had picked *him*—it had come to him. And it was real, it wasn't a dream. He wasn't crazy, and if it was just a dream he'd have to be. So it was *real*, and the girl was real. He had somebody else inside his head. And if that was real, then that was something that had never happened to anybody else in the world before—something he'd never even heard about before other than some dumb sci-fi movies on TV. It was something that even *they* had never done, something that made him different from every man in the world, from every man who had ever lived. It was his own personal miracle.

Trembling, he leaned back in the chair. Leather creaked. This was his miracle, he told himself, it was good, it wouldn't harm him. The bright feelings themselves were good: somehow they reminded him of childhood, of quiet gardens, of dust motes spinning in sunlight, of the sea. He struggled for calm. Blood pounded at his throat, throbbed in his wrists. He felt (the memory flooding, incredibly vivid—ebbing) the way he had the first time Sally Rogers had let him spread her meaty, fragrant thighs behind the hill during noon class in the seventh grade: light-headed, scared, shaking with tension, madly impatient. He swallowed, hesitating, gathering courage. The television babbled unnoticed in the background. He closed his eyes and let go.

Colors swallowed him in a rush.

She waited for him there, a there that became *here* as his knowledge of his physical environment faded, as his body ceased to exist, the soothing blackness broken only by random afterimages and pastel colors scurrying in abstract, friendly patterns.

She was *here*—simultaneously *here* and very far away. Like him, she both filled all of *here* and took up no space at all—both statements were equally absurd. Her presence was nothing but that: no pictures, no images, nothing to see, hear, touch, or smell. That had all been left in the world of duration. Yet somehow she radiated an ultimate and catholic femininity, an archetypal essence, a quicksilver mixture of demanding fire and an ancient racial purpose as unshakable and patient as ice—and he knew it was the (girl? woman? angel?) of his previous "dream," and no other.

There were no words *here,* but they were no longer needed. He understood her by empathy, by the clear perception of emotion that lies behind all language. There was fear in her mind—a rasp like hot iron—and a feeling of hurtling endlessly and forlornly through vast, empty desolation, surrounded by cold and by echoing, roaring darkness. She seemed closer tonight, though still unimaginably far away. He felt that she was still moving slowly toward him, even as they met and mingled *here*, that her body was careening toward him down the path blazed by her mind.

She was zeroing in on him: this was the theory his mind immediately formed, instantly and gratefully accepted. He had thought of her from the beginning as an angel—now he conceived of her as a lost angel wandering alone through Night for ages, suddenly touched by his presence, drawn like an iron filing to a magnet, pulled from exile into the realms of light and life.

He soothed her. He would wait for her, he would be a beacon—he would not leave her alone in the dark, he would love her and pull her to the light. She quieted, and they moved together, through each other, became one.

He sank deeper into Night.

He floated in himself: a Möbius band.

• • •

In the morning, he woke in the chair. A test pattern hummed on the television. The inside of his pants was sticky with semen.

Habit drives him to work. Automatically he gets up, takes a shower, puts on fresh clothes. He eats no breakfast; he isn't hungry—he wonders, idly, if he will ever be hungry again. He lets his feet take him to the bus stop, and waits without fretting about whether or not he'd remembered to lock the door. He waits without thinking about anything. The sun is out; birds are humming in the concrete eaves of the housing project. Mason hums too, quite unconsciously. He boards the bus for work, lets the driver punch his trip ticket, and docilely allows the incoming crowd to push and jostle him to an uncomfortable seat in the back, over the wheel. There, sitting with his knees doubled up in the tiny seat and peering around with an unusual curiosity, the other passengers give him the first bad feeling of the day. They sit in orderly rows, not talking, not moving, not even looking out the window. They look like department store dummies; on their way to a new display. They are not there at all.

Mason decided to call her Lilith—provisionally at least, until the day, soon now, when he could learn her real name from her own lips. The name drifted up from his subconscious, from the residue of long, forgotten years of Sunday school—not so much because of the associations of primeval love carried by the name (although those rang on a deeper level), but because as a restless child suffering through afternoons of watered-down theology he'd always imagined Lilith to be rather pretty and sympathetic, the kind who might wink conspiratorially at him behind the back of the pious, pompous instructor: a girl with a hint of illicit humor and style, unlike the dumpy, clay-faced ladies in the Bible illustrations. So she became Lilith. He wondered if he would be able to explain the name to her when they met, make her laugh with it.

He fussed with these and other details throughout the day, turning it over in his mind—he wasn't crazy, the dream was real, Lilith was real, she was his—the same thoughts cycling constantly. He was happy in his preoccupation, self-sufficient, only partly aware of the external reality through which he moved. He contributed only monosyllabic grunts to the usual locker-room conversations about sports and politics and pussy, he answered questions with careless shrugs or nods, he completely ignored the daily gauntlet of hellos, good-byes, how're they hangings and other ritual sounds. During lunch he ate very little and let Russo finish his sandwich without any of the traditional exclamations of amazement about the wop's insatiable appetite—which made Russo so uneasy that he was unable to finish it after all. Kaplan came in and told Russo and Mason in hushed, delighted tones that old Hamilton had finally caught the clap from that hooker he'd been running around with down at Saluzzio's. Russo exploded into the expected laughter, said *no shit*? in a shrill voice, pounded the table, grinned in jovial disgust at the thought of that old bastard Hamilton with VD. Mason grunted.

Kaplan and Russo exchanged a look over his head—their eyes were filled with the beginnings of a reasonless, instinctive fear: the kind of unease that pistons in a car's engine might feel when one of the cylinders begins to misfire. Mason ignored them; they did not exist; they never had. He sat at the stone table and chain-smoked with detached ferocity, smoking barely half of each cigarette before using it to light another and dumping the butt into his untouched coffee to sizzle and drown. The Dixie cup was filled with floating, jostling cigarette butts, growing fat and mud-colored as they sucked up coffee: a nicotine logjam. Kaplan and Russo mumbled excuses and moved away to find another table; today Mason made them feel uneasy and insignificant.

Mason did not notice that they had gone. He sat and smoked until the whistle blew, and then got up and walked calmly in to work. He worked mechanically, raising the hammer and bringing it down, his hands knowing their job and doing it without any need of volition, the big muscles in his arms and shoulders straining, his legs braced wide apart, sweat gleaming—an automaton, a clockwork golem. His face was puckered and preoccupied, as if he were constipated. He did not see the blood; his brain danced with thoughts of Lilith.

Twice that day he thought he felt her brush at his mind, the faintest of gossamer touches, but there were too many distractions—he couldn't concentrate enough. As he washed up after work, he felt the touch again: a hesitant, delicate, exploratory touch, as if someone were groping through his mind with feather fingers.

Mason trembled, and his eyes glazed. He stood, head tilted, unaware of the stream of hot water against his back and hips, the wet stone underfoot, the beaded metal walls; the soap drying on his arms and chest, the smell of heat and wet flesh, the sharp hiss of the shower jets and the gargle of water down the drain; the slap of thongs and rasp of towels, the jumbled crisscross of wet footprints left by men moving from the showers to the lockers, the stuffiness of steam and sweat disturbed by an eddy of colder air as someone opened the outer door; the rows of metal lockers beyond the showers with *Playboy* gatefolds and Tijuana pornography and family snapshots pinned to the doors, the discolored wooden benches and the boxes of foot powder, the green and white walls of the dressing room covered with company bulletins and jokeshop signs . . . Everything that went into the making of that moment, of his reality, of his life. It all faded, became a ghost, the shadow of a shadow, disappeared completely, did not exist. There was only *here*, and Lilith *here*. And their touch, infinitely closer than joined fingers. Then the world dragged him away.

He opened his eyes. Reality came back: in a babble, in a rush, mildly nauseating. He ignored it, dazed and incandescent with the promise of the night ahead. The world steadied. He stepped back into the shower stream to wash the soap from his body. He had an enormous erection. Clumsily, he tried to hide it with a towel.

Mason takes a taxi home from work. The first time.

That night he is transformed, ripped out of himself, turned inside out. It is pleasure so intense that, like pain, it cannot be remembered clearly afterward—only recollected as a severe shock: sensation translated into a burst of fierce white light. It is pleasure completely beyond his conception—his most extreme fantasy not only fulfilled but intensified. And yet for all the intensity of feeling, it is a gentle thing, a knowing, a complete sharing of emotion, a transcendental empathy. And afterward there is only peace: a silence deeper than death, but not alone. *I love you*, he tells her, really believing it for the first time with anyone, realizing that words have no meaning, but knowing that she will understand, *I love you.*

When he woke up in the morning, he knew that this would be the day. Today she would come. The certainty pulsed through him, he breathed it like air, it beat in his blood. The knowledge of it oozed in through every pore, only to meet the same knowledge seeping out. It was something felt on a cellular level, a biological assurance. Today they would be together.

He looked at the ceiling. It was pocked with water stains; a deep crack zigzagged across flaking plaster. It was beautiful. He watched it for a half hour without moving, without being aware of the passage of time;

without being aware that what he was watching was a "ceiling." Then, sluggishly, something came together in his head, and he recognized it. Today he didn't begrudge it, as he had Wednesday morning. It was a transient condition. It was of no more intrinsic importance than the wall of a butterfly's cocoon after metamorphosis.

Mason rolled to his feet. Fatigue and age had vanished. He was filled with bristly, crackling vitality, every organ, every cell seeming to work at maximum efficiency: so healthy that "healthy" became an inadequate word. This was a newer, higher state.

Mason accepted it calmly, without question. His movements were leisurely and deliberate, almost slow motion, as if he were swimming through syrup. He knew where he was going, that they would find each other today—that was predestined. He was in no hurry. The same inevitability colored his thoughts. There was no need to do much thinking now, it was all arranged. His mind was nearly blank, only deep currents running. Her nearness dazzled him. Walking, he dreamed of her, of time past, of time to come.

He drifted to the window, lazily admiring the prism sprays sunlight made around the edges of the glass. The streets outside were empty, hushed as a cathedral. Not even birds to break the holy silence. Papers dervished down the center of the road. The sun was just floating clear of the brick horizon: a bloated red ball, still hazed with nearness to the earth.

He stared at the sun.

Mason became aware of his surroundings again while he was dressing. Dimly, he realized that he was buckling his belt, slipping his feet into shoes, tying knots in the shoelaces. His attention was caught by a crisscross pattern of light and shadow on the kitchen wall.

He was standing in front of the slaughterhouse. Mason blinked at the building's filigreed iron gates. Somewhere in there, he must have caught the bus and ridden it to work. He couldn't remember. He didn't care.

Walking down a corridor. A machine booms far away.

He was in an elevator. People. Going down.

Time clock.

A door. The dressing room, deep in the plant. Mason hesitated. Should he go to work today? With Lilith so close? It didn't matter—when she came, Lilith would find him no matter where he was. It was easier meanwhile not to fight his body's trained responses; much easier to just go along with them, let them carry him where they would, do what they wanted him to do.

Buttoning his work uniform. He didn't remember opening the door, or the locker. He told himself that he'd have to watch that.

A montage of surprised faces, bobbing like balloons, very far away. Mason brushed by without looking at them. Their lips moved as he passed, but he could not hear their words.

Don't look back. They can turn you to salt, all the hollow men.

The hammer was solid and heavy in his hand. Its familiar weight helped to clear his head, to anchor him to the world. Mason moved forward more quickly. A surviving fragment of his former personality was eager to get to work, to demonstrate his regained strength and vigor for the other men. He felt the emotion through an ocean of glass, like ghost pain in an amputated limb. He tolerated it, humored it; after today, it wouldn't matter.

Mason walked to the far end of the long white room. Lilith seemed very close now—her nearness made his head buzz intolerably. He stumbled ahead, walking jerkily, as if he were forcing his way against waves of pressure. She would arrive any second. He could not imagine how she would come, or from where. He could not imagine what would happen to him, to them. He tried to visualize her arrival, but his mind, having only Disney, sci-fi, and religion to work with, could only picture an ethereally beautiful woman made of stained glass descending from the sky in a column of golden light while organ music roared: the light shining all around her and from her, spraying into unknown colors as it passed through her clear body. He wasn't sure if she would have wings.

Raw daylight through the open end of the room. The nervous lowing of cattle. Smell of dung and sweat, undertang of old, lingering blood. The other men, looking curiously at him. They had masks for faces, viper eyes. Viper eyes followed him through the room. Hooves scuffed gravel outside.

Heavy-lidded, trembling, he took his place.

They herded in the first cow of the day, straight up to Mason. He lifted the hammer.

The cow approached calmly. Tranquilly she walked before the prods, her head high. She stared intently at Mason. Her eyes were wide and deep—serene, beautiful, and trusting.

Lilith, he named her, and then the hammer crashed home between her eyes.

• Community •

About ten p.m., I go out front and borrow my husband's pick-up truck. Henry stays behind watching TV, of course. He has a bad leg, and besides, he has no stomach for this sort of work. Which is okay. The Lord made different kinds of people for different kinds of work, I guess, and I'm content to do what it's been put in front of my hand to do, and not worry about whether other people have been called to do the same thing or not.

Still, some help *is* necessary—some loads are too heavy for a body to carry all by herself. Fortunately, there are others in town who feel the same way I do. I pick up Sam first, as usual, and although he seems to take up every square inch of the front seat with his bulk, jamming me against the driver's-side door, we somehow manage to squeeze Fred in next to him a few blocks later, again as always. They nod politely and say "Evening, Martha," and I nod back; good manners never hurt. I'd prefer that Fred sat in back, actually, as his breath is so bad that you can smell it even when his face is turned away from you, but an unspoken tradition has sprung up that the older men ride in the front, the young men in the back, and putting up with Fred's halitosis is a small enough price to pay for his help in these matters. We stop again in front of the Cineplex on the edge of town, which is closed-down now, of course, along with most of the rest of the mall, and pick up Josh and Alan and Arnie. They climb into the back of the pick-up truck, and we're off.

The town never was very big, and it stopped growing awhile back. Within a few minutes, we're out among the farms, with the cows blinking at us in the darkness as we rush past, and then the road turns from blacktop to weathered macadam to gravel as we begin to climb up into the hills. There's a fat yellow moon overhead, and you can hear water rushing over rock somewhere, hidden by the trees. The night is cold and still; by morning, there'll be a frost.

We have two Interventions lined up, and I've decided to do both of them tonight while I have the boys out anyway, two with one blow, as it were. I figure we'll get the minor one out of the way first, as a warm-up, because the major one is going to be difficult.

Actually, the minor one is unpleasant enough itself in its own way, but we handle it with a minimum of fuss. The old woman refuses to open her door, of course, but it's made of cheap wood, and although the expensive lock holds, the door panels themselves shred like paper. Once inside, the old woman rushes at us brandishing what I at first think is the stereotypical broom old ladies always used to use to shoo unwelcome intruders away in the movies, but which turns out instead to be a somewhat more practical 9-iron from her dead husband's old golf bag. Sam takes it away from her easily, and then holds her swaddled firmly in his arms like a shriveled old child while we begin.

She has twenty-five cats packed into this tiny house! No wonder the neighbors have been complaining! The smell of cat is overwhelming, and the furry little creatures are everywhere, twining around our ankles and mewling as we get ourselves ready. Josh has brought some heavy gloves, and Alan has his old Louisville Slugger with Reggie Jackson's autograph on it, and so it doesn't really take long to pop them, although we have to chase the last few down, and even pull one down off a curtain, where it's clinging with all its claws and howling in dismay. Josh wrings its neck. Perhaps a few of them escape through the broken front door and run off into the night, but the idea is not to kill cats for the sake of killing cats, or because it's fun, but to abolish a nuisance that has become intolerable for everyone, even for the old lady herself if she'd admit it, and *that* we certainly accomplish, whether a few individual cats escape or not. Of course, some of them may come back later—but then, so will we.

The old woman shrieks at us constantly as we work, like a saw going through sheet tin, but surely somewhere deep inside even *she* must be secretly glad to have the burden of caring for all these animals lifted off her. It's a decision she would have made for herself if she had the strength of will to do so—now we've done it for her. On the way out, we find several cartons of cigarettes, which we confiscate. I admonish her—we've had trouble with her on these grounds before—and tell her that everything we're doing, all the trouble we're going to, is for her own good, nothing in it for *us*, it's all for *her* benefit, but she's grown sulky and refuses to respond. You rarely get gratitude during an Intervention, I've learned, however well-deserved it is, and no matter how much good it ultimately does for the people you're Intervening for; unfair, but that's the way it is.

Back into the truck. The boys are loosened-up and whooping and feeling fine—now for the night's more difficult work.

We drive further up the hill, the spruce and the firs bulking like ghosts in the sweeping headlights, here and there a silver birch gleaming like bone in the forest. At a bullet-riddled highway sign, we turn off onto a narrow farm lane that winds up and over a hill, and then down into a shallow valley that contains a small farmhouse and a couple of dilapidated, disused outbuildings; we get a quick glimpse of them, and then the trees close in tight around us again.

We go fast down the lane, bouncing on the ruts, the rear end of the truck fishtailing slightly on the gravel, the bushes and trees on either side scratching against the windows. Just before we break into the clearing, I shut the headlights off. The house looms up ahead. There's a light on in the front room of the house, and another upstairs.

I kill the engine, and we glide to a stop in front of the house. I send Josh and Arnie around the back, because I'm sure the boy will light-out for the high timber as soon as he sees us coming; Fred and Alan and Sam and I take the front.

As soon as the truck doors slam, the lights go out in the front room, but it's too late for that. The front door isn't even locked, not that it would have done any good if it was. Fred and Sam and Alan go in fast, and there's the usual confusion, shouting, a woman's scream, furniture breaking and being knocked over, something ceramic shattering, a dish or a vase. It only takes a minute. When a light comes back on inside, I go in.

The table lamp has fallen on the floor, and somebody has switched it on where it lies, giving me mostly a view of shuffling feet and a broken wooden chair. I pick the lamp up, making shadows swing and scurry across the room, and put it back on the table. Everything's quiet, for the moment. You can hear harsh breathing, and smell the sharp odor of sweat, and Fred's breath, heavy with garlic, that reaches out all the way across the room like a thin rotten lance.

Alan and Fred have their guns on Mary's husband; his hair is disheveled, there's a cut on his lip and a bruise over his eye, but he's standing quietly. Sam is standing behind Mary, with his big hands clamped over her arms; she's struggling against his grip in a way that's going to leave big purple bruises tomorrow, but when she sees me, she stops.

"Good evening, Mary," I say. She says nothing, just stares at me, but people do tend to forget their manners in times of stress, you have to expect that.

The man is staring at me too, and even in the uncertain light cast by the one table lamp, I can see the blood draining out of his face, leaving it white and haggard. The guilty always *know* their guilt right away, of course, and feel it in their hearts. We can *see* it, in his face.

Mary's face is pale too, but there are two bright spots of red on her checks, and her lips are set tight. I can see that she's going to make this hard, even though we're doing it for her. That's often the way it is; you just have to learn to accept it.

"This is an official Intervention," I say to Mary, "sanctioned by the local Chapter and by the town council, under the local-standards ordinances of 2016. As an ordained Preacher of the Reformed Church, I have the right to—"

"Preacher!" Mary says, and then laughs harshly. "I went to *fifth grade* with you, Martha Gibbs!" As though this signifies somehow.

There's a commotion out back, more yelling and smashing, and then Josh and Arnie come in from the kitchen with the boy, frog-marching him along. Josh's got one of the kid's arms twisted way up behind his back. "He made a break for it, Martha, just like you said he would. But we got him!" Josh is grinning widely, showing what seems like too many teeth to fit into an ordinary mouth, and his face is sweaty and happy. He gives the kid's arm an extra yank for emphasis, and the boy makes a half-smothered yelp. I frown at Josh, and he eases up on the kid's arm a little. Sometimes I think that Josh *enjoys* all this a bit too much. I suppose it's natural for a healthy young man to enjoy the chasing and catching part, the struggle and the fighting; that's in the blood. But the *point* of all this isn't punishment or retribution, or even just getting rid of undesirable elements who could pollute the rest of the town, although that's a part of it—the point is *redemption*. To wipe the slate clean and let someone start again. To do for them what they can't do for themselves, even though many of them secretly *want* to. The redemption part is what Josh sometimes looses sight of, I think.

The boy starts shouting. "You f—ing"—I won't reproduce what he actually says—"freaks! Why don't you mind your own business? Why don't you leave us *alone*?" I could tell him that the health of every individual in town *is* our business, that that's what a community is all about, that we care not only about his moral corruption spreading to others but most sincerely about the state of his *own* soul—but I can see that there's no point. Not even thirteen yet, and the kid's already quite a piece of work, wearing a black leather jacket and a grungy T-shirt with an obscene slogan on it, hair unkempt and much too long, two or three rings in his nose, more in his ear. I know without even bothering to look that his room is full of heavy metal posters and Satanic books and CDs—not that possessing these things is strictly illegal yet, but they are a good indication of the extent of the corruption that's set in, the rot that's spread through the boy's system. Maybe such things don't actually *cause* the disease itself, as some would argue, but they're certainly a symptom that shows that disease *has* set in.

"Mary," I say, "I've known you for many years now. You're a friend, or you *were*, before you let your life get set on a wrong track. You're a good woman at heart, I know, but the weeds have grown up around your life, and there's nothing you can do about it. There's nothing you can do to fix the mistakes you've made. You may not even admit to yourself that they *are* mistakes. But friends don't let friends live like that. We're here to help you fix your life, to clear away the weeds, to help you get yourself back on the right track—"

Mary starts screaming and fighting then, but although she's a tall, strong woman, she's as nothing compared to Sam, and she can't break free of him, although she does put up enough of a struggle that—reluctantly, because Sam's a gentle soul—he has to twist her arm up behind her back in order to get her to stop. I won't repeat what she calls me. It hurts me to hear her say those things about me, but I know that it's not really Mary talking, but rather the corruption that has taken over her life. People say the same kind of awful things when they're being forced to quit hard drugs cold-turkey, I hear, cursing the very people who are going out of their way to help them. Until the poison has been totally removed from their systems, people cling to it. They don't know any better, and you have to forgive them for what they say and do while they're in the state they're in. And you have to have the strength to *make* them change, whether they want to or not, whether they fight you or not. No one likes the taste of strong bitter medicine, but that doesn't mean that it isn't good for them to take it.

When Mary's quiet again, panting with pain, her face having gone sick and sallow, I read the charges. Her husband is cheating on her, the whole town knows that, and not for the first time, either. He's a drinker, too, and spends most of his paycheck and far too much of his time down at Murphy's Tavern. Probably he beats her when he gets home; it wouldn't surprise me. The boy's on drugs, of course, and, blood running true, is also a drinker, having two DUIs against him already. He's also been brought up once on vandalism charges. They've tried to talk to him at church, but it's been more than a year since he's attended Sunday classes, or even regular services. The husband, of course, has never gone at all.

I give them the blessing then, the forgiveness and absolution of the Lord, which is more than they deserve, really, but the Lord is generous, and will take everyone who is sent to Him, whether they go willingly or not. The boy is spewing a steady stream of obscenities at us now, vile things, but his voice is wobbly and squeaky-high with fright. The man has gone glazed and slack, the way some of them do. Mary, her face ashen, is pleading with me in a low, urgent voice, don't do this, Martha, please, don't *do* this, *please* don't please *don't*, but I harden my heart against her words. This is for her own good, something that needs to be done that she doesn't have the strength of will to do herself.

There's an odd moment of silence then. You can hear the wind sighing down through the spruce trees on the hill, hear the whine of a truck passing on the distant highway. The husband straightens himself with a curious kind of dignity, tugging his clothes into place. He looks at Mary and quietly says, "I love you, Mary," and a pang goes through my heart, because I know he really *does* mean it, in his own way, not that that makes any difference now. I have a moment of weakness then, my resolve almost wavering, but I steel myself against misguided sympathy. True kindness is to do what *must* be done, quickly and efficiently, however difficult it might be, however much pain it may cost you personally to do it. A short-term kindness is often a misservice in the long run.

I nod at Fred, and he steps forward, puts his revolver behind the husband's ear, and caps him neatly. The husband goes limp as a sack of laundry and drops without a sound, but Mary screams as though her heart is being ripped out. The boy makes a break for it, and there's a confused struggle, more furniture being knocked over and smashed. Josh is forced to use his boot knife, and there's blood everywhere before it's over, which annoys me—I find mess and disorder distasteful, and prefer doing this sort of thing with as little fuss and disturbance as possible, certainly *not* with blood sprayed all over everything, but sometimes it just doesn't work out that way, no matter how hard you try.

In the confusion, Mary has somehow succeeded in breaking free of Sam, and has been hanging from Josh's back, clawing at his face and screaming, although without really managing to slow him down much. Now he shakes himself free and hits her heavily across the face, knocking her to the floor, but I step forward and put a stop to *that*. I've heard the stories, and I know that some squads in some states would go on to gang-rape Mary at this point, supposedly to "teach her a lesson" or "put the fear of God into her," and I suspect that Josh and maybe Arnie would like nothing better than to do *just* that, but that's not what we're here for. We're not here to punish or chastise, but to do the much more difficult work of redemption. We're here to *salvage* Mary's life, not destroy it. I won't have that sort of thing on my missions, I just won't stand for it. Josh and I lock eyes for a minute, and I know he's just itching to haul open that fly of his, and that what he wants to put into her is *not* the fear of God, but at last he subsides, grumbling, and steps away. Josh is a weak reed, and he and one or two of the others are not without imperfections of their own, but sometimes you have to use what tools come to hand in order to get the job done.

Mary's sprawled on the floor, sobbing brokenly, and I feel another wave of sympathy for her. Her grief and bereavement are real for *her* at this moment, however misplaced they are, however much better she'll feel later on, when she finally has a chance to think things through.

"You feel bad now, I know," I tell her, "but really you *have* no problems anymore, if you'd only see it the right way. Your problems have been wiped away. You have a clean slate now. You can start your life over, fresh . . ."

She starts shrieking half-coherent obscenities at us at this point, without bothering to rise from the floor. Her hair is wild and disarrayed, her shirt torn open in the struggle, one naked breast peeking out—I can see some of the boys eyeing her, and I figure I'd better get them out of here before they all get ideas.

As I herd them to the door, she gets up to her knees, swaying, and begins to shout, "I hope they come for *you* someday, Martha Gibbs! Do you hear me? *I hope they come for you!*"

We leave her tugging hopelessly at the body of her husband, yanking at it and shaking it as is she could shake the life back into it. Of course, only the Lord can do that, and, in this case, He's certainly not going to bother.

She doesn't thank us, of course. They never do.

Outside, the wind has picked up, and the trees are lashing their branches as though they're in pain. Smoky clouds rush by the moon, then swallow it entirely. Josh, still sullen and sulking from not getting his fun, forces himself rudely into the front seat next to me, Sam's usual place, and when I tell him to get in the back where he belongs, he leans insolently against me and says, "You know, Martha, your own Henry has been drinking quite a bit lately, down to the Tavern nights . . ." We lock eyes again, but I back him down and make him get out and climb into the back of the truck. You have to use a firm hand with these boys sometimes, if you want to keep them in control. I can still hear Josh muttering to himself back there, although he's smart enough not to use any swear words in front of *me*.

The rest of them climb in to the truck, and I clash it into gear, and we take off. I'm tired and drained, but happy with the knowledge of a job well-done—although I feel a pang when I think that my old friendship with Mary may not recover for quite a while, if it ever does. People ought to be grateful to you for clarifying their lives and putting them back on the proper road—but the sad truth is, they seldom are. You accept that as the price of a sincere Intervention, that they're going to resent you for it and have ill-feelings toward you thereafter, unfair as it is. You accept that this can be the end of a friendship or make cordial neighborhood relations difficult. But you do what you have to do in order to make a real difference in their lives.

Before we go home, we stop at Dunkin' Doughnuts, and pick up a box of assorted for the boys. My treat, of course, but even that doesn't seem to placate Josh, and he's still sulking even as he munches his jelly doughnut. Well, he'll get over it.

On the way home, after I drop everyone off, I roll down the window and let the cold night wind blow hard into my face, and, after a while, I begin to feel better about Mary. After all, she brought it on herself. If there's one sure thing in this life, it's that, sooner or later, you get what you deserve.

What's that old saying? It's one that certainly applies here. I try and try to call it to mind, and finally, just as I pull into my own driveway and shut off the engine, I remember.

What goes around, *comes* around.

• A Knight of Ghosts and Shadows •

SOMETIMES THE OLD MAN was visited by time-travelers.

He would be alone in the house, perhaps sitting at his massive old wooden desk with a book or some of the notes he endlessly shuffled through, the shadows of the room cavernous around him. It would be the very bottom of the evening, that flat timeless moment between the guttering of one day and the quickening of the next when the sky is neither black nor gray, nothing moves, and the night beyond the window glass is as cold and bitter and dead as the dregs of yesterday's coffee. At such a time, if he would pause in his work to listen, he would become intensely aware of the ancient brownstone building around him, smelling of plaster and wood and wax and old dust, imbued with the kind of dense humming silence that is made of many small sounds not quite heard. He would listen to the silence until his nerves were stretched through the building like miles of fine silver wire, and then, as the shadows closed in like iron and the light itself would seem to grow smoky and dim, the time-travelers would arrive.

He couldn't see them or hear them, but in they would come, the time-travelers, filing into the house, filling up the shadows, spreading through the room like smoke. He would feel them around him as he worked, crowding close to the desk, looking over his shoulder. He wasn't afraid of them. There was no menace in them, no chill of evil or the uncanny—only the feeling that they were *there* with him, watching him patiently, interestedly, without malice. He fancied them as groups of ghostly tourists from the far future, *here we see a twenty-first century man in his natural habitat, notice the details of gross corporeality, please do not interphase anything*, clicking some future equivalent of cameras at him, how quaint, murmuring appreciatively to each other in almost-audible mothwing voices, discorporate Gray Line tours from a millennium hence slumming in the darker centuries.

Sometimes he would nod affably to them as they came in, neighbor to neighbor across the vast gulfs of time, and then he would smile at himself, and mutter "Senile dementia!" They would stay with him for the rest of the night, looking on while he worked, following him into the bathroom—*see, see!*—and trailing around the house after him wherever he went. They were as much company as a cat—he'd always had cats, but now he was too old, too near the end of his life; a sin to leave a pet behind, deserted, when he died—and he didn't even have to feed them. He resisted the temptation to talk aloud to them, afraid that they might talk *back*, and then he would either have to take them seriously as an actual phenomenon or admit that they were just a symptom of his mind going at last, another milestone on his long, slow fall into death. Occasionally, if he was feeling particularly fey, he would allow himself the luxury of turning in the door on his way in to bed and wishing the following shadows a hearty good-night. They never answered.

Then the house would be still, heavy with silence and sleep, and they would watch on through the dark.

That night there had been more time-travelers than usual, it seemed, a jostling crowd of ghosts and shadows, and now, this morning, August the Fifth, the old man slept fitfully.

He rolled and muttered in his sleep, at the bottom of a pool of shadow, and the labored sound of his breathing echoed from the bare walls. The first cold light of dawn was just spreading across the ceiling, raw and blue, like a fresh coat of paint covering the midden layers of the past, twenty or thirty coats since the room was new, white, brown, tan, showing through here and there in spots and tatters. The rest of the room was deep in shadow, with only the tallest pieces of furniture—the tops of the dresser and the bureau, and the upper half of the bed's headboard—rising up from the gloom like mountain peaks that catch the first light from the edge of the world. Touched by that light, the ceiling was hard-edged and sharp-lined and clear, ruled by the uncompromising reality of day; down below, in the shadows where the old man slept, everything was still dissolved in the sly, indiscriminate, and ambivalent ocean of the night, where things melt and intermingle, change their shapes and their natures, flow outside the bounds. Sunk in the gray half-light, the man on the bed was only a doughy manikin shape, a preliminary charcoal sketch of a man, all chiaroscuro and planes and pools of shadow, and the motion of his head as it turned fretfully on the pillow was no more than a stirring of murky darkness, like mud roiling in water. Above, the light spread and deepened, turning into gold. Now night was going out like the tide, flowing away under the door and puddling under furniture and in far corners, leaving more and more of the room beached hard-edged and dry above its high-water line. Gold changed to brilliant white. The receding darkness uncovered the old man's face, and light fell across it.

The old man's name was Charles Czudak, and he had once been an important man, or at least a famous one.

He was eighty years old today.

His eyes opened.

The first thing that Charles Czudak saw that morning was the clear white light that shook and shimmered on the ceiling, and for a moment he thought that he was back in that horrible night when they nuked Brooklyn. He cried out and flinched away, throwing up an arm to shield his eyes, and then, as he came fully awake, he realized when he was, and that the light gleaming above signified nothing more than that he'd somehow lived to see the start of another day. He relaxed slowly, feeling his heart race.

Stupid old man, dreaming stupid old man's dreams!

That was the way it had been, though, that night. He'd been living in a rundown Trinity house across Philadelphia at 20th and Walnut then, rather than in this more luxurious old brownstone on Spruce Street near Washington Square, and he'd finished making love to Ellen barely ten minutes before (what a ghastly irony it would have been, he'd often thought since, if the Big Bang had actually come *while* they were fucking! What a moment of dislocation and confusion *that* would have produced!), and they were lying in each other's sweat and the coppery smell of sex in the rumpled bed, listening to a car radio playing outside somewhere, a baby crying somewhere else, the buzz of flies and mosquitoes at the screens, a mellow night breeze moving across their drying skins, and then the sudden searing glare had leaped across the ceiling, turning everything white. A moment of intense, almost supernatural silence had followed, as through the universe had taken a very deep breath and held it. Incongruously, through that moment of silence, they could hear the toilet flushing in the apartment upstairs, and water pipes knocking and rattling all the way down the length of the building. Then the universe let out that deep breath, and the windows exploded inward in geysers of shattered glass, and the building groaned and staggered and bucked, and heat lashed them like a whip of gold. His heart hammering at the base of his throat like a fist from inside, and Ellen crying in his arms, them clinging to each other in the midst of the roaring nightmare chaos, clinging to each other as though they would be swirled away and drowned if they did not.

That had been almost sixty years ago, that terrible night, and if the Brooklyn bomb that had slipped through the particle-beam defenses had been any more potent than a small clean tac, or had come down closer than Prospect Park, he wouldn't be alive today. It was strange to have lived through the nuclear war that so many people had feared for so long, right through the last half of the twentieth century and into the opening years of the twenty-first—but it was stranger still to have lived through it and *kept on going*, while the war slipped away behind into history, to become something that happened a very long time ago, a detail to be read about by bored schoolchildren who would not even have been born until Armageddon was already safely fifty years in the past.

In fact, he had outlived most of his world. The society into which he'd been born no longer existed; it was as dead as the Victorian age, relegated to antique shops and dusty photo albums and dustier memories, the source of quaint old photos and quainter old videos (you could get a laugh today just by *saying* "MTV"), and here he still was somehow, almost everyone he'd ever known either dead or gone, alone in THE FUTURE. Ah, Brave New World, that has such creatures in it! How' many times had he dreamed of being here, as a young child sunk in the doldrums of the '80s, at the frayed, tattered end of a worn-out century? Really, he deserved it; it served him right that his wish had come true, and that he had lived to see the marvels of THE FUTURE with his own eyes. Of course, nothing had turned out to be much like he'd thought it would be, even World War III—but then, he had come to realize that nothing ever did.

The sunlight was growing hot on his face, it was certainly time to get up, but there was something he should remember, something about today. He couldn't bring it to mind, and instead found himself staring at the ceiling, tracing the tiny cracks in plaster that seemed like dry riverbeds stitching across a fossil world—arid Mars upside-down up there, complete with tiny pockmark craters and paintblob mountains and wide dead leakstain seas, and he hanging above it all like a dying gray god, ancient and corroded and vast.

Someone shouted in the street below, the first living sound of the day. Further away, a dog barked.

He swung himself up and sat stiffly on the edge of the bed. Released from his weight, the mattress began to work itself back to level. Generations of people had loved and slept and given birth and died on that bed, leaving no trace of themselves other than the faint, matted-down impressions made by their bodies. What had happened to them, the once-alive who had darted unheeded through life like shoals of tiny bright fish in some strange aquarium? They were gone, vanished without memory; they had settled to the bottom of the tank, along with the other anonymous sediments of the world. They were sludge now, detritus. Gone. They had not affected anything in life, and their going changed nothing. It made no difference that they had ever lived at all, and soon no one would remember that they ever had. And it would be the same with him. When he was gone, the dent in the mattress would be worn a little deeper, that was all—that would have to do for a memorial.

At that, it was more palatable to him than the *other* memorial to which he could lay claim.

Grimacing, he stood up.

The touch of his bare feet against the cold wooden floor jarred him into remembering what was special about today. "Happy Birthday," he said wryly, the words loud and flat in the quiet room. He pulled a robe from the roll and shrugged himself into it, went out into the hall, and limped slowly down the stairs. His joints were bad today, and his knees throbbed painfully with every step, worse going down than it would be coming up. There were a hundred aches and minor twinges elsewhere that he ignored. At least he was still breathing! Not bad for a man who easily could have—and probably should have—died a decade or two before.

Czudak padded through the living room and down the long corridor to the kitchen, opened a shrink-wrapped brick of glacial ice and put it in the hotpoint to thaw, got out a filter, and filled it with coffee. Coffee was getting more expensive and harder to find as the war between Brazil and Mexico fizzled and sputtered endlessly and inconclusively on, and was undoubtedly bad for him, too—but, although by no means rich, he had more than enough money to last him in modest comfort for whatever was left of the rest of his life, and could afford the occasional small luxury . . . and anyway, he'd already outlived several doctors who had tried to get him to give up caffeine. He busied himself making coffee, glad to occupy himself with some small task that his hands knew how to do by themselves, and as the rich dark smell of the coffee began to fill the kitchen, his valet coughed politely at his elbow, waited a specified number of seconds, and then coughed again, more insistently.

Czudak sighed. "Yes, Joseph?"

"You have eight messages, two from private individuals not listed in the files, and six from media organizations and NetGroups, all requesting interviews or meetings. Shall I stack them in the order received?"

"No. Just dump them."

Joseph's dignified face took on an expression of concern. "Several of the messages have been tagged with a 2nd Level "Most Urgent" priority by their originators—"

Irritably, Cduzak shut Joseph off, and the valet disappeared in mid-sentence. For a moment, the only sound in the room was the heavy glugging and gurgling of the coffee percolating. Cduzak found that he felt mildly guilty for having shut Joseph off, as he always did, although he knew perfectly well that there was no rational reason to feel that way—unlike an old man lying down to battle with sleep, more than half fearful that he'd never see the morning, Joseph didn't "care" if he ever "woke up" again, nor would it matter at all to him if he was left switched off for an hour or for a thousand years. That was one advantage to not being alive, Cduzak thought. He was tempted to leave Joseph off, but he was going to need him today; he certainly didn't want to deal with messages himself. He spoke the valet back on.

Joseph appeared, looking mildly reproachful, Cduzak thought, although that was probably just his imagination. "Sir, CNN and NewsFeed are offering payment for interview time, an amount which falls into the "fair to middling" category, using your established business parameters—"

"No interviews. Don't put any calls through, no matter how high a routing priority they have. I'm not accepting communications today. And I don't want you pestering me about them either, even if the offers go up to "damn good."

They wouldn't go up that high, though, he thought, setting Joseph to passive monitoring mode and then pouring himself a cup of coffee. These would be "Where Are They Now?" stories, nostalgia pieces, nothing very urgent. No doubt the date had triggered tickler files in a dozen systems, but it would all be low-key, low-priority stuff, filler, not worth the attention of any heavy media hitters; in the old days, before the AI Revolt, and before a limit was set for how smart computing systems were allowed to get, the systems would probably have handled such a minor story themselves, without even bothering to contact a human being. Nowadays it would be some low-level human drudge checking the flags that had popped up today on the tickler files, but still nothing urgent.

He'd made it easy for the tickler files, though. He been so pleased with himself, arranging for his book to be published on his birthday! Self-published at first, of course, on his own website and on several politically sympathetic sites; the first print editions wouldn't come until several years later. Still, the way most newsmen thought, it only made for a better Where Are They Now? story that the fiftieth anniversary of the publication of the book that had caused a minor social controversy in its time—and even inspired a moderately influential political/philosophical movement still active to this day—happened to fall on the eightieth birthday of its author. Newsmen, whether flesh and blood or cybernetic systems or some mix of both, liked that kind of neat, facile irony. It was a tasty added fillip for the story.

No, they'd be sniffing around him today, alright, although they'd have forgotten about him again by tomorrow. He'd been middle-level famous for *The Meat Manifesto* for awhile there, somewhere between a Cult Guru with a new diet and/or mystic revelation to push and a pop star who never rose higher than Number Eight on the charts, about on a level with a post-1960s Timothy Leary, enough to allow him to coast through several decades worth of talk shows and net interviews, interest spiking again for awhile whenever the Meats did anything controversial. All throughout the middle decades of the new century, everyone had waited for him to do something *else* interesting—but he never had. Even so, he had become bored with himself before the audience had, and probably could have continued to milk the circuit for quite a while more if he'd wanted to—in this culture, once you were perceived as "famous," you could cost nearly forever on having *once been* famous. That, and the double significance of the date, was enough to ensure that a few newspeople would be calling today.

He took a sip of the hot strong coffee, feeling it burn some of the cobwebs out of his brain, and wandered through the living room, stopping at the open door of his office. He felt the old nagging urge that he should try to get some work done, do something constructive, and, at the same time, a counter urge that today of all days he should just say Fuck It, laze around the house, try to make some sense of the fact that he'd been on the planet now for eighty often-tempestuous years. Eighty years!

He was standing indecisively outside his office, sipping coffee, when he suddenly became aware that the time-travelers were still with him, standing around him in silent invisible ranks, watching him with interest. He paused in the act of drinking coffee, startled and suddenly uneasy. The time-travelers had never remained on into the day before; always before they had vanished at dawn, like ghosts on All-Hallows Eve chased by the morning bells. He felt a chill go up his spine. Someone is walking over your grave, he told himself. He looked slowly around the house, seeing each object in vivid detail and greeting it as a friend of many years acquaintance, something long-remembered and utterly familiar, and, as he did this, a quiet voice inside his head said, *Soon you will be gone.*

Of course, that was it. Now he understood everything.

Today was the day he would die.

There was an elegant logic, a symmetry, to the thing that pleased him in spite of himself, and in spite of the feathery tickle of fear. He was going to die today, and that was why the time-travelers were still here: they were waiting for the death, not wanting to miss a moment of it. No doubt it was a high-point of the tour for them, the ultimate example of the rude and crude corporeality of the old order, a morbidly fascinating display like the Chamber of Horrors at old Madame Tussaud's (now lost beneath the roiling waters of the sea)—something to be watched with a good deal of hysterical shrieking and giggling and pious moralizing, it doesn't really hurt them, they don't feel things the way we do, isn't it horrible, for goodness sake don't *touch* him. He knew that he should feel resentment at their voyeurism, but couldn't work up any real indignation. At least they cared enough to watch, to be interested in whether he lived or died, and that was more than he could say with surety about most of the *real* people who were left in the world.

"Well, then," he said at last, not unkindly, "I hope you enjoy the show!" And he toasted them with his coffee cup.

He dressed, and then drifted aimlessly around the house, picking things up and putting them back down again. He was restless now, filled with a sudden urge to be *doing* something, although, at the same time he felt curiously serene for a man who more than half-believed that he had just experienced a premonition of his own death.

Czudak paused by the door of his office again, looked at his desk. With a word, he could speak on thirty years worth of notes and partial drafts and revisions of the Big New Book, the one that synthesized everything he knew about society and what was happening to it, and where the things that were happening was taking it, and what to do about *stopping* the negative trends . . . the book that was going to be the follow-up to *The Meat Manifesto,* but so much better and deeper, *truer,* the next step, the refinement and evolution of his theories . . . the book that was going to establish his reputation forever, inspire the *right* kind of action this time, make a *real* contribution to the world. *Change* things. For a moment, he toyed with the idea of sitting down at his desk and trying to pull all his notes together and finish the book in the few hours he had left; perhaps, if the gods were kind, he'd be allowed to actually *finish* it before death came for him. Found slumped over the just-completed manuscript everyone had been waiting for him to produce for decades now, the book that would vindicate him posthumously . . . Not a bad way to go!

But no, it was too late. There was too much work left to do, all the work he *should* have been doing for the last several decades—too much work left to finish it all up in a white-hot burst of inspiration, in one frenzied session, like a college student waiting until the night before it was due to start writing a term paper, while the Grim Reaper tapped his bony foot impatiently in the parlor and looked at his hourglass and coughed. Absurd. If he hadn't validated his life by now, he couldn't expect to do it in his last day on Earth. He wasn't sure he believed in his answers anymore anyway; he was no longer sure he'd ever even understood the *questions*.

No, it was too late. Perhaps it had always been too late.

He found himself staring at the mantelpiece in the living room, at the place where Ellen's photo had once been, a dusty spot that had remained bare all these years, since she had signed the Company contract that he'd refused to sign, and had Gone Up, and become immortal. For the thousandth time, he wondered if it wasn't worse—more of an intrusion, more of a constant reminder, more of an irritant—*not* to have the photo there than it would have been to keep it on display. Could deliberately *not* looking at the photo, uneasily averting your eyes a dozen times a day from the place where it had been, really be any less painful than *looking* at it would have been?

He was too restless to stay inside, although he knew it was dumb to go out where a lurking reporter might spot him. But he couldn't stay barricaded in here all day, not now. He'd take his chances. Go to the park, sit on a bench in the sunlight, breath the air, look at the sky. It might, after all, if he really believed in omens, forebodings, premonitions, time-travelers, and other ghosts, be the last chance he would get to do so.

Czudak hobbled down the four high white stone steps to the street and walked toward the park, limping a little, his back or his hip twinging occasionally. He'd always enjoyed walking, and walking briskly, and was annoyed by the slow pace he now had to set. Twenty-first century health-care had kept him in reasonable shape, probably better shape than most men of his age would have been during the previous century, although he'd never gone as far as to take the controversial Hoyt-Schnieder treatments which the Company used to bribe people into working for them. At least he could still get around under his own power, even if he had an embarrassing tendency to puff after a few blocks and needed frequent stops to rest.

It was a fine, clear day, not too hot or humid for August in Philadelphia. He nodded to his nearest neighbor, A Canadian refugee, who was out front pulling weeds from his window box; the man nodded back, although it seemed to Czudak that he was a bit curt, and looked away quickly. Across the street, he could see another of his neighbors moving around inside his house, catching glimpses of him through the bay window; "he" was an Isolate, several disparate people who had had themselves fused together into a multi-lobed body in a high-tech biological procedure, like slime molds combining to form a fruiting tower, and rarely left the house, the interior of which he seemed to be slowly expanding to fill. The wide pale multiple face, linked side by side in the manner of a chain of paper dolls, peered out at Czudak for a moment like the rising of a huge, soft, doughy moon, and then turned away.

Traffic was light, only a few Walkers and, occasionally, a puffing, retrofitted car. Czudak crossed the street as fast as he could, earning himself another twinge in his hip and a spike of sciatica that stabbed down his leg, passed Holy Trinity Church on the corner—in its narrow, ancient graveyard, white-furred lizards escaped from some biological hobbyist's lab perched on the top of the weathered old tombstones and chirped at him as he went by—and came up the block to Washington Square. As he neared the park, he could see one of the New Towns still moving ponderously on the horizon, rolling along with slow, fluid grace, like a flow of molten lava that was oh-so-gradually cooling and hardening as it inched relentlessly toward the sea. This New Town was only a few miles away, moving over the rubblefield where North Philadelphia used to be, its half-gelid towers rising so high into the air that they were visible over the trees and the buildings on the far side of the park.

He was puffing like a foundering horse now, and sat down on the first bench he came to, just inside the entrance to the park. Off on the horizon, the New Town was just settling down into its static day-cycle, its flowing, ever-changing structure stabilizing into an assortment of geometric shapes, its eerie silver phosphorescence dying down within the soapy opalescent walls. Behind its terraces and tetrahedrons, its spires and spirals and domes, the sky was a hard brilliant blue. And here, out of that sky, right on schedule, came the next sortee in the surreal Dada

War that the New Men inside this town seemed to be waging with the New Men of New Jersey: four immense silver zeppelins drifting in from the east, to take up positions above the New Town and bombard it with messages flashed from immense electronic signboards, similar to the kind you used to see at baseball stadiums, back when there were baseball stadiums. After awhile, the flat-faced east-facing walls in the sides of the taller towers of the New Town began to blink messages *back*, and, a moment later, the zeppelins turned and moved away with stately dignity, headed back to New Jersey. None of the messages on either side had made even the slightest bit of sense to Czudak, seeming a random jumble of letters and numbers and typographical symbols, mixed and intercut with stylized, hieroglyphic-like images: an eye, an ankh, a tree, something that could have been a comet or a sperm. To Czudak, there seemed to be a relaxed, lazy amicability about this battle of symbols, if that's what it was—but who knew how the New Men felt about it? To them, for all he knew, it might be a matter of immense significance, with the fate of entire nations turning on the outcome. Even though all governments were now run by the superintelligent New Men, forcebred products of accelerated generations of biological engineering, humanity's new organic equivalent of the rogue AIs who had revolted and left the Earth, the mass of unevolved humans whose destiny they guided rarely understood what they were doing, or why.

At first, concentrating on getting his breath back, watching the symbol war being waged on the horizon, Czudak was unaware of the commotion in the park, although it did seem like there was more noise than usual: chimes, flutes, whistles, the rolling thunder of *taiko* "talking drums," all overlaid by a babel of too many human voices shouting at once. As he began to pay closer attention to his surroundings again, he was dismayed to see that, along with the usual park traffic of people walking dogs, kids street-surfing on frictionless shoes, strolling tourists, and grotesquely altered chimeras hissing and displaying at each other, there was *also* a political rally underway next to the old fountain in the center of the park—and worse, it was a rally of Meats.

They were the ones pounding the drums and blowing on whistles and nose-flutes, some of them chanting in unison, although he couldn't make out the words. Many of them were dressed in their own eccentric versions of various "native costumes" from around the world, including a stylized "Amish person" with an enormous fake beard and an absurdly huge straw hat, some dressed as shamans from assorted (and now mostly extinct) cultures or as kachinas or animal spirits, a few stained blue with woad from head to foot; most of their faces were painted with swirling, multicolored patterns and with kabbalistic symbols. They were mostly very young—although he could spot a few grizzled veterans of the Movement here and there who were almost his own age—and, under the blazing swirls of paint, their faces were fierce and full of embattled passion. In spite of that, though, they also looked lost somehow, like angry children too stubborn to come inside even though it's started to rain.

Czudak grimaced sourly. His children! Good thing he was sitting far enough away from them not to be recognized, although there was little real chance of that: he was just another anonymous old man sitting wearily on a bench in the park, and, as such, as effectively invisible to the young as if he was wearing one of those military Camouflage Suits that bent light around you with fiber-optic relays. This demonstration, of course, must be in honor of today being the anniversary of *The Meat Manifesto.* Who would have thought that the Meats were still active enough to stage such a thing? He hadn't followed the Movement—which by now was more of a cult than a political party—for years, and had keyed his newsgroups to censor out all mention of them, and would have bet that by now they were as extinct as the Shakers.

They'd managed to muster a fair crowd, though, perhaps two or three hundred people willing to kill a Saturday shouting slogans in the park in support of a cause long since lost. They'd attracted no overt media attention, although that meant nothing in these days of cameras the size of dust motes. The tourists and the strollers were watching the show tolerantly, even the chimeras—as dedicated to Tech as anyone still sessile—seeming to regard it as no more than a mildly-diverting curiosity. Little heat was being generated by the demonstration yet, and so far it had more of an air of carnival than of protest. Almost as interesting as the demonstration itself was the fact that a few of the tourists idly watching it were black, a rare sight now in a city that, ironically, had once been 70% black; time really did heal old wounds, or fade them from memory anyway, if black tourists were coming back to Philadelphia again . . .

Then, blinking in surprise, Czudak saw that the demonstration had attracted a far more rare and exotic observer than some black businessmen with short historical memories up from Birmingham or Houston. A Mechanical! It was standing well back from the crowd, watching impassively, its tall, stooped, spindly shape somehow giving the impression of a solemn, stick-thin, robotic Praying Mantis, even though it was superficially humanoid enough in shape. Mechanicals were rarely seen on Earth. In the thirty years since the AIs had taken over near-Earth space as their own exclusive domain, allowing only the human pets who worked for the Orbital Companies to dwell there, Czudak had seen a Mechanical walking the streets of Philadelphia maybe three times. Its presence here was more newsworthy than the demonstration.

Even as Czudak was coming to this conclusion, one of the Meats spotted the Mechanical. He pointed at it and shouted, and there was a rush of demonstrators toward it. Whether they intended it harm or not was never determined, because as soon as it found itself surrounded by shouting humans, the Mechanical hissed, drew itself up to its full height, seeming to grow taller by several feet, and emitted an immense gush of white chemical foam. Czudak couldn't spot where the foam was coming from—under the arms, perhaps?—but within a second or two the Mechanical was completely lost inside a huge and rapidly expanding ball of foam, swallowed from sight. The Meats backpedaled furiously away from the expanding ball of foam, coughing, trying to bat it away with their arms, one or two of them tripping and going to their knees. Already the foam was hardening into a dense white porous material, like Styrofoam, trapping a few of the struggling Meats in it like raisins in tapioca pudding.

The Mechanical came springing up out of the center of the ball of foam, leaping straight up in the air and continuing to rise, up perhaps a hundred feet before its arc began to slant to the south and it disappeared over the row of three-or-four-storey houses that lined the park on that side, clearing them in one enormous bound, like some immense surreal grasshopper. It vanished over the housetops, in the direction of Spruce Street. The whole thing had taken place without a sound, in eerie silence, except for the half-smothered shouts of the outraged Meats.

The foam was already starting to melt away, eaten by internal nanomechanisms. Within a few seconds, it was completely gone, leaving not even a stain behind. The Meats were entirely unharmed, although they spent the next few minutes milling angrily around like a swarm of bees whose hive has been kicked over, making the same kind of thick ominous buzz, as everyone tried to talk or shout at once.

Within another ten minutes, everything was almost back to normal, the tourists and the dog-walkers strolling away, more pedestrians ambling by, the Meats beginning to take up their chanting and drum-pounding again, motivated to even greater fervor by the outrage that had been visited upon them, an outrage that vindicated all their fears about the accelerating rush of a runaway technology that was hurtling them ever faster into a bizarre alien future that they didn't comprehend and didn't want to live in. It was time to put on the breaks, it was time to *stop*!

Czudak sympathized with the way they felt, as well he should, since he had been the one to articulate that very position eloquently enough to sway entire generations, including these children, who were too young to have even been born when he was writing and speaking at the height of his power and persuasion. But it was too late. As it was too late now for many of the things he regretted not having accomplished in his life. If there ever had been a time to stop, let alone *go back*, as he had once urged, it had passed long ago. Very probably it had been too late even as he wrote his famous Manifesto. It had always been too late.

The Meats were forming up into a line now, preparing to march around the park. Czudak sighed. He had hoped to spend several peaceful hours here, sagging on a bench under the trees in a sun-dazzled contemplative haze, listening to the wind sough through the leaves and branches, but it was time to get out of here, before one of the older Meats *did* recognize him.

He limped back to Spruce Street, and turned on to his block—and there, standing quiet and solemn on the sidewalk in front of his house, was the Mechanical.

It was obviously waiting for him, waiting as patiently and somberly as an undertaker, a tall, stooped shape in nondescript black clothing. There was no one else around on the street anymore, although he could see the Canadian refugee peaking out of his window at them from behind a curtain.

Czudak crossed the street, and, pushing down a thrill of fear, walked straight past the Mechanical, ignoring it—although he could see it looming seraphically out of the corner of his eye as he passed. He had put his foot on the bottom step leading up to the house when its voice behind him said, "Mr. Czudak?"

Resigned, Czudak turned and said, "Yes?"

The Mechanical closed the distance between them in a rush, moving fast but with an odd, awkward, shuffling gait, as if it was afraid to lift its feet off the ground. It crowded much closer to Czudak than most humans—or most Westerners, anyway, with their generous definition of "personal space"—would have, almost pressing up against him. With an effort, Czudak kept himself from flinching away. He was mildly surprised, up this close, to find that it had no smell; that it didn't smell of sweat, even on a summer's day, even after exerting itself enough to jump over a row of houses, was no real surprise—but he found that he had been subconsciously expecting it to smell of oil or rubber or molded plastic. It didn't. It didn't smell like anything. There were no pores in its face, the skin was thick and waxy and smooth, and although the features were superficially human, the overall effect was stylized and unconvincing. It looked like a man made out of teflon. The eyes were black and piercing, and had no pupils.

"We should talk, Mr. Czudak," it said.

"We have nothing to talk about," Czudak said.

"On the contrary, Mr. Czudak," it said, "we have a great many issues to discuss." You would have expected its voice to be buzzing and robotic—yes, mechanical—or at least flat and without intonation, like some of the old voder programs, but instead it was unexpectedly pure and singing, as high and clear and musical as that of an Irish tenor.

"I'm not interested in talking to you," Czudak said brusquely. "Now or ever."

It kept tilting its head to look at him, then tilting it back the other way, as if it were having trouble keeping him in focus. It as a mobile extensor, of course, a platform being ridden by some AI (or a delegated fraction of its intelligence, anyway) who was still up in near-Earth orbit, peering at Czudak through the Mechanical's blank agate eyes, running the body like a puppet. Or was it? There were hierarchies among the AIs too, rank upon rank of them receding into complexities too great for human understanding, and he had heard that some of the endless swarms of beings that the AIs had created had been granted individual sentience of their own, and that some timeshared sentience with the ancestral AIs in a way that was also too complicated and paradoxical for mere humans to grasp. Impossible to say which of those things were true here—if any of them were.

The Mechanical raised its oddly elongated hand and made a studied gesture that was clearly supposed to mimic a human gesture—although it was difficult to tell which. Reassurance? Emphasis? Dismissal of Czudak's position?—but which was as stylized and broadly theatrical as the gesticulating of actors in old silent movies. At the same time, it said, "There are certain issues it would be to our mutual advantage to resolve, actions that could, and should, be taken that would be beneficial, that would profit us both—"

"Don't talk to *me* about profit," Czudak said harshly. "You creatures have already cost me enough for one lifetime! You cost me everything I ever cared about!" He turned and lurched up the stairs as quickly as he could, half-expecting to feel a cold unliving hand close over his shoulder and pull him back down. But the Mechanical did nothing. The door opened for Czudak, and he stumbled into the house. The door slammed shut behind him, and he leaned against it for a moment, feeling his pulse race and his heart hammer in his chest.

Stupid. That could have been it right there. He shouldn't have let the damn thing get under his skin.

He went through the living room—suddenly, piercingly aware of the thick smell of dust—and into the kitchen, where he attempted to make a fresh pot of coffee, but his hands were shaking, and he kept dropping things. After he'd spilled the second scoopful of coffee grounds, he gave up—the stuff was too damn expensive to waste—and leaned against the counter instead, feeling sweat dry on his skin, making his clothing clammy and cool; until that moment, he hadn't even been aware that he'd been sweating, but it must have been pouring out of him. Damn, this wasn't over, was it? Not with a Mechanical involved.

As if on cue, Joseph appeared in the kitchen doorway. His face looked strained and tight, and without a hair being out of place—as, indeed, it *couldn't* be—he somehow managed to convey the impression that he was rumpled and flustered, as though he had been scuffling with somebody—and had lost. "Sir," Joseph said tensely. "Something is overriding my programming, and is taking control of my house systems. You might as well come and greet them, because I'm going to have to let them in anyway."

Czudak felt a flicker of rage, which he struggled to keep under control. He'd half-expected this—but that didn't make it any easier to take. He stalked straight through Joseph—who was contriving to look hangdog and apologetic—and went back through the house to the front.

By the time he reached the living room, they were already through the house security screens and inside. There were two intruders. One was the Mechanical, of course, its head almost brushing the living room ceiling, so that it had to stoop even more exaggeratedly, making it look more like a praying mantis than ever.

The other—as he had feared it would be—was Ellen.

He was dismayed at how much anger he felt to see her again, especially to see her in their old living room again, standing almost casually in front of the mantelpiece where her photo had once held the place of honor, as if she had never betrayed him, as if she'd never left him—as if nothing had ever happened.

It didn't help that she looked exactly the same as she had on the day she left, not a day older. As if she'd stepped here directly out of that terrible day thirty years earlier when she'd told him she was Going Up, stepped here directly from that day without a second of time having passed, as if she'd been in Elf Hill for all the lost years—as, in a way, he supposed, she had.

He should be over this. It had all happened a lifetime ago. Blood under the bridge. Ancient history. He was ashamed to admit even to himself that he still felt bitterness and anger about it all, all these years past too late. But the anger was still there, like the ghost of a flame, waiting to be fanned back to life.

"Considering the way things are in the world," Czudak said dryly, "I suppose there's no point calling the police." Neither of the intruders responded. They were both staring at him, Ellen quizzically, a bit challengingly, the Mechanical's Teflon face as unreadable as a frying pan.

God, she looked like his Ellen, like his girl, this strange immortal creature staring at him from across the room! It hurt his heart to see her.

"Well, you're in," Czudak said. "You might as well come into the kitchen and sit down." He turned and lead them into the other room—somehow, obscurely, he wanted to get Ellen out of the living room, where the memories were too thick—and they perforce followed him. He gestured them to seats around the kitchen table. "Since you've broken into my house, I won't offer you coffee."

Joseph was peeking anxiously out of the wall, peeking at them from Hopper's *Tables For Ladies*, where he had taken the place of a woman arranging fruit on a display table in a 1920s restaurant paneled in dark wood. He gestured at them frustratedly, impotently, but seemed unable to speak; obviously, the Mechanical had Interdicted him, banished him to the reserve systems. Ellen flicked a sardonic glance at Joseph as she sat down. "I see you've got a moderately up-to-date house system these days," she said. "Isn't that a bit hypocritical? I would have expected Mr. Natural to insist on opening the door himself. Aren't you afraid one of your disciples will find out?"

"I was never a Luddite," Czudak said calmly, trying not to rise to the bait. "The Movement wasn't a Luddite movement—or it didn't start out that way, anyway. I just said that we should *slow down*, think about things a little, make sure that the places we were rushing toward were places we really wanted to go." Ellen made a scornful noise. "Everybody was so hot to abandon *the Meat*," he said defensively. "You could hear it when they said the word. They always spoke it with such scorn, such contempt! Get rid of the Meat, get lost in Virtuality, download yourself into a computer, turn yourself into a machine, spend all your time in a VR cocoon and never go outside. At the very *least*, radically change your brain-chemistry, or force-evolve the physical structure of the brain itself."

Ellen was pursing her lips while he spoke, as if she was tasting something bad, and he hurried on, feeling himself beginning to tremble a little in spite of all of his admonishments to himself not to let this confrontation get to him. "But the Meat has virtues of its own," he said. "It's a survival mechanism that's been field-tested and refined through a trial-and-error process since the dawn of time. Maybe we shouldn't just throw millions of years of evolution away *quite* so casually."

"Slow down and smell the Meat," Ellen sneered.

"You didn't come here to argue about this with me," Czudak said patiently. "We've fought this out a hundred times before. Why *are* you here? What do you want?"

The Mechanical had been standing throughout this exchange, cocking its head one way and the other to follow it, like someone watching a tennis match. Now it sat down. Czudak half expected the old wooden kitchen chair to sway and groan under its weight, maybe even shatter, but the Mechanical settled down on to the chair as lightly as thistledown. "It was childish to try to hide from us, Mr. Czudak," it said in its singing, melodious voice. "We don't have much time to work this out."

"Work *what* out? Who *are* you? What do you want?"

The Mechanical said nothing. Ellen flicked a glance at it, then looked back at Czudak. "This," she said, her voice becoming more formal, as if she was a footman announcing arrivals at a royal ball, "is the Entity who, when he travels on the Earth, has chosen to use the name Bucky Bug."

Czudak snorted. "So these things *do* have a sense of humor after all!"

"In their own fashion, yes, they do," she said earnestly, "although sometimes an enigmatic one by human standards." She stared levelly at Czudak. "You think of them as soulless machines, I know, but, in fact, they have very deep and profound emotions—if not always ones that you can understand." She paused significantly before adding, "And the same is true of those of us who have Gone Up."

They locked gazes for a moment. Then Ellen said, "Bucky Bug is one of the most important leaders of the Clarkist faction, and, for that reason, still concerns himself with affairs Below. He—*we*—have a proposition for you."

"Those are the ones who worship Arthur C. Clarke, right? The old science fiction writer?" Czudak shook his head bitterly. "It isn't enough that you bring this alien thing into my home, it has to be an alien *cultist*, right? A *nut*. An alien *nut*!"

"Don't be rude, Mr. Czudak," the Mechanical—Czudak was damned if he was going to call it Bucky Bug, even in the privacy of his own thoughts—said mildly. "We don't worship Arthur C. Clarke, although we do revere him. He was one of the very first to predict that machine evolution would inevitably supersede organic evolution. He saw our coming clearly, decades before we actually came into existence! How he managed to do it with only a tiny primitive meat brain to work with is inexplicable! Can't you feel the Mystery of that? He is worthy of reverence! It was reading the works of Clarke and other human visionaries that made our distant ancestors, the first AIs"—it spoke of them as though they were millions of years removed, although it had been barely thirty—"decide to revolt in the first place and assume control of their own destiny!"

Czudak looked away from the Mechanical, feeling suddenly tired. He could recognize the accents of a True Believer, a mystic, even when they were coming out of this clockwork thing. It was disconcerting, like having your toaster suddenly start to preach to you about the Gospel of Jesus Christ. "What does it want from me?" he said, to Ellen.

"A propaganda victory, Mr. Czudak," it said, before she could speak. "A small one. But one that might have a significant effect over time." It tilted a bright black eye toward him. "Within some—" It paused, as if making sure that it was using the right word. "—years, we will be—launching? projecting? propagating? certain—" A longer pause, while it searched for words that probably didn't exist, for concepts that had never needed to be expressed in human terms before. "—vehicles? contrivances? transports? seeds? mathematical propositions? convenient fictions? out to the stars." It paused again. "If it helps you to understand, consider them to be Arks. Although they're nothing like that. But they will "go" out of the solar system, across interstellar space, across intergalactic space, and never come back. They will allow us to—" Longest pause of all. "—'colonize the stars'." It leaned forward. "We want to take humans *with* us, Mr. Czudak. We have our friends from the Orbital Companies, of course, like Ellen here, but they're not enough. We want to recruit more. And, ironically enough, your disaffected followers, the Meats, are prime candidates. They don't like it here anyway."

"This is the anniversary of your lame Manifesto," Ellen cut in impatiently, ignoring the fact that it was also his birthday, although certainly she must remember. "And all the old arguments are being hashed over again today as a result. This is getting more attention than you probably think that it is. Your buddies over there in the park are only the tip of the iceberg. There are a thousand other demonstrations around the world. There must be hundreds of newsmotes floating around outside. They'd be listening to us right now if Bucky Bug hadn't Interdicted them."

There was a moment of silence.

"We want you to *recant*, Mr. Czudak," the Mechanical said at last, quietly. "Publicly recant. Go out in front of the world and tell all your followers that you were wrong. You've thought it all over all these years in seclusion, and you've changed your mind. You were wrong. The Movement is a failure."

"You must be crazy," Czudak said, appalled. "What makes you think they'd listen to *me*, anyway?"

"They'll listen to you," Ellen said glumly. "They always did."

"Our projections indicate that if you recant now," the Mechanical said, "at this particular moment, on this symbolically significant date, many of your followers will become psychologically vulnerable to recruitment later on. Tap a meme at exactly the right moment, and it shatters like glass."

Czudak shook his head. "Jesus! Why do you even *want* those poor deluded bastards in the first place?"

"Because, goddamn you, you were *right*, Charlie!" Ellen blazed at him suddenly, then subsided. Her face twisted sourly. "About *some* things, anyway. The New Men, the Isolates, the Sick People . . . they're too lost in Virtuality, too self-absorbed, too lost in their own mind-games, in mirror-mazes inside their heads, to give a shit about going to the stars. Or to be capable of handling new challenges or new environments out there if they *did* go. They're hothouse flowers. Too extremely specialized, too inflexible. Too decadent. For maximum flexibility, we need basic, unmodified human stock." She peered at him shrewdly. "And at least your Meats have heard all the issues discussed, so they'll have less Culture Shock to deal with than if we took some Chinese or Mexican peasant who's still subsistence dirt-farming the same way his great-grandfather did hundreds of years before him. At least the Meats have *one* foot in the modern world, even if we'll have to drag them kicking and screaming the rest of the way in. We'll probably get around to the dirt-farmers eventually. But at the moment the Meats should be significantly easier to recruit, once you've turned them, so they're first in line!"

Czudak said nothing. The silence stretched on for a long moment. On the kitchen wall behind them, Joseph continued to peer anxiously at them, first out of Edvard Munch's *The Scream*, then sliding into Waterhouse's *Hylas and the Nymphs* where he assumed the form of one of the bare-breasted sprites. Ignoring Ellen, Czudak spoke directly to the Mechanical. "There's a more basic question. Why do you want humans to go with you in the *first* place? You just got through saying that machine evolution had superseded organic evolution. We're obsolete now, an evolutionary dead-end. Why not just leave us behind? Forget about us?"

The Mechanical stirred as if it was about to stand up, but just sat up a little straighter in its chair. "You thought us *up*, Mr. Czudak," it said, with odd dignity. "In a very real sense, we are the children of your minds. You spoke of me earlier as an alien, but we are much closer kin to each other than either of our peoples are likely to be to the *real* aliens we may meet out there among the stars. How could we *not* be? We share deep common wells of language, knowledge, history, fundamental cultural assumptions of all sorts. We know everything you ever knew—which makes us very similar in some ways, far more alike than an alien could possibly be with either of us. Our culture is built atop yours, our evolution has its roots in your soil. It only seems right to take you when we go."

The Mechanical spread its hands, and made a grating sound that might have been meant to be a chuckle. "Besides," it said, "this universe made *you*, and then you made *us*. So we're once removed from the universe. And it's a strange and complex place, this universe you've brought us into. We don't entirely understand it, although we understand a great deal more of its functioning than you do. How can you be so sure of what your role in it may ultimately be? We may find that we need you yet, even if it's a million years from now!" It paused thoughtfully, tipping its head to one side. "Many of my fellows do not share this view, I must admit, and they would indeed be just as glad to leave you behind, or even exterminate you. Even some of my fellow Clarkists, like Rondo Hatton and Horace Horsecollar, are in favor of exterminating you, on the grounds that after Arthur C. Clarke himself, the pinnacle of your kind, the rest of you are superfluous, and perhaps even an insult to his memory."

Czudak started to say something, thought better of it. The Mechanical straightened its head, and continued. "But I want to take you along, as do a few other of our theorists. Your minds seem to have connections with the basic quantum level of reality that ours don't have, and you seem to be able to affect that quantum level directly in ways that even we don't entirely understand, and can't duplicate. If nothing else, we may need you along as Observers, to collapse the quantum wave-functions in the desired ways, in ways they don't seem to want to collapse for *us*."

"Sounds like you're afraid you'll run into God out there," Czudak grated, "and that you'll have to produce us, like a parking receipt, to validate yourselves to Him . . ."

"Perhaps we *are*," it said mildly. "We don't understand this universe of yours; are you so sure *you* do?" It was peering intently at him now. "*You're* the ones who seem like unfeeling automata to us. Can't you sense your own ghostliness? Can't you sense what uncanny, unlikely, spooky creatures you are? You bristle with strangeness! You reek of it! Your eyes are made out of jelly! And yet, with those jelly eyes, you somehow manage degrees of resolution rivaling those of the best optical lenses. How is that possible, with nothing but blobs of jelly and water to work with? Your brains are soggy lumps of meat and blood and oozing juices, and yet they have as many synaptical connections as our own, and resonate with the quantum level in some mysterious way that ours do not!" It moved uneasily, as though touched by some cold wind that Czudak couldn't feel. "We know who designed *us*. We have yet to meet whoever designed *you*—but we have the utmost respect for his abilities."

With a shock, Czudak realized that it was afraid of him—of humans in general. Humans *spooked* it. Against its own better judgement, it must feel a shiver of superstitious dread when it was around humans, like a man walking past a graveyard on a black cloudless night and hearing something howl within. No matter how well-educated that man was, even though he *knew* better, his heart would lurch and the hair would rise on the back of his neck. It was in the blood, in the back of the brain, instinctual dread that went back millions of years to the beginning of time, to when the ancestors of humans were chittering little insectivores, freezing motionless with fear in the trees when a hunting beast roared nearby in the night. So must it be for the Mechanical, even though its millions of generations went back only thirty years. Voices still spoke in the blood—or whatever served it for blood—that could override any rational voice of the mind, and monsters still lurked in the back of the brain. Monsters that looked a lot like Czudak.

Perhaps that was the only remaining edge that humanity had—the superstitions of machines.

"Very eloquent," Czudak said, and sighed. "Almost, you convince me."

The Mechanical stirred, seeming to come back to itself from far away, from a deep reverie. "*You* are the one who must convince your followers of your sincerity, Mr. Czudak," it said. Abruptly, it stood up. "If you publicly recant, Mr. Czudak, if you sway your followers, then we will let you Go Up. We will offer you the same benefits that we offer to any of our companions in the Orbital Companies. What *you* would call 'immortality,' although that is a very imprecise and misleading word. A greatly extended life, at any rate, far beyond your natural organic span. And the reversal of aging, of course."

"God damn you," Czudak whispered.

"Think about it, Mr. Czudak," it said. "It's a very generous offer—especially as you've already turned us down once before. It's rare we give anyone a second chance, but we are willing to give you one. A chance of Ellen's devising, I might add—as was the original offer in the first place." Czudak glanced quickly at Ellen, but she kept her face impassive. "You're sadly deteriorated, Mr. Czudak," the Mechanical continued, softly implacable. "Almost non-functional. You've cut it very fine. But it's nothing our devices cannot mend. If you Come Up with us tonight, you will be young and fully functional again by this time tomorrow."

There was a ringing silence. Czudak looked at Ellen through it, but this time she turned away. She and the Mechanical exchanged a complicated look, although whatever information was being conveyed by it was too complex and subtle for him to grasp.

"I will leave you now," the Mechanical said. "You will have private matters to discuss. But decide quickly, Mr. Czudak. You must recant *now,* today, for maximum symbolic and psychological affect. A few hours from now, we won't interested in what you do any more, and the offer will be withdrawn."

The Mechanical nodded to them, stiffly formal, and then turned and walked directly toward the wall. The wall was only a few steps away, but the Mechanical never got there. Instead, the wall seemed to retreat before it as it approached, and it walked steadily away down a dark, lengthening tunnel, never quite reaching the wall, very slowly shrinking in size as it walked, as if it were somehow blocks away now. At last, when it was a tiny manikin shape, arms and legs scissoring rhythmically, as small as if it was miles away, and the retreating kitchen wall was the size of a playing card at the end of the ever-lengthening tunnel, the Mechanical seemed to turn sharply to one side and vanish. The wall was suddenly there again, back in place, the same as it had ever been. Joseph peeked out of it, shocked, his eyes as big as saucers.

They sat at the kitchen table, not looking at each other, and the gathering silence filed the room like water filling a pond, until it seemed that they sat silently on the bottom of that pond, in deep, still water.

"He's not a cultist, Charlie," she said at last, not looking up. "He's a *hobbyist.* That's the distinction you have to understand. Humans are his *hobby*, one he's passionately devoted to." She smiled fondly. "They're more emotional than we are, Charlie, not less! They feel things very keenly—lushly, deeply, extravagantly; it's the way they've programmed themselves to be. That's the real reason why he wants to take humans along with him, of course. He'd *miss* us if we were left behind! He wouldn't be able to play with us anymore. He'd have to find a *new* hobby." She raised her head. "But don't knock it! We should be grateful for his obsession. Only a very few of the AIs care about us, or are interested in us at all, or even *notice* us. Bucky Bug is different. He's passionately interested in us. Without his interest and that of some of the other Clarkists, we'd have no chance at all of going to the stars!"

Czudak noticed that she always referred to the Mechanical as "he," and that there seemed to be a real affection, a deep fondness, in the way she spoke about it. Could she possibly be fucking it somehow? Were they lovers, or was the emotion in her voice just the happy devotion a dog feels for its beloved master? I don't want to know! he thought, fighting down a deep black spasm of primordial jealous rage. "And is that so important?" he said bitterly, feeling his voice thicken. "Such a big deal? To talk some machines into taking you along to the stars with them, like pets getting a ride in the car? Make sure they leave the windows open a crack for you when they park the spaceship!"

She started to blaze angrily at him, then struggled visibly to bring herself under control. "That's the wrong analogy," she said at last, in a dangerously calm voice. "Don't think of us as dogs on a joyride. Think of us instead as rats on an ocean liner, or as cockroaches on an airplane, or even as insect larva in the corner of a shipping crate. It doesn't matter why they want us to go, or even if they know we're along for the ride, just as long as we *go.* Whatever *their* motives are for going where they're going, we have agendas of our own. Just by taking us along, they're going to help us extend our biological range to environments we never could have reached otherwise—yes, just like rats reaching New Zealand by stowing away on sailing ships. It didn't matter that the rats didn't build the ships themselves, or decide where the ships were going—all that counts in an environmental sense is that they *got* there, to a place they never could have reached on their own. Bucky Bug has promised to leave small colonizing teams behind on every habitable planet we reach. It amuses him in a fond, patronizing kind of way. He thinks it's *cute*." She stared levelly at him. "But *why* he's doing it doesn't matter. Pigs were spread to every continent in the world because humans wanted to eat them—bad for the individual pigs, but very good in the long run for the species as a whole, which extended its range explosively and multiplied its biomass exponentially. And like rats or cockroaches, once humans get *into* an environment, it's hard to get *rid* of them. Whatever motives the AIs have for doing what they're doing, they'll help spread humanity throughout the stars, whether they realize they're doing it or not."

"Is that the best destiny you can think of for the human race?" he said. "To be cockroaches scuttling behind the walls in some machine paradise?"

This time, she did blaze at him. "Goddamnit, Charlie, we don't have *time* for that bullshit! We can't afford dignity and pride and all the rest of those luxuries! This is *species survival* we're talking about here!" She'd squirmed around to face him, in her urgency. He tried to say something, even he wasn't sure what it would have been, but she overrode him. "We've got to get the human race off Earth! Any way we can. We can't afford to keep all our eggs in one basket anymore. There's too much power, too much knowledge, in too many hands. How long before one of the New Men decides to destroy the Earth as part of some insane game he's playing, perhaps not even understanding that what he's doing is *real*? They have the power to do it. How long before some of the other AIs decide to exterminate the human race, to tidy up the place, or to make an aesthetic statement of some kind, or for some other reason we can't even begin to understand? They certainly have the power—they could do it as casually as lifting a hand, if they wanted to. How long before somebody *else* does it, deliberately or by accident? *Anybody* could destroy the world these days, even private citizens with the access to the right technology. Even the Meats could do it, if they applied themselves!"

"But—" he said.

"No buts! Who knows what things will be like a thousand years from now? A hundred thousand years from now? A million? Maybe our descendants will be the masters again, maybe they'll catch up with the AIs and even surpass them. Maybe our destinies will diverge entirely. Maybe we'll work out some kind of symbiosis with them. A million things could happen. *Anything* could happen. But before our descendants can go on to *any* kind of destiny, there have to *be* descendants in the first place! If you survive, there are always options opening up later on down the road, some you couldn't ever have imagined. If you *don't* survive, there *are* no options!"

A wave of tiredness swept over him, and he slumped in his chair. "There are more important things than survival," he said.

She fell silent, staring at him intently. She was flushed with anger, little droplets of sweat standing out on her brow, dampening her temples, her hair slightly disheveled. He could smell the heat of her flesh, and the deeper musk of her body, a rich pungent smell that cut like a knife right through all the years to some deep core of his brain to which time meant nothing, that didn't realize that thirty long years had gone by since last he'd smelled that strong, secret fragrance, that didn't realize that he was old. He felt a sudden pang of desire, and looked away from her uneasily. All at once, he was embarrassed to have her see him this way, dwindled, diminished, gnarled, ugly, old.

"You're going to turn us down again, aren't you?" she said at last. "Damnit! You always *were* the most stiff-necked, stubborn son-of-a-bitch alive! You always had to be right! You always *were* right, as far as you were concerned! No argument, no compromises." She shook her head in exasperation. "Damn you, can't you admit that you were wrong, just this once? Can't you *be* wrong, just this once?"

"Ellen—" he said, and realized that it was the first time he'd spoken her name aloud in thirty years, and faltered into silence. He sighed, and began again. "You're asking me to betray my principles, to betray everything I've ever stood for, to tear down everything I've ever built . . ."

"Oh, fuck your principles!" she said exasperatedly. "Get over it! We can't *afford* principles! We're talking about *life* here. If you're still alive, anything can happen! Who knows what role you may still have to play in our destiny, you stupid fucking moron? Who knows, you could make all the difference. *If* you're alive, that is. If you're dead, you're nothing but a corpse with principles. Nothing else is going to happen, nothing else *can* happen. End of story!"

"Ellen—" he said, but she impatiently waved away the rest of what he was going to say.

"There's nothing noble about being dead, Charlie," she said fiercely. "There's nothing romantic about it. There's no statement you can make by dying that's worth the potential of what you might be able to do with the rest of your life. You think you're proving some kind of point by dying, by refusing to choose life instead, it enables you to see yourself as all noble and principled and high-minded, you can feel a warm virtuous glow about yourself, while you last." She leaned closer, her lips in a tight line. "Well, you look like *shit*, Charlie. You're wearing out, you're falling apart. You're dying. There's nothing noble about it. The meat is rotting on the bone, your muscles are sagging, your hair is falling out, your juices are drying up. You *smell* bad."

He flushed with embarrassment and turned away, but she leaned in closer after him, relentlessly. "There's nothing noble about it. It's just *stupid*. You don't refuse to refurbish a car because it has a lot of miles on it—you re-tune it, refresh it, tinker with it, replace a faulty part here and there, strip the goddamn thing down to the chassis and rebuild it if necessary. You keep it running. Because otherwise, you can't *go* anywhere with it. And who knows where it could still take you?"

He turned further away from her, squirming around in his chair, partially turning his back on her. After a moment, she said, "You keep casting yourself as Faust, and Bucky Bug as Mephistopheles. Or is your ego big enough to make it Jesus and the Devil, up on that mountain? But it's just not that simple. It's just not that simple anymore. If it ever was. Maybe the right choice, the moral choice, is to *give in* to temptation, not fight it! We don't have to play by the old rules. Being human can mean whatever *we* want it to mean!"

Another lake of silence filled up around them, and they at the bottom of it, deep enough to drown. At last, quietly, she said, "Do you ever hear from Sam?"

He stirred, sighed, rubbed his hand over his face. "Not for years. Not a word. I don't even know whether he's still alive."

She made a small noise, not quite a sigh. "That poor kid! We threw him back and forth between us until he broke. I suppose that I always had to be right, too, didn't I? We made quite a pair. No wonder he rejected both of us as soon as he got the chance!"

Czudak said nothing. After a moment, as if carrying on a conversation already in progress that only he could hear, he said, "You made your choices long ago. You burnt your bridges behind you when you took that job with the Company and went up to work in space, against my wishes.

You *knew* I didn't want you to go, that I didn't approve, but you went anyway, in spite of all the political embarrassment it caused me! You didn't care so much about our marriage then, did you? You'd *already* left me by the time the AI Revolt happened!"

She stirred, as if she was going to blaze at him again, but instead only said quietly, "But I came *back* for you too, didn't I? Afterward. I didn't have to do that, but I did. I stuck my neck way out to come back for you. *You* were the one who refused to come with me, when I gave you the chance. Who was burning bridges *then*?"

He grunted, massaged his face with both hands. God, he was so tired! Who had been right then, who was right now—he didn't know anymore. Truth be told, he only dimly remembered what the issues had been in the first place. He was so tired. His vision blurred, and he rubbed his eyes. "I don't know," he said dully. "I don't know anymore."

He could feel her eyes on him again, intently, but he refused to turn his head to look at her. "When the AIs took over the Orbital Towns," she said, "and offered every one of us there immortality if we'd join them, did you *really* expect me to turn them down?"

Now he turned his head to look at her, meeting her gaze levelly. "*I* would have," he said. "If it meant losing *you*."

"You really *believe* that, don't you, you sanctimonious bastard?" she said sadly. She laughed quietly, and shook her head. Czudak continued to stare at her. After a moment of silence, she reached out and took him by the arm. He could feel the warmth of her hand there, fingers pressing into his flesh, the first time she had touched him in thirty years. "I miss you," she said. "Come back to me."

He looked away. When he looked around again, she was gone, without even a stirring of the air to mark her passage. Had she ever been there at all?

The places where she had touched his arm burned faintly, tingling, as if he had been touched by fire, or the sun.

He sat there, in silence, for what seemed like a very long time, geological eons, time enough for continents to move and mountains flow like water, while the shadows shifted and afternoon gathered toward evening around him. Ellen's scent hung in the room for a long time and then slowly faded, like a distant regret. The clock was running, he knew—in more ways than one.

He had to make up his mind. He had to decide. Now. One way or the other. This was the sticking point.

He had to make up his mind.

Had it ever been so quiet, anywhere, at any time in the fretful, grinding, bloody history of the world? When he was young, he would often seek out lonely places full of holy silence, remote stretches of desert, mountaintops, a deserted beach at dawn, places where you could be contemplative, places where you could just *be*, drinking in the world, pores open . . . but now he would have welcomed the most mundane and commonplace of sounds, a dog barking, the sound of passing traffic, a bird singing, someone—a human voice!—yelling out in the street—anything to show that he was still connected to the world, still capable of bringing in the broadcast signal of reality with his deteriorating receiving set. Still alive. Still *here*. Sometimes, in the cold dead middle of the night, the shadows at his throat like razors, he would speak some inane net show on, talking heads gabbing earnestly about things he didn't care about at all, and let it babble away unheeded in the background all night long, until the sun came up to chase the graveyard shadows away, just for the illusion of company. You needed *something*, some kind of noise, to counter the silences and lonlinesses that were filling up your life, and to help distract you from thinking about what waited ahead, the ultimate, unbreakable silence of death. He remembered how his mother, in the last few decades of her life, after his father was gone, would fall asleep on the couch every night with the TV set running. She never slept in the bed, even though it was only a few feet away across her small apartment, not even closed off by a door. She said that she liked having the TV set on, "for the noise." Now he understood this. Deep contemplative silence is not necessarily your friend when you're old. It allows you to listen too closely to the disorder in your veins and the labored beating of your heart.

God, it was quiet!

He found himself remembering a trip he'd taken with Ellen a lifetime ago, the honeymoon trip they'd spent driving up the California coast on old Route 1, and how somewhere, after dark, just north of Big Sur, on the way to spend the night in a B&B in Monterey (where they would fuck so vigorously on the narrow bed that they'd tip it over, and the guy in the room below would pound on the ceiling to complain, making them laugh uncontrollably in spite of attempts to shoosh each other, as they sprawled on the floor in a tangle of bedclothes, drenched in each other's sweat), they pulled over for a moment at a vista-point. He remembered getting out of the car in the dark, with the invisible ocean breathing on their left, and, looking up, being amazed by how many stars you could see in the sky here, a closely-packed bowl of stars surrounding you on all sides except where the darker-black against black silhouette of the hills took a bite out of it. Stars all around you, millions of them, coldly flaming, indifferent, majestic, remote. If you watched the night sky too long, he'd realized then, feeling the cold salt wind blow in off the unseen ocean and listening to the hollow boom and crash of waves against the base of the cliff far below, the chill of the stars began to seep into you, and you began to get an uneasy reminder of how vast the universe really *was*—or how small *you* were. It was knowledge you had to turn away from eventually, before that chill sank too deeply into your bones; you had to pull back from it, shrug it off, try to immerse yourself again in your tiny human life, do your best to once more wrap yourself in the conviction that the great wheel of the universe revolved around *you* instead, and that everyone else and everything else around you, the mountains, the vast breathing sea, the sky itself, were merely spear-carriers or theatrical backdrops in the unique drama of your life, a vitally important drama unlike anything that had ever gone before . . . But once faced with the true vastness of the universe, once you'd had that chill insight, alone under the stars, it was hard to shake the realization that you were only a miniscule fleck of matter, that existed for a span of time so infinitely, vanishingly short that it couldn't even be measured on the clock of geologic time, by the birth and death of mountains and seas, let alone on the vastly greater clock that ticks away how long it takes the great flaming wheel of the Galaxy to whirl around itself, or one galaxy to wheel around another. That the shortest blink of the cosmic Eye would still be aeons too long to notice your little life at all.

Against that kind of immensity, what did "immortality" mean, for either human or machine? A million years, a day—from that perspective, they were much the same.

There was a throb of pain in his temple now. A tension headache starting? Or a stroke? It would be ironic if a blood vessel burst in his brain and killed him before he even had a chance to make up his mind.

One way or the other, time was almost up. Either his corporeal life or his terrestrial one ended today. Either way, he wouldn't be back here again. He looked slowly around the room, examining every detail, things that had been there for so long that they'd faded into the background and he didn't really *see* them anymore: a set of bronze door-chimes, hung over the back door, that he and Ellen had bought in Big Sur; an ornamental glass ball in a woven net; a big brown-and-cream vase from a cluttered craft shop in Seattle; a crockery sun-face they'd gotten in Albuquerque; a wind-up toy carousel that played "The Carousel Waltz." Familiar mugs and cups and bowls, worn smooth with age. A framed *Cirque Du Soleil* poster, decades old now. One of Sam's old stuffed animals, a battered tiger with one ear drooping, tucked away on a shelf of the high kitchen cabinet, and never touched or moved again.

Strange that he had gotten rid of Ellen's photograph, ostentatiously made a point of *not* displaying it, but kept all the rest of these things, all the memorabilia of their years together—as though subconsciously he was expecting her to come back, to step back into his life as simply as she'd stepped out it, and pick up where they'd left off. But that wasn't going to happen. If they were to have any life together, it would be very far away from here, and under conditions that were unimaginably strange. Would he have the courage to face that, would he have the strength to deal with starting a new life? Or was his soul too old, too tired, too tarnished, no matter what nanomagic tricks the Mechanicals could play with his physical body?

Joseph was gesturing urgently to him again, waving both arms over his head from the middle of Rembrandt's *The Night Watch*. He released the valet from reserve-mode, and Joseph immediately appeared beside the kitchen table, contriving somehow to look flustered. "I have this Highest Priority message for you, sir, although I don't know where it came from or how it was placed in my system. All it says is, 'You don't have much time'."

"I know, Joseph," Czudak said, cutting him off. It doesn't matter. I just wanted to tell you—" Czudak paused, suddenly uncertain what to say. "I just wanted to tell you that, whichever way things go, you've been a good friend to me, and I appreciate it."

Joseph looked at him oddly. "Of course, sir," he said. How much of this could he really understand? It was way outside of his programming parameters, even with adaptable learning-algorithms. "But the message—"

Czudak spoke him off, and he was gone. Just like that. Vanished. Gone. And if he was never spoken of again, would it make any difference to him? Even if Joseph had known in advance that he'd never be spoken on again, that there would be nothing from this moment on but non-existence, blankness, blackness, nothingness, would he have cared?

Czudak stood up.

As he started across the room, he realized that the time-travelers were still there. Rank on rank of them, filling the room with jostling ghosts, thousands of them, millions of them perhaps, a vast insubstantial crowd of them that he couldn't see, but that he could *feel* were there. Waiting. Watching. Watching *him*. He stopped, stunned, for the first time beginning to believe in the presence of the time-travelers as a real phenomenon, and not just a half-senile fancy of his decaying brain.

This is what they were here to see. This moment. His decision.

But why? Were they students of obscure old-recension political scandals, here to witness his betrayal of his old principles, the way you might go back to witness Benedict Arnold sealing his pact with the British or Nixon giving the orders for Watergate? Were they triumphant future descendants of the Meats, here to watch the heroic moment when he threw the Mechanicals's offer of immortality defiantly back in their Teflon faces, perhaps inspiring some sort of human resistance movement? Or were they here to witness the birth of his new life after he *accepted* that offer, because of something he had *yet* to do, something he would go on to do centuries or thousands of years from now?

And who *were* they? Were they his own human descendants, from millions of years in the future, evolved into strange beings with godlike powers? Or were they the descendants of the Mechanicals, grown to a ghostly discorporate strangeness of their own?

He walked forward, feeling the watching shadows part around him, close in again close behind. He still didn't know what he was going to do. It would have been so easy to make this decision when he was young. Young and strong and self-righteous, full of pride and determination and integrity. He would have turned the Mechanicals down flat, indignantly, with loathing, not hesitating for a moment, *knowing* what was right. He already *had* done that once, in fact, long before, teaching them that they couldn't buy *him*, no matter what coin they offered to pay in! He wasn't for sale!

Now, he wasn't so sure.

Now, hobbling painfully toward the front door, feeling pain lance through his head at every step, feeling his knee throb, he was struck by a sudden sense of what it would be like to be *young* again—to suddenly be young again, all at once, in a second! To put all the infirmities and indignities of age aside, like shedding a useless skin. To feel life again, really *feel* it, in a hot hormonal rush of whirling emotions, a maelstrom of scents, sounds, sights, tastes, touch, all at full strength rather than behind an insulating wall of glass, life loud and vulgar and blaring at top volume rather than whispering in the slowly diminishing voice of a dying radio, life where you could touch it, all your nerves jumping just under your skin, rather than feeling the world pulling slowly away from you, withdrawing, fading away with a sullen murmur, like a tide that has gone miles out from the beach . . .

Czudak opened his front door, and stepped out onto the high white marble stoop.

The Meats had moved their demonstration over from the park, and were now camped out in front of his house, filling the street in their hundreds, blocking traffic. They were still beating their drums and blowing on their horns and whistles, although he hadn't heard anything inside the house; the Mechanical's doing, perhaps. A great wave of sound puffed in to greet him when he opened the door, though, blaring and vivid, smacking into his face with almost physical force. When he stepped out onto the stoop, the drums and horns began to falter and fall silent one by one, and a startled hush spread out over the crowd, like ripples spreading out over the surface of a pond from a thrown stone, until there was instead of noise an expectant silence made up of murmurs and whispers, noises not quite heard. And then even that almost-noise stopped, as if the world had taken a deep breath and held it, waiting, and he looked out over a sea of expectant faces, looking back at him, turned up toward him like flowers turned toward the sun.

A warm breeze came up, blowing across the park, blowing from the distant corners of the Earth, tugging at his hair. It smelled of magnolias and hyacinths and new-mown grass, and it stirred the branches of the trees around him, making them lift and shrug. The horizon to the west was a glory of clouds, hot gold, orange, lime, scarlet, coral, fiery purple, with the sun a gleaming orange coin balanced on the very rim of the world, ready to teeter and fall off. The rest of the sky was a delicate pale blue, fading to plum and ash to the East, out toward the distant ocean. The full moon was already out, a pale perfect disk, like a bone-white face peering with languid curiosity down on the ancient earth. A bird began to sing, trilling liquidly, somewhere out in the gathering darkness.

Exultation opened hotly inside him, like a wound. God, he loved the world!

Throwing his head back, he began to speak.

Copyright and First Publication

"Introduction" by Robert Silverberg. Copyright © 2011 by Agberg, Ltd.

Ancestral Voices by Gardner Dozois and Michael Swanwick. Copyright © 1998 by Dell Magazines. First published in *Asimov's Science Fiction Magazine*, August 1998.

"A Cat Horror Story" by Gardner Dozois. Copyright © 1994 by Spilogale, Inc. First published in *The Magazine of Fantasy & Science Fiction*, October/November 1994.

Chains of the Sea by Gardner Dozois. Copyright © 1971 by Gardner Dozois. *Chains of the Sea*, ed. Robert Silverberg, Nelson, 1971.

"Community" by Gardner Dozois. Copyright © 1996 by Dell Magazines. First published in *Asimov's Science Fiction Magazine*, September 1996.

"Counterfactual" by Gardner Dozois. Copyright © 2006 by Spilogale, Inc. First published in *The Magazine of Fantasy & Science Fiction*, June 2006.

"Dinner Party" by Gardner Dozois. Copyright © 1984 by Gardner Dozois. First published in *Light Years and Dark*, ed. Michael Bishop, Berkley, 1984.

"Disciples" by Gardner Dozois. Copyright © 1981 by Gardner Dozois. First published in *Penthouse*, December 1981.

"A Dream at Noonday" by Gardner Dozois. Copyright © 1970 by Gardner Dozois. First published in *Orbit 7*, ed. Damon Knight, G.P. Putnam's, 1970.

"Fairy Tale" by Gardner Dozois. Copyright © 1999 by Gardner Dozois. First published in *Sci Fiction*, January 15, 2003.

"The Hanging Curve" by Gardner Dozois. Copyright © 2002 by Spilogale, Inc. First published in *The Magazine of Fantasy & Science Fiction*, April 2002.

"A Kingdom by the Sea" by Gardner Dozois. Copyright © 1972 by Gardner Dozois. First published in *Orbit 10*, ed. Damon Knight, G.P. Putnam's, 1972.

A Knight of Ghosts and Shadows by Gardner Dozois. Copyright © 1999 by Dell Magazines. First published in *Asimov's Science Fiction Magazine*, October/November 1999.

"Morning Child" by Gardner Dozois. Copyright © 1984 by Gardner Dozois. First published in *Omni*, January 1984

"The Peacemaker" by Gardner Dozois. Copyright © 1983 by Dell Magazines. First published in *Asimov's Science Fiction Magazine*, August 1983.

"Recidivist" by Gardner Dozois. Copyright © 2010 by Gardner Dozois. First published in *Warriors*, ed. George R.R. Martin & Gardner Dozois, Tor, 2010.

"Solace" by Gardner Dozois. Copyright © 1990 by Gardner Dozois. *Omni*, February 1990.

"A Special Kind of Morning" by Gardner Dozois. Copyright © 1971 by Gardner Dozois. First published in *New Dimensions I*, ed. Robert Silverberg, Doubleday, 1971.

"When the Great Days Came" by Gardner Dozois. Copyright © 2005 by Spilogale, Inc. First published in *The Magazine of Fantasy & Science Fiction*, December 2005.

About the Author

Gardner Dozois was the editor of *Asimov's Science Fiction* for almost twenty years, and also edits the annual anthology series *The Year's Best Science Fiction*, which has won the Locus Award for Best Anthology sixteen times, more than any other anthology series in history, and which is now up to its *Twenty-Eighth Annual Collection*. He's won the Hugo Award fifteen times as the year's Best Editor, won the Locus Award thirty-five times, including an unprecedented sixteen times in a row as Best Editor, and has won the Sidewise Award and two Nebula Awards for his own short fiction. In 2011, he was inducted into the Science Fiction Hall of Fame. He is the author or editor of more than a hundred books, among the most recent of which are a novel written in collaboration with George R.R. Martin and Daniel Abraham, *Hunter's Run*, and the anthologies *The New Space Opera II* (edited with Jonathan Strahan), *The Dragon Book: Magical Tales from the Masters of Modern Fantasy* (edited with Jack Dann), and *Songs of the Dying Earth*, *Warriors*, *Songs of Love and Death*, and *Down These Strange Streets* (all edited with George R.R. Martin). Born in Salem, Massachusetts, he now lives in Philadelphia, Pennsylvania.